THE GUNS OF NAVARONE

Twelve hundred British soldiers isolated on the small
island of Kheros off the Turkish coast waiting . . .
waiting . . . waiting to die. Twelve hundred lives in jeo-
pardy, lives that must be snatched from the remorseless grip of an exultant enemy—and would be—if
the guns of Navarone could be silenced. The guns
of Navarone, vigilant, venomous and damnably
accurate, hungrily guarded their destined prey.
Navarone itself, grim bastion of the narrow straits
manned by a mixed garrison of Germans and Italians,
an apparently impregnable iron fortress, was the
supreme obstacle to any rescue attempt by the
Royal Navy. To Captain Keith Mallory, skilled
saboteur, trained mountaineer, fell the task of leading the small party detailed to scale the vast, impossible precipice of Navarone and to blow up the guns.
The Guns of Navarone is a story of that mission, the
tale of a calculated risk in time of war typical of
many undertaken in days and nights of danger and
now more happily recorded in tranquillity.

Alistair MacLean

THE GUNS OF NAVARONE

COLLINS
ST JAMES'S PLACE, LONDON
1957

To my mother

PRINTED IN GREAT BRITAIN

COLLINS CLEAR-TYPE PRESS: LONDON AND GLASGOW

CONTENTS

N

KHEROS

C
Y
C
L
A
D
E
S

MAIDOS

CAPE
DEMIRCI

MAIDOS STRAITS

FORTRESS

CASTLE VYGOS

CAROB GROVE
COAST ROAD

DEVIL'S
PLAYGROUND

MARGARITHA

SHEPHERD'S
HUT

CAVE

MT. KOSTOS

SOUTH
CLIFF

CAIQUE WRECKED
HERE

T U R K E Y

CHARLES GREEN·

CHAPTER ONE

PRELUDE: SUNDAY

0100-0900

THE MATCH scratched noisily across the rusted metal of the corrugated iron shed, fizzled, then burst into a sputtering pool of light, the harsh sound and sudden brilliance alike strangely alien in the stillness of the desert night. Mechanically, Mallory's eyes followed the cupped sweep of the flaring match to the cigarette jutting out beneath the Group-Captain's clipped moustache, saw the light stop inches away from the face, saw too the sudden stillness of that face, the unfocused vacancy of the eyes of a man lost in listening. Then the match was gone, ground into the sand of the airfield perimeter.

" I can hear them," the Group-Captain said softly. " I can hear them coming in. Five minutes, no more. No wind to-night—they'll be coming in on Number two. Come on, let's meet them in the interrogation room." He paused, looked quizzically at Mallory and seemed to smile. But the darkness deceived, for there was no humour in his voice. " Just curb your impatience, young man—just for a little longer. Things haven't gone too well to-night. You're going to have all your answers, I'm afraid, and have them all too soon." He turned abruptly, strode off towards the squat buildings that loomed vaguely against the pale darkness that topped the level horizon.

Mallory shrugged, then followed on more slowly, step for step with the third member of the group, a broad stocky, figure with a very pronounced roll in his gait. Mallory

7

wondered sourly just how much practice Jensen had required
to achieve that sailorly effect. Thirty years at sea, of course—
and Jensen had done exactly that—were sufficient warrant for
a man to dance a hornpipe as he walked: but that wasn't the
point. As the brilliantly successful Chief of Operations of the
Subversive Operation Executive in Cairo, intrigue, deception,
imitation and disguise were the breath of life to Captain James
Jensen, D.S.O., R.N. As a Levantine stevedore agitator, he
had won the awed respect of the dock-labourers from Alexan-
dretta to Alexandria: as a camel-driver, he had blasphemously
out-camel-driven all available Bedouin competition: and no
more pathetic beggar had ever exhibited such realistic sores
in the bazaars and market-places of the East. To-night,
however, he was just the bluff and simple sailor. He was
dressed in white from cap-cover to canvas shoes   the starlight
glinted softly on the golden braid on epaulettes and cap
peak.

Their footsteps crunched in companionable unison over the
hard-packed sand, rang sharply as they moved on to the
concrete of the runway. The hurrying figure of the Group-
Captain was already almost lost to sight. Mallory took a
deep breath and turned suddenly towards Jensen.

"Look, sir, just what *is* all this? What's all the flap, all the
secrecy about? And why am *I* involved in it? Good lord, sir,
it was only yesterday that I was pulled out of Crete, relieved
at eight hours' notice. A month's leave, I was told. And what
happens?"

"Well," Jensen murmured, "what did happen?"

"No leave," Mallory said bitterly. "Not even a night's
sleep. Just hours and hours in the S.O.E. Headquarters,
answering a lot of silly, damnfool questions about climbing in
the Southern Alps. Then hauled out of bed at midnight, told
I was to meet you, and then driven for hours across the blasted
desert by a mad Scotsman who sang drunken songs and asked
hundreds of even more silly, damnfool questions!"

" One of my more effective disguises, I've always thought," Jensen said smugly. " Personally, I found the journey most entertaining! "

" One of your——" Mallory broke off, appalled at the memory of the things he had said to the elderly, bewhiskered Scots captain who had driven the command vehicle. " I—I'm terribly sorry, sir. I never realised——"

" Of course you didn't! " Jensen cut in briskly. " You weren't supposed to. Just wanted to find out if you were the man for the job. I'm sure you are—I was pretty sure you were before I pulled you out of Crete. But where you got the idea about leave I don't know. The sanity of the S.O.E. has often been questioned, but even *we* aren't given to sending a flying-boat for the sole purpose of enabling junior officers to spend a month wasting their substance among the flesh-pots of Cairo," he finished dryly.

" I still don't know——"

" Patience, laddie, patience—as our worthy Group-Captain has just advocated. Time is endless. To wait, and to keep on waiting—that is to be of the East."

" To total four hours' sleep in three days is not," Mallory said feelingly. " And that's all I've had. . . . Here they come! "

Both men screwed up their eyes in automatic reflex as the fierce glare of the landing lights struck at them, the flare path arrowing off into the outer darkness. In less than a minute the first bomber was down, heavily, awkwardly, taxi-ing to a standstill just beside them. The grey camouflage paint of the after fuselage and tail-planes was riddled with bullet and cannon shells, an aileron was shredded and the port outer engine out of commission, saturated in oil. The cabin Perspex was shattered and starred in a dozen places.

For a long time Jensen stared at the holes and scars of the damaged machine, then shook his head and looked away.

"Four hours' sleep, Captain Mallory," he said quietly. "Four hours. I'm beginning to think that you can count yourself damn' lucky to have had even that much."

The interrogation room, harshly lit by two powerful, un-shaded lights, was uncomfortable and airless. The furniture consisted of some battered wall-maps and charts, a score or so of equally scuffed chairs and an unvarnished deal table. The Group-Captain, flanked by Jensen and Mallory, was sitting behind this when the door opened abruptly and the first of the flying crews entered, blinking rapidly in the fierceness of the unaccustomed light. They were led by a dark-haired, thick-set pilot, trailing helmet and flying-suit in his left hand. He had an Anzac bush helmet crushed on the back of his head, and the word "Australia" emblazoned in white across each khaki shoulder. Scowling, wordlessly and without permission, he sat down in front of them, produced a pack of cigarettes and rasped a match across the surface of the table. Mallory looked furtively at the Group-Captain. The Group-Captain just looked resigned. He even sounded resigned.

"Gentlemen, this is Squadron Leader Torrance. Squadron Leader Torrance," he added unnecessarily, "is an Australian." Mallory had the impression that the Group-Captain rather hoped this would explain some things, Squadron Leader Torrance among them. "He led to-night's attack on Navarone. Bill, these gentlemen here—Captain Jensen of the Royal Navy, Captain Mallory of the Long Range Desert Group—have a very special interest in Navarone. How did things go to-night?"

Navarone! So that's why I'm here to-night, Mallory thought. Navarone. He knew it well, rather, knew of it. So did everyone who had served any time at all in the Eastern Mediterranean: a grim, impregnable iron fortress off the coast of Turkey, heavily defended by—it was thought—a mixed garrison of Germans and Italians, one of the few Ægean islands

on which the Allies had been unable to establish a mission, far
less recapture, at some period of the war. . . . He realised that
Torrance was speaking, the slow drawl heavy with controlled
anger.

" Bloody awful, sir. A fair cow, it was, a real suicide do."
He broke off abruptly, stared moodily with compressed lips
through his own drifting tobacco smoke. " But we'd like to
go back again," he went on. " Me and the boys here. Just
once. We were talking about it on the way home." Mallory
caught the deep murmur of voices in the background, a growl
of agreement. " We'd like to take with us the joker who
thought this one up and shove him out at ten thousand over
Navarone, without benefit of parachute."

" As bad as that, Bill ? "

" As bad as that, sir. We hadn't a chance. Straight up,
we really hadn't. First off, the weather was against us—the
jokers in the Met. office were about as right as they usually
are."

" They gave you clear weather ? "

" Yeah. Clear weather. It was ten-tenths over the target,"
Torrance said bitterly. " We had to go down to fifteen hundred.
Not that it made any difference. We would have to have gone
down lower than that anyway—about three thousand feet
below sea-level then fly up the way: that cliff overhang shuts
the target clean off. Might as well have dropped a shower of
leaflets asking them to spike their own bloody guns. . . . Then
they've got every second A.A. gun in the south of Europe concentrated along this narrow 50-degree vector—the only way
you can approach the target, or anywhere near the target.
Russ and Conroy were belted good and proper on the way in.
Didn't even get half-way towards the harbour. . . . They never
had a chance."

" I know, I know." The Group-Captain nodded heavily.
" We heard. W/T reception was good. . . . And McIlveen
ditched just north of Alex ? "

" Yeah. But he'll be all right. The old crate was still awash when we passed over, the big dinghy was out and it was as smooth as a millpond. He'll be all right," Torrance repeated.

The Group-Captain nodded again, and Jensen touched his sleeve.

" May I have a word with the Squadron Leader? "

" Of course, Captain. You don't have to ask."

" Thanks." Jensen looked across at the burly Australian and smiled faintly.

" Just one little question, Squadron Leader. You don't fancy going back there again? "

" Too bloody right, I don't! " Torrance growled.

" Because? "

" Because I don't believe in suicide. Because I don't believe in sacrificing good blokes for nothing. Because I'm not God and I can't do the impossible." There was a flat finality in Torrance's voice that carried conviction, that brooked no argument.

" It is impossible, you say? " Jensen persisted. " This is terribly important."

" So's my life. So are the lives of all these jokers." Torrance jerked a big thumb over his shoulder. " It's impossible, sir. At least, it's impossible for us." He drew a weary hand down his face. " Maybe a Dornier flying-boat with one of these new-fangled radio-controlled glider-bombs might do it and get off with it. I don't know. But I do know that nothing we've got has a snowball's chance in hell. Not," he added bitterly, " unless you cram a Mosquito full of T.N.T. and order one of us to crash-dive it at four hundred into the mouth of the gun cave. That way there's always a chance."

" Thank you, Squadron Leader—and all of you." Jensen was on his feet. " I know you've done your very best, no one could have done more. And I'm sorry. . . . Group-Captain? "

" Right with you, gentlemen." He nodded to the be-spectacled Intelligence officer who had been sitting behind them to take his place, led the way out through a side door and into his own quarters.

" Well, that is that, I suppose." He broke the seal of a bottle of Talisker, brought out some glasses. " You'll have to accept it as final, Jensen. Bill Torrance's is the senior, most experienced squadron left in Africa to-day. Used to pound the Ploesti oil well and think it a helluva skylark. If anyone could have done to-night's job it was Bill Torrance, and if he says it's impossible, believe me, Captain Jensen, it can't be done."

" Yes." Jensen looked down sombrely at the golden amber of the glass in his hand. " Yes, I know now. I *almost* knew before, but I couldn't be sure, and I couldn't take the chance of being wrong. . . . A terrible pity that it took the lives of a dozen men to prove me right. . . . There's just the one way left, now."

" There's just the one," the Group-Captain echoed. He lifted his glass, shook his head. " Here's luck to Kheros! "

" Here's luck to Kheros! " Jensen echoed in turn. His face was grim.

" Look! " Mallory begged. " I'm completely lost. Would somebody please tell me——"

" Kheros," Jensen interrupted. " That was your cue call, young man. All the world's a stage, laddie, etc., and this is where you tread the boards in this particular little comedy." Jensen's smile was quite mirthless. " Sorry you've missed the first two acts, but don't lose any sleep over that. This is no bit part: you're going to be the star, whether you like it or not. This is it. Kheros, Act 3, Scene 1. Enter Captain Keith Mallory."

Neither of them had spoken in the last ten minutes. Jensen drove the big Humber command car with the same sureness, the same relaxed efficiency that hall-marked everything he did: Mallory still sat hunched over the map on his knees, a large-scale Admiralty chart of the Southern Ægean illuminated by the hooded dashboard light, studying an area of the Sporades and Northern Dodecanese heavily squared off in red pencil. Finally he straightened up and shivered. Even in Egypt these late November nights could be far too cold for comfort. He looked across at Jensen.

"I think I've got it now, sir."

"Good!" Jensen gazed straight ahead along the winding grey ribbon of dusty road, along the white glare of the head-lights that cleaved through the darkness of the desert. The beams lifted and dipped, constantly, hypnotically, to the cushioning of the springs on the rutted road. "Good!" he repeated. "Now, have another look at it and imagine yourself standing in the town of Navarone—that's on that almost circular bay on the north of the island. Tell me, what would you see from there?"

Mallory smiled.

"I don't have to look again, sir. Four miles or so away to the east I'd see the Turkish coast curving up north and west to a point almost due north of Navarone—a very sharp promontory, that, for the coastline above curves back almost due east. Then, about sixteen miles away, due north beyond this promontory—Cape Demirci, isn't it?—and practically in a line with it I'd see the island of Kheros. Finally, six miles to the west is the island of Maidos, the first of the Lerades group. They stretch away in a north-westerly direction, maybe fifty miles."

"Sixty." Jensen nodded. "You have the eye, my boy. You've got the guts and the experience—a man doesn't survive eighteen months in Crete without both. You've got one or two special qualifications I'll mention by and by." He paused for a moment, shook his head slowly. "I only hope you have the luck—all the luck. God alone knows you're going to need it."

Mallory waited expectantly, but Jensen had sunk into some

private reverie. Three minutes passed, perhaps five, and there was only the swish of the tyres, the subdued hum of the powerful engine. Presently Jensen stirred and spoke again, quietly, still without taking his eyes off the road.

" This is Saturday—rather, it's Sunday morning now. There are one thousand two hundred men on the island of Kheros—one thousand two hundred British soldiers—who will be dead, wounded or prisoner by next Saturday. Mostly, they'll be dead." For the first time he looked at Mallory and smiled, a brief smile, a crooked smile, and then it was gone. " How does it feel to hold a thousand lives in your hands, Captain Mallory? "

For long seconds Mallory looked at the impassive face beside him, then looked away again. He stared down at the chart. Twelve hundred men on Kheros, twelve hundred men waiting to die. Kheros and Navarone, Kheros and Navarone. What was that poem again, that little jingle that he'd learnt all these long years ago in that little upland village in the sheeplands outside Queenstown? Chimborazo—that was it. " Chimborazo and Cotopaxi, you have stolen my heart away." Kheros and Navarone—they had the same ring, the same indefinable glamour, the same wonder of romance that took hold of a man and stayed with him. Kheros and—angrily, almost, he shook his head, tried to concentrate. The pieces of the jigsaw were beginning to click into place, but slowly.

Jensen broke the silence.

" Eighteen months ago, you remember, after the fall of Greece, the Germans had taken over nearly all the islands of the Sporades: the Italians, of course, already held most of the Dodecanese. Then, gradually, we began to establish missions on these islands, usually spear-headed by your people, the Long Range Desert Group or the Special Boat Service. By last September we had retaken nearly all the larger islands except Navarone—it was too damned hard a nut, so we just by-passed it—and brought some of the garrisons up to, and beyond, battalion strength." He grinned at Mallory. "You were lurking in your cave somewhere in the White Mountains at the time, but you'll remember how the Germans reacted?"

" Violently?"

Jensen nodded.

" Exactly. Very violently indeed. The political importance of Turkey in this part of the world is impossible to over-estimate—and she's always been a potential partner for either Axis or Allies. Most of these islands are only a few miles off the Turkish coast. The question of prestige, of restoring confidence in Germany, was urgent."

" So?"

" So they flung in everything—paratroopers, airborne troops, crack mountain brigades, hordes of Stukas—I'm told they stripped the Italian front of dive-bombers for these operations. Anyway, they flung everything in—the lot. In a few weeks we'd lost over ten thousand troops and every island we'd ever recaptured—except Kheros."

" And now it's the turn of Kheros?"

" Yes." Jensen shook out a pair of cigarettes, sat silently until Mallory had lit them and sent the match spinning through the window towards the pale gleam of the Mediterranean lying north below the coast road. " Yes, Kheros is for the hammer. Nothing that we can do can save it. The Germans have absolute air superiority in the Ægean. . . ."

" But—but how can you be so sure that it's this week?"

Jensen sighed.

" Laddie, Greece is fairly hotching with Allied agents. We have over two hundred in the Athens-Piraeus area alone and——"

" Two hundred!" Mallory interrupted incredulously. " Did you say——"

" I did." Jensen grinned. " A mere bagatelle, I assure you, compared to the vast hordes of spies that circulate freely

among our noble hosts in Cairo and Alexandria." He was
suddenly serious again. "Anyway, our information is accurate.
An armada of caiques will sail from the Piraeus on Thursday
at dawn and island-hop across the Cyclades, holing up in the
islands at night." He smiled. "An intriguing situation, don't
you think? We daren't move in the Ægean in the daytime or
we'd be bombed out of the water. The Germans don't dare
move at night. Droves of our destroyers and M.T.B.s and gun-
boats move into the Ægean at dusk: the destroyers retire to
the south before dawn, the small boats usually lie up in isolated
islands creeks. But we can't stop them from getting across.
They'll be there Saturday or Sunday—and synchronise their
landings with the first of the airborne troops: they've scores
of Junkers 52s waiting just outside Athens. Kheros won't last
a couple of days." No one could have listened to Jensen's
carefully casual voice, his abnormal matter-of-factness and not
have believed him.

Mallory believed him. For almost a minute he stared down
at the sheen of the sea, at the faerie tracery of the stars shimmering across its darkly placid surface. Suddenly he swung round
on Jensen.

"But the Navy, sir! Evacuation! Surely the Navy——"

"The Navy," Jensen interrupted heavily, "is not keen.
The Navy is sick and tired of the Eastern Med. and the Ægean,
sick and tired of sticking out its long-suffering neck and having
it regularly chopped off—and all for sweet damn all. We've
had two battleships wrecked, eight cruisers out of commission
—four of them sunk—and over a dozen destroyers gone. . . . I
couldn't even start to count the number of smaller vessels
we've lost. And for what? I've told you—for sweet damn all!
Just so's our High Command can play round-and-round-the-
rugged-rocks and who's-the-king-of-the-castle with their opposite
numbers in Berlin. Great fun for all concerned—except, of
course, for the thousand or so sailors who've been drowned in
the course of the game, the ten thousand or so Tommies and

Anzacs and Indians who suffered and died on these same islands—and died without knowing why."

Jensen's hands were white-knuckled on the wheel, his mouth tight-drawn and bitter. Mallory was surprised, shocked almost, by the vehemence, the depth of feeling; it was so completely out of character. . . . Or perhaps it was in character, perhaps Jensen knew a very great deal indeed about what went on on the inside. . . .

" Twelve hundred men, you said, sir? " Mallory asked quietly. " You said there were twelve hundred men on Kheros? "

Jensen flickered a glance at him, looked away again.

" Yes. Twelve hundred men." Jensen sighed. " You're right, laddie, of course you're right. I'm just talking off the top of my head. Of course we can't leave them there. The Navy will do its damnedest. What's two or three more destroyers—sorry, boy, sorry, there I go again. . . . Now listen, and listen carefully.

" Taking 'em off will have to be a night operation. There isn't a ghost of a chance in the daytime—not with two-three hundred Stukas just begging for a glimpse of a Royal Naval destroyer. It'll have to be destroyers—transports and tenders are too slow by half. And they can't possibly go north about the northern tip of the Lerades—they'd never get back to safety before daylight. It's too long a trip by hours."

" But the Lerades is a pretty long string of islands," Mallory ventured. " Couldn't the destroyers go through——"

" Between a couple of them? Impossible." Jensen shook his head. " Mined to hell and back again. Every single channel. You couldn't take a dinghy through."

" And the Maidos-Navarone channel. Stiff with mines also, I suppose? "

" No, that's a clear channel. Deep water—you can't moor mines in deep water."

" So that's the route you've got to take, isn't it, sir? I

mean, they're Turkish territorial waters on the other side and we——"

" We'd go through Turkish territorial waters to-morrow, and in broad daylight, if it would do any good," Jensen said flatly. " The Turks know it and so do the Germans. But all other things being equal, the Western channel is the one we're taking. It's a clearer channel, a shorter route—and it doesn't involve any unnecessary international complications."

" All other things being equal? "

" The guns of Navarone." Jensen paused for a long time, then repeated the words, slowly, expressionlessly, as one would repeat the name of some feared and ancient enemy. " The guns of Navarone. They make everything equal. They cover the Northern entrances to both channels. We could take the twelve hundred men off Kheros to-night—if we could silence the guns of Navarone."

Mallory sat silent, said nothing. He's coming to it now, he thought.

" These guns are no ordinary guns," Jensen went on quietly. " Our naval experts say they're about nine-inch rifle barrels. I think myself they're more likely a version of the 210 mm. ' crunch ' guns that the Germans are using in Italy—our soldiers up there hate and fear those guns more than anything on earth. A dreadful weapon—shell extremely slow in flight and damnably accurate. Anyway," he went on grimly, " whatever they were they were good enough to dispose of the *Sybaris* in five minutes flat."

Mallory nodded slowly.

" The *Sybaris*? I think I heard——"

" An eight-inch cruiser we sent up there about four months ago to try conclusions with the Hun. Just a formality, a routine exercise, we thought. The *Sybaris* was blasted out of the water. There were seventeen survivors."

" Good God! " Mallory was shocked. " I didn't know——"

"Two months ago we mounted a large-scale amphibious attack on Navarone." Jensen hadn't even heard the interruption. "Commandos, Royal Marine Commandos and Jellicoe's Special Boat Service. Less than an even chance, we knew—Navarone's practically solid cliff all the way round. But then these were very special men, probably the finest assault troops in the world to-day." Jensen paused for almost a minute, then went on very quietly. "They were cut to ribbons. They were massacred almost to a man.

"Finally, twice in the past ten days—we've seen this attack on Kheros coming for a long time now—we sent in parachute saboteurs: Special Boat Service men." He shrugged his shoulders helplessly. "They just vanished."

"Just like that?"

"Just like that. And then to-night—the last desperate fling of the gambler and what have you." Jensen laughed, briefly and without humour. "That interrogation hut—I kept pretty quiet in there to-night, I tell you. I was the 'joker' that Torrance and his boys wanted to heave out over Navarone. I don't blame them. But I had to do it, I just had to do it. I knew it was hopeless—but it had to be done."

The big Humber was beginning to slow down now, running silently between the tumble-down shacks and hovels that line the Western approach to Alexandria. The sky ahead was already beginning to streak in the first tenuous greys of the false dawn.

"I don't think I'd be much good with a parachute," Mallory said doubtfully. "In fact, quite frankly, I've never even *seen* a parachute."

"Don't worry," Jensen said briefly. "You won't have to use one. You're going into Navarone the hard way."

Mallory waited for more, but Jensen had fallen silent, intent on avoiding the large potholes that were beginning to pock the roadway. After a time Mallory asked:

"Why me, Captain Jensen?"

Jensen's smile was barely visible in the greying darkness. He swerved violently to avoid a gaping hole and straightened up again.

" Scared? "

" Certainly I'm scared. No offence intended, sir, but the way you talk you'd scare anyone. . . . But that wasn't what I meant."

" I know it wasn't. Just my twisted humour. . . . Why you? Special qualifications, laddie, just like I told you. You speak Greek like a Greek. You speak German like a German. Skilled saboteur, first-class organiser and eighteen unscathed months in the White Mountains of Crete—a convincing demonstration of your ability to survive in enemy-held territory." Jensen chuckled. " You'd be surprised to know just how complete a dossier I have on you! "

" No, I wouldn't." Mallory spoke with some feeling. " And," he added, " I know of at least three other officers with the same qualifications."

" There are others," Jensen agreed. " But there are no other Keith Mallorys. Keith Mallory," Jensen repeated rhetorically. " Who hadn't heard of Keith Mallory in the palmy, balmy days before the war? The finest mountaineer, the greatest rock climber New Zealand has ever produced— and by that, of course, New Zealanders mean the world. The human fly, the climber of the unclimbable, the scaler of vertical cliffs and impossible precipices. The entire south coast of Navarone," said Jensen cheerfully, " consists of one vast, impossible precipice. Nary a hand or foot-hold in sight."

" I see," Mallory murmured. " I see indeed. ' Into Navarone the hard way.' That was what you said."

" That was," Jensen acknowledged. " You and your gang —just four others. Mallory's Merry Mountaineers. Handpicked. Every man a specialist. You'll meet them all tomorrow—this afternoon, rather."

They travelled in silence for the next ten minutes, turned up right from the dock area, jounced their uncomfortable way over the massive cobbles of the Rue Souers, slewed round into Mohammed Ali square, passed in front of the Bourse and turned right down the Sherif Pasha.

Mallory looked at the man behind the wheel. He could see his face quite clearly now in the gathering light.

" Where to, sir? "

" To see the only man in the Middle East who can give you any help now. Monsieur Eugene Vlachos of Navarone."

" You are a brave man, Captain Mallory." Nervously Eugene Vlachos twisted the long, pointed ends of his black moustache. " A brave man and a foolish one, I would say— but I suppose we cannot call a man a fool when he only obeys his orders." His eyes left the large drawing lying before him on the table and sought Jensen's impassive face.

" Is there no other way, Captain? " he pleaded.

Jensen shook his head slowly.

" There are. We've tried them all, sir. They all failed. This is the last."

" He must go, then? "

" There are over a thousand men on Kheros, sir."

Vlachos bowed his head in silent acceptance, then smiled faintly at Mallory.

" He calls me ' sir.' Me, a poor Greek hotel-keeper and Captain Jensen of the Royal Navy calls me ' sir.' It makes an old man feel good." He stopped, gazed off vacantly into space, the faded eyes and tired, lined face soft with memory. " An old man, Captain Mallory, an old man now, a poor man and a sad one. But I wasn't always, not always. Once I was just middle-aged, and rich and well content. Once I owned a lovely land, a hundred square miles of the most beautiful country God ever sent to delight the eyes of His creatures here below, and how well I loved that land! " He laughed self-consciously and ran a hand through his thick, greying hair. " Ah, well, as you people say, I suppose it's all in the eye of the beholder. ' A lovely land,' I say. ' That blasted rock,' as Captain Jensen has been heard to describe it out of my hearing." He smiled at Jensen's sudden discomfiture. " But we both give it the same name—Navarone."

Startled, Mallory looked at Jensen. Jensen nodded.

" The Vlachos family has owned Navarone for generations. We had to remove Monsieur Vlachos in a great hurry eighteen months ago. The Germans didn't care overmuch for his kind of collaboration."

" It was—how do you say—touch and go," Vlachos nodded. " They had reserved three very special places for my two sons and myself in the dungeons in Navarone. . . . But enough of the Vlachos family. I just wanted you to know, young man, that I spent forty years on Navarone and almost four days "— he gestured to the table—" on that map. My information and that map you can trust absolutely. Many things will have changed, of course, but some things never change. The mountains, the bays, the passes, the caves, the roads, the houses and, above all, the fortress itself—these have remained unchanged for centuries, Captain Mallory."

" I understand, sir." Mallory folded the map carefully, stowed it away in his tunic. " With this, there's always a chance. Thank you very much."

" It is little enough, God knows." Vlachos's fingers drummed on the table for a moment, then he looked up at Mallory. " Captain Jensen informs me that most of you speak Greek fluently, that you will be dressed as Greek peasants and will carry forged papers. That is well. You will be—what is the word?—self-contained, will operate on your own." He paused, then went on very earnestly.

" Please do not try to enlist the help of the people of Navarone. At all costs you must avoid that. The Germans are ruthless. I know. If a man helps you and is found out, they will destroy not only that man but his entire village—men, women and children. It has happened before. It will happen again."

"It happened in Crete," Mallory agreed quietly. "I've seen it for myself."

"Exactly." Vlachos nodded. "And the people of Navarone have neither the skill nor the experience for successful guerrilla operations. They have not had the chance—German surveillance has been especially severe in our island."

"I promise you, sir——" Mallory began.

Vlachos held up his hand.

"Just a moment. If your need is desperate, really desperate, there are two men to whom you may turn. Under the first plane tree in the village square of Margaritha—at the mouth of the valley about three miles south of the fortress—you will find a man called Louki. He has been the steward of our family for many years. Louki has been of help to the British before—Captain Jensen will confirm that—and you can trust him with your life. He has a friend, Panayis: he, too, has been useful in the past."

"Thank you, sir. I'll remember. Louki and Panayis and Margaritha—the first plane tree in the square."

"And you will refuse all other aid, Captain?" Vlachos asked anxiously. "Louki and Panayis—only these two," he pleaded.

"You have my word, sir. Besides, the fewer the safer for us as well as your people." Mallory was surprised at the old man's intensity.

"I hope so, I hope so." Vlachos sighed heavily.

Mallory stood up, stretched out his hand to take his leave.

"You're worrying about nothing, sir. They'll never see us," he promised confidently. "Nobody will see us—and we'll see nobody. We're after only one thing—the guns."

"Ay, the guns—those terrible guns." Vlachos shook his head. "But just suppose——"

"Please. It will be all right," Mallory insisted quietly. "We will bring harm to none—and least of all to your islanders."

"God go with you to-night," the old man whispered. "God go with you to-night. I only wish that I could go too."

CHAPTER TWO

SUNDAY NIGHT

1900-0200

"COFFEE, SIR?"

Mallory stirred and groaned and fought his way up from the depths of exhausted sleep. Painfully he eased himself back on the metal-framed bucket-seat, wondering peevishly when the Air Force was going to get round to upholstering these fiendish contraptions. Then he was fully awake, tired, heavy eyes automatically focusing on the luminous dial of his wristwatch. Seven o'clock. Just seven o'clock—he'd been asleep barely a couple of hours. Why hadn't they let him sleep on?

"Coffee, sir?" The young air-gunner was still standing patiently by his side, the inverted lid of an ammunition box serving as a tray for the cups he was carrying.

"Sorry, boy, sorry." Mallory struggled upright in his seat, reached up for a cup of the steaming liquid, sniffed it appreciatively. "Thank you. You know, this smells just like real coffee."

"It is, sir." The young gunner smiled proudly. "We have a percolator in the galley."

"He has a percolator in the galley." Mallory shook his head in disbelief. "Ye gods, the rigours of war in the Royal Air Force!" He leaned back, sipped the coffee luxuriously and sighed in contentment. Next moment he was on his feet, the hot coffee splashing unheeded on his bare knees as he stared out the window beside him. He looked at the gunner, gestured

26

in disbelief at the mountainous landscape unrolling darkly beneath them.

" What the hell goes on here? We're not due till two hours after dark—and it's barely gone sunset! Has the pilot——? "

" That's Cyprus, sir." The gunner grinned. " You can just see Mount Olympus on the horizon. Nearly always, going to Castelrosso, we fly a big dog-leg over Cyprus. It's to escape observation, sir; and it takes us well clear of Rhodes."

" To escape observation, he says! " The heavy trans-atlantic drawl came from the bucket-seat diagonally across the passage: the speaker was lying collapsed—there was no other word for it—in his seat, the bony knees topping the level of the chin by several inches. " My Gawd! To escape observation! " he repeated in awed wonder. " Dog-legs over Cyprus. Twenty miles out from Alex by launch so that nobody ashore can see us takin' off by plane. And then what? " He raised himself painfully in his seat, eased an eyebrow over the bottom of the window, then fell back again, visibly exhausted by the effort. " And then what? Then they pack us into an old crate that's painted the whitest white you ever saw, guaranteed visible to a blind man at a hundred miles—'specially now that it's gettin' dark."

" It keeps the heat out," the young gunner said defensively.

" The heat doesn't worry me, son." The drawl was tireder, more lugubrious than ever. " I like the heat. What I don't like are them nasty cannon shells and bullets that can ventilate a man in all the wrong places." He slid his spine another impossible inch down the seat, closed his eyes wearily and seemed asleep in a moment.

The young gunner shook his head admiringly and smiled at Mallory.

" Worried to hell, isn't he, sir? "

Mallory laughed and watched the boy disappear for'ard into the control cabin. He sipped his coffee slowly, looked again at the sleeping figure across the passage. The blissful

unconcern was magnificent: Corporal Dusty Miller of the
United States, and more recently of the Long Range Desert
Force, would be a good man to have around.

He looked round at the others and nodded to himself in
satisfaction. They would all be good men to have around.
Eighteen months in Crete had developed in him an unerring
sense for assessing a man's capacity for survival in the peculiar
kind of irregular warfare in which he himself had been so long
engaged. Off-hand he'd have taken long odds on the capacity
of these four to survive. In the matter of picking an outstanding
team Captain Jensen, he reckoned, had done him proud. He
didn't know them all yet—not personally. But he was intimately
acquainted with the exhaustive dossier that Jensen held on
each one of them. These were reassuring, to say the least.

Or was there perhaps a slight question mark against
Stevens? Mallory wondered, looked across the passage at the
fair-haired, boyish figure gazing out eagerly beneath the
gleaming white wing of the Sunderland. Lieutenant Andy
Stevens, R.N.V.R., had been chosen for this assignment for
three reasons. He would navigate the craft that was to take
them to Navarone: he was a first-class Alpinist, with several
outstanding climbs to his record: and, the product of the
classical side of a red-brick university, he was an almost
fanatical philhellene, fluent in both Ancient and Modern
Greek, and had spent his last two long vacations before the
war as a tourist courier in Athens. But he was young, absurdly
young, Mallory thought as he looked at him, and youth could
be dangerous. Too often, in that island guerrilla warfare, it had
been fatal. The enthusiasm, the fire, the zeal of youth was not
enough: rather, it was too much, a positive handicap. This
was not a war of bugle calls and roaring engines and magnificent defiance in the clamour of battle: this was a war of
patience and endurance and stability, of cunning and craft and
stealth, and these were not commonly the attributes of youth.
. . . But he looked as if he might learn fast.

Mallory stole another glance at Miller. Dusty Miller, he decided, had learnt it all a long, long time ago. Dusty Miller on a white charger, the bugle to his lips—no, his mind just refused to encompass the incongruity of it. He just didn't look like Sir Launcelot. He just looked as if he had been around for a long, long time and had no illusions left.

Corporal Miller, had, in fact, been around for exactly forty years. By birth a Californian, by descent three parts Irish and one part Central European, he had lived and fought and adventured more in the previous quarter of a century than most men would in a dozen lifetimes. Silver-miner in Nevada, tunneller in Canada and oil-fire shooter all over the globe, he had been in Saudi Arabia when Hitler attacked Poland. One of his more remote maternal ancestors, some time around the turn of the century, had lived in Warsaw, but that had been affront enough for Miller's Irish blood. He had taken the first available plane to Britain and lied his way into the Air Force, where, to his immense disgust, and because of his age, he was relegated to the rear turret of a Wellington.

His first operational flight had been his last. Within ten minutes of taking off from the Menidi airfield outside Athens on a January night in 1941, engine failure had brought them to an ignominious though well-cushioned end in a paddy field some miles north-west of the city. The rest of the winter he had spent seething with rage in a cookhouse back in Menidi. At the beginning of April he resigned from the Air Force without telling anyone and was making his way north towards the fighting and the Albanian frontier when he met the Germans coming south. As Miller afterwards told it, he reached Nauplion two blocks ahead of the nearest panzer division, was evacuated by the transport *Slamat*, sunk, picked up by the destroyer *Wryneck*, sunk, and finally arrived in Alexandria in an ancient Greek caique, with nothing left him in the world but a fixed determination never again to venture in the air or on the sea. Some months later he was operating with a long-range striking force behind the enemy lines in Libya.

He was, Mallory mused, the complete antithesis to Lieutenant Stevens. Stevens, young, fresh, enthusiastic, correct and immaculately dressed, and Miller, dried-up, lean, stringy, immensely tough and with an almost pathological aversion to spit and polish. How well the nickname " Dusty" suited him: there could hardly have been a greater contrast. Again, unlike Stevens, Miller had never climbed a mountain in his life and the only Greek words he knew were invariably omitted from the dictionaries. And both these facts were of no importance at all. Miller had been picked for one reason only. A genius with explosives, resourceful and cool, precise and deadly in action, he was regarded by Middle East Intelligence in Cairo as the finest saboteur in southern Europe.

Behind Miller sat Casey Brown. Short, dark and compact, Petty Officer Telegraphist Brown was a Clydesider, in peacetime an installation and testing engineer in a famous yachtbuilder's yard on the Gareloch. The fact that he was a born and ready-made engine-room artificer had been so blindingly obvious that the Navy had missed it altogether and stuck him in the Communications Branch. Brown's ill luck was Mallory's good fortune. Brown would act as the engineer of the boat taking them to Navarone and would maintain radio contact with base. He had also the further recommendation of being a first-class guerrilla fighter: a veteran of the Special Boat Service, he held the D.C.M. and D.S.M. for his exploits in the Ægean and off the coast of Libya.

The fifth and last member of the party sat directly behind Mallory. Mallory did not have to turn round to look at him. He already knew him, knew him better than he knew anyone else in the world, better even than he knew his own mother. Andrea, who had been his lieutenant for all these eighteen interminable months in Crete, Andrea of the vast bulk, the continual rumbling laughter and tragic past, with whom he had eaten, lived and slept in caves, rock-shelters and abandoned shepherd's huts while constantly harried by German patrols and aircraft— that Andrea had become his *alter ego*, his *doppelganger*: to look at Andrea was to look in a mirror to remind himself what he was like. . . . There was no question as to why Andrea had come along. He wasn't there primarily because he was a Greek himself, with an intimate knowledge of the islanders' language, thought and customs, nor even because of his perfect understanding with Mallory, although all these things helped. He was, instead, there exclusively for the protection and safety he afforded. Endlessly patient, quiet and deadly, tremendously fast in spite of his bulk, and with a feline stealth that exploded into berserker action, Andrea was the complete fighting machine. Andrea was their insurance policy against failure.

Mallory turned back to look out the window again, then nodded to himself in imperceptible satisfaction. Jensen probably couldn't have picked a better team if he'd scoured the whole Mediterranean theatre. It suddenly occurred to Mallory that Jensen probably had done just that. Miller and Brown had been recalled to Alexandria almost a month ago. It was almost as long since Stevens's relief had arrived aboard his cruiser in Malta. And if their battery-charging engine hadn't slipped down that ravine in the White Mountains, and if the sorely harassed runner from the nearest listening post hadn't taken a week to cover fifty miles of snowbound, enemy patrolled mountains and another five days to find them, he and Andrea would have been in Alexandria almost a fortnight earlier. Mallory's opinion of Jensen, already high, rose another notch. A far-seeing man who planned accordingly, Jensen must have had all his preparations for this made even before the first of the two abortive parachute landings on Navarone.

It was eight o'clock and almost totally dark inside the plane when Mallory rose and made his way for'ard to the control cabin. The captain, face wreathed in tobacco smoke, was drinking coffee: the co-pilot waved a languid hand at his approach and resumed a bored scanning of the scene ahead.

" Good evening." Mallory smiled. " Mind if I come in? "

" Welcome in my office any time," the pilot assured him. " No need to ask."

" I only thought you might be busy. . . ." Mallory stopped and looked again at the scene of masterly inactivity. " Just who is flying this plane? " he asked.

" George. The automatic pilot." He waved a coffee-cup in the direction of a black, squat box, it's blurred outlines just visible in the near darkness. " An industrious character, and makes a damn' sight fewer mistakes than that idle hound who's supposed to be on watch. . . Anything on your mind, Captain?"

" Yes. What were your instructions for to-night? "

" Just to set you blokes down in Castelrosso when it was good and dark." The pilot paused, then said frankly, " I don't get it. A ship this size for only five men and a couple of hundred odd pounds of equipment. Especially to Castelrosso. Especially after dark. Last plane that came down here after dark just kept on going down. Underwater obstruction—dunno what it was. Two survivors."

" I know. I heard. I'm sorry, but I'm under orders too. As for the rest, forget it—and I mean forget. Impress on your crew that they mustn't talk. They've never seen us."

The pilot nodded glumly. " We've all been threatened with court-martial already. You'd think there was a ruddy war on."

" There is. . . . We'll be leaving a couple of cases behind. We're going ashore in different clothes. Somebody will be waiting for our old stuff when you get back."

" Roger. And the best of luck, Captain. Official secrets, or no official secrets, I've got a hunch you're going to need it."

" If we are, you can give us a good send-off." Mallory grinned. " Just set us down in one piece, will you? "

" Reassure yourself, brother," said the pilot firmly. " Just set your mind at ease. Don't forget—I'm in this ruddy plane too."

The clamour of the Sunderland's great engines was still echoing in their ears when the stubby little motor-boat chugged softly out of the darkness and nosed alongside the gleaming hull of the flying-boat. There was no time lost, there were no words spoken; within a minute the five men and all their gear had been embarked; within another the little boat was rubbing to a stop against the rough stone Navy jetty of Castelrosso. Two ropes went spinning up into the darkness, were caught and quickly secured by practised hands. Amidships, the rust-scaled iron ladder, recessed deep into the stone, stretched up into the star-dusted darkness above: as Mallory reached the top, a figure stepped forward out of the gloom.

" Captain Mallory? "

" Yes."

" Captain Briggs, Army. Have your men wait here, will you? The colonel would like to see you." The nasal voice, peremptory in its clipped affectation, was far from cordial. Mallory stirred in slow anger, but said nothing. Briggs sounded like a man who might like his bed or his gin, and maybe their late visitation was keeping him from either or both. War was hell.

They were back in ten minutes, a third figure following behind them. Mallory peered at the three men standing on the edge of the jetty, identified them, then peered around again.

" Where's Miller got to? " he asked.

" Here, boss, here." Miller groaned, eased his back off a big, wooden bollard, climbed wearily to his feet. " Just restin', boss. Recuperatin', as you might say, from the nerve-rackin' rigours of the trip."

" When you're all *quite* ready," Briggs said acidly,

" Matthews here will take you to your quarters. You are to remain on call for the Captain, Matthews. Colonel's orders." Briggs's tone left no doubt that he thought the colonel's orders a piece of arrant nonsense. " And don't forget, Captain—two hours, the Colonel said."

" I know, I know," Mallory said wearily. " I was there when he said it. It was to me he was talking. Remember? All right, boys, if you're ready."

" Our gear, sir? " Stevens ventured.

" Just leave it there. Right, Matthews, lead the way, will you? "

Matthews led the way along the jetty and up interminable flights of steep, worn steps, the others following in Indian file, rubber soles noiseless on the stone. He turned sharply right at the top, went down a narrow, winding alley, into a passage, climbed a flight of creaking, wooden stairs, opened the first door in the corridor above.

" Here you are, sir. I'll just wait in the corridor outside."

" Better wait downstairs," Mallory advised. " No offence, Matthews, but the less you know of this the better."

He followed the others into the room, closing the door behind him. It was a small, bleak room, heavily curtained. A table and half a dozen chairs took up most of the space. Over in the far corner the springs of the single bed creaked as Corporal Miller stretched himself out luxuriously, hands clasped behind his head.

" Gee! " he murmured admiringly. " A hotel room. Just like home. Kinda bare, though." A thought occurred to him. " Where are all you other guys gonna sleep? "

" We aren't," Mallory said briefly. " Neither are you. We're pulling out in less than two hours." Miller groaned. " Come on, soldier," Mallory went on relentlessly. " On your feet."

Miller groaned again, swung his legs over the edge of the bed and looked curiously at Andrea. The big Greek was quartering the room methodically, pulling out lockers, turning pictures, peering behind curtains and under the bed.

" What's he doin'? " Miller asked. " Lookin' for dust? "

" Testing for listening devices," Mallory said curtly. " One of the reasons why Andrea and I have lasted so long." He dug into the inside pocket of his tunic, a dark naval battledress with neither badge nor insignia, pulled out a chart and the map Vlachos had given him, unfolded and spread them out. " Round the table, all of you. I know you've been bursting with curiosity for the past couple of weeks, asking yourselves a hundred questions. Well, here are all the answers. I hope you like them. . . . Let me introduce you to the island of Navarone."

Mallory's watch showed exactly eleven o'clock when he finally sat back, folded away the map and chart. He looked quizzically at the four thoughtful faces round the table.

" Well, gentlemen, there you have it. A lovely set-up, isn't it? " He smiled wryly. " If this was a film, my next line should be, ' Any questions, men? ' But we'll dispense with that because I just wouldn't have any of the answers. You all know as much as I do."

" A quarter of a mile of sheer cliff, four hundred feet high, and he calls it the only break in the defences." Miller, his head bent moodily over his tobacco tin, rolled a long, thin cigarette with one expert hand. " This is just crazy, boss. Me, I can't even climb a bloody ladder without falling off." He puffed strong, acrid clouds of smoke into the air. " Suicidal. That's the word I was lookin' for. Suicidal. One buck gets a thousand we never get within five miles of them gawddamned guns! "

" One in a thousand, eh? " Mallory looked at him for a long time without speaking. " Tell me, Miller, what odds are you offering on the boys on Kheros? "

" Yeah." Miller nodded heavily. " Yeah, the boys on

Kheros. I'd forgotten about them. I just keep thinkin' about me and that damned cliff." He looked hopefully across the table at the vast bulk of Andrea. " Or maybe Andrea there would carry me up. He's big enough, anyway."

Andrea made no reply. His eyes were half-closed, his thoughts could have been a thousand miles away.

" We'll tie you hand and foot and haul you up on the end of a rope," Stevens said unkindly. " We'll try to pick a fairly sound rope," he added carelessly. The words, the tone, were jocular enough, but the worry on his face belied them. Mallory apart, only Stevens appreciated the almost insuperable technical difficulties of climbing a sheer, unknown cliff in the darkness. He looked at Mallory questioningly. " Going up alone, sir, or——"

" Excuse me, please." Andrea suddenly sat forward, his deep rumble of a voice rapid in the clear, idiomatic English he had learnt during his long association with Mallory. He was scribbling quickly on a piece of paper. " I have a plan for climbing this cliff. Here is a diagram. Does the Captain think this is possible? "

He passed the paper across to Mallory. Mallory looked at it, checked, recovered, all in the one instant. There was no diagram on it. There were only two large, printed words: " Keep talking."

" I see," Mallory said thoughtfully. " Very good indeed, Andrea. This has distinct possibilities." He reversed the paper, held it up before him so that they could all see the words. Andrea had already risen to his feet, was padding cat-footed towards the door. " Ingenious, isn't it, Corporal Miller," he went on conversationally. " Might solve quite a lot of our difficulties."

" Yeah." The expression on Miller's face hadn't altered a fraction, the eyes were still half-closed against the smoke drifting up from the cigarette dangling between his lips. " Reckon that might solve the problem, Andrea—and get me

up in one piece, too." He laughed easily, concentrated on
screwing a curiously-shaped cylinder on to the barrel of an
automatic that had magically appeared in his left hand. "But
I don't quite get that funny line and the dot at——"

It was all over in two seconds—literally. With a deceptive
ease and nonchalance Andrea opened the door with one hand,
reached out with the other, plucked a wildly-struggling figure
through the gap, set him on the ground again and closed the
door, all in one concerted movement. It had been as soundless
as it had been swift. For a second the eavesdropper, a hatchet-
faced, swarthy Levantine in badly-fitting white shirt and blue
trousers, stood there in shocked immobility, blinking rapidly in
the unaccustomed light. Then his hand dived in under his
shirt.

"Look out!" Miller's voice was sharp, the automatic
lining up as Mallory's hand closed over his.

"Watch!" Mallory said softly.

The men at the table caught only a flicker of blued steel as
the knife arm jerked convulsively back and plunged down with
vicious speed. And then, incredibly, hand and knife were
stopped dead in mid-air, the gleaming point only two inches
from Andrea's chest. There was a sudden scream of agony, the
ominous cracking of wrist bones as the giant Greek tightened his
grip, and then Andrea had the blade between finger and thumb,
had removed the knife with the tender, reproving care of a
parent saving a well-loved but irresponsible child from himself.
Then the knife was reversed, the point was at the Levantine's
throat and Andrea was smiling down pleasantly into the dark
and terror-stricken eyes.

Miller let out a long breath, half-sigh, half-whistle.

"Well, now," he murmured, "I guess mebbe Andrea has
done that sort of thing before?"

"I guess maybe he has," Mallory mimicked. "Let's have
a closer look at exhibit A, Andrea."

Andrea brought his prisoner close up to the table, well

within the circle of light. He stood there sullenly before them, a thin, ferret-faced man, black eyes dulled in pain and fear, left hand cradling his crushed wrist.

"How long do you reckon this fellow's been outside, Andrea?" Mallory asked.

Andrea ran a massive hand through his thick, dark, curling hair, heavily streaked with grey above the temples.

"I cannot be sure, Captain. I imagined I heard a noise—a kind of shuffle—about ten minutes ago, but I thought my ears were playing tricks. Then I heard the same sound a minute ago. So I am afraid——"

"Ten minutes, eh?" Mallory nodded thoughtfully, then looked at the prisoner. "What's your name?" he asked sharply. "What are you doing here?"

There was no reply. There were only the sullen eyes, the sullen silence—a silence that gave way to a sudden yelp of pain as Andrea cuffed the side of his head.

"The Captain is asking you a question," Andrea said reproachfully. He cuffed him again, harder this time. "Answer the Captain."

The stranger broke into rapid, excitable speech, gesticulating wildly with both hands. The words were quite unintelligible. Andrea sighed, shut off the torrent by the simple expedient of almost encircling the scrawny throat with his left hand.

Mallory looked questioningly at Andrea. The giant shook his head.

"Kurdistan or Armenian, Captain, I think. But I don't understand it."

"I certainly don't," Mallory admitted. "Do you speak English?" he asked suddenly.

Black, hate-filled eyes glared back at him in silence. Andrea cuffed him again.

"Do you speak English?" Mallory repeated relentlessly.

"Eenglish? Eenglish?" Shoulders and upturned palms

lifted in the age-old gesture of incomprehension. "Ka Eenglish!"

"He says he don't speak English," Miller drawled.

"Maybe he doesn't and maybe he does," Mallory said evenly. "All we know is that he *has* been listening and that we can't take any chances. There are far too many lives at stake." His voice suddenly hardened, the eyes were grim and pitiless. "Andrea!"

"Captain?"

"You have the knife. Make it clean and quick. Between the shoulder blades!"

Stevens cried out in horror, sent his chair crashing back as he leapt to his feet.

"Good God, sir, you can't——"

He broke off and stared in amazement at the sight of the prisoner catapulting himself bodily across the room to crash into a distant corner, one arm up-curved in rigid defence, stark, unreasoning panic limned in every feature of his face. Slowly Stevens looked away, saw the triumphant grin on Andrea's face, the dawning comprehension in Brown's and Miller's. Suddenly he felt a complete fool. Characteristically, Miller was the first to speak.

"Waal, waal, whaddya know! Mebbe he *does* speaka da Eenglish after all."

"Maybe he does," Mallory admitted. "A man doesn't spend ten minutes with his ear glued to a keyhole if he doesn't understand a word that's being said. . . . Give Matthews a call, will you, Brown?"

The sentry appeared in the doorway a few seconds later.

"Get Captain Briggs here, will you, Matthews?" he asked. "At once, please."

The soldier hesitated.

"Captain Briggs has gone to bed, sir. He left strict orders that he wasn't to be disturbed."

"My heart bleeds for Captain Briggs and his broken

slumbers," Mallory said acidly. "He's had more sleep in a day than I've had in the past week." He glanced at his watch and the heavy brows came down in a straight line over the tired, brown eyes. "We've no time to waste. Get him here at once. Understand? At once!"

Matthews saluted and hurried away. Miller cleared his throat and clucked his tongue sadly.

"These hotels are all the same. The goin's-on—you'd never believe your eyes. Remember once I was at a convention in Cincinnati——"

Mallory shook his head wearily.

"You have a fixation about hotels, Corporal. This is a military establishment and these are army officers' billets."

Miller made to speak but changed his mind. The American was a shrewd judge of people. There were those who could be ribbed and those who could not be ribbed. An almost hopeless mission, Miller was quietly aware, and as vital as it was, in his opinion, suicidal; but he was beginning to understand why they'd picked this tough, sunburnt New Zealander to lead it.

They sat in silence for the next five minutes, then looked up as the door opened. Captain Briggs was hatless and wore a white silk muffler round his throat in place of the usual collar and tie. The white contrasted oddly with the puffed red of the heavy neck and face above. These had been red enough when Mallory had first seen them in the colonel's office—high blood pressure and even higher living, Mallory had supposed: the extra deeper shades of red and purple now present probably sprang from a misplaced sense of righteous indignation. A glance at the choleric eyes, gleaming light-blue prawns afloat in a sea of vermilion, was quite enough to confirm the obvious.

"I think this is a bit much, Captain Mallory!" The voice was high pitched in anger, more nasal than ever. "I'm not the duty errand-boy, you know. I've had a damned hard day and——"

"Save it for your biography," Mallory said curtly, "and take a gander at this character in the corner."

Briggs's face turned an even deeper hue. He stepped into the room, fists balled in anger, then stopped in his tracks as his eye lit on the crumpled, dishevelled figure still crouched in the corner of the room.

"Good God!" he ejaculated. "Nicolai!"

"You know him." It was a statement, not a question.

"Of course I know him!" Briggs snorted. "Everybody knows him. Nicolai. Our laundry-boy."

"Your laundry-boy! Do his duties entail snooping around the corridors at night, listening at keyholes?"

"What do you mean?"

"What I say." Mallory was very patient. "We caught him listening outside the door."

"Nicolai? I don't believe it!"

"Watch it, mister," Miller growled. "Careful who you call a liar. We all saw him."

Briggs stared in fascination at the black muzzle of the automatic waving negligently in his direction, gulped, looked hastily away.

"Well, what if you did?" He forced a smile. "Nicolai can't speak a word of English."

"Maybe not," Mallory agreed dryly. "But he understands it well enough." He raised his hand. "I've no desire to argue all night and I certainly haven't the time. Will you please have this man placed under arrest, kept in solitary confinement and incommunicado for the next week at least. It's vital. Whether he's a spy or just too damned nosy, he knows far too much. After that, do what you like. My advice is to kick him out of Castelrosso."

"*Your* advice, indeed!" Briggs's colour returned, and with it his courage. "Who the hell are you to give me advice or to give me orders, Captain Mallory?" There was a heavy emphasis on the word "captain."

" Then I'm asking it as a favour," Mallory pleaded wearily. " I can't explain, but it's terribly important. There are hundreds of lives——"

"Hundreds of lives! " Briggs sneered. "Melodramatic stuff and nonsense! " He smiled unpleasantly. " I suggest you keep that for *your* cloak-and-dagger biography, Captain Mallory."

Mallory rose, walked round the table, stopped a foot away from Briggs. The brown eyes were still and very cold.

" I could go and see your colonel, I suppose. But I'm tired of arguing. You'll do exactly as I say or I'll go straight to Naval H.Q. and get on the radio-telephone to Cairo. And if I do," Mallory went on, " I swear to you that you'll be on the next ship home to England—and on the troop-deck, at that."

His last words seemed to echo in the little room for an interminable time: the stillness was intense. And then, as suddenly as it had arisen, the tension was gone and Briggs's face, a now curiously mottled white and red, was slack and sullen in defeat.

" All right, all right," he said. " No need for all these damned stupid threats—not if it means all that much to you." The attempt to bluster, to patch up the shredded rags of his dignity, was pathetic in its transparency. " Matthews—call out the guard."

The torpedo-boat, great aero engines throttled back half speed, pitched and lifted, pitched and lifted with monotonous regularity as it thrust its way into the long, gentle swell from the W.N.W. For the hundredth time that night Mallory looked at his watch.

" Running behind time, sir? " Stevens suggested.

Mallory nodded.

" We should have stepped straight into this thing from the Sunderland—there was a hold-up."

Brown grunted. " Engine trouble, for a fiver." The Clyde-side accent was very heavy.

"Yes, that's right." Mallory looked up, surprised. "How did you know?"

"Always the same with these blasted M.T.B. engines," Brown growled. "Temperamental as a film star."

There was silence for a time in the tiny blacked-out cabin, a silence broken only by the occasional clink of a glass. The Navy was living up to its traditional hospitality.

"If we're late," Miller observed at last, "why doesn't the skipper open her up? They tell me these crates can do forty to fifty knots."

"You look green enough already," Stevens said tactlessly. "Obviously, you've never been in an M.T.B. full out in a heavy sea."

Miller fell silent a moment. Clearly, he was trying to take his mind off his internal troubles. "Captain?"

"Yes, what is it?" Mallory answered sleepily. He was stretched full length on a narrow settee, an almost empty glass in his fingers.

"None of my business, I know, boss, but—would you have carried out that threat you made to Captain Briggs?"

Mallory laughed.

"It *is* none of your business, but—well, no, Corporal, I wouldn't. I wouldn't because I couldn't. I haven't all that much authority invested in me—and I didn't even know whether there was a radio-telephone in Castelrosso."

"Yeah. Yeah, do you know, I kinda suspected that." Corporal Miller rubbed a stubbled chin. "If he'd called your bluff, what would you have done, boss?"

"I'd have shot Nicolai," Mallory said quietly. "If the colonel had failed me, I'd have had no choice left."

"I knew that too. I really believe you would. For the first time I'm beginning to believe we've got a chance. . . . But I kinda wish you *had* shot him—*and* little Lord Fauntleroy. I didn't like the expression on old Briggs's face when you went out that door. Mean wasn't the word. He coulda killed you then. You trampled right over his pride, boss—and to a phony like that nothin' else in the world matters."

Mallory made no reply. He was already sound asleep, his empty glass fallen from his hand. Not even the banshee clamour of the great engines opening full out as they entered the sheltered calm of the Rhodes channel could plumb his bottomless abyss of sleep.

CHAPTER THREE

MONDAY

0700-1700

"My dear fellow, you make me feel dreadfully embarrassed."
Moodily the officer switched his ivory-handled fly-swat against
an immaculately trousered leg, pointed a contemptuous but
gleaming toe-cap at the ancient caique, broad-beamed and two-
masted, moored stern on to the even older and more dilapidated
wooden pier on which they were standing. " I am positively
ashamed. The clients of Rutledge and Company, I assure you,
are accustomed only to the best."

Mallory smothered a smile. Major Rutledge of the Buffs,
Eton and Sandhurst as to intonation, millimetrically tooth-
brushed as to moustache, Savile Row as to the quite dazzling
sartorial perfection of his khaki drill, was so magnificently out
of place in the wild beauty of the rocky, tree-lined bluffs of that
winding creek that his presence there seemed inevitable. Such
was the major's casual assurance, so dominating his majestic
unconcern, that it was the creek, if anything, that seemed
slightly out of place.

" It *does* look as if it has seen better days," Mallory admitted.
" Nevertheless, sir, it's exactly what we want."

" Can't understand it, I really can't understand it." With
an irritable but well-timed swipe the major brought down a
harmless passing fly. " I've been providing chaps with everything during the past eight or nine months—caiques, launches,
yachts, fishing boats, everything—but no one has ever yet

specified the oldest, most dilapidated derelict I could lay hands on. Quite a job laying hands on it, too, I tell you." A pained expression crossed his face. " The chaps know I don't usually deal in this line of stuff."

" What chaps? " Mallory asked curiously.

" Oh, up the islands, you know." Rutledge gestured vaguely to the north and west.

" But—but those are enemy held——"

" So's this one. Chap's got to have his H.Q. somewhere." Rutledge explained patiently. Suddenly his expression brightened. " I say, old boy, I know just the thing for you. A boat to escape observation and investigation—that was what Cairo insisted I get. How about a German E-boat, absolutely perfect condition, one careful owner. Could get ten thou. for her at home. Thirty-six hours. Pal of mine over in Bodrum——"

" Bodrum? " Mallory questioned. " Bodrum? But—but that's in Turkey, isn't it? "

" Turkey? Well, yes, actually, I believe it is," Rutledge admitted. " Chap has to get his supplies from somewhere, you know," he added defensively.

" Thanks all the same "—Mallory smiled—" but this is exactly what we want. We can't wait, anyway."

" On your own heads be it! " Rutledge threw up his hands in admission of defeat. " I'll have a couple of my men shove your stuff aboard."

" I'd rather we did it ourselves, sir. It's—well, it's a very special cargo."

" Right you are," the major acknowledged. " No questions Rutledge, they call me. Leaving soon? "

Mallory looked at his watch.

" Half an hour, sir."

" Bacon, eggs and coffee in ten minutes? "

" Thanks very much." Mallory grinned. " That's one offer we'll be very glad to accept."

He turned away, walked slowly down to the end of the pier. He breathed deeply, savouring the heady, herb-scented air of an Ægean dawn. The salt tang of the sea, the drowsily sweet perfume of honeysuckle, the more delicate, sharper fragrance of mint all subtly merged into an intoxicating whole, indefinable, unforgettable. On either side, the steep slopes, still brilliantly green with pine and walnut and holly, stretched far up to the moorland pastures above, and from these, faintly borne on the perfumed breeze, came the distant, melodic tinkling of goats' bells, a haunting, a nostalgic music, true symbol of the leisured peace the Ægean no longer knew.

Unconsciously almost, Mallory shook his head and walked more quickly to the end of the pier. The others were still sitting where the torpedo boat had landed them just before dawn. Miller, inevitably, was stretched his full length, hat tilted against the golden, level rays of the rising sun.

"Sorry to disturb you and all that, but we're leaving in half an hour; breakfast in ten minutes. Let's get the stuff aboard." He turned to Brown. "Maybe you'd like to have a look at the engine?" he suggested.

Brown heaved himself to his feet, looked down unenthusiastically at the weather-beaten, paint-peeled caique.

"Right you are, sir. But if the engine is on a par with this bloody wreck . . ." He shook his head in prophetic gloom and swung nimbly over the side of the pier.

Mallory and Andrea followed him, reaching up for the equipment as the other two passed it down. First they stowed away a sackful of old clothes, then the food, pressure stove and fuel, the heavy boots, spikes, mallets, rock axes and coils of wire-centred rope to be used for climbing, then, more carefully, the combined radio receiver and transmitter and the firing generator fitted with the old-fashioned plunge handle. Next came the guns—two Schmeissers, two Brens, a Mauser and a Colt—then a case containing a weird but carefully selected hodge-podge of torches, mirrors, two sets of identity papers and, incredibly, bottles of Hock, Moselle, *ouzo* and *retsima*.

Finally, and with exaggerated care, they stowed away for'ard in the forepeak two wooden boxes, one green in colour, medium sized and bound in brass, the other small and black. The green box held high explosive—T.N.T., amatol and a few standard sticks of dynamite, together with grenades, gun-cotton primers and canvas hosing; in one corner of the box was a bag of emery dust, another of ground glass, and a sealed jar of potassium, these last three items having been included against the possibility of Dusty Miller's finding an opportunity to exercise his unique talents as a saboteur. The black box held only detonators, percussion and electrical, detonators with fulminates so unstable that their exposed powder could be triggered off by the impact of a falling feather.

The last box had been stowed away when Casey Brown's head appeared above the engine hatch. Slowly he examined the mainmast reaching up above his head, as slowly turned for'ard to look at the foremast. His face carefully expression-less, he looked at Mallory.

" Have we got sails for these things, sir? "

" I suppose so. Why? "

" Because God only knows we're going to need them! " Brown said bitterly. " Have a look at the engine-room, you said. This isn't an engine-room. It's a bloody scrap-yard. And the biggest, most rusted bit of scrap down there is attached to the propeller shaft. And what do you think it is? An old Kelvin two-cylinder job built more or less on my own doorstep —about thirty years ago." Brown shook his head in despair, his face as stricken as only a Clydeside engineer's can be at the abuse of a beloved machine. " And it's been falling to bits for years, sir. Place is littered with discarded bits and spares. I've seen junk heaps off the Gallowgate that were palaces compared to this."

" Major Rutledge said it was running only yesterday,"

Mallory said mildly. " Anyway, come on ashore. Breakfast.
Remind me we're to pick up a few heavy stones on the way
back, will you? "

" Stones! " Miller looked at him in horror. " Aboard that
thing? "

Mallory nodded, smiling.

" But that gawddamned ship is sinkin' already! " Miller
protested. " What do you want stones for? "

" Wait and see."

Three hours later Miller saw. The caique was chugging
steadily north over a glassy, windless sea, less than a mile off
the coast of Turkey, when he mournfully finished lashing his
blue battledress into a tight ball and heaved it regretfully over
the side. Weighted by the heavy stone he had carried aboard,
it was gone from sight in a second.

Morosely he surveyed himself in the mirror propped up
against the for'ard end of the wheelhouse. Apart from a deep
violet sash wrapped round his lean middle and a fancifully
embroidered waistcoat with its former glory mercifully faded,
he was dressed entirely in black. Black lacing jackboots, black
baggy trousers, black shirt and black jacket: even his sandy
hair had been dyed to the same colour.

He shuddered and turned away.

" Thank Gawd the boys back home can't see me now! "
he said feelingly. He looked critically at the others, dressed,
with some minor variations, like himself. " Waal, mebbe I ain't
quite so bad after all. . . . Just what is all this quick-change
business for, boss? "

" They tell me you've been behind the German lines twice,
once as a peasant, once as a mechanic." Mallory heaved his
own ballasted uniform over the side. " Well, now you see what
the well-dressed Navaronian wears."

" The double change, I meant. Once in the plane, and
now."

" Oh, I see. Army khaki and naval whites in Alex., blue battledress in Castelrosso and now Greek clothes? Could have been—almost certainly were—snoopers in Alex. or Castelrosso or Major Rutledge's island. And we've changed from launch to plane to M.T.B. to caique. Covering our tracks, Corporal. We just can't take any chances."

Miller nodded, looked down at the clothes sack at his feet, wrinkled his brows in puzzlement, stooped and dragged out the white clothing that had caught his eye. He held up the long, voluminous clothes for inspection.

" To be used when passing through the local cemeteries, I suppose." He was heavily ironic. " Disguised as ghosts."

" Camouflage," Mallory explained succinctly. " Snow-smocks."

" What ! "

" Snow. That white stuff. There are some pretty high mountains in Navarone, and we may have to take to them. So—snow-smocks."

Miller looked stunned. Wordlessly he stretched his length on the deck, pillowed his head and closed his eyes. Mallory grinned at Andrea.

" Picture of a man getting his full quota of sunshine before battling with the Arctic wastes. . . . Not a bad idea. Maybe you should get some sleep, too. I'll keep watch for a couple of hours."

For five hours the caique continued on its course parallel to the Turkish coast, slightly west of north and rarely more than two miles off-shore. Relaxed and warm in the still kindly November sun, Mallory sat wedged between the bulwarks of the blunt bows, his eyes ceaselessly quartering sky and horizon. Amidships, Andrea and Miller lay asleep. Casey Brown still defied all attempts to remove him from the engine-room. Occasionally—very occasionally—he came up for a breath of fresh air, but the intervals between his appearances steadily lengthened as he concentrated more and more on the aged Kelvin engine, regulating the erratic drip-fed lubrication, constantly adjusting the air intake: an engineer to his finger-tips, he was unhappy about that engine: he was drowsy, too, and headachy—the narrow hatchway gave hardly any ventilation at all.

Alone in the wheelhouse—an unusual feature in so tiny a caique—Lieutenant Andy Stevens watched the Turkish coast slide slowly by. Like Mallory's, his eyes moved ceaselessly, but not with the same controlled wandering. They shifted from the coast to the chart: from the chart to the islands up ahead off the port bow, islands whose position and relation to each other changed continually and deceptively, islands gradually lifting from the sea and hardening in definition through the haze of blue refraction: from the islands to the old alcohol compass swinging almost imperceptibly on corroded gimbals, and from the compass back to the coast again. Occasionally, he peered up into the sky, or swung a quick glance through a 180-degree sweep of the horizon. But one thing his eyes avoided all the time. The chipped, fly-blown mirror had been hung up in the wheelhouse again, but it was as if his eyes and the mirror were of opposite magnetic poles: he could not bring himself to look at it.

His forearms ached. He had been spelled at the wheel twice, but still they ached, abominably: his lean, tanned hands were ivory-knuckled on the cracked wheel. Repeatedly, con-sciously, he tried to relax, to ease the tension that was bunching up the muscles of his arms; but always, as if possessed of independent volition, his hands tightened their grip again. There was a funny taste in his mouth, too, a sour and salty taste in a dry, parched mouth, and no matter how often he swallowed. or drank from the sun-warmed pitcher at his side, the taste and the dryness remained. He could no more exorcise them than he could that twisting, cramping ball that was knot-ting up his insides, just above the solar plexus, or the queer, uncontrollable tremor that gripped his right leg from time to time.

Lieutenant Andy Stevens was afraid. He had never been in action before, but it wasn't that. This wasn't the first time he had been afraid. He had been afraid all his life, ever since he could remember: and he could remember a long way back, even to his early prep-school days when his famous father, Sir Cedric Stevens, the most celebrated explorer and mountaineer of his time, had thrown him bodily into the swimming pool at home, telling him that this was the only way he could learn to swim. He could remember still how he had fought and spluttered his way to the side of the pool, panic-stricken and desperate, his nose and mouth blocked with water, the pit of his stomach knotted and constricted in that nameless, terrifying ache he was to come to know so well: how his father and two elder brothers, big and jovial and nerveless like Sir Cedric himself, had wiped the tears of mirth from their eyes and pushed him in again. . . .

His father and brothers. . . . It had been like that all through his schooldays. Together, the three of them had made his life thoroughly miserable. Tough, hearty, open-air types who worshipped at the shrine of athleticism and physical fitness, they could not understand how anyone could fail to revel in diving from a five-metre springboard or setting a hunter at a five-barred gate or climbing the crags of the Peak district or sailing a boat in a storm. All these things they had made him do and often he had failed in the doing, and neither his father nor his brothers could ever have understood how he had come to dread those violent sports in which they excelled, for they were not cruel men, nor even unkind, but simply stupid. And so to the simple physical fear he sometimes and naturally felt was added the fear of failure, the fear that he was bound to fail in whatever he had to do next, the fear of the inevitable mockery and ridicule: and because he had been a sensitive boy and feared the ridicule above all else, he had come to fear these things that provoked the ridicule. Finally, he had come to fear fear itself, and it was in a desperate attempt to overcome this double fear that he had devoted himself—this in his late teens—to crag and mountain climbing: in this he had ultimately become so proficient, developed such a reputation, that father and brothers had come to treat him with respect and as an equal, and the ridicule had ceased. But the fear had not ceased; rather it had grown by what it fed on, and often, on a particularly difficult climb, he had all but fallen to his death, powerless in the grip of sheer, unreasoning terror. But this terror he had always sought, successfully so far, to conceal. As now. He was trying to overcome, to conceal that fear now. He was afraid of failing—in what he wasn't quite sure—of not measuring up to expectation: he was afraid of being afraid: and he was desperately afraid, above all things, of being seen, of being known to be afraid. . . .

The startling, incredible blue of the Ægean; the soft, hazy silhouette of the Anatolian mountains against the washed-out cerulean of the sky; the heart-catching, magical blending of the blues and violets and purples and indigoes of the sun-soaked islands drifting lazily by, almost on the beam now; the iridescent rippling of the water fanned by the gentle, scent-laden breeze newly sprung from the south-east; the peaceful scene on deck, the reassuring, interminable thump-thump, thump-thump of the old Kelvin engine. . . . All was peace and quiet and contentment and warmth and languor, and it seemed impossible that anyone could be afraid. The world and the war were very far away that afternoon.

Or perhaps, after all, the war wasn't so far away. There were occasional pin-pricks—and constant reminders. Twice a German Arado seaplane had circled curiously overhead, and a Savoia and Fiat, flying in company, had altered course, dipped to have a look at them and flown off, apparently satisfied: Italian planes, these, and probably based on Rhodes, they were almost certainly piloted by Germans who had rounded up their erstwhile Rhodian allies and put them in prison camps after the surrender of the Italian Government. In the morning they had passed within half a mile of a big German caique—it flew the German flag and bristled with mounted machine-guns and a two-pounder far up in the bows; and in the early afternoon a high-speed German launch had roared by so closely that their caique had rolled wickedly in the wash of its passing: Mallory and Andrea had shaken their fists and cursed loudly and fluently at the grinning sailors on deck. But there had been no attempts to molest or detain them: neither British nor German hesitated at any time to violate the neutrality of Turkish territorial waters, but by the strange quixotry of a tacit gentlemen's agreement hostilities between passing vessels and planes were almost unknown. Like the envoys of warring countries in a neutral capital, their behaviour ranged from the impeccably and frigidly polite to a very pointed unawareness of one another's existence.

These, then, were the pin-pricks—the visitations and by-goings, harmless though they were, of the ships and planes of the enemy. The other reminders that this was no peace but an illusion, an ephemeral and a frangible thing, were more permanent. Slowly the minute hands of their watches circled, and every tick took them nearer to that great wall of cliff, barely eight hours away, that had to be climbed somehow: and almost dead ahead now, and less than fifty miles distant, they could see the grim, jagged peaks of Navarone topping the shimmering horizon and reaching up darkly against the sapphired sky, desolate and remote and strangely threatening.

At half-past two in the afternoon the engine stopped. There had been no warning coughs or splutters or missed strokes. One moment the regular, reassuring thump-thump: the next, sudden, completely unexpected silence, oppressive and foreboding in its absoluteness.

Mallory was the first to reach the engine hatch.

"What's up, Brown?" His voice was sharp with anxiety. "Engine broken down?"

"Not quite, sir." Brown was still bent over the engine, his voice muffled. "I shut it off just now." He straightened his back, hoisted himself wearily through the hatchway, sat on deck with his feet dangling, sucking in great draughts of fresh air. Beneath the heavy tan his face was very pale.

Mallory looked at him closely.

"You look as if you had the fright of your life."

"Not that." Brown shook his head. "For the past two-three hours I've been slowly poisoned down that ruddy hole. Only now I realise it." He passed a hand across his brow and groaned. "Top of my blinkin' head just about lifting off, sir. Carbon monoxide ain't a very healthy thing."

"Exhaust leak?"

"Aye. But it's more than a leak now." He pointed down at the engine. "See that stand-pipe supporting that big iron ball above the engine—the water-cooler? That pipe's as thin as paper, must have been leaking above the bottom flange for hours. Blew out a bloody great hole a minute ago. Sparks, smoke and flames six inches long. Had to shut the damned thing off at once, sir."

Mallory nodded in slow understanding.

"And now what? Can you repair it, Brown?"

"Not a chance, sir." The shake of the head was very definite. "Would have to be brazed or welded. But there's a spare down there among the scrap. Rusted to hell and about as shaky as the one that's on. . . . I'll have a go, sir."

"I'll give him a hand," Miller volunteered.

"Thanks, Corporal. How long, Brown, do you think?"

"Lord only knows, sir. Two hours, maybe four. Most of the nuts and bolts are locked solid with rust: have to shear or saw 'em—and then hunt for others."

Mallory said nothing. He turned away heavily, brought up beside Stevens who had abandoned the wheelhouse and was

now bent over the sail locker. He looked up questioningly as
Mallory approached.

Mallory nodded. " Just get them out and up. Maybe four
hours, Brown says. Andrea and I will do our landlubberly best
to help."

Two hours later, with the engine still out of commission,
they were well outside territorial waters, closing on a big island
some eight miles away to the W.N.W. The wind, warm and
oppressive now, had backed to a darkening and thundery east,
and with only a lug and a jib—all the sails they had found—
bent to the foremast, they could make no way at all into it.
Mallory had decided to make for the island—the chances of
being observed there were far less than in the open sea.
Anxiously he looked at his watch then stared back moodily
at the receding safety of the Turkish shore. Then he stiffened,
peered closely at the dark line of sea, land and sky that lay
to the east.

" Andrea! Do you see——"

" I see it, Captain." Andrea was at his shoulder. " Caique.
Three miles. Coming straight towards us," he added softly.

" Coming straight towards us," Mallory acquiesced. " Tell
Miller and Brown. Have them come here."

Mallory wasted no time when they were all assembled.

" We're going to be stopped and investigated," he said
quickly. " Unless I'm much mistaken, it's that big caique that
passed us this morning. Heaven only knows how, but they've
been tipped off and they're going to be as suspicious as hell.
This'll be no kid-glove, hands-in-the-pockets inspection. They'll
be armed to the teeth and hunting trouble. There's going to
be no half-measures. Let's be quite clear about that. Either
they go under or we do: we can't possibly survive an inspection
—not with all the gear *we've* got aboard. And," he added softly,
" we're not going to dump that gear." Rapidly he explained
his plans. Stevens, leaning out from the wheelhouse window,
felt the old sick ache in his stomach, felt the blood leaving his

face. He was glad of the protection of the wheelhouse that hid
the lower part of his body: that old familiar tremor in his leg
was back again. Even his voice was unsteady.

"But, sir—sir——"

"Yes, yes, what is it, Stevens?" Even in his hurry Mallory
paused at the sight of the pale, set face, the bloodless nails
clenched over the sill of the window.

"You—you can't do *that*, sir!" The voice burred harshly
under the sharp edge of strain. For a moment his mouth
worked soundlessly, then he rushed on. "It's massacre, sir,
it's—it's just murder!"

"Shut up, kid!" Miller growled.

"That'll do, Corporal!" Mallory said sharply. He looked
at the American for a long moment then turned to Stevens,
his eyes cold. "Lieutenant, the whole concept of directing a
successful war is aimed at placing your enemy at a disadvantage,
at *not* giving him an even chance. We kill them or they kill us.
They go under or we do—and a thousand men on Kheros.
It's just as simple as that, Lieutenant. It's not even a question
of conscience."

For several seconds Stevens stared at Mallory in complete
silence. He was vaguely aware that everyone was looking at
him. In that instant he hated Mallory, could have killed him.
He hated him because—suddenly he was aware that he hated
him only for the remorseless logic of what he said. He stared
down at his clenched hands. Mallory, the idol of every young
mountaineer and cragsman in pre-war England, whose
fantastic climbing exploits had made world headlines, in '38
and '39: Mallory, who had twice been baulked by the most
atrocious ill-fortune from surprising Rommel in his desert
headquarters: Mallory, who had three times refused promotion
in order to stay with his beloved Cretans who worshipped him
the other side of idolatry. Confusedly these thoughts tumbled
through his mind and he looked up slowly, looked at the lean,
sunburnt face, the sensitive, chiselled mouth, the heavy, dark

eyebrows bar-straight over the lined brown eyes that could be so cold or so compassionate, and suddenly he felt ashamed, knew that Captain Mallory lay beyond both his understanding and his judgment.

" I am very sorry, sir." He smiled faintly. " As Corporal Miller would say, I was talking out of turn." He looked aft at the caique arrowing up from the south-east. Again he felt the sick fear, but his voice was steady enough as he spoke. " I won't let you down, sir."

" Good enough. I never thought you would." Mallory smiled in turn, looked at Miller and Brown. " Get the stuff ready and lay it out, will you? Casual, easy and keep it hidden. They'll have the glasses on you."

He turned away, walked for'ard. Andrea followed him.

" You were very hard on the young man." It was neither criticism nor reproach—merely statement of fact.

" I know." Mallory shrugged. " I didn't like it either. . . . I had to do it."

" I think you had," Andrea said slowly. " Yes, I think you had. But it was hard. . . . Do you think they'll use the big gun in the bows to stop us? "

" Might—they haven't turned back after us unless they're pretty sure we're up to something fishy. But the warning shot across the bows—they don't go in for that Captain Teach stuff normally."

Andrea wrinkled his brows.

" Captain Teach? "

" Never mind." Mallory smiled. " Time we were taking up position now. Remember, wait for me. You won't have any trouble in hearing my signal," he finished dryly.

The creaming bow-wave died away to a gentle ripple, the throb of the heavy diesel muted to a distant murmur as the German boat slid alongside, barely six feet away. From where he sat on a fish-box on the port of the fo'c'sle, industriously sewing a button on to the old coat lying on the deck between his legs, Mallory could see six men, all dressed in the uniform of the regular German Navy—one crouched behind a belted Spandau mounted on its tripod just aft of the two-pounder, three others bunched amidships each armed with an automatic machine carbine—Schmeissers, he thought—the captain, a hard, cold-faced young lieutenant with the Iron Cross on his tunic, looking out the open door of the wheelhouse and, finally, a curious head peering over the edge of the engine-room hatch. From where he sat, Mallory couldn't see the poop-deck—the intermittent ballooning of the lug-sail in the uncertain wind blocked his vision; but from the restricted fore-and-aft lateral sweep of the Spandau, hungrily traversing only the for'ard half of their own caique, he was reasonably sure that there was another machine-gunner similarly engaged on the German's poop.

The hard-faced, young lieutenant—a real product of the Hitler Jugend that one, Mallory thought—leaned out of the wheelhouse, cupped his hand to his mouth.

" Lower your sails! " he shouted.

Mallory stiffened, froze to immobility. The needle had jammed hard into the palm of his hand, but he didn't even notice it. The lieutenant had spoken in English! Stevens was so young, so inexperienced. He'll fall for it, Mallory thought with a sudden sick certainty, he's bound to fall for it.

But Stevens didn't fall for it. He opened the door, leaned out, cupped his hand to his ear and gazed vacantly up to the sky, his mouth wide open. It was so perfect an imitation of dull-witted failure to catch or comprehend a shouted message that it was almost a caricature. Mallory could have hugged him. Not in his actions alone, but in his dark, shabby clothes and hair as blackly counterfeit as Miller's, Stevens was the slow, suspicious island fisherman to the life.

" Eh ? " he bawled.

" Lower your sails! We are coming aboard! " English again, Mallory noted; a persistent fellow this.

Stevens stared at him blankly, looked round helplessly at Andrea and Mallory: their faces registered a lack of comprehension as convincing as his own. He shrugged his shoulders in despair.

" I am sorry, I do not understand German," he shouted. " Can you not speak my language? " Stevens's Greek was perfect, fluent and idiomatic. It was also the Greek of Attica, not of the islands; but Mallory felt sure that the lieutenant wouldn't know the difference.

He didn't. He shook his head in exasperation, called in slow, halting Greek: " Stop your boat at once. We are coming aboard."

" Stop my boat! " The indignation was so genuine, the accompanying flood of furious oaths so authentic, that even the lieutenant was momentarily taken aback. " And why should I stop my boat for you, you—you——"

" You have ten seconds," the lieutenant interrupted. He was on balance again, cold, precise. " Then we will shoot."

Stevens gestured in admission of defeat and turned to Andrea and Mallory.

" Our conquerors have spoken," he said bitterly. " Lower the sails."

Quickly they loosened the sheets from the cleats at the foot of the mast. Mallory pulled the jib down, gathered the sail in his arms and squatted sullenly on the deck—he knew a dozen hostile eyes were watching him—close by the fish-box. The sail covering his knees and the old coat, his forearms on his thighs, he sat with head bowed and hands dangling between his knees, the picture of heart-struck dejection. The lug-sail, weighted by the boom at the top, came down with a rush. Andrea stepped over it, walked a couple of uncertain paces aft, then stopped, huge hands hanging emptily by his sides.

A sudden deepening in the muted throbbing of the diesel, a spin of the wheel and the big German caique was rubbing alongside. Quickly, but carefully enough to keep out of the

line of fire of the mounted Spandaus—there was a second
clearly visible now on the poop—the three men armed with
the Schmeissers leapt aboard. Immediately one ran forward,
whirled round level with the foremast, his automatic carbine
circling gently to cover all of the crew. All except Mallory—
and he was leaving Mallory in the safe hands of the Spandau
gunner in the bows. Detachedly, Mallory admired the precision, the timing, the clockwork inevitability of an old routine.

He raised his head, looked around him with a slow, peasant
indifference. Casey Brown was squatting on the deck abreast
the engine-room, working on the big ball-silencer on top of the
hatch-cover. Dusty Miller, two paces farther for'ard and with
his brows furrowed in concentration, was laboriously cutting a
section of metal from a little tin box, presumably to help in the
engine repairs. He was holding the wire-cutting pliers in his
left hand—and Miller, Mallory knew, was right-handed.
Neither Stevens nor Andrea had moved. The man beside the
foremast still stood there, eyes unwinking. The other two were
walking slowly aft, had just passed Andrea, their carriage
relaxed and easy, the bearing of men who know they have
everything so completely under control that even the idea of
trouble is ridiculous.

Carefully, coldly and precisely, at point-blank range and
through the folds of both coat and sail, Mallory shot the
Spandau machine-gunner through the heart, swung the still
chattering Bren round and saw the guard by the mast crumple
and die, half his chest torn away by the tearing slugs of the
machine-gun. · But the dead man was still on his feet, still had
not hit the deck, when four things happened simultaneously.
Casey Brown had had his hand on Miller's silenced automatic,
lying concealed beneath the ball-silencer, for over a minute.
Now he squeezed the trigger four times, for he wanted to mak'
siccar; the after machine-gunner leaned forward tiredly over
his tripod, lifeless fingers locked on the firing-guard. Miller
crimped the three-second chemical fuse with the pliers, lobbed

the tin box into the enemy engine-room, Stevens spun the armed stick-grenade into the opposite wheelhouse and Andrea, his great arms reaching out with all the speed and precision of striking cobras, swept the Schmeisser gunners' heads together with sickening force. And then all five men had hurled themselves to the deck and the German caique was erupting in a roar of flame and smoke and flying debris: gradually the echoes faded away over the sea and there was left only the whining stammer of the Spandau, emptying itself uselessly skyward; and then the belt jammed and the Ægean was as silent as ever, more silent than it had ever been.

Slowly, painfully, dazed by the sheer physical shock and the ear-shattering proximity of the twin explosions, Mallory pushed himself off the wooden deck and stood shakily on his feet. His first conscious reaction was that of surprise, incredulity almost: the concussive blast of a grenade and a couple of lashed blocks of T.N.T., even at such close range, was far beyond anything he had expected.

The German boat was sinking, sinking fast. Miller's home-made bomb must have torn the bottom out of the engine-room. She was heavily on fire amidships, and for one dismayed instant Mallory had an apprehensive vision of towering black columns of smoke and enemy reconnaissance planes. But only for an instant: timbers and planking, tinder-dry and resinous, were burning furiously with hardly a trace of smoke, and the flaming, crumbling deck was already canted over sharply to port: she would be gone in seconds. His eyes wandered to the shattered skeleton of the wheelhouse, and he caught his breath suddenly when he saw the lieutenant impaled on the splintered wreck of the wheel, a ghastly, mangled caricature of what had once been a human being, decapitated and wholly horrible: vaguely, some part of Mallory's mind registered the harsh sound of retching, violent and convulsive, coming from the wheelhouse, and he knew Stevens must have seen it too. From deep within the sinking caique came the muffled roar of rupturing fuel tanks: a flame-veined gout of oily black smoke erupted from the engine-room and the caique miraculously struggled back on even keel, her gunwales almost awash, and then the hissing waters had overflowed and overcome the decks and the twisting flames, and the caique was gone, her slender masts sliding vertically down and vanishing in a turbulent welter of creaming foam and oil-filmed bubbles. And now the Ægean was calm and peaceful again, as placid as if the caique had never been, and almost as empty: a few charred planks and an inverted helmet drifted lazily on the surface of the shimmering sea.

With a conscious effort of will, Mallory turned slowly to look to his own ship and his own men. Brown and Miller were on their feet, staring down in fascination at where the caique had been, Stevens was standing at the wheelhouse door. He, too, was unhurt, but his face was ashen: during the brief action he had been a man above himself, but the aftermath, the brief glimpse he'd had of the dead lieutenant had hit him badly. Andrea, bleeding from a gash on the cheek, was looking down at the two Schmeisser gunners lying at his feet. His face was expressionless. For a long moment Mallory looked at him, looked in slow understanding.

" Dead? " he asked quietly.

Andrea inclined his head.

" Yes." His voice was heavy. " I hit them too hard."

Mallory turned away. Of all the men he had ever known, Andrea, he thought, had the most call to hate and to kill his enemies. And kill them he did, with a ruthless efficiency appalling in its single-mindedness and thoroughness of execution. But he rarely killed without regret, without the most bitter self-condemnation, for he did not believe that the lives of his fellow-men were his to take. A destroyer of his fellow-man, he loved his fellow-man above all things. A simple man, a good man, a killer with a kindly heart, he was for ever troubled by his conscience, ill at ease with his inner self. But over and above the wonderings and the reproaches, he was informed by an honesty of thought, by a clear-sighted wisdom which sprang from and transcended his innate simplicity. Andrea killed neither for revenge, nor from hate, nor nationalism, nor for the sake of any of the other " isms " which self-seekers and fools and knaves employ as beguilement to the battlefield and justification for the slaughter of millions too young and too unknowing to comprehend the dreadful futility of it all. Andrea killed simply that better men might live.

" Anybody else hurt? " Mallory's voice was deliberately brisk, cheerful. " Nobody? Good! Right, let's get under way as fast as possible. The farther and the faster we leave this place behind, the better for all of us." He looked at his watch. " Almost four o'clock—time for our routine check with Cairo. Just leave that scrapyard of yours for a couple of minutes, Chief. See if you can pick them up." He looked at the sky to the east, a sky now purply livid and threatening, and shook his head. " Could be that the weather forecast might be worth hearing."

It was. Reception was very poor—Brown blamed the violent static on the dark, convoluted thunderheads steadily creeping up astern, now overspreading almost half the sky— but adequate. Adequate enough to hear information they had never expected to hear, information that left them silenced, eyes stilled in troubled speculation. The tiny loudspeaker boomed and faded, boomed and faded, against the scratchy background of static.

" Rhubarb calling Pimpernel! Rhubarb calling Pimpernel! " These were the respective code names for Cairo and Mallory. " Are you receiving me? "

Brown tapped an acknowledgment. The speaker boomed again.

" Rhubarb calling Pimpernel. Now X minus one. Repeat, X minus one." Mallory drew in his breath sharply. X—dawn on Saturday—had been the assumed date for the German attack on Kheros. It must have been advanced by one day— and Jensen was not the man to speak without certain knowledge. Friday, dawn—just over three days.

" Send ' X minus one understood,' " Mallory said quietly.

" Forecast, East Anglia," the impersonal voice went on: the Northern Sporades, Mallory knew. " Severe electrical storms probable this evening, with heavy rainfall. Visibility poor. Temperature falling, continuing to fall next twenty-four hours. Winds east to south-east, force six, locally eight, moderating early to-morrow."

Mallory turned away, ducked under the billowing lug-sail, walked slowly aft. What a set-up, he thought, what a bloody mess. Three days to go, engine u. s. and a first-class storm building up. He thought briefly, hopefully, of Squadron Leader Torrance's low opinion of the backroom boys of the Met. Office, but the hope was never really born. It couldn't be, not unless he was blind. The steep-piled buttresses of the thunderheads towered up darkly terrifying, now almost directly above.

" Looks pretty bad, huh ? " The slow nasal drawl came from immediately behind him. There was something oddly reassuring about that measured voice, about the steadiness of the washed-out blue of the eyes enmeshed in a spider's web of fine wrinkles.

" It's not so good," Mallory admitted.

" What's all this force eight business, boss ? "

" A wind scale," Mallory explained. " If you're in a boat this size and you're good and tired of life, you can't beat a force eight wind."

Miller nodded dolefully.

" I knew it. I might have known. And me swearing they'd never get me on a gawddamned boat again." He brooded a while, sighed, slid his legs over the engine-room hatchway, jerked his thumb in the direction of the nearest island, now less than three miles away. "That doesn't look so hot, either."

"Not from here," Mallory agreed. "But the chart shows a creek with a right-angle bend. It'll break the sea and the wind."

"Inhabited?"

"Probably."

"Germans?"

"Probably."

Miller shook his head in despair and descended to help Brown. Forty minutes later, in the semi-darkness of the overcast evening and in torrential rain, lance-straight and strangely chill, the anchor of the caique rattled down between the green walls of the forest, a dank and dripping forest, hostile in its silent indifference.

CHAPTER FOUR

MONDAY EVENING

1700-2330

"BRILLIANT!" said Mallory bitterly. "Ruddy well brilliant!
'Come into my parlour, said the spider to the fly.'" He swore
in chagrin and exasperated disgust, eased aside the edge of the
tarpaulin that covered the for'ard hatchway, peered out
through the slackening curtain of rain and took a second and
longer look at the rocky bluff that elbowed out into the bend
of the creek, shutting them off from the sea. There was no
difficulty in seeing now, none at all: the drenching cloudburst
had yielded to a gentle drizzle, and grey and white cloud
streamers, shredding in the lifting wind, had already pursued
the blackly towering cumulo-nimbus over the far horizon. In a
clear band of sky far to the west, the sinking, flame-red sun
was balanced on the rim of the sea. From the shadowed waters
of the creek it was invisible, but its presence unmistakable from
the gold-shot gauze of the falling rain, high above their heads.

The same golden rays highlighted the crumbling old watch-
tower on the very point of the cliff, a hundred feet above the
river. They burnished its fine-grained white Parian marble,
mellowed it to a delicate rose: they gleamed on the glittering
steel, the evil mouths of the Spandau machine-guns reaching
out from the slotted embrasures in the massive walls, illumined
the hooked cross of the swastika on the flag that streamed out
stiffly from the staff above the parapet. Solid even in its decay,
impregnable in its position, commanding in its lofty outlook,

67

the tower completely dominated both waterborne approaches, from the sea and, upriver, down the narrow, winding channel that lay between the moored caique and the foot of the cliff.

Slowly, reluctantly almost, Mallory turned away and gently lowered the tarpaulin. His face was grim as he turned round to Andrea and Stevens, ill-defined shadows in the twilit gloom of the cabin.

" Brilliant! " he repeated. " Sheer genius. Mastermind Mallory. Probably the only bloody creek within a hundred miles—and in a hundred islands—with a German guard post on it. And of course I had to go and pick it. Let's have another look at that chart, will you, Stevens? "

Stevens passed it across, watched Mallory study it in the pale light filtering in under the tarpaulin, leaned back against the bulkhead and drew heavily on his cigarette. It tasted foul, stale and acrid, but the tobacco was fresh enough, he knew. The old, sick fear was back again, as strongly as ever. He looked at the great bulk of Andrea across from him, felt an illogical resentment towards him for having spotted the emplacement a few minutes ago. They'll have cannon up there, he thought dully, they're bound to have cannon—couldn't control the creek otherwise. He gripped his thigh fiercely, just above the knee, but the tremor lay too deep to be controlled: he blessed the merciful darkness of the tiny cabin. But his voice was casual enough as he spoke.

" You're wasting your time, sir, looking at that chart and blaming yourself. This is the only possible anchorage within hours of sailing time from here. With that wind there was nowhere else we could have gone."

" Exactly. That's just it." Mallory folded the chart, handed it back. " There was nowhere else we could have gone. There was nowhere else anyone could have gone. Must be a very popular port in a storm, this—a fact which must have become apparent to the Germans a long, long time ago. That's why I should have known they were almost bound to have a post here. However, spilt milk, as you say." He raised his voice. " Chief! "

" Hallo! " Brown's muffled voice carried faintly from the depths of the engine-room.

" How's it going? "

" Not too bad, sir. Assembling it now."

Mallory nodded in relief.

" How long? " he called. " An hour? "

" Aye, easy, sir."

" An hour." Again Mallory glanced through the tarpaulin, looked back at Andrea and Stevens. " Just about right. We'll leave in an hour. Dark enough to give us some protection from our friends up top, but enough light left to navigate our way out of this damned corkscrew of a channel."

" Do you think they'll try to stop us, sir? " Stevens's voice was just too casual, too matter of fact. He was pretty sure Mallory would notice.

" It's unlikely they'll line the banks and give us three hearty cheers," Mallory said dryly. " How many men do you reckon they'll have up there, Andrea? "

" I've seen two moving around," Andrea said thoughtfully. " Maybe three or four altogether, Captain. A small post. The Germans don't waste men on these."

" I think you're about right," Mallory agreed. " Most of them'll be in the garrison in the village—about seven miles from here, according to the chart, and due west. It's not likely——"

He broke off sharply, stiffened in rigid attention. Again the call came, louder this time, imperative in its tone. Cursing himself for his negligence in not posting a guard—such carelessness would have cost him his life in Crete—Mallory pulled the tarpaulin aside, clambered slowly on to the deck. He carried no arms, but a half-empty bottle of Moselle dangled from his left hand: as part of a plan prepared before they had left

Alexandria, he'd snatched it from a locker at the foot of the tiny companionway.

He lurched convincingly across the deck, grabbed at a stay in time to save himself from falling overboard. Insolently he stared down at the figure on the bank, less than ten yards away —it hadn't mattered about a guard, Mallory realised, for the soldier carried his automatic carbine slung over his shoulder—insolently he tilted the wine to his mouth and swallowed deeply before condescending to talk to him.

He could see the mounting anger in the lean, tanned face of the young German below him. Mallory ignored it. Slowly, an inherent contempt in the gesture, he dragged the frayed sleeve of his black jacket across his lips, looked the soldier even more slowly up and down in a minutely provocative inspection as disdainful as it was prolonged.

" Well? " he asked truculently in the slow speech of the islands. " What the hell do you want? "

Even in the deepening dusk he could see the knuckles whitening on the stock of the carbine, and for an instant Mallory thought he had gone too far. He knew he was in no danger—all noise in the engine-room had ceased, and Dusty Miller's hand was never far from his silenced automatic—but he didn't want trouble. Not just yet. Not while there were a couple of manned Spandaus in that watch-tower.

With an almost visible effort the young soldier regained his control. It needed little help from the imagination to see the draining anger, the first tentative stirrings of hesitation and bewilderment. It was the reaction Mallory had hoped for. Greeks—even half-drunken Greeks—didn't talk to their over-lords like that—not unless they had an overpoweringly good reason.

" What vessel is this? " The Greek was slow and halting but passable. " Where are you bound for? "

Mallory tilted the bottle again, smacked his lips in noisy

satisfaction. He held the bottle at arm's length, regarded it with a loving respect.

" One thing about you Germans," he confided loudly. " You do know how to make a fine wine. I'll wager _you_ can't lay your hands on this stuff, eh? And the swill they're making up above "—the island term for the mainland—" is so full of resin that it's only good for lighting fires." He thought for a moment. " Of course, if you know the right people in the islands, they _might_ let you have some ouzo. But some of us can get ouzo _and_ the best Hocks _and_ the best Moselles."

The soldier wrinkled his face in disgust. Like almost every fighting man he despised Quislings, even when they were on his side: in Greece they were very few indeed.

" I asked you a question," he said coldly. " What vessel, and where bound? "

" The caique _Aigion_," Mallory replied loftily. " In ballast, for Samos. Under orders," he said significantly.

" Whose orders? " the soldier demanded. Shrewdly Mallory judged the confidence as superficial only. The guard was impressed in spite of himself.

" Herr Commandant in Vathy. General Graebel," Mallory said softly. " You will have heard of the Herr General before, yes? " He was on safe ground here, Mallory knew. The reputation of Graebel, both as a paratroop commander and an iron disciplinarian, had spread far beyond these islands.

Even in the half-light Mallory could have sworn that the guard's complexion turned paler. But he was dogged enough.

" You have papers? Letters of authority? "

Mallory sighed wearily, looked over his shoulder.

" Andrea! " he bawled.

" What do you want? " Andrea's great bulk loomed through the hatchway. He had heard every word that passed, had taken his cue from Mallory: a newly-opened wine bottle was almost engulfed in one vast hand and he was scowling hugely. " Can't you see I'm busy? " he asked surlily. He stopped short at the sight of the German and scowled again, irritably. " And what does this halfling want? "

" Our passes and letters of authority from Herr General. They're down below."

Andrea disappeared, grumbling deep in his throat. A rope was thrown ashore, the stern pulled in against the sluggish current and the papers passed over. The papers—a set different from those to be used if emergency arose in Navarone—proved to be satisfactory, eminently so. Mallory would have been surprised had they been anything else. The preparation of these, even down to the photostatic facsimile of General Graebel's signature, was all in the day's work for Jensen's bureau in Cairo.

The soldier folded the papers, handed them back with a muttered word of thanks. He was only a kid, Mallory could see now—if he was more than nineteen, his looks belied him. A pleasant, open-faced kid—of a different stamp altogether from the young fanatics of the S.S. Panzer Division—and far too thin. Mallory's chief reaction was one of relief: he would have hated to have to kill a boy like this. But he had to find out all he could. He signalled to Stevens to hand him up the almost empty crate of Moselle. Jensen, he mused, had been very thorough indeed: the man had literally thought of every-thing. . . . Mallory gestured lazily in the direction of the old watch-tower.

" How many of you are up there? " he asked.

The boy was instantly suspicious. His face had tightened up, stilled in hostile surmise.

" Why do you want to know? " he asked stiffly.

Mallory groaned, lifted his hands in despair, turned sadly to Andrea.

" You see what it is to be one of them? " he asked in mournful complaint. " Trust nobody. Think everyone is as twisted as . . ." He broke off hurriedly, turned to the soldier again. " It's just that we don't want to have the same trouble every time we come in here," he explained. "We'll be back in Samos in a couple of days, and we've still another case of Moselle to work through. General Graebel keeps his—ah—special envoys well supplied. . . . It must be thirsty work up there in the sun. Come on, now, a bottle each. How many bottles?"

The reassuring mention that they would be back again, the equally reassuring mention of Graebel's name, plus, probably, the attraction of the offer and his comrades' reaction if he told them he had refused it, tipped the balance, overcame scruples and suspicions.

"There are only three of us," he said grudgingly.

"Three it is," Mallory said cheerfully. "We'll bring you some Hock next time we return." He tilted his own bottle. "*Prosit!*" he said, an islander proud of airing his German, and then, more proudly still, "*Auf Wiedersehen!*"

The boy murmured something in return. He stood hesitating for a moment, slightly shame-faced, then wheeled abruptly, walked off slowly along the river bank, clutching his bottles of Moselle.

"So!" Mallory said thoughtfully. "There are only three of them. That should make things easier——"

"Well done, sir!" It was Stevens who interrupted, his voice warm, his face alive with admiration. "Jolly good show!"

"Jolly good show!" Miller mimicked. He heaved his lanky length over the coaming of the engine hatchway. "'Good' be damned! I couldn't understand a gawddamned word, but for my money that rates an Oscar. That was terrific, boss!"

"Thank you, one and all," Mallory murmured. "But I'm afraid the congratulations are a bit premature." The sudden chill in his voice struck at them, so that their eyes aligned along his pointing finger even before he went on. "Take a look," he said quietly.

The young soldier had halted suddenly about two hundred

yards along the bank, looked into the forest on his left in startled surprise, then dived in among the trees. For a moment the watchers on the boat could see another soldier, talking excitedly to the boy and gesticulating in the direction of their boat, and then both were gone, lost in the gloom of the forest.

" That's torn it! " Mallory said softly. He turned away. " Right, that's enough. Back to where you were. It would look fishy if we ignored that incident altogether, but it would look a damned sight fishier if we paid too much attention to it. Don't let's appear to be holding a conference."

Miller slipped down into the engine-room with Brown, and Stevens went back to the little for'ard cabin. Mallory and Andrea remained on deck, bottles in their hands. The rain had stopped now, completely, but the wind was still rising, climbing the scale with imperceptible steadiness, beginning to bend the tops of the tallest of the pines. Temporarily the bluff was affording them almost complete protection. Mallory deliberately shut his mind to what it must be like outside. They had to put out to sea—Spandaus permitting—and that was that.

" What do you think has happened, sir? " Stevens's voice carried up from the gloom of the cabin.

" Pretty obvious, isn't it? " Mallory asked. He spoke loudly enough for all to hear. " They've been tipped off. Don't ask me how. This is the second time—and their suspicions are going to be considerably reinforced by the absence of a report from the caique that was sent to investigate us. She was carrying a wireless aerial, remember? "

" But why should they get so damned suspicious all of a sudden? " Miller asked. " It doesn't make sense to me, boss."

" Must be in radio contact with their H.Q. Or a telephone —probably a telephone. They've just been given the old tic-tac. Consternation on all sides."

" So mebbe they'll be sending a small army over from their H.Q. to deal with us," Miller said lugubriously.

Mallory shook his head definitely. His mind was working

quickly and well, and he felt oddly certain, confident of himself.

" No, not a chance. Seven miles as the crow flies. Ten, maybe twelve miles over rough hill and forest tracks—and in pitch darkness. They wouldn't think of it." He waved his bottle in the direction of the watch-tower. " To-night's their big night."

" So we can expect the Spandaus to open up any minute? " Again the abnormal matter-of-factness of Stevens's voice.

Mallory shook his head a second time.

"They won't. I'm positive of that. No matter how suspicious they may be, how certain they are that we're the big bad wolf, they are going to be shaken to the core when that kid tells them we're carrying papers and letters of authority signed by General Graebel himself. For all they know, curtains for us may be the firing squad for them. Unlikely, but you get the general idea. So they're going to contact H.Q., and the commandant on a small island like this isn't going to take a chance on rubbing out a bunch of characters who may be the special envoys of the Herr General himself. So what? So he codes a message and radios it to Vathy in Samos and bites his nails off to the elbow till a message comes back saying Graebel has never heard of us and why the hell haven't we all been shot dead? " Mallory looked at the luminous dial of his watch. " I'd say we have at least half an hour."

" And meantime we all sit around with our little bits of paper and pencil and write out our last wills and testaments." Miller scowled. " No percentage in that, boss. We gotta *do* somethin'."

Mallory grinned.

" Don't worry, Corporal, we are going to do something. We're going to hold a nice little bottle party, right here on the poop."

The last words of their song—a shockingly corrupted

Grecian version of "Lilli Marlene," and their third song in the past few minutes—died away in the evening air. Mallory doubted whether more than faint snatches of the singing would be carried to the watch-tower against the wind, but the rhythmical stamping of feet and waving of bottles were in themselves sufficient evidence of drunken musical hilarity to all but the totally blind and deaf. Mallory grinned to himself as he thought of the complete confusion and uncertainty the Germans in the tower must have been feeling then. This was not the behaviour of enemy spies, especially enemy spies who know that suspicions had been aroused and that their time was running out.

Mallory tilted the bottle to his mouth, held it there for several seconds, then set it down again, the wine untasted. He looked round slowly at the three men squatting there with him on the poop, Miller, Stevens and Brown. Andrea was not there, but he didn't have to turn his head to look for him. Andrea, he knew, was crouched in the shelter of the wheelhouse, a waterproof bag with grenades and a revolver strapped to his back.

"Right!" Mallory said crisply. "Now's your big chance for *your* Oscar. Let's make this as convincing as we can." He bent forward, jabbed his finger into Miller's chest and shouted angrily at him.

Miller shouted back. For a few moments they sat there, gesticulating angrily and, to all appearances, quarrelling furiously with each other. Then Miller was on his feet, swaying in drunken imbalance as he leaned threateningly over Mallory, clenched fists ready to strike. He stood back as Mallory struggled to his feet, and in a moment they were fighting fiercely, raining apparently heavy blows on each other. Then a haymaker from the American sent Mallory reeling back to crash convincingly against the wheelhouse.

"Right, Andrea." He spoke quietly, without looking round. "This is it. Five seconds. Good luck." He scrambled to his feet, picked up a bottle by the neck and rushed at Miller, upraised arm and bludgeon swinging fiercely down. Miller dodged, swung a vicious foot, and Mallory roared in pain as his shins caught on the edge of the bulwarks. Silhouetted against the pale gleam of the creek, he stood poised for a second, arms flailing wildly, then plunged heavily, with a loud splash, into the waters of the creek.

For the next half-minute—it would take about that time for Andrea to swim underwater round the next upstream corner of the creek—everything was a confusion and a bedlam of noise. Mallory trod water as he tried to pull himself aboard: Miller had seized a boathook and was trying to smash it down on his head: and the others, on their feet now, had flung their arms round Miller, trying to restrain him: finally they managed to knock him off his feet, pin him to the deck and help the dripping Mallory aboard. A minute later, after the immemorial fashion of drunken men, the two combatants had shaken hands with one another and were sitting on the engine-room hatch, arms round each others' shoulders and drinking in perfect amity from the same freshly-opened bottle of wine.

" Very nicely done," Mallory said approvingly. " Very nicely indeed. An Oscar, definitely, for Corporal Miller."

Dusty Miller said nothing. Taciturn and depressed, he looked moodily at the bottle in his hand. At last he stirred.

" I don't like it, boss," he muttered unhappily. " I don't like the set-up one little bit. You shoulda let me go with Andrea. It's three to one up there, and they're waiting and ready." He looked accusingly at Mallory. " Dammit to hell, boss, you're always telling us how desperately important this mission is! "

" I know," Mallory said quietly. " That's why I didn't send you with him. That's why none of us has gone with him. We'd only be a liability to him, get in his way." Mallory shook his head. " You don't know Andrea, Dusty." It was the first time Mallory had called him that: Miller was warmed by the unexpected familiarity, secretly pleased. " None of you know him. But I know him." He gestured towards the watch-tower, its square-cut lines in sharp silhouette against the darkening sky. " Just a big, fat, good-natured chap, always laughing and joking." Mallory paused, shook his head again, went on slowly. " He's up there now, padding through that forest like a cat, the biggest and most dangerous cat you'll ever see. Unless they offer no resistance—Andrea never kills un-necessarily—when I send him up there after these three poor bastards I'm executing them just as surely as if they were in the electric chair and I was pulling the switch."

In spite of himself Miller was impressed, profoundly so.

" Known him a long time, boss, huh? " It was half question, half statement.

" A long time. Andrea was in the Albanian war—he was in the regular army. They tell me the Italians went in terror of him—his long-range patrols against the Iulia division, the Wolves of Tuscany, did more to wreck the Italian morale in Albania than any other single factor. I've heard a good many stories about them—not from Andrea—and they're all in-credible. And they're all true. But it was afterwards I met him, when we were trying to hold the Servia Pass. I was a very junior liaison lieutenant in the Anzac brigade at the time. Andrea "—he paused deliberately for effect—" Andrea was a lieutenant-colonel in the 19th Greek Motorised Division."

" A *what*? " Miller demanded in astonishment. Stevens and Brown were equally incredulous.

" You heard me. Lieutenant-colonel. Outranks me by a fairish bit, you might say." He smiled at them quizzically. " Puts Andrea in rather a different light, doesn't it? "

They nodded silently but said nothing. The genial, hail-fellow Andrea— a good-natured, almost simple-minded buffoon — a senior army officer. The idea had come too suddenly, was too incongruous for easy assimilation and immediate comprehension. But, gradually, it began to make sense to them. It explained many things about Andrea to them—his repose, his confidence, the unerring sureness of his lightning reactions, and, above all, the implicit faith Mallory had in him, the respect he showed for Andrea's opinions whenever he consulted him, which was frequently. Without surprise now, Miller slowly recalled that he'd never yet heard Mallory give Andrea a direct order. And Mallory never hesitated to pull his rank when necessary.

"After Servia," Mallory went on, "everything was pretty confused. Andrea had heard that Trikkala—a small country town where his wife and three daughters lived—had been flattened by the Stukas and Heinkels. He reached there all right, but there was nothing he could do. A land-mine had landed in the front garden and there wasn't even rubble left."

Mallory paused, lit a cigarette. He stared through the drifting smoke at the fading outlines of the tower.

"The only person he found there was his brother-in-law, George. George was with us in Crete—he's still there. From George he heard for the first time of the Bulgarian atrocities in Thrace and Macedonia—and his parents lived there. So they dressed in German uniforms—you can imagine how Andrea got those—commandeered a German army truck and drove to Protosami." The cigarette in Mallory's hand snapped suddenly, was sent spinning over the side. Miller was vaguely surprised: emotion, or rather, emotional displays, were so completely foreign to that very tough New Zealander. But Mallory went on quietly enough.

"They arrived in the evening of the infamous Protosami massacre. George has told me how Andrea stood there, clad in his German uniform and laughing as he watched a party of nine or ten Bulgarian soldiers lash couples together and throw them into the river. The first couple in were his father and stepmother, both dead."

"My Gawd above!" Even Miller was shocked out of his usual equanimity. "It's just not possible——"

"You know nothing," Mallory interrupted impatiently. "Hundreds of Greeks in Macedonia died the same way—but usually alive when they were thrown in. Until you know how the Greeks hate the Bulgarians, you don't even begin to know what hate is. . . . Andrea shared a couple of bottles of wine with the soldiers, found out that they had killed his parents earlier in the afternoon—they had been foolish enough to resist. After dusk he followed them up to an old corrugated-iron shed where they were billeted for the night. All he had was a knife. They left a guard outside. Andrea broke his neck, went inside, locked the door and smashed the oil lamp. George doesn't know what happened except that Andrea went berserk. He was back outside in two minutes, completely sodden, his uniform soaked in blood from head to foot. There wasn't a sound, not even a groan to be heard from the hut when they left, George says."

He paused again, but this time there was no interruption, nothing said. Stevens shivered, drew his shabby jacket closer round his shoulders: the air seemed to have become suddenly chill. Mallory lit another cigarette, smiled faintly at Miller, nodded towards the watch-tower.

"See what I mean by saying we'd only be a liability to Andrea up there?"

"Yeah. Yeah, I guess I do," Miller admitted. "I had no idea, I had no idea. . . . Not *all* of them, boss! He couldn't have killed——"

"He did," Mallory interrupted flatly. "After that he formed his own band, made life hell for the Bulgarian outposts in Thrace. At one time there was almost an entire division chasing him through the Rhodope mountains. Finally he was betrayed and captured, and he, George and four others were shipped to Stavros—they were to go on to Salonika for trial. They overpowered their guards—Andrea got loose among them on deck at night—and sailed the boat to Turkey. The Turks tried to intern him—they might as well have tried to intern an earthquake. Finally he arrived in Palestine, tried to join the Greek Commando Battalion that was being formed in the Middle East—mainly veterans of the Albanian campaign, like himself." Mallory laughed mirthlessly. " He was arrested as a deserter. He was released eventually, but there was no place for him in the new Greek Army. But Jensen's bureau heard about him, knew he was a natural for Subversive Operations. . . . And so we went to Crete together."

Five minutes passed, perhaps ten, but nobody broke the silence. Occasionally, for the benefit of any watchers, they went through the motions of drinking; but even the half-light was fading now and Mallory knew they could only be half-seen blurs, shadowy and indistinct, from the heights of the watch-tower. The caique was beginning to rock in the surge from the open sea round the bluff. The tall, reaching pines, black now as midnight cypress and looming impossibly high against the star-dusted cloud wrack that scudded palely overhead, were closing in on them from either side, sombre, watchful and vaguely threatening, the wind moaning in lost and mournful requiem through their swaying topmost branches. A bad night, an eerie and an ominous night, pregnant with that indefinable foreboding that reaches down and touches the well-springs of the nameless fears, the dim and haunting memories of a million years ago, the ancient racial superstitions of mankind: a night that sloughed off the tissue veneer of civilisation and the shivering man complains that someone is walking over his grave.

Suddenly, incongruously, the spell was shattered and Andrea's cheerful hail from the bank had them all on their feet in a moment. They heard his booming laugh and even the forests seemed to shrink back in defeat. Without waiting for the stern to be pulled in, he plunged into the creek, reached the caique in half a dozen powerful strokes and hoisted himself easily aboard. Grinning down from his great height, he shook

himself like some shaggy mastiff and reached out a hand for
a convenient wine bottle.

"No need to ask how things went, eh?" Mallory asked,
smiling.

"None at all. It was just too easy. They were only boys,
and they never even saw me." Andrea took another long swig
from the bottle and grinned in sheer delight. "And I didn't
lay a finger on them," he went on triumphantly. "Well, maybe
a couple of little taps. They were all looking down here, staring
out over the parapet when I arrived. Held them up, took their
guns off them and locked them in a cellar. And then I bent
their Spandaus—just a little bit."

This is it, Mallory thought dully, this is the end. This is
the finish of everything, the strivings, the hopes, the fears, the
loves and laughter of each one of us. This is what it all comes
to. This is the end, the end for us, the end for a thousand boys
on Kheros. In unconscious futility his hand came up, slowly
wiped lips salt from the spray bulleting off the wind-flattened
wave-tops, then lifted farther to shade bloodshot eyes that
peered out hopelessly into the storm-filled darkness ahead. For
a moment the dullness lifted, and an almost intolerable bitterness welled through his mind. All gone, everything—everything except the guns of Navarone. The guns of Navarone.
They would live on, they were indestructible. Damn them,
damn them, damn them! Dear God, the blind waste, the
terrible uselessness of it all!

The caique was dying, coming apart at the seams. She was
literally being pounded to death, being shaken apart by the
constant battering shocks of wind and sea. Time and time
again the poop-deck dipped beneath the foam-streaked
cauldron at the stern, the fo'c'sle rearing crazily into the air,
dripping forefoot showing clear: then the plummetting drop,
the shotgun, shuddering impact as broad-beamed bows crashed
vertically down into the cliff-walled trough beyond, an explosive

collision that threw so unendurable a strain on the ancient timbers and planks and gradually tore them apart.

It had been bad enough when they'd cleared the creek just as darkness fell, and plunged and wallowed their way through a quartering sea on a northward course for Navarone. Steering the unwieldy old caique had become difficult in the extreme: with the seas fine on the starboard quarter she had yawed wildly and unpredictably through a fifty degree arc, but at least her seams had been tight then, the rolling waves overtaking her in regular formation and the wind settled and steady somewhere east of south. But now all that was gone. With half a dozen planks sprung from the stem-post and working loose from the apron, and leaking heavily through the stuffing-gland of the propeller shaft, she was making water far faster than the ancient, vertical hand-pump could cope with: the wind-truncated seas were heavier, but broken and confused, sweeping down on them now from this quarter, now from that: and the wind itself, redoubled in its shrieking violence, veered and backed insanely from south-west to south-east. Just then it was steady from the south, driving the unmanageable craft blindly on to the closing iron cliffs of Navarone, cliffs that loomed invisibly ahead, somewhere in that all-encompassing darkness.

Momentarily Mallory straightened, tried to ease the agony of the pincers that were clawing into the muscles of the small of his back. For over two hours now he had been bending and straightening, bending and straightening, lifting a thousand buckets that Dusty Miller filled interminably from the well of the hold. God only knew how Miller felt. If anything, he had the harder job of the two and he had been violently and almost continuously seasick for hours on end. He looked ghastly, and he must have been feeling like death itself: the sustained effort, the sheer iron will-power to drive himself on in that condition reached beyond the limits of understanding. Mallory shook his head wonderingly. " My God, but he's tough, that Yank."

Unbidden, the words framed themselves in his mind, and he shook his head in anger, vaguely conscious of the complete inadequacy of the words.

Fighting for his breath, he looked aft to see how the others were faring. Casey Brown, of course, he couldn't see. Bent double in the cramped confines of the engine-room, he, too, was constantly sick and suffering a blinding headache from the oil fumes and exhaust gases still filtering from the replacement stand-pipe, neither of which could find any escape in the unventilated engine-room: but, crouched over the engine, he had not once left his post since they had cleared the mouth of the creek, had nursed the straining, ancient Kelvin along with the loving care, the exquisite skill of a man born into a long and proud tradition of engineering. That engine had only to falter once, to break down for the time in which a man might draw a deep breath, and the end would be as immediate as it was violent. Their steerage way, their lives, depended entirely on the continuous thrust of that screw, the laboured thudding of that rusted old two-cylinder. It was the heart of the boat, and when that heart stopped beating the boat died too, slewed broadside on and foundering in the waiting chasms between the waves.

For'ard of the engine-room, straddle-legged and braced against the corner pillar of the splintered skeleton that was all that remained of the wheelhouse, Andrea laboured unceasingly at the pump, never once lifting his head, oblivious of the crazy lurching of the deck of the caique, oblivious, too, of the biting wind and stinging, sleet-cold spray that numbed bare arms and moulded the sodden shirt to the hunched and massive shoulders. Ceaselessly, tirelessly, his arm thrust up and down, up and down, with the metronomic regularity of a piston. He had been there for close on three hours now, and he looked as if he could go on for ever. Mallory, who had yielded him the pump in complete exhaustion after less than twenty minutes' cruel labour, wondered if there was any limit to the man's endurance.

He wondered, too, about Stevens. For four endless hours now Andy Stevens had fought and overcome a wheel that leapt and struggled in his hands as if possessed of a convulsive life and will of its own—the will to wrench itself out of exhausted hands and turn them into the troughs: he had done a superb job, Mallory thought, had handled the clumsy craft magnificently. He peered at him closely, but the spray lashed viciously across his eyes and blinded him with tears. All he could gather was a vague impression of a tightly-set mouth, sleepless, sunken eyes and little patches of skin unnaturally pale against the mask of blood that covered almost the entire face from hairline to throat. The twisting, towering comber that had stove in the planks of the wheelhouse and driven in the windows with such savage force had been completely unexpected: Stevens hadn't had a chance. The cut above the right temple was particularly bad, ugly and deep: the blood still pulsed over the ragged edge of the wound, dripped monotonously into the water that sloshed and gurgled about the floor of the wheelhouse.

Sick to his heart, Mallory turned away, reached down for another bucket of water. What a crew, he thought to himself, what a really terrific bunch of—of . . . He sought for words to describe them, even to himself, but he knew his mind was far too tired. It didn't matter anyway, for there were no words for men like that, nothing that could do them justice.

He could almost taste the bitterness in his mouth, the bitterness that washed in waves through his exhausted mind. God, how wrong it was, how terribly unfair! Why did such men have to die, he wondered savagely, why did they have to die so uselessly. Or maybe it wasn't necessary to justify dying, even dying ingloriously empty of achievement. Could one not die for intangibles, for the abstract and the ideal? What had the martyrs at the stake achieved? Or what was the old tag— *dulce et decorumest pro patria mori*. If one lives well, what matter how one dies. Unconsciously his lips tightened in quick re-

vulsion and he thought of Jensen's remarks about the High
Commands playing who's-the-king-of-the-castle. Well, they
were right bang in the middle of their playground now, just a
few more pawns sliding into the limbo. Not that it mattered—
they had thousands more left to play with.

For the first time Mallory thought of himself. Not with
bitterness or self-pity or regret that it was all over. He thought
of himself only as the leader of this party, his responsibility for
the present situation. It's my fault, he told himself over and
over again, it's all my fault. I brought them here, I made them
come. Even while one part of his mind was telling him that he'd
had no option, that his hand had been forced, that if they had
remained in the creek they would have been wiped out long
before the dawn, irrationally he still blamed himself the more.
Shackleton, of all the men that ever lived, maybe Ernest
Shackleton could have helped them now. But not Keith
Mallory. There was nothing he could do, no more than the
others were doing, and they were just waiting for the end. But
he was the leader, he thought dully, he should be planning
something, he should be doing something. . . . But there was
nothing he could do. There was nothing anyone on God's
earth could do. The sense of guilt, of utter inadequacy, settled
and deepened with every shudder of the ancient timbers.

He dropped his bucket, grabbed for the security of the mast
as a heavy wave swept over the deck, the breaking foam
quicksilver in its seething phosphorescence. The waters swirled
hungrily round his legs and feet, but he ignored them, stared
out into the darkness. The darkness—that was the devil of it.
The old caique rolled and pitched and staggered and plunged,
but as if disembodied, in a vacuum. They could see nothing—
not where the last wave had gone, nor where the next was
coming from. A sea invisible and strangely remote, doubly
frightening in its palpable immediacy.

Mallory stared down into the hold, was vaguely conscious
of the white blur of Miller's face: he had swallowed some sea-

water and was retching painfully, salt water laced with blood. But Mallory ignored it, involuntarily: all his mind was concentrated elsewhere, trying to reduce some fleeting impression, as vague as it had been evanescent, to a coherent realisation. It seemed desperately urgent that he should do so. Then another and still heavier wave broke over the side and all at once he had it.

The wind! The wind had dropped away, was lessening with every second that passed. Even as he stood there, arms locked round the mast as the second wave fought to carry him away, he remembered how often in the high hills at home he had stood at the foot of a precipice as an onrushing wind, seeking the path of least resistance, had curved and lifted up the sheer face, leaving him standing in a pocket of relative immunity. It was a common enough mountaineering phenomenon. And these two freak waves—the surging backwash! The significance struck at him like a blow. The cliffs! They were on the cliffs of Navarone!

With a hoarse, wordless cry of warning, reckless of his own safety, he flung himself aft, dived full length through the swirling waters for the engine-room hatchway.

" Full astern! " he shouted. The startled white smudge that was Casey Brown's face twisted up to his. " For God's sake, man, full astern! We're heading for the cliffs! "

He scrambled to his feet, reached the wheelhouse in two strides, hand pawing frantically for the flare pocket.

" The cliffs, Stevens! We're almost on them! Andrea—Miller's still down below! "

He flicked a glance at Stevens, caught the slow nod of the set, blood-masked face, followed the line of sight of the expressionless eyes, saw the whitely phosphorescent line ahead, irregular but almost continuous, blooming and fading, blooming and fading, as the pounding seas smashed against and fell back from cliffs still invisible in the darkness. Desperately his hands fumbled with the flare.

And then, abruptly, it was gone, hissing and spluttering along the near-horizontal trajectory of its flight. For a moment, Mallory thought it had gone out, and he clenched his fists in impotent bitterness. Then it smashed against the rock face, fell back on to a ledge about a dozen feet above the water, and lay there smoking and intermittently burning in the driving rain, in the heavy spray that cascaded from the booming breakers.

The light was feeble, but it was enough. The cliffs were barely fifty yards away, black and wetly shining in the fitful radiance of the flare—a flare that illuminated a vertical circle of less than five yards in radius, and left the cliff below the ledge shrouded in the treacherous dark. And straight ahead, twenty, maybe fifteen yards from the shore, stretched the evil length of a reef, gap-toothed and needle-pointed, vanishing at either end into the outer darkness.

" Can you take her through? " he yelled at Stevens.

" God knows! I'll try! " He shouted something else about " steerage way," but Mallory was already half-way to the for'ard cabin. As always in an emergency, his mind was racing ahead with that abnormal sureness and clarity of thought for which he could never afterwards account.

Grasping spikes, mallet and a wire-cored rope, he was back on deck in seconds. He stood stock still, rooted in an almost intolerable tension as he saw the towering, jagged rock bearing down upon them, fine on the starboard bow, a rock that reached half-way up the wheelhouse. It struck the boat with a crash that sent him to his knees, rasped and grated along half the length of the buckled, splintered gunwales: and then the caique had rolled over to port and she was through, Stevens frantically spinning the wheel and shouting for full astern.

Mallory's breath escaped in a long, heavy sigh of relief—he had been quite unaware that he had stopped breathing—and he hurriedly looped the coil of rope round his neck and under his left shoulder and stuck spikes and hammer in his belt. The

caique was slewing heavily round now, port side to, plunging
and corkscrewing violently as she began to fall broadside into
the troughs of the waves, waves shorter and steeper than ever
under the double thrust of the wind and the waves and the
backwash recoiling from the cliffs: but she was still in the grip
of the sea and her own momentum, and the distance was closing
with frightening speed. It's a chance I have to take, Mallory
repeated to himself over and over again; it's a chance I have
to take. But that little ledge, remote and just inaccessible, was
fate's last refinement of cruelty, the salt in the wound of
extinction, and he knew in his heart of hearts that it wasn't a
chance at all, but just a suicidal gesture. And then Andrea
had heaved the last of the fenders—worn truck tyres—out
board, and was towering above him, grinning down hugely
into his face: and suddenly Mallory wasn't so sure any
more.

"The ledge?" Andrea's vast, reassuring hand was on his
shoulder.

Mallory nodded, knees bent in readiness, feet braced on the
plunging, slippery deck.

"Jump for it," Andrea boomed. "Then keep your legs
stiff."

There was no time for any more. The caique was swinging
in broadside to, teetering on the crest of a wave, as high up the
cliff as she would ever be, and Mallory knew it was now or
never. His hands swung back behind his body, his knees bent
farther, and then, in one convulsive leap he had flung himself
upwards, fingers scrabbling on the wet rock of the cliff, then
hooking over the rim of the ledge. For an instant he hung
there at the length of his arms, unable to move, wincing as he
heard the foremast crash against the ledge and snap in two,
then his fingers left the ledge without their own volition, and
he was almost half-way over, propelled by one gigantic heave
from below.

He was not up yet. He was held only by the buckle of his

belt, caught on the edge of the rock, a buckle now dragged up to his breastbone by the weight of his body. But he did not paw frantically for a handhold, or wriggle his body or flail his legs in the air—and any of these actions would have sent him crashing down again. At last, and once again, he was a man utterly at home in his own element. The greatest rock climber of his time, men called him, and this was what he had been born for.

Slowly, methodically, he felt the surface of the ledge, and almost at once he discovered a crack running back from the face. It would have been better had it been parallel to the face —and more than the width of a matchstick. But it was enough for Mallory. With infinite care he eased the hammer and a couple of spikes from his belt, worked a spike into the crack to obtain a minimal purchase, slid the other in some inches nearer, hooked his left wrist round the first, held the second spike with the fingers of the same hand and brought up the hammer in his free hand. Fifteen seconds later he was standing on the ledge.

Working quickly and surely, catlike in his balance on the slippery, shelving rock, he hammered a spike into the face of the cliff, securely and at a downward angle, about three feet above the ledge, dropped a clove hitch over the top and kicked the rest of the coil over the ledge. Then, and only then, he turned round and looked below him.

Less than a minute had passed since the caique had struck, but already she was a broken-masted, splintered shambles, sides caving in and visibly disintegrating as he watched. Every seven or eight seconds a giant comber would pick her up and fling her bodily against the cliff, the heavy truck tyres taking up only a fraction of the impact that followed, the sickening, rending crash that reduced the gunwales to matchwood, holed and split the sides and cracked the oaken timbers: and then she would roll clear, port side showing, the hungry sea pouring in through the torn and ruptured planking.

Three men were standing by what was left of the wheelhouse. *Three* men—suddenly, he realised that Casey Brown was missing, realised, too, that the engine was still running, its clamour rising and falling then rising again, at irregular intervals. Brown was edging the caique backwards and forwards along the cliff, keeping her as nearly as humanly possible in the same position, for he knew their lives depended on Mallory—and on himself. " The fool! " Mallory swore. " The crazy fool! "

The caique surged back in a receding trough, steadied, then swept in against the cliff again, heeling over so wildly that the roof of the wheelhouse smashed and telescoped against the wall of the cliff. The impact was so fierce, the shock so sudden, that Stevens lost both hand-grip and footing and was catapulted into the rock face, upflung arms raised for protection. For a moment he hung there, as if pinned against the wall, then fell back into the sea, limbs and head relaxed, lifeless in his limp quiescence. He should have died then, drowned under the hammer-blows of the sea or crushed by the next battering-ram collision of caique and cliff. He should have died and he would have died but for the great arm that hooked down and plucked him out of the water like a limp and sodden rag doll and heaved him inboard a bare second before the next bludgeoning impact of the boat against the rock would have crushed the life out of him.

" Come on, for God's sake! " Mallory shouted desperately. " She'll be gone in a minute! The rope—use the rope! " He saw Andrea and Miller exchange a few quick words, saw them shake and pummel Stevens and stand him on his feet, dazed and retching sea-water, but conscious. Andrea was speaking in his ear, emphasising something and guiding the rope into his hands, and then the caique was swinging in again, Stevens automatically shortening his grip on the rope. A tremendous boost from below by Andrea, Mallory's long arm reaching out and Stevens was on the ledge, sitting with his back to the cliff and hanging on to the spike, dazed still and shaking a muzzy head, but safe.

"You're next, Miller!" Mallory called. "Hurry up, man —jump for it!"

Miller looked at him and Mallory could have sworn that he was grinning. Instead of taking the rope from Andrea, he ran for'ard to the cabin.

"Just a minute, boss!" he bawled. "I've forgotten my toothbrush."

He reappeared in a few seconds, but without the toothbrush. He was carrying the big, green box of explosives, and before Mallory had appreciated what was happening the box, all fifty pounds of it, was curving up into the air, upthrust by the Greek's tireless arms. Automatically Mallory's hands reached for and caught it. He over-balanced, stumbled and toppled forward, still clutching the box, then was brought up with a jerk. Stevens, still clutching the spike, was on his feet now, free hand hooked in Mallory's belt: he was shivering violently, with cold and exhaustion and an oddly fear-laced excitement. But, like Mallory, he was a hillman at home again.

Mallory was just straightening up when the waterproofed radio set came soaring up. He caught it, placed it down, looked over the side.

"Leave that bloody stuff alone!" he shouted furiously. "Get up here yourselves—now!"

Two coils of rope landed on the ledge beside him, then the first of the rucksacks with the food and clothing. He was vaguely aware that Stevens was trying to stack the equipment in some sort of order.

"Do you hear me?" Mallory roared. "Get up here at once! That's an order. The boat's sinking, you bloody idiots!"

The caique *was* sinking. She was filling up quickly and Casey Brown had abandoned the flooded Kelvin. But she was a far steadier platform now, rolling through a much shorter arc, less violent in her soggy, yielding collisions with the cliff wall. For a moment Mallory thought the sea was dropping away, then he realised that the tons of water in the caique's hold had drastically lowered her centre of gravity, were acting as a counter-balancing weight.

Miller cupped a hand to his ear. Even in the near darkness of the sinking flare his face had an oddly greenish pallor.

" Can't hear a word you say, boss. Besides, she ain't sinkin' yet." Once again he disappeared into the for'ard cabin.

Within thirty seconds, with all five men working furiously, the remainder of the equipment was on the ledge. The caique was down by the stern, the poop-deck covered and water pouring down the engine-room hatchway as Brown struggled up the rope, the fo'c'sle awash as Miller grabbed the rope and started after him, and as Andrea reached up and swung in against the cliff his legs dangled over an empty sea. The caique had foundered, completely gone from sight: no drifting flotsam, not even an air bubble marked where she had so lately been.

The ledge was narrow, not three feet wide at its broadest, tapering off into the gloom on either side. Worse still, apart from the few square feet where Stevens had piled the gear, it shelved sharply outwards, the rock underfoot treacherous and slippery. Backs to the wall, Andrea and Miller had to stand on their heels, hands outspread and palms inward against the cliff, pressing in to it as closely as possible to maintain their balance. But in less than a minute Mallory had another two spikes hammered in about twenty inches above the ledge, ten feet apart and joined with a rope, a secure lifeline for all of them.

Wearily Miller slid down to a sitting position, leaned his chest in heartfelt thankfulness against the safe barrier of the rope. He fumbled in his breast pocket, produced a pack of cigarettes and handed them round, oblivious to the rain that soaked them in an instant. He was soaking wet from the waist downwards and both his knees had been badly bruised against the cliff wall: he was bitterly cold, drenched by heavy rain and the sheets of spray that broke continually over the ledge: the sharp edge of the rock bit cruelly into the calves of his legs, the tight rope constricted his breathing and he was still ashen-faced and exhausted from long hours of labour and seasickness: but when he spoke, it was with a voice of utter sincerity.

"My Gawd!" he said reverently. "Ain't this wonderful!"

CHAPTER FIVE

MONDAY NIGHT

0100-0200

NINETY MINUTES later Mallory wedged himself into a natural rock chimney on the cliff face, drove in a spike beneath his feet and tried to rest his aching, exhausted body. Two minutes' rest, he told himself, only two minutes while Andrea comes up: the rope was quivering and he could just hear, above the shrieking of the wind that fought to pluck him off the cliff face, the metallic scraping as Andrea's boots struggled for a foothold on that wicked overhang immediately beneath him, the overhang that had all but defeated him, the obstacle that he had impossibly overcome only at the expense of torn hands and body completely spent, of shoulder muscles afire with agony and breath that rasped in great gulping inhalations into his starving lungs. Deliberately he forced his mind away from the pains that racked his body, from its insistent demands for rest, and listened again to the ringing of steel against rock, louder this time, carrying clearly even in the gale. . . . He would have to tell Andrea to be more careful on the remaining twenty feet or so that separated them from the top.

At least, Mallory thought wryly, no one would have to tell him to be quiet. He couldn't have made any noise with his feet if he'd tried—not with only a pair of torn socks as cover for his bruised and bleeding feet. He'd hardly covered the first twenty feet of the climb when he'd discovered that his climbing boots

95

were quite useless, had robbed his feet of all sensitivity, the ability to locate and engage the tiny toe-holds which afforded the only sources of purchase. He had removed them with great difficulty, tied them to his belt by the laces—and lost them, had them torn off, when forcing his way under a projecting spur of rock.

The climb itself had been a nightmare, a brutal, gasping agony in the wind and the rain and the darkness, an agony that had eventually dulled the danger and masked the suicidal risks in climbing that sheer unknown face, an interminable agony of hanging on by fingertips and toes, of driving in a hundred spikes, of securing ropes then inching on again up into the darkness. It was a climb such as he had not ever made before, such as he knew he would not ever make again, for this was insanity. It was a climb that had extended him to the utmost of his great skill, his courage and his strength, and then far beyond that again, and he had not known that such reserves, such limitless resources, lay within him or any man. Nor did he know the well-spring, the source of that power that had driven him to where he was, within easy climbing reach of the top. The challenge to a mountaineer, personal danger, pride in the fact that he was probably the only man in southern Europe who could have made the climb, even the sure knowledge that time was running out for the men on Kheros—it was none of these things, he knew that: in the last twenty minutes it had taken him to negotiate that overhang beneath his feet his mind had been drained of all thought and all emotion, and he had climbed only as a machine.

Hand over hand up the rope, easily, powerfully, Andrea hauled himself over the smoothly swelling convexity of the overhang, legs dangling in mid-air. He was festooned with heavy coils of rope, girdled with spikes that protruded from his belt at every angle and lent him the incongruous appearance of a comic-opera Corsican bandit. Quickly he hauled himself up beside Mallory, wedged himself in the chimney and mopped his sweating forehead. As always, he was grinning hugely.

Mallory looked at him, smiled back. Andrea, he reflected, had no right to be there. It was Stevens's place, but Stevens had still been suffering from shock, had lost much blood: besides, it required a first-class climber to bring up the rear, to coil up the ropes as he came and to remove the spikes—there must be no trace left of the ascent: or so Mallory had told him, and Stevens had reluctantly agreed, although the hurt in his face had been easy to see. More than ever now Mallory was glad he had resisted the quiet plea in Stevens's face: Stevens was undoubtedly a fine climber, but what Mallory had required that night was not another mountaineer but a human ladder. Time and time again during the ascent he had stood on Andrea's back, his shoulders, his upturned palm and once—for at least ten seconds and while he was still wearing his steel-shod boots—on his head. And not once had Andrea protested or stumbled or yielded an inch. The man was indestructible, as tough and enduring as the rock on which he stood. Since dusk had fallen that evening, Andrea had laboured un-ceasingly, done enough work to kill two ordinary men, and, looking at him then, Mallory realised, almost with despair, that even now he didn't look particularly tired.

Mallory gestured at the rock chimney, then upwards at its shadowy mouth limned in blurred rectangular outline against the pale glimmer of the sky. He leant forward, mouth close to Andrea's ear.

"Twenty feet, Andrea," he said softly. His breath was still coming in painful gasps. "It'll be no bother—it's fissured on my side and the chances are that it goes up to the top."

Andrea looked up the chimney speculatively, nodded in silence.

"Better with your boots off," Mallory went on. "And any spikes we use we'll work in by hand."

"Even on a night like this—high winds and rain, cold and

black as a pig's inside—and on a cliff like this?" There was neither doubt nor question in Andrea's voice: rather it was acquiescence, unspoken confirmation of an unspoken thought. They had been so long together, had reached such a depth of understanding that words between them were largely superfluous.

Mallory nodded, waited while Andrea worked home a spike, looped his ropes over it and secured what was left of the long ball of twine that stretched four hundred feet below to the ledge where the others waited. Andrea then removed boots and spikes, fastened them to the ropes, eased the slender, double-edged throwing knife in its leather shoulder scabbard, looked across at Mallory and nodded in turn.

The first ten feet were easy. Palms and back against one side of the chimney and stocking-soled feet against the other, Mallory jack-knifed his way upwards until the widening sheer of the walls defeated him. Legs braced against the far wall, he worked in a spike as far up as he could reach, grasped it with both hands, dropped his legs across and found a toe-hold in the crevice. Two minutes later his hands hooked over the crumbling edge of the precipice.

Noiselessly and with an infinite caution he fingered aside earth and grass and tiny pebbles until his hands were locked on the solid rock itself, bent his knee to seek lodgment for the final toe-hold, then eased a wary head above the cliff-top, a movement imperceptible in its slow-motion, millimetric stealth. He stopped moving altogether as soon as his eyes had cleared the level of the cliff, stared out into the unfamiliar darkness, his whole being, the entire field of consciousness, concentrated into his eyes and his ears. Illogically, and for the first time in all that terrifying ascent, he became acutely aware of his own danger and helplessness, and he cursed himself for his folly in not borrowing Miller's silenced automatic.

The darkness below the high horizon of the lifting hills beyond was just one degree less than absolute: shapes and

angles, heights and depressions were resolving themselves in
nebulous silhouette, contours and shadowy profiles emerging
reluctantly from the darkness, a darkness suddenly no longer
vague and unfamiliar but disturbingly reminiscent in what it
revealed, clamouring for recognition. And then abruptly,
almost with a sense of shock, Mallory had it. The cliff-top
before his eyes was exactly as Monsieur Vlachos had drawn and
described it—the narrow, bare strip of ground running parallel
to the cliff, the jumble of huge boulders behind them and then,
beyond these, the steep scree-strewn lower slopes of the mountains. The first break they'd had yet, Mallory thought
exultantly—but what a break! The sketchiest navigation but
the most incredible luck, right bang on the nose of the target—
the highest point of the highest, most precipitous cliffs in
Navarone: the one place where the Germans never mounted a
guard, because the climb was impossible! Mallory felt the
relief, the high elation wash through him in waves. Jubilantly
he straightened his leg, hoisted himself half-way over the edge,
arms straight, palms down on the top of the cliff. And then
he froze into immobility, petrified as the solid rock beneath his
hands, his heart thudding painfully in his throat.

     One of the boulders had moved. Seven, maybe eight yards
away, a shadow had gradually straightened, detached itself
stealthily from the surrounding rock, was advancing slowly
towards the edge of the cliff. And then the shadow was no
longer " it." There could be no mistake now—the long jack-
boots, the long greatcoat beneath the waterproof cape, the
close-fitting helmet were all too familiar. Damn Vlachos! Damn
Jensen! Damn all the know-alls who sat at home, the pundits
of Intelligence who gave a man wrong information and sent
him out to die. And in the same instant Mallory damned
himself for his own carelessness, for he had been expecting this
all along.

     For the first two or three seconds Mallory had lain rigid and
unmoving, temporarily paralysed in mind and body: already

the guard had advanced four or five steps, carbine held in readiness before him, head turned sideways as he listened into the high, thin whine of the wind and the deep and distant booming of the surf below, trying to isolate the sound that had aroused his suspicions. But now the first shock was over and Mallory's mind was working again. To go up on to the top of the cliff would be suicidal: ten to one the guard would hear him scrambling over the edge and shoot him out of hand: and if he did get up he had neither the weapons nor, after that exhausting climb, the strength to tackle an armed, fresh man. He would have to go back down. But he would have to slide down slowly, an inch at a time. At night, Mallory knew, side vision is even more acute than direct, and the guard might catch a sudden movement out of the corner of his eye. And then he would only have to turn his head and that would be the end: even in that darkness, Mallory realised, there could be no mistaking the bulk of his silhouette against the sharp line of the edge of the cliff.

Gradually, every movement as smooth and controlled as possible, every soft and soundless breath a silent prayer, Mallory slipped gradually back over the edge of the cliff. Still the guard advanced, making for a point about five yards to Mallory's left, but still he looked away, his ear turned into the wind. And then Mallory was down, only his finger-tips over the top, and Andrea's great bulk was beside him, his mouth to his ear.

" What is it? Somebody there? "

" A sentry," Mallory whispered back. His arms were beginning to ache from the strain. " He's heard something and he's looking for us."

Suddenly he shrank away from Andrea, pressed himself as closely as possible to the face of the cliff, was vaguely aware of Andrea doing the same thing. A beam of light, hurtful and dazzling to eyes so long accustomed to the dark, had suddenly stabbed out at an angle over the edge of the cliff, was moving slowly along towards them. The German had his torch out, was methodically examining the rim of the cliff. From the angle of the beam, Mallory judged that he was walking along about a couple of feet from the edge. On that wild and gusty night he was taking no chances on the crumbly, treacherous top-soil of the cliff: even more likely, he was taking no chances on a pair of sudden hands reaching out for his ankles and jerking him to a mangled death on the rocks and reefs four hundred feet below.

Slowly, inexorably, the beam approached. Even at that slant, it was bound to catch them. With a sudden sick certainty Mallory realised that the German wasn't just suspicious: he *knew* there was someone there, and he wouldn't stop looking until he found them. And there was nothing they could do, just nothing at all. . . . Then Andrea's head was close to his again.

" A stone," Andrea whispered. " Over there, behind him."

Cautiously at first, then frantically, Mallory pawed the cliff-top with his right hand. Earth, only earth, grass roots and tiny pebbles—there was nothing even half the size of a marble. And then Andrea was thrusting something against him and his hand closed over the metallic smoothness of a spike: even in that moment of desperate urgency, with the slender, searching beam only feet away, Mallory was conscious of a sudden, brief anger with himself—he had still a couple of spikes stuck in his belt and had forgotten all about them.

His arm swung back, jerked convulsively forward, sent the spike spinning away into the darkness. One second passed, then another, he knew he had missed, the beam was only inches from Andrea's shoulders, and then the metallic clatter of the spike striking a boulder fell upon his ear like a benison. The beam wavered for a second, stabbed out aimlessly into the darkness and then whipped round, probing into the boulders to the left. And then the sentry was running towards them, slipping and stumbling in his haste, the barrel of the carbine gleaming in the light of the torch held clamped to it. He'd gone less than ten yards when Andrea was over the top of the cliff like a great, black cat, was padding noiselessly across the ground to the shelter of the nearest boulder. Wraith-like, he flitted in behind it and was gone, a shadow long among shadows.

The sentry was about twenty yards away now, the beam of his torch darting fearfully from boulder to boulder when Andrea struck the haft of his knife against a rock, twice. The sentry whirled round, torch shining along the line of the boulders, then started to run clumsily back again, the skirts of the greatcoat fluttering grotesquely in the wind. The torch was swinging wildly now, and Mallory caught a glimpse of a white, straining face, wide-eyed and fearful, incongruously at variance with the gladiatorial strength of the steel helmet above. God only knew, Mallory thought, what wild and panic-stricken thoughts were passing through his confused mind: noises from the cliff-top, metallic sound from either side among the boulders, the long, eerie vigil, afraid and companionless, on a deserted cliff edge on a dark and tempest-filled night in a hostile land—suddenly Mallory felt a deep stab of compassion for this man, a man like himself, someone's well-loved husband or brother or son who was only doing a dirty and dangerous job as best he could and because he was told to, compassion for his loneliness and his anxieties and his fears, for the sure knowledge that before he had drawn breath another three times he would be dead. . . . Slowly, gauging his time and distance, Mallory raised his head.

" Help! " he shouted. " Help me! I'm falling! "

The soldier checked in mid-stride and spun round, less than five feet from the rock that hid Andrea. For a second the beam of his torch waved wildly around, then settled on Mallory's head. For another moment he stood stock still, then the carbine in his right hand swung up, the left hand reaching down for the barrel. Then he grunted once, a violent and convulsive exhalation of breath, and the thud of the hilt of Andrea's knife striking home against the ribs carried clearly to Mallory's ears, even against the wind. . . .

Mallory stared down at the dead man, at Andrea's impassive face as he wiped the blade of his knife on the greatcoat, rose slowly to his feet, sighed and slid the knife back in its scabbard.

" So, my Keith! " Andrea reserved the punctilious " Captain " for company only. " This is why our young lieutenant eats his heart out down below."

" That is why," Mallory acknowledged. " I knew it—or I almost knew it. So did you. Too many coincidences—the German caique investigating, the trouble at the watch-tower—and now this." Mallory swore, softly and bitterly. " This is the end for our friend Captain Briggs of Castelrosso. He'll be cashiered within the month. Jensen will make certain of that."

Andrea nodded.

" He let Nicolai go? "

" Who else could have known that we were to have landed here, tipped off everyone all along the line? " Mallory paused, dismissed the thought, caught Andrea by the arm. " The Germans are thorough. Even although they must know it's almost an impossibility to land on a night like this, they'll have a dozen sentries scattered along the cliffs." Unconsciously Mallory had lowered his voice. " But they wouldn't depend on one man to cope with five. So——"

" Signals," Andrea finished for him. " They must have some way of letting the others know. Perhaps flares——"

" No, not that," Mallory disagreed. " Give their position away. Telephone. It has to be that. Remember how they were in Crete—miles of field telephone wire all over the shop? "

Andrea nodded, picked up the dead man's torch, hooded it in his huge hand and started searching. He returned in less than a minute.

"Telephone it is," he announced softly. "Over there, under the rocks."

"Nothing we can do about it," Mallory said. "If it does ring, I'll have to answer or they'll come hot-footing along. I only hope to heaven they haven't got a bloody password. It would be just like them."

He turned away, stopped suddenly.

"But someone's got to come sometime—a relief, sergeant of the guard, something like that. Probably he's supposed to make an hourly report. Someone's bound to come—and come soon. My God, Andrea, we'll have to make it fast!"

"And this poor devil?" Andrea gestured to the huddled shadow at his feet.

"Over the side with him." Mallory grimaced in distaste. "Won't make any difference to the poor bastard now, and we can't leave any traces. The odds are they'll think he's gone over the edge—this top soil's as crumbly and treacherous as hell. . . . You might see if he's any papers on him—never know how useful they might be."

"Not half as useful as these boots on his feet." Andrea waved a large hand towards the scree-strewn slopes. "You are not going to walk very far there in your stocking soles."

Five minutes later Mallory tugged three times on the string that stretched down into the darkness below. Three answering tugs came from the ledge, and then the cord vanished rapidly down over the edge of the overhang, drawing with it the long, steel-cored rope that Mallory paid out from the coil on the top of the cliff.

The box of explosives was the first of the gear to come up. The weighted rope plummetted straight down from the point of the overhang, and padded though the box was on every side with lashed rucksacks and sleeping-bags it still crashed terrifyingly against the cliff on the inner arc of every wind-driven swing of the pendulum. But there was no time for finesse, to wait for the diminishing swing of the pendulum after each tug.

Securely anchored to a rope that stretched around the base of a great boulder, Andrea leaned far out over the edge of the precipice and reeled in the seventy-pound deadweight as another man would a trout. In less than three minutes the ammunition box lay beside him on the cliff-top: five minutes later the firing generator, guns and pistols, wrapped in a couple of other sleeping-bags and their lightweight, reversible tent— white on one side, brown and green camouflage on the other —lay beside the explosives.

A third time the rope went down into the rain and the darkness, a third time the tireless Andrea hauled it in, hand over hand. Mallory was behind him, coiling in the slack of the rope, when he heard Andrea's sudden exclamation: two quick strides and he was at the edge of the cliff, his hand on the big Greek's arm.

"What's up, Andrea? Why have you stopped——?"

He broke off, peered through the gloom at the rope in Andrea's hand, saw that it was being held between only finger and thumb. Twice Andrea jerked the rope up a foot or two, let it fall again: the weightless rope swayed wildly in the wind.

"Gone?" Mallory asked quietly.

Andrea nodded without speaking.

"Broken?" Mallory was incredulous. "A wire-cored rope?"

"I don't think so." Quickly Andrea reeled in the remaining forty feet. The twine was still attached to the same place, about a fathom from the end. The rope was intact.

"Somebody tied a knot." Just for a moment the giant's voice sounded tired. "They didn't tie it too well."

Mallory made to speak, then flung up an instinctive arm as a great, forked tongue of flame streaked between the cliff-top and unseen clouds above. Their cringing eyes were still screwed tight shut, their nostrils full of the acrid, sulphurous smell of burning, when the first volley of thunder crashed in

Titan fury almost directly overhead, a deafening artillery to mock the pitiful efforts of embattled man, doubly terrifying in the total darkness that followed that searing flash. Gradually the echoes pealed and faded inland in diminishing reverberation, were lost among the valleys of the hills.

" My God! " Mallory murmured. " That was close. We'd better make it fast, Andrea—this cliff is liable to be lit up like a fairground any minute. . . . What was in that last load you were bringing up? " He didn't really have to ask—he himself had arranged for the breaking up of the equipment into three separate loads before he'd left the ledge. It wasn't even that he suspected his tired mind of playing tricks on him; but it was tired enough, too tired, to probe the hidden compulsion, the nameless hope that prompted him to grasp at nameless straws that didn't even exist.

" The food," Andrea said gently. " *All* the food, the stove, the fuel—and the compasses."

For five, perhaps ten seconds, Mallory stood motionless. One half of his mind, conscious of the urgency, the desperate need for haste, was jabbing him mercilessly: the other half held him momentarily in a vast irresolution, an irresolution of coldness and numbness that came not from the lashing wind and sleety rain but from his own mind, from the bleak and comfortless imaginings of lost wanderings on that harsh and hostile island, with neither food nor fire. . . . And then Andrea's great hand was on his shoulder, and he was laughing softly.

" Just so much less to carry, my Keith. Think how grateful our tired friend Corporal Miller is going to be. . . . This is only a little thing."

" Yes," Mallory said. " Yes, of course. A little thing." He turned abruptly, tugged the cord, watched the rope disappear over the edge.

Fifteen minutes later, in drenching, torrential rain, a great, sheeting downpour almost constantly illuminated by the jagged, branching stilettos of the forked lightning, Casey Brown's bedraggled head came into view over the edge of the cliff. The thunder, too, emptily cavernous in that flat and explosive intensity of sound that lies at the heart of a thunderstorm, was almost continuous: but in the brief intervals, Casey's voice, rich in his native Clydeside accent, carried clearly. He was expressing himself fluently in basic Anglo-Saxon, and with cause. He had had the assistance of two ropes on the way up— the one stretched from spike to spike and the one used for raising supplies, which Andrea had kept pulling in as he made the ascent. Casey Brown had secured the end of this round his waist with a bowline, but the bowline had proved to be nothing of the sort but a slip-knot, and Andrea's enthusiastic help had almost cut him in half. He was still sitting on the cliff-top, exhausted head between his knees, the radio still strapped to his back, when two tugs on Andrea's rope announced that Dusty Miller was on his way up.

Another quarter of an hour elapsed, an interminable fifteen minutes when, in the lulls between the thunderclaps, every slightest sound was an approaching enemy patrol, before Miller materialised slowly out of the darkness, half-way down the rock chimney. He was climbing steadily and methodically, then checked abruptly at the cliff-top, groping hands pawing uncertainly on the top-soil of the cliff. Puzzled, Mallory bent down, peered into the lean face: both the eyes were clamped tightly shut.

" Relax, Corporal," Mallory advised kindly. " You have arrived."

Dusty Miller slowly opened his eyes, peered round at the edge of the cliff, shuddered and crawled quickly on hands and knees to the shelter of the nearest boulders. Mallory followed and looked down at him curiously.

" What was the idea of closing your eyes coming over the top? "

" I did not," Miller protested.

Mallory said nothing.

" I closed them at the bottom," Miller explained wearily.
" I opened them at the top."

Mallory looked at him incredulously.

" What! All the way? "

" It's like I told you, boss," Miller complained. " Back in
Castelrosso. When I cross a street and step up on to the side-
walk I gotta hang on to the nearest lamp-post. More or less."
He broke off, looked at Andrea leaning far out over the side
of the cliff, and shivered again. " Brother! Oh, brother! Was
I scared! "

Fear. Terror. Panic. Do the thing you fear and the death
of fear is certain. Do the thing you fear and the death of fear
is certain. Once, twice, a hundred times, Andy Stevens
repeated the words to himself, over and over again, like a
litany. A psychiatrist had told him that once and he'd read it
a dozen times since. Do the thing you fear and the death of
fear is certain. The mind is a limited thing, they had said. It
can only hold one thought at a time, one impulse to action.
Say to yourself, I am brave, I am overcoming this fear, this
stupid, unreasoning panic which has no origin except in my
own mind, and because the mind *can* only hold one thought at
a time, and because thinking and feeling are one, then you
will be brave, you *will* overcome and the fear will vanish like
a shadow in the night. And so Andy Stevens said these things
to himself, and the shadows only lengthened and deepened,
lengthened and deepened, and the icy claws of fear dug ever
more savagely into his dull exhausted mind, into his twisted,
knotted stomach.

His stomach. That knotted ball of jangled, writhing nerve-
ends beneath the solar plexus. No one could ever know how
it was, how it felt, except those whose shredded minds were
going, collapsing into complete and final breakdown. The
waves of panic and nausea and faintness that flooded up through

a suffocating throat to a mind dark and spent and sinewless, a mind fighting with woollen fingers to cling on to the edge of the abyss, a tired and lacerated mind, only momentarily in control, wildly rejecting the clamorous demands of a nervous system, which had already taken far too much, that he should let go, open the torn fingers that were clenched so tightly round the rope. It was just that easy. " Rest after toil, port after stormy seas." What was that famous stanza of Spenser's? Sobbing aloud, Stevens wrenched out another spike, sent it spinning into the waiting sea three hundred long feet below, pressed himself closely into the face and inched his way despairingly upwards.

Fear. Fear had been at his elbow all his life, his constant companion, his *alter ego*, at his elbow, or in close prospect or immediate recall. He had become accustomed to that fear, at times almost reconciled, but the sick agony of this night lay far beyond either tolerance or familiarity. He had never known anything like this before, and even in his terror and confusion he was dimly aware that the fear did not spring from the climb itself. True, the cliff was sheer and almost vertical, and the lightning, the ice-cold rain, the darkness and the bellowing thunder were a waking nightmare. But the climb, technically, was simple: the rope stretched all the way to the top and all he had to do was to follow it and dispose of the spikes as he went. He was sick and bruised and terribly tired, his head ached abominably and he had lost a great deal of blood: but then, more often than not, it is in the darkness of agony and exhaustion that the spirit of man burns most brightly.

Andy Stevens was afraid because his self-respect was gone. Always, before, that had been his sheet anchor, had tipped the balance against his ancient enemy—the respect in which other men had held him, the respect he had had for himself. But now these were gone, for his two greatest fears had been realised —he was known to be afraid, he had failed his fellow-man.

Both in the fight with the German caique and when anchored above the watch-tower in the creek, he had known that Mallory and Andrea knew. He had never met such men before, and he had known all along that he could never hide his secrets from such men. He should have gone up that cliff with Mallory, but Mallory had made excuses and taken Andrea instead—Mallory *knew* he was afraid. And twice before, in Castelrosso and when the German boat had closed in on them, he had almost failed his friends—and to-night he had failed them terribly. He had not been thought fit to lead the way with Mallory—and it was he, the sailor of the party, who had made such a botch of tying that last knot, had lost all the food and the fuel that had plummetted into the sea a bare ten feet from where he had stood on the ledge . . . and a thousand men on Kheros were depending on a failure so abject as himself. Sick and spent, spent in mind and body and spirit, moaning aloud in his anguish of fear and self-loathing, and not knowing where one finished and the other began, Andy Stevens climbed blindly on.

The sharp, high-pitched call-up buzz of the telephone cut abruptly through the darkness on the cliff-top. Mallory stiffened and half-turned, hands clenching involuntarily. Again it buzzed, the jarring stridency carrying clearly above the bass rumble of the thunder, fell silent again. And then it buzzed again and kept on buzzing, peremptory in its harsh insistence.

Mallory was half-way towards it when he checked in mid-step, turned slowly round and walked back towards Andrea. The big Greek looked at him curiously.

" You have changed your mind? "

Mallory nodded but said nothing.

" They will keep on ringing until they get an answer," Andrea murmured. " And when they get no answer, they will come. They will come quickly and soon."

" I know, I know." Mallory shrugged. " We have to take
that chance—certainty rather. The question is—how long will
it be before anyone turns up." Instinctively he looked both
ways along the windswept cliff-top: Miller and Brown were
posted one on either side about fifty yards away, lost in the
darkness. " It's not worth the risk. The more I think of it, the
poorer I think my chances would be of getting away with it.
In matters of routine the old Hun tends to be an inflexible sort
of character. There's probably a set way of answering the
phone, or the sentry has to identify himself by name, or there's
a password—or maybe my voice would give me away. On the
other hand the sentry's gone without trace, all our gear is up
and so's everyone except Stevens. In other words, we've
practically made it. We've landed—and nobody knows we're
here."

" Yes." Andrea nodded slowly. " Yes, you are right—and
Stevens should be up in two or three minutes. It would be
foolish to throw away everything we've gained." He paused,
then went on quietly: " But they are going to come running."
The phone stopped ringing as suddenly as it had started.
" They are going to come now."

" I know. I hope to hell Stevens . . ." Mallory broke off,
spun on his heel, said over his shoulder, " Keep your eye open
for him, will you? I'll warn the others we're expecting
company."

Mallory moved quickly along the cliff-top, keeping well
away from the edge. He hobbled rather than walked—the
sentry's boots were too small for him and chafed his toes cruelly.
Deliberately he closed his mind to the thought of how his feet
would be after a few hour's walking over rough territory in
these boots: time enough for the reality, he thought grimly,
without the added burden of anticipation. . . . He stopped
abruptly as something hard and metallic pushed into the small
of his back.

" Surrender or die! " The drawling, nasal voice was

positively cheerful: after what he had been through on the caique and the cliff face, just to set feet on solid ground again was heaven enough for Dusty Miller.

"Very funny," Mallory growled. "Very funny indeed." He looked curiously at Miller. The American had removed his oilskin cape—the rain had ceased as abruptly as it had come—to reveal a jacket and braided waistcoat even more sodden and saturated than his trousers. It didn't make sense. But there was no time for questions.

"Did you hear the phone ringing just now?" he asked.

"Was that what it was? Yeah, I heard it."

"The sentry's phone. His hourly report, or whatever it was, must have been overdue. We didn't answer it. They'll be hot-footing along any minute now, suspicious as hell and looking for trouble. Maybe your side, maybe Brown's. Can't approach any other way unless they break their necks climbing over these boulders." Mallory gestured at the shapeless jumble of rocks behind them. "So keep your eyes skinned."

"I'll do that, boss. No shootin', huh?"

"No shooting. Just get back as quickly and quietly as you can and let us know. Come back in five minutes anyway."

Mallory hurried away, retracing his steps. Andrea was stretched full length on the cliff-top, peering over the edge. He twisted his head round as Mallory approached.

"I can hear him. He's just at the overhang."

"Good." Mallory moved on without breaking step. "Tell him to hurry, please."

Ten yards farther on Mallory checked, peered into the gloom ahead. Somebody was coming along the cliff-top at a dead run, stumbling and slipping on the loose gravelly soil.

"Brown?" Mallory called softly.

"Yes, sir. It's me." Brown was up to him now, breathing heavily, pointing back in the direction he had just come. "Somebody's coming, and coming fast! Torches waving and jumping all over the place—must be running."

" How many? " Mallory asked quickly.

" Four or five at least." Brown was still gasping for breath.
" Maybe more—four or five torches, anyway. You can see
them for yourself." Again he pointed backwards, then
blinked in puzzlement. " That's bloody funny! They're all
gone." He turned back swiftly to Mallory. " But I can
swear——"

" Don't worry," Mallory said grimly. " You saw them all
right. I've been expecting visitors. They're getting close now
and taking no chances. . . . How far away? "

" Hundred yards—not more than a hundred and fifty."

" Go and get Miller. Tell him to get back here fast."

Mallory ran back along the cliff edge and knelt beside the
huge length of Andrea.

" They're coming, Andrea," he said quickly. " From the
left. At least five, probably more. Two minutes at the most.
Where's Stevens? Can you see him? "

" I can see him." Andrea was magnificently unperturbed.
" He is just past the overhang . . ." The rest of his words were
lost, drowned in a sudden, violent thunderclap, but there was
no need for more. Mallory could see Stevens now, climbing
up the rope, strangely old and enfeebled in action, hand over
hand in paralysing slowness, half-way now between the overhang and the foot of the chimney.

" Good God! " Mallory swore. " What's the matter with
him? He's going to take all day . . ." He checked himself,
cupped his hands to his mouth. " Stevens! Stevens! " But
there was no sign that Stevens had heard. He still kept climbing
with the same unnatural over-deliberation, a robot in slow
motion.

" He is very near the end," Andrea said quietly. " You see
he does not even lift his head. When a climber does not lift
his head, he is finished." He stirred. " I will go down for
him."

" No." Mallory's hand was on his shoulder. " Stay here.

I can't risk you both. . . . Yes, what is it?" He was aware that
Brown was back, bending over him, his breath coming in
great heaving gasps.

" Hurry, sir; hurry, for God's sake! " A few brief words
but he had to suck in two huge gulps of air to get them out.
" They're on top of us! "

" Get back to the rocks with Miller," Mallory said urgently.
" Cover us. . . . Stevens! Stevens! " But again the wind swept
up the face of the cliff, carried his words away.

" Stevens! For God's sake, man! Stevens! " His voice was
low-pitched, desperate, but this time some quality in it must
have reached through Stevens's fog of exhaustion and touched
his consciousness, for he stopped climbing and lifted his head,
hand cupped to his ear.

" Some Germans coming! " Mallory called through
funnelled hands, as loudly as he dared. " Get to the foot of
the chimney and stay there. Don't make a sound. Understand? "

Stevens lifted his hand, gestured in tired acknowledgment,
lowered his head, started to climb up again. He was going
even more slowly now, his movements fumbling and clumsy.

" Do you think he understands? " Andrea was troubled.

" I think so. I don't know." Mallory stiffened and caught
Andrea's arm. It was beginning to rain again, not heavily yet,
and through the drizzle he'd caught sight of a hooded torch
beam probing among the rocks thirty yards away to his left.
" Over the edge with the rope," he whispered. " The spike at
the bottom of the chimney will hold it. Come on—let's get
out of here! "

Gradually, meticulous in their care not to dislodge the
smallest pebble, Mallory and Andrea inched back from the
edge, squirmed round and headed back for the rocks, pulling
themselves along on their elbows and knees. The few yards
were interminable and without even a gun in his hand Mallory
felt defenceless, completely exposed. An illogical feeling, he

knew, for the first beam of light to fall on them meant the end not for them but for the man who held the torch. Mallory had complete faith in Brown and Miller. . . . That wasn't important. What mattered was the complete escape from detection. Twice during the last endless few feet a wandering beam reached out towards them, the second a bare arm's length away: both times they pressed their faces into the sodden earth, lest the pale blur of their faces betray them, and lay very still. And then, all at once it seemed, they were among the rocks and safe.

In a moment Miller was beside them, a half-seen shadow against the darker dusk of the rocks around them.

" Plenty of time, plenty of time," he whispered sarcastically. " Why didn't you wait another half-hour ? " He gestured to the left, where the flickering of torches, the now clearly audible murmur of guttural voices, were scarcely twenty yards away. " We'd better move farther back. They're looking for him among the rocks."

" For him or for his telephone," Mallory murmured in agreement. " You're right, anyway. Watch your guns on these rocks. Take the gear with you. . . . And if they look over and find Stevens we'll have to take the lot. No time for fancy work and to hell with the noise. Use the automatic carbines."

Andy Stevens had heard, but he had not understood. It was not that he panicked, was too terrified to understand, for he was no longer afraid. Fear is of the mind, but his mind had ceased to function, drugged by the last stages of exhaustion, crushed by the utter, damnable tiredness that held his limbs, his whole body, in leaden thrall. He did not know it, but fifty feet below he had struck his head against a spur of rock, a sharp, wicked projection that had torn his gaping temple wound open to the bone. His strength drained out with the pulsing blood.

He had heard Mallory, had heard something about the

chimney he had now reached, but his mind had failed to register the meaning of the words. All that Stevens knew was that he was climbing, and that one always kept on climbing until one reached the top. That was what his father had always impressed upon him, his brothers too. You must reach the top.

He was half-way up the chimney now, resting on the spike that Mallory had driven into the fissure. He hooked his fingers in the crack, bent back his head and stared up towards the mouth of the chimney. Ten feet away, no more. He was conscious of neither surprise nor elation. It was just there: he had to reach it. He could hear voices, carrying clearly from the top. He was vaguely surprised that his friends were making no attempt to help him, that they had thrown away the rope that would have made those last few feet so easy, but he felt no bitterness, no emotion at all: perhaps they were trying to test him. What did it matter anyway—he had to reach the top.

He reached the top. Carefully, as Mallory had done before him, he pushed aside the earth and tiny pebbles, hooked his fingers over the edge, found the same toe-hold as Mallory had and levered himself upwards. He saw the flickering torches, heard the excited voices, and then for an instant the curtain of fog in his mind lifted and a last tidal wave of fear washed over him and he knew that the voices were the voices of the enemy and that they had destroyed his friends. He knew now that he was alone, that he had failed, that this was the end, one way or another, and that it had all been for nothing. And then the fog closed over him again, and there was nothing but the emptiness of it all, the emptiness and the futility, the overwhelming lassitude and despair and his body slowly sinking down the face of the cliff. And then the hooked fingers—they, too, were slipping away, opening gradually, reluctantly as the fingers of a drowning man releasing their final hold on a spar of wood. There was no fear now, only a vast and heedless indifference as his hands slipped away and he fell like a stone, twenty vertical feet into the cradling bottle-neck at the foot of the chimney.

He himself made no sound, none at all: the soundless scream of agony never passed his lips, for the blackness came with the pain: but the straining ears of the men crouching in the rocks above caught clearly the dull, sickening crack as his right leg fractured cleanly in two, snapping like a rotten bough.

CHAPTER SIX

MONDAY NIGHT

0200-0600

THE GERMAN PATROL was everything that Mallory had feared —efficient, thorough and very, very painstaking. It even had imagination, in the person of its young and competent sergeant, and that was more dangerous still.

There were only four of them, in high boots, helmets and green, grey and brown mottled capes. First of all they located the telephone and reported to base. Then the young sergeant sent two men to search another hundred yards or so along the cliff, while he and the fourth soldier probed among the rocks that paralleled the cliff. The search was slow and careful, but the two men did not penetrate very far into the rocks. To Mallory, the sergeant's reasoning was obvious and logical. If the sentry had gone to sleep or taken ill, it was unlikely that he would have gone far in among that confused jumble of boulders. Mallory and the others were safely back beyond their reach.

And then came what Mallory had feared—an organised, methodical inspection of the cliff-top itself: worse still, it began with a search along the very edge. Securely held by his three men with interlinked arms—the last with a hand hooked round his belt—the sergeant walked slowly along the rim, probing every inch with the spot-lit beam of a powerful torch. Suddenly he stopped short, exclaimed suddenly and stooped, torch and face only inches from the ground. There was no question as to what he had found—the deep gouge made in the soft, crumbling soil by the climbing rope that had been belayed round the boulder and gone over the edge of the cliff. . . . Softly, silently, Mallory and his three companions straightened to their knees or to their feet, gun barrels lining along the tops of boulders or peering out between cracks in the rocks. There was no doubt in any of their minds that Stevens was lying there helplessly in the crutch of the chimney, seriously injured or dead. It needed only one German carbine to point down that cliff face, however carelessly, and these four men would die. They would have to die.

The sergeant was stretched out his length now, two men holding his legs. His head and shoulders were over the edge of the cliff, the beam from his torch stabbing down the chimney. For ten, perhaps fifteen seconds, there was no sound on the cliff-top, no sound at all, only the high, keening moan of the wind and the swish of the rain in the stunted grass. And then the sergeant had wriggled back and risen to his feet, slowly shaking his head. Mallory gestured to the others to sink down behind the boulders again, but even so the sergeant's soft Bavarian voice carried clearly in the wind.

" It's Ehrich all right, poor fellow." Compassion and anger blended curiously in the voice. " I warned him often enough about his carelessness, about going too near the edge of that cliff. It is very treacherous." Instinctively the sergeant stepped back a couple of feet and looked again at the gouge in the soft earth. " That's where his heel slipped—or maybe the butt of his carbine. Not that it matters now."

" Is he dead, do you think, Sergeant? " The speaker was only a boy, nervous and unhappy.

" It's hard to say. . . . Look for yourself."

Gingerly the youth lay down on the cliff-top, peering cautiously over the lip of the rock. The other soldiers were talking among themselves, in short staccato sentences when Mallory turned to Miller, cupped his hands to his mouth and the American's ear. He could contain his puzzlement no longer.

" Was Stevens wearing his dark suit when you left him? " he whispered.

" Yeah," Miller whispered back. " Yeah, I think he was." A pause. " No, dammit, I'm wrong. We both put on our rubber camouflage capes about the same time."

Mallory nodded. The waterproofs of the Germans were almost identical with their own: and the sentry's hair, Mallory remembered, had been jet black—the same colour as Stevens's dyed hair. Probably all that was visible from above was a crumpled, cape-shrouded figure and a dark head. The sergeant's mistake in identity was more than understandable: it was inevitable.

The young soldier eased himself back from the edge of the cliff and hoisted himself carefully to his feet.

" You're right, Sergeant. It *is* Ehrich." The boy's voice was unsteady. " He's alive, I think. I saw his cape move, just a little. It wasn't the wind, I'm sure of that."

Mallory felt Andrea's massive hand squeezing his arm, felt the quick surge of relief, then elation, wash through him. So Stevens *was* alive! Thank God for that! They'd save the boy yet. He heard Andrea whispering the news to the others, then grinned wryly to himself, ironic at his own gladness. Jensen definitely would not have approved of this jubilation. Stevens had already done his part, navigated the boat to Navarone and climbed the cliff: and now he was only a crippled liability, would be a drag on the whole party, reduce what pitiful chances of success remained to them. For a High Command who pushed the counters around crippled pawns slowed up the whole game, made the board so damnably untidy. It was most inconsiderate of Stevens not to have killed himself so that they could have disposed of him neatly and without trace in the deep and hungry waters that boomed around the foot of the cliff. . . . Mallory clenched his hands in the darkness and swore to himself that the boy would live, come home again, and to hell with total war and all its inhuman demands. . . . Just a kid, that was all, a scared and broken kid and the bravest of them all.

The young sergeant was issuing a string of orders to his men, his voice quick, crisp and confident. A doctor, splints, rescue stretcher, anchored sheer-legs, ropes, spikes—the trained, well-ordered mind missing nothing. Mallory waited tensely, wondering how many men, if any, would be left on guard, for the guards would have to go and that would inevitably betray them. The question of their quick and silent disposal never entered his mind—a whisper in Andrea's ear and the guards would have no more chance than penned lambs against a marauding wolf. Less chance even than that—the lambs could always run and cry out before the darkness closed over them.

The sergeant solved the problem for them. The assured competence, the tough, unsentimental ruthlessness that made the German N.C.O. the best in the world gave Mallory the chance he never expected to have. He had just finished giving his orders when the young soldier touched him on the arm, then pointed over the edge.

" How about poor Ehrich, Sergeant? " he asked uncertainly. " Shouldn't—don't you think one of us ought to stay with him? "

" And what could you do if you did stay—hold his hand? " the sergeant asked acidly. " If he stirs and falls, then he falls, that's all, and it doesn't matter then if a hundred of us are standing up here watching him. Off you go, and don't forget the mallets and pegs to stay the sheer-legs."

The three men turned and went off quickly to the east without another word. The sergeant walked over to the phone, reported briefly to someone, then set off in the opposite direction—to check the next guard post, Mallory guessed. He was still in sight, a dwindling blur in the darkness, when

Mallory whispered to Brown and Miller to post themselves on guard again: and they could still hear the measured crunch of his firm footfalls on a patch of distant gravel as their belayed rope went snaking over the edge of the cliff, Andrea and Mallory sliding swiftly down even before it had stopped quivering.

Stevens, a huddled, twisted heap with a gashed and bleeding cheek lying cruelly along a razor-sharp spur of rock, was still unconscious, breathing stertorously through his open mouth. Below the knee his right leg twisted upwards and outwards against the rock at an impossible angle. As gently as he could, braced against either side of the chimney and supported by Andrea, Mallory lifted and straightened the twisted limb. Twice, from the depths of the dark stupor of his unconsciousness, Stevens moaned in agony, but Mallory had no option but to carry on, his teeth clenched tight until his jaws ached. Then slowly, with infinite care, he rolled up the trouser leg, winced and screwed his eyes shut in momentary horror and nausea as he saw the dim whiteness of the shattered tibia sticking out through the torn and purply swollen flesh.

" Compound fracture, Andrea." Gently his exploring fingers slid down the mangled leg, beneath the lip of the jack-boot, stopped suddenly as something gave way beneath his feather touch. " Oh, my God! " he murmured. " Another break, just above the ankle. This boy is in a bad way, Andrea."

" He is indeed," Andrea said gravely. " We can do nothing for him here? "

" Nothing. Just nothing. We'll have to get him up first." Mallory straightened, gazed up bleakly at the perpendicular face of the chimney. " Although how in the name of heaven——"

" I will take him up." There was no suggestion in Andrea's voice either of desperate resolve or consciousness of the almost incredible effort involved. It was simply a statement of intention, the voice of a man who never questioned his ability to do what he said he would. "If you will help me to raise him, to tie him to my back. . . ."

"With his broken leg loose, dangling from a piece of skin and torn muscle?" Mallory protested. "Stevens can't take much more. He'll die if we do this."

"He'll die if we don't," Andrea murmured.

Mallory stared down at Stevens for a long moment, then nodded heavily in the darkness.

"He'll die if we don't," he echoed tiredly. "Yes, we have to do this." He pushed outwards from the rock, slid half a dozen feet down the rope and jammed a foot in the crutch of the chimney just below Stevens's body. He took a couple of turns of rope round his waist and looked up.

"Ready, Andrea?" he called softly.

"Ready." Andrea stooped, hooked his great hands under Stevens's armpits and lifted slowly, powerfully, as Mallory pushed from below. Twice, three times before they had him up, the boy moaned deep down in his tortured throat, the long, quavering "Aahs" of agony setting Mallory's teeth on edge: and then his dangling, twisted leg had passed from Mallory's reach and he was held close and cradled in Andrea's encircling arm, the rain-lashed, bleeding mask of a face lolling grotesquely backwards, forlorn and lifeless with the dead pathos of a broken doll. Seconds later Mallory was up beside them, expertly lashing Stevens's wrists together. He was swearing softly as his numbed hands looped and tightened the rope, softly, bitterly, continuously, but he was quite unaware of this: he was aware only of the broken head that lolled stupidly against his shoulder, of the welling, rain-thinned blood that filmed the upturned face, of the hair above the gashed temple emerging darkly fair as the dye washed slowly out. Inferior bloody boot-blacking, Mallory thought savagely: Jensen shall know of this—it could cost a man's life. And then he became aware of his own thoughts and swore again, still more savagely and at himself this time, for the utter triviality of what he was thinking.

With both hands free—Stevens's bound arms were looped round his neck, his body lashed to his own—Andrea took less than thirty seconds to reach the top: if the dragging, one hundred and sixty pound deadweight on his back made any difference to Andrea's climbing speed and power, Mallory couldn't detect it. The man's endurance was fantastic. Once, just once, as Andrea scrambled over the edge of the cliff, the broken leg caught on the rock, and the crucifying torture of it seared through the merciful shell of insensibility, forced a brief shriek of pain from his lips, a hoarse, bubbling whisper of sound all the more horrible for its muted agony. And then Andrea was standing upright and Mallory was behind him, cutting swiftly at the ropes that bound the two together.

"Straight into the rocks with him, Andrea, will you?" Mallory whispered. "Wait for us at the first open space you come to." Andrea nodded slowly and without raising his head, his hooded eyes bent over the boy in his arms, like a man sunk in thought. Sunk in thought or listening, and all unawares Mallory, too, found himself looking and listening into the thin, lost moaning of the wind, and there was nothing there, only the lifting, dying threnody and the chill of the rain hardening to an ice-cold sleet. He shivered, without knowing why, and listened again; then he shook himself angrily, turned abruptly towards the cliff face and started reeling in the rope. He had it all up, lying round his feet in a limp and rain-sodden tangle when he remembered about the spike still secured to the foot of the chimney, the hundreds of feet of rope suspended from it.

He was too tired and cold and depressed even to feel exasperated with himself. The sight of Stevens and the knowledge of how it was with the boy had affected him more than he knew. Moodily, almost, he kicked the rope over the side again, slid down the chimney, untied the second rope and sent the spike spinning out into the darkness. Less than ten minutes later, the wetly-coiled ropes over his shoulder, he led Miller and Brown into the dark confusion of the rocks.

They found Stevens lying under the lee of a huge boulder, less than a hundred yards inland, in a tiny, cleared space barely the size of a billiard table. An oilskin was spread beneath him on the sodden, gravelly earth, a camouflage cape covered most of his body: it was bitterly cold now, but the rock broke the force of the wind, sheltered the boy from the driving sleet. Andrea looked up as the three men dropped into the hollow and lowered their gear to the ground; already, Mallory could see, Andrea had rolled the trouser up beyond the knee and cut the heavy jackboot away from the mangled leg.

" Sufferin' Christ! " The words, half-oath, half-prayer, were torn involuntarily from Miller: even in the deep gloom the shattered leg looked ghastly. Now he dropped on one knee and stooped low over it. " What a mess! " he murmured slowly. He looked up over his shoulder. " We've gotta do something about that leg, boss, and we've no damned time to lose. This kid's a good candidate for the mortuary."

" I know. We've got to save him, Dusty, we've just *got* to." All at once this had become terribly important to Mallory. He dropped down on his knees. " Let's have a look at him."

Impatiently Miller waved him away.

" Leave this to me, boss." There was a sureness, a sudden authority in his voice that held Mallory silent. " The medicine pack, quick—and undo that tent."

" You sure you can handle this? " God knew, Mallory thought, he didn't really doubt him—he was conscious only of gratitude, of a profound relief, but he felt he had to say something. " How are you going——"

" Look, boss," Miller said quietly. " All my life I've worked with just three things—mines, tunnels and explosives. They're kinda tricky things, boss. I've seen hundreds of busted arms and legs—and fixed most of them myself." He grinned wryly in the darkness. "I was boss myself, then—just one of my privileges, I reckon."

"Good enough!" Mallory clapped him on the shoulder. "He's all yours, Dusty. But the tent!" Involuntarily he looked over his shoulder in the direction of the cliff. "I mean——"

"You got me wrong, boss." Miller's hands, steady and precise with the delicate certainty of a man who has spent a lifetime with high explosive, were busy with a swab and disinfectant. "I wasn't fixin' on settin' up a base hospital. But we need tent-poles—splints for his legs."

"Of course, of course. The poles. Never occurred to me for splints—and I've been thinking of nothing else for——"

"They're not too important, boss." Miller had the medicine pack open now, rapidly selecting the items he wanted with the aid of a hooded torch. "Morphine—that's the first thing, or this kid's goin' to die of shock. And then shelter, warmth, dry clothin'——"

"Warmth! Dry clothing!" Mallory interrupted incredulously. He looked down at the unconscious boy, remembering how Stevens had lost them the stove and all the fuel, and his mouth twisted in bitterness. His own executioner. . . . "Where in God's name are we going to find them?"

"I don't know, boss," Miller said simply. "But we gotta find them. And not just to lessen shock. With a leg like this and soaked to the skin, he's bound to get pneumonia. And then as much sulfa as that bloody great hole in his leg will take—one touch of sepsis in the state this kid's in . . ." His voice trailed away into silence.

Mallory rose to his feet.

"I reckon you're the boss." It was a very creditable imitation of the American's drawl, and Miller looked up quickly, surprise melting into a tired smile, then looked away again. Mallory could hear the chatter of his teeth as he bent over Stevens, and sensed rather than saw that he was shivering violently, continuously, but oblivious to it all in his complete concentration on the job in hand. Miller's clothes, Mallory remembered again, were completely saturated: not for the first time, Mallory wondered how he had managed to get himself into such a state with a waterproof covering him.

" You fix him up. I'll find a place." Mallory wasn't as confident as he felt: still, on the scree-strewn, volcanic slopes of these hills behind, there ought to be a fair chance of finding a rock shelter, if not a cave. Or there would have been in daylight: as it was they would just have to trust to luck to stumble on one. . . . He saw that Casey Brown, grey-faced with exhaustion and illness—the after-effects of carbon monoxide poisoning are slow to disappear—had risen unsteadily to his feet and was making for a gap between the rocks.

" Where are you going, Chief? "

" Back for the rest of the stuff, sir."

" Are you sure you can manage? " Mallory peered at him closely. " You don't look any too fit to me."

" I don't feel it either," Brown said frankly. He looked at Mallory. " But with all respects, sir, I don't think you've seen yourself recently."

" You have a point," Mallory acknowledged. " All right then, come on. I'll go with you."

For the next ten minutes there was silence in the tiny clearing, a silence broken only by the murmurs of Miller and Andrea working over the shattered leg, and the moans of the injured man as he twisted and struggled feebly in his dark abyss of pain: then gradually the morphine took effect and the struggling lessened and died away altogether, and Miller was able to work rapidly, without fear of interruption. Andrea had an oilskin outstretched above them. It served a double purpose —it curtained off the sleet that swept round them from time to time and blanketed the pin-point light of the rubber torch he held in his free hand. And then the leg was set and bandaged and as heavily splinted as possible and Miller was on his feet, straightening his aching back.

" Thank Gawd that's done," he said wearily. He gestured at Stevens. " I feel just the way that kid looks." Suddenly he stiffened, stretched out a warning arm. " I can hear something, Andrea," he whispered.

Andrea laughed. " It's only Brown coming back, my friend. He's been coming this way for over a minute now."

" How do you know it's Brown? " Miller challenged. He felt vaguely annoyed with himself and unobtrusively shoved his ready automatic back into his pocket.

" Brown is a good man among rocks," Andrea said gently; " but he is tired. But Captain Mallory . . ." He shrugged. " People call me ' the big cat ' I know, but among the mountains and rocks the captain is more than a cat. He is a ghost, and that was how men called him in Crete. You will know he is here when he touches you on the shoulder."

Miller shivered in a sudden icy gust of sleet.

" I wish you people wouldn't creep around so much," he complained. He looked up as Brown came round the corner of a boulder, slow with the shambling, stumbling gait of an exhausted man. " Hi, there, Casey. How are things goin'? "

" Not too bad." Brown murmured his thanks as Andrea took the box of explosives off his shoulder and lowered it easily to the ground. " This is the last of the gear. Captain sent me back with it. We heard voices some way along the cliff. He's staying behind to see what they say when they find Stevens gone." Wearily he sat down on top of the box. " Maybe he'll get some idea of what they're going to do next, if anything."

" Seems to me he could have left you there and carried that damned box back himself," Miller growled. Disappointment in Mallory made him more outspoken than he'd meant to be. " He's much better off than you are right now, and I think it's a bit bloody much . . ." He broke off and gasped in pain as Andrea's fingers caught his arm like giant steel pincers.

"It is not fair to talk like that, my friend," Andrea said reproachfully. "You forget, perhaps, that Brown here cannot talk or understand a word of German?"

Miller rubbed his bruised arm tenderly, shaking his head in slow self-anger and condemnation.

"Me and my big mouth," he said ruefully. "Always talkin' outa turn Miller, they call me. Your pardon, one and all. . . . And what is next on the agenda, gentlemen?"

"Captain says we're to go straight on into the rocks and up the right shoulder of this hill here." Brown jerked a thumb in the direction of the vague mass, dark and strangely foreboding, that towered above and beyond them. "He'll catch us up within fifteen minutes or so." He grinned tiredly at Miller. "And we're to leave this box and a rucksack for him to carry."

"Spare me," Miller pleaded. "I feel only six inches tall as it is." He looked down at Stevens, lying quietly under the darkly gleaming wetness of the oilskins, then up at Andrea. "I'm afraid, Andrea——"

"Of course, of course!" Andrea stooped quickly, wrapped the oilskins round the unconscious boy and rose to his feet, as effortlessly as if the oilskins had been empty.

"I'll lead the way," Miller volunteered. "Mebbe I can pick an easy path for you and young Stevens." He swung generator and rucksacks on to his shoulder, staggering under the sudden weight; he hadn't realised he was so weak. "At first, that is," he amended. "Later on, you'll have to carry us both."

Mallory had badly miscalculated the time it would require to overtake the others; over an hour had elapsed since Brown had left him, and still there were no signs of the others. And with seventy pounds on his back, he wasn't making such good time himself.

It wasn't all his fault. The returning German patrol, after

the first shock of discovery, had searched the cliff-top again, methodically and with exasperating slowness. Mallory had waited tensely for someone to suggest descending and examining the chimney—the gouge-marks of the spikes on the rock would have been a dead giveaway—but nobody even mentioned it. With the guard obviously fallen to his death, it would have been a pointless thing to do anyway. After an unrewarding search, they had debated for an unconscionable time as to what they should do next. Finally they had done nothing. A replacement guard was left, and the rest made off along the cliff, carrying their rescue equipment with them.

The three men ahead had made surprisingly good time, although the conditions, admittedly, were now much easier. The heavy fall of boulders at the foot of the slope had petered out after another fifty yards, giving way to broken scree and rain-washed rubble. Possibly he had passed them, but it seemed unlikely: in the intervals between these driving sleet showers —it was more like hail now—he was able to scan the bare shoulder of the hill, and nothing moved. Besides, he knew that Andrea wouldn't stop until he reached what promised at least a bare minimum of shelter, and as yet these exposed, windswept slopes had offered nothing that even remotely approached that.

In the end, Mallory almost literally stumbled upon both men and shelter. He was negotiating a narrow, longitudinal spine of rock, had just crossed its razor-back, when he heard the murmur of voices beneath him and saw a tiny glimmer of light behind the canvas stretching down from the overhang of the far wall of the tiny ravine at his feet.

Miller started violently and swung round as he felt the hand on his shoulder; the automatic was half-way out of his pocket before he saw who it was and sunk back heavily on the rock behind him.

" Come, come, now! Trigger-happy." Thankfully Mallory slid his burden from his aching shoulders and looked across at the softly laughing Andrea. " What's so funny? "

"Our friend here." Andrea grinned again. "I told him that the first thing he would know of your arrival would be when you touched him on the shoulder. I don't think he believed me."

"You might have coughed or somethin'," Miller said defensively. "It's my nerves, boss," he added plaintively. "They're not what they were forty-eight hours ago."

Mallory looked at him disbelievingly, made to speak, then stopped short as he caught sight of the pale blur of a face propped up against a rucksack. Beneath the white swathe of a bandaged forehead the eyes were open, looking steadily at him. Mallory took a step forward, sank down on one knee.

"So you've come round at last!" He smiled into the sunken parchment face and Stevens smiled back, the bloodless lips whiter than the face itself. He looked ghastly. "How do you feel, Andy?"

"Not too bad, sir. Really I'm not." The bloodshot eyes were dark and filled with pain. His gaze fell and he looked down vacantly at his bandaged leg, looked up again, smiled uncertainly at Mallory. "I'm terribly sorry about all this, sir. What a bloody stupid thing to do."

"It wasn't a stupid thing." Mallory spoke with slow, heavy emphasis. "It was criminal folly." He knew everyone was watching them, but knew, also, that Stevens had eyes for him alone. "Criminal, unforgivable folly," he went on quietly, "—and I'm the man in the dock. I'd suspected you'd lost a lot of blood on the boat, but I didn't know you had these big gashes on your forehead. I should have made it my business to find out." He smiled wryly. "You should have heard what these two insubordinate characters had to say to me about it when they got to the top. . . . And they were right. You should never have been asked to bring up the rear in the state you were in. It was madness." He grinned again. "You should have been hauled up like a sack of coals like the intrepid mountaineering team of Miller and Brown. . . . God knows how you ever made it—I'm sure you'll never know." He leaned forward, touched Stevens's sound knee. " Forgive me, Andy. I honestly didn't realise how far through you were."

Stevens stirred uncomfortably, but the dead pallor of the high-boned cheeks was stained with embarrassed pleasure.

" Please, sir," he pleaded. " Don't talk like that. It was just one of these things." He paused, eyes screwed shut and indrawn breath hissing sharply through his teeth as a wave of pain washed up from his shattered leg. Then he looked at Mallory again. " And there's no credit due to me for the climb," he went on quietly. " I hardly remember a thing about it."

Mallory looked at him without speaking, eyebrows arched in mild interrogation.

" I was scared to death every step of the way up," Stevens said simply. He was conscious of no surprise, no wonder that he was saying the thing he would have died rather than say. " I've never been so scared in all my life."

Mallory shook his head slowly from side to side, stubbled chin rasping in his cupped palm. He seemed genuinely puzzled. Then he looked down at Stevens and smiled quizzically.

" Now I know you *are* new to this game, Andy." He smiled again. " Maybe you think I was laughing and singing all the way up that cliff? Maybe you think *I* wasn't scared? " He lit a cigarette and gazed at Stevens through a cloud of drifting smoke. " Well, I wasn't. ' Scared ' isn't the word—I was bloody well terrified. So was Andrea here. We know too much not to be scared."

" Andrea! " Stevens laughed, then cried out as the movement triggered off a crepitant agony in his bone-shattered leg. For a moment Mallory thought he had lost consciousness, but almost at once he spoke again, his voice husky with pain. " Andrea! " he whispered. " Scared! I don't believe it! "

" Andrea *was* afraid." The big Greek's voice was very gentle. " Andrea *is* afraid. Andrea is always afraid. That is why I have lived so long." He stared down at his great hands. "And why so many have died. They were not so afraid as I. They were not afraid of everything a man could be afraid of, there was always something they forgot to fear, to guard against. But Andrea was afraid of everything—and he forgot nothing. It is as simple as that."

He looked across at Stevens and smiled.

"There are no brave men and cowardly men in the world, my son. There are only brave men. To be born, to live, to die —that takes courage enough in itself, and more than enough. We are all brave men and we are all afraid, and what the world calls a brave man, he, too, is brave and afraid like all the rest of us. Only he is brave for five minutes longer. Or sometimes ten minutes, or twenty minutes—or the time it takes a man sick and bleeding and afraid to climb a cliff."

Stevens said nothing. His head was sunk on his chest, and his face was hidden. He had seldom felt so happy, seldom so at peace with himself. He had known that he could not hide things from men like Andrea and Mallory, but he had not known that it would not matter. He felt he should say something, but he could not think what and he was deathly tired. He knew, deep down, that Andrea was speaking the truth, but not the whole truth; but he was too tired to care, to try to work things out.

Miller cleared his throat noisily.

"No more talkin', Lieutenant," he said firmly. "You gotta lie down, get yourself some sleep."

Stevens looked at him, then at Mallory in puzzled inquiry.

"Better do what you're told, Andy," Mallory smiled. "Your surgeon and medical adviser talking. He fixed your leg."

"Oh! I didn't know. Thanks, Dusty. Was it very— difficult?"

Miller waved a deprecatory hand.

"Not for a man of my experience. Just a simple break," he

lied easily. " Almost let one of the others do it. . . . Give him a hand to lie down, will you, Andrea? " He jerked his head towards Mallory. " Boss? "

The two men moved outside, turning their backs to the icy wind.

" We gotta get a fire, dry clothing, for that kid," Miller said urgently. " His pulse is about 140, temperature 103. He's runnin' a fever, and he's losin' ground all the time."

" I know, I know," Mallory said worriedly. " And there's not a hope of getting any fuel on this damned mountain. Let's go in and see how much dried clothing we can muster between us."

He lifted the edge of the canvas and stepped inside. Stevens was still awake, Brown and Andrea on either side of him. Miller was on his heels.

" We're going to stay here for the night," Mallory announced, " so let's make things as snug as possible. Mind you," he admitted, " we're a bit too near the cliff for comfort, but old Jerry hasn't a clue we're on the island, and we're out of sight of the coast. Might as well make ourselves comfortable."

" Boss . . ." Miller made to speak, then fell silent again. Mallory looked at him in surprise, saw that he, Brown and Stevens were looking at one another, uncertainty, then doubt and a dawning, sick comprehension in their eyes. A sudden anxiety, the sure knowledge that something was far wrong, struck at Mallory like a blow.

" What's up? " he demanded sharply. " What is it? "

" We have bad news for you, boss," Miller said carefully. " We should have told you right away. Guess we all thought that one of the others would have told you. . . . Remember that sentry you and Andrea shoved over the side? "

Mallory nodded, sombrely. He knew what was coming.

" He fell on top of that reef twenty-thirty feet or so from the cliff," Miller went on. " Wasn't much of him left, I guess, but what was was jammed between two rocks. He was really stuck good and fast."

" I see," Mallory murmured. " I've been wondering all night how you managed to get so wet under your rubber cape."

" I tried four times, boss," Miller said quietly. " The others had a rope round me." He shrugged his shoulders. " Not a chance. Them gawddamned waves just flung me back against the cliff every time."

" It will be light in three or four hours," Mallory murmured. " In four hours they will know we are on the island. They will see him as soon as it's dawn and send a boat to investigate."

" Does it really matter, sir," Stevens suggested. " He could still have fallen."

Mallory eased the canvas aside and looked out into the night. It was bitterly cold and the snow was beginning to fall all around them. He dropped the canvas again.

" Five minutes," he said absently. " We will leave in five minutes." He looked at Stevens and smiled faintly. " We are forgetful, too. We should have told you. Andrea stabbed the sentry through the heart."

The hours that followed were hours plucked from the darkest nightmare, endless, numbing hours of stumbling and tripping and falling and getting up again, of racked bodies and aching, tortured muscles, of dropped loads and frantic pawing around in the deepening snow, of hunger and thirst and all-encompassing exhaustion.

They had retraced their steps now, were heading W.N.W. back across the shoulder of the mountain—almost certainly the Germans would think they had gone due north, heading for the centre of the island. Without compass, stars or moon to guide, Mallory had nothing to orientate them but the feel of the slope of the mountain and the memory of the map Vlachos had shown them in Alexandria. But by and by he was reasonably certain that they had rounded the mountain and were pushing up some narrow gorge into the interior.

The snow was the deadly enemy. Heavy, wet and feathery, it swirled all around them in a blanketing curtain of grey, sifted down their necks and jackboots, worked its insidious way under their clothes and up their sleeves, blocked their eyes and ears and mouths, pierced and then anæsthetised exposed faces, and turned gloveless hands into leaden lumps of ice, benumbed and all but powerless. All suffered, and suffered badly, but Stevens most of all. He had lost consciousness again within minutes of leaving the cave and clad in clinging, sodden clothes as he was, he now lacked even the saving warmth generated by physical activity. Twice Andrea had stopped and felt for the beating of the heart, for he thought that the boy had died: but he could feel nothing for there was no feeling left in his hands, and he could only wonder and stumble on again.

About five in the morning, as they were climbing up the steep valley head above the gorge, a treacherous, slippery slope with only a few stunted carob trees for anchor in the sliding scree, Mallory decided that they must rope up for safety's sake. In single file they scrambled and struggled up the ever-steepening slope for the next twenty minutes: Mallory, in the lead, did not even dare to think how Andrea was getting on behind him. Suddenly the slope eased, flattened out completely, and almost before they realised what was happening they had crossed the high divide, still roped together and in driving, blinding snow with zero visibility, and were sliding down the valley on the other side.

They came to the cave at dawn, just as the first grey stirrings of a bleak and cheerless day struggled palely through the lowering, snow-filled sky to the east. Monsieur Vlachos had told them that the south of Navarone was honey-combed with caves, but this was the first they had seen, and even then it was no cave but a dark, narrow tunnel in a great heap of piled volcanic slabs, huge, twisted layers of rock precariously poised in a gully that threaded down the slope towards some broad and unknown valley a thousand, two thousand feet, beneath them, a valley still shrouded in the gloom of night.

It was no cave, but it was enough. For frozen, exhausted, sleep-haunted men, it was more than enough, it was more than they had ever hoped for. There was room for them all, the few cracks were quickly blocked against the drifting snow, the entrance curtained off by the boulder-weighted tent. Somehow, impossibly almost in the cramped darkness, they stripped Stevens of his sea- and rain-soaked clothes, eased him into a providentially zipped sleeping-bag, forced some brandy down his throat and cushioned the blood-stained head on some dry clothing. And then the four men, even the tireless Andrea, slumped down to the sodden, snow-chilled floor of the cave and slept like men already dead, oblivious alike of the rocks on the floor, the cold, their hunger and their clammy, saturated clothing, oblivious even to the agony of returning circulation in their frozen hands and faces.

CHAPTER SEVEN

TUESDAY

1500-1900

THE SUN, rime-ringed and palely luminous behind the drifting cloud-wrack, was far beyond its zenith and dipping swiftly westwards to the snow-limned shoulder of the mountain when Andrea lifted the edge of the tent, pushed it gently aside and peered out warily down the smooth sweep of the mountainside. For a few moments he remained almost motionless behind the canvas, automatically easing cramped and aching leg muscles, narrowed, roving eyes gradually accustoming themselves to the white glare of the glistening, crystalline snow. And then he had flitted noiselessly out of the mouth of the tunnel and reached far up the bank of the gully in half a dozen steps; stretched full length against the snow, he eased himself smoothly up the slope, lifted a cautious eye over the top.

Far below him stretched the great, curved sweep of an almost perfectly symmetrical valley—a valley born abruptly in the cradling embrace of steep-walled mountains and falling away gently to the north. That towering, buttressed giant on his right that brooded darkly over the head of the valley, its peak hidden in the snow clouds—there could be no doubt about that, Andrea thought. Mt. Kostos, the highest mountain in Navarone: they had crossed its western flank during the darkness of the night. Due east and facing his own at perhaps five miles' distance, the third mountain was barely less high: but its northern flank fell away more quickly, debouching on to the plains that lay to the north-east of Navarone. And about four miles away to the north-north-east, far beneath the snowline and the isolated shepherds' huts, a tiny, flat-roofed township lay in a fold in the hills, along the bank of the little stream that wound its way through the valley. That could only be the village of Margaritha.

Even as he absorbed the topography of the valley, his eyes probing every dip and cranny in the hills for a possible source of danger, Andrea's mind was racing back over the last two minutes of time, trying to isolate, to remember the nature of the alien sound that had cut through the cocoon of sleep and brought him instantly to his feet, alert and completely awake, even before his conscious mind had time to register the memory of the sound. And then he heard it again, three times in as many seconds, the high-pitched, lonely wheep of a whistle, shrill peremptory blasts that echoed briefly and died along the lower slopes of Mt. Kostos: the final echo still hung faintly on the air as Andrea pushed himself backwards and slid down to the floor of the gully.

He was back on the bank within thirty seconds, cheek muscles contracting involuntarily as the ice-chill eyepieces of Mallory's Zeiss-Ikon binoculars screwed into his face. There was no mistaking them now, he thought grimly, his first, fleeting impression had been all too accurate. Twenty-five, perhaps thirty soldiers in all, strung out in a long, irregular line, they were advancing slowly across the flank of Kostos, combing every gully, each jumbled confusion of boulders that lay in their path. Every man was clad in a snow-suit, but even at a distance of two miles they were easy to locate: the arrow-heads of their strapped skis angled up above shoulders and hooded heads: startlingly black against the sheer whiteness of the snow, the skis bobbed and weaved in disembodied drunkenness as the men slipped and stumbled along the scree-strewn slopes of the mountain. From time to time a man near the centre of the line pointed and gestured with an alpenstock, as if co-ordinating the efforts of the search party. The man with the whistle, Andrea guessed.

"Andrea!" The call from the cave mouth was very soft. "Anything wrong?"

Finger to his lips, Andrea twisted round in the snow. Mallory was standing by the canvas screen. Dark-jowled and crumple-clothed, he held up one hand against the glare of the snow while the other rubbed the sleep from his bloodshot eyes. And then he was limping forward in obedience to the crooking of Andrea's finger, wincing in pain at every step he took. His toes were swollen and skinned, gummed together with congealed blood. He had not had his boots off since he had taken them from the feet of the dead German sentry: and now he was almost afraid to remove them, afraid of what he would find. . . . He clambered slowly up the bank of the gully and sank down in the snow beside Andrea.

"Company?"

"The very worst of company," Andrea murmured. "Take a look, my Keith." He handed over the binoculars, pointed down to the lower slopes of Mt. Kostos. "Your friend Jensen never told us that they were here."

Slowly, Mallory quartered the slopes with the binoculars. Suddenly the line of searchers moved into his field of vision. He raised his head, adjusted the focus impatiently, looked briefly once more, then lowered the binoculars with a restrained deliberation of gesture that held a wealth of bitter comment.

"The W.G.B.," he said softly.

"A Jaeger battalion," Andrea conceded. "Alpine Corps —their finest mountain troops. This is most inconvenient, my Keith."

Mallory nodded, rubbed his stubbled chin.

"If anyone can find us, they can. And they'll find us." He lifted the glasses to look again at the line of advancing men. The painstaking thoroughness of the search was disturbing enough: but even more threatening, more frightening, was the snail-like relentlessness, the inevitability of the approach of these tiny figures. " God knows what the Alpenkorps is doing here," Mallory went on. " It's enough that they are here. They must know that we've landed and spent the morning searching the eastern saddle of Kostos—that was the obvious route for us to break into the interior. They've drawn a blank there, so now they're working their way over to the other saddle. They must be pretty nearly certain that we're carrying a wounded man with us and that we can't have got very far. It's only going to be a matter of time, Andrea."

" A matter of time," Andrea echoed. He glanced up at the sun, a sun all but invisible in a darkening sky. " An hour, an hour and a half at the most. They'll be here before the sun goes down. And we'll still be here." He glanced quizzically at Mallory. " We cannot leave the boy. And we cannot get away if we take the boy—and then he would die anyway."

" We will not be here," Mallory said flatly. " If we stay we all die. Or finish up in one of these nice little dungeons that Monsieur Vlachos told us about."

" The greatest good of the greatest number," Andrea nodded slowly. " That's how it has to be, has it not, my Keith ? The greatest number. That is what Captain Jensen would say." Mallory stirred uncomfortably, but his voice was steady enough when he spoke.

" That's how I see it, too, Andrea. Simple proportion— twelve hundred to one. You know it has to be this way." Mallory sounded tired.

" Yes, I know. But you are worrying about nothing." Andrea smiled. " Come, my friend. Let us tell the others the good news."

Miller looked up as the two men came in, letting the canvas screen fall shut behind them. He had unzipped the side of Stevens's sleeping-bag and was working on the mangled leg. A pencil flashlight was propped on a rucksack beside him.

"When are we goin' to do somethin' about this kid, boss?"
The voice was abrupt, angry, like his gesture towards the sleep-
drugged boy beside him. "This damned waterproof sleeping-
bag is soaked right through. So's the kid—and he's about
frozen stiff: his leg feels like a side of chilled beef. He's gotta
have heat, boss, a warm room and hot drinks—or he's
finished. Twenty-four hours." Miller shivered and looked
slowly round the broken walls of the rock-shelter. "I reckon
he'd have less than an even chance in a first-class general
hospital. . . . He's just wastin' his time keepin' on breathin' in
this gawddamned ice-box."

Miller hardly exaggerated. Water from the melting snow
above trickled continuously down the clammy, green-lichened
walls of the cave or dripped directly on to the half-frozen
gravelly slush on the floor of the cave. With no through
ventilation and no escape for the water accumulating at the
sides of the shelter, the whole place was dank and airless and
terribly chill.

"Maybe he'll be hospitalised sooner than you think,"
Mallory said dryly. "How's his leg?"

"Worse." Miller was blunt. "A helluva sight worse. I've
just chucked in another handful of sulpha and tied things up
again. That's all I can do, boss, and it's just a waste of
time anyway. . . . What was that crack about a hospital?" he
added suspiciously.

"That was no crack," Mallory said soberly, "but one of
the more unpleasant facts of life. There's a German search party
heading this way. They mean business. They'll find us, all
right."

Miller swore. "That's handy, that's just wonderful," he
said bitterly. "How far away, boss?"

"An hour, maybe a little more."

"And what are we goin' to do with Junior, here? Leave
him? It's his only chance, I reckon."

"Stevens comes with us." There was a flat finality in

Mallory's voice. Miller looked at him for a long time in silence: his face was very cold.

"Stevens comes with us," Miller repeated. "We drag him along with us until he's dead—that won't take long—and then we leave him in the snow. Just like that, huh?"

"Just like that, Dusty." Absently Mallory brushed some snow off his clothes, and looked up again at Miller. "Stevens knows too much. The Germans will have guessed why we're on the island, but they don't know how we propose to get inside the fortress—and they don't know when the Navy's coming through. But Stevens does. They'll make him talk. Scopolamine will make anyone talk."

"Scopolamine! On a dying man?" Miller was openly incredulous.

"Why not? I'd do the same myself. If you were the German commandant and you knew that your big guns and half the men in your fortress were liable to be blown to hell any moment, you'd do the same."

Miller looked at him, grinned wryly, shook his head.

"Me and my——"

"I know. You and your big mouth." Mallory smiled and clapped him on the shoulder. "I don't like it one little bit more than you do, Dusty." He turned away and crossed to the other side of the cave. "How are you feeling, Chief?"

"Not too bad, sir." Casey Brown was only just awake, numbed and shivering in sodden clothes. "Anything wrong?"

"Plenty," Mallory assured him. "Search party moving this way. We'll have to pull out inside half an hour." He looked at his watch. "Just on four o'clock. Do you think you could raise Cairo on the set?"

"Lord only knows," Brown said frankly. He rose stiffly to his feet. "The radio didn't get just the best of treatment yesterday. I'll have a go."

"Thanks, Chief. See that your aerial doesn't stick up above the sides of the gully." Mallory turned to leave the cave, but halted abruptly at the sight of Andrea squatting on a boulder just beside the entrance. His head bent in concentration, the big Greek had just finished screwing telescopic sights on to the barrel of his 7.92 mm. Mauser and was now deftly wrapping a sleeping-bag lining round its barrel and butt until the entire rifle was wrapped in a white cocoon.

Mallory watched him in silence. Andrea glanced up at him, smiled, rose to his feet and reached out for his rucksack. Within thirty seconds he was clad from head to toe in his mountain camouflage suit, was drawing tight the purse-strings of his snow-hood and easing his feet into the rucked elastic anklets of his canvas boots. Then he picked up the Mauser and smiled slightly.

" I thought I might be taking a little walk, Captain," he said apologetically. " With your permission, of course."

Mallory nodded his head several times in slow recollection.

" You said I was worrying about nothing," he murmured. " I should have known. You might have told me, Andrea." But the protest was automatic, without significance. Mallory felt neither anger nor even annoyance at this tacit arrogation of his authority. The habit of command died hard in Andrea: on such occasions as he ostensibly sought approval for or consulted about a proposed course of action it was generally as a matter of courtesy and to give information as to his intentions. Instead of resentment, Mallory could feel only an overwhelming relief and gratitude to the smiling giant who towered above him: he had talked casually to Miller about driving Stevens till he died and then abandoning him, talked with an indifference that masked a mind sombre with bitterness at what he must do, but even so he had not known how depressed, how sick at heart this decision had left him until he knew it was no longer necessary.

" I am sorry." Andrea was half-contrite, half-smiling. " I should have told you. I thought you understood. . . . It is the best thing to do, yes? "

" It is the only thing to do," Mallory said frankly. " You're going to draw them off up the saddle? "

" There is no other way. With their skis they would overtake me in minutes if I went down into the valley. I cannot come back, of course, until it is dark. You will be here? "

" Some of us will." Mallory glanced across the shelter where a waking Stevens was trying to sit up, heels of his palms screwing into his exhausted eyes. " We must have food and fuel, Andrea," he said softly. " I am going down into the valley to-night."

" Of course, of course. We must do what we can." Andrea's face was grave, his voice only a murmur. " As long as we can. He is only a boy, a child almost. . . . Perhaps it will not be long." He pulled back the curtain, looked out at the evening sky. " I will be back by seven o'clock."

" Seven o'clock," Mallory repeated. The sky, he could see, was darkening already, darkening with the gloom of coming snow, and the lifting wind was beginning to puff little clouds of air-spun, flossy white into the little gully. Mallory shivered and caught hold of the massive arm. " For God's sake, Andrea," he urged quietly, " look after yourself! "

" Myself? " Andrea smiled gently, no mirth in his eyes, and as gently he disengaged his arm. " Do not think about me." The voice was very quiet, with an utter lack of arrogance. " If you must speak to God, speak to Him about these poor devils who are looking for us." The canvas dropped behind him and he was gone.

For some moments Mallory stood irresolutely at the mouth of the cave, gazing out sightlessly through the gap in the curtain. Then he wheeled abruptly, crossed the floor of the shelter and knelt in front of Stevens. The boy was propped up against Miller's anxious arm, the eyes lack-lustre and expressionless, bloodless cheeks deep-sunken in a grey and parchment face. Mallory smiled at him: he hoped the shock didn't show in his face.

"Well, well, well. The sleeper awakes at last. Better late than never." He opened his waterproof cigarette case, proferred it to Stevens. "How are you feeling now, Andy?"

"Frozen, sir." Stevens shook his head at the case and tried to grin back at Mallory, a feeble travesty of a smile that made Mallory wince.

"And the leg?"

"I think it must be frozen, too." Stevens looked down incuriously at the sheathed whiteness of his shattered leg. "Anyway, I can't feel a thing."

"Frozen!" Miller's sniff was a masterpiece of injured pride. "Frozen, he says! Gawddamned ingratitude. It's the first-class medical care, if I do say so myself!"

Stevens smiled, a fleeting, absent smile that flickered over his face and was gone. For long moments he kept staring down at his leg, then suddenly lifted his head and looked directly at Mallory.

"Look, sir, there's no good kidding ourselves." The voice was soft, quite toneless. "I don't want to seem ungrateful and I hate even the idea of cheap heroics, but—well, I'm just a damned great millstone round your necks and——"

"Leave you, eh?" Mallory interrupted. "Leave you to die of the cold or be captured by the Germans. Forget it, laddie. We can look after you—and these ruddy guns—at the same time."

"But, sir——"

"You insult us, Lootenant." Miller sniffed again. "Our feelings are hurt. Besides, as a professional man I gotta see my case through to convalescence, and if you think I'm goin' to do that in any gawddamned dripping German dungeon, you can——"

"Enough!" Mallory held up his hand. "The subject is closed." He saw the stain high up on the thin cheeks, the glad light that touched the dulled eyes, and felt the self-loathing and the shame well up inside him, shame for the gratitude of a sick man who did not know that their concern stemmed not from solicitude but from fear that he might betray them. . . . Mallory bent forward and began to unlace his high jack-boots. He spoke without looking up.

"Dusty."

"Yeah?"

"When you're finished boasting about your medical prowess, maybe you'd care to use some of it. Come and have a look at these feet of mine, will you? I'm afraid the sentry's boots haven't done them a great deal of good."

Fifteen painful minutes later Miller snipped off the rough edges of the adhesive bandage that bound Mallory's right foot, straightened up stiffly and contemplated his handiwork with pride.

"Beautiful, Miller, beautiful," he murmured complacently. "Not even in John Hopkins in the city of Baltimore . . ." He broke off suddenly, frowned down at the thickly bandaged feet and coughed apologetically. "A small point has just occurred to me, boss."

"I thought it might eventually," Mallory said grimly. "Just how do you propose to get my feet into these damned boots again?" He shivered involuntarily as he pulled on a pair of thick woollen socks, matted and sodden with melted snow, picked up the German sentry's boots, held them at arm's length and examined them in disgust. "Sevens, at the most— and a darned small sevens at that!"

"Nines," Stevens said laconically. He handed over his own jack-boots, one of them slit neatly down the side where Andrea had cut it open. "You can fix that tear easily enough, and they're no damned good to me now. No arguments, sir, please." He began to laugh softly, broke off in a sharply indrawn hiss of pain as the movement jarred the broken bones, took a couple of deep, quivering breaths, then smiled whitely. "My first— and probably my last—contribution to the expedition. What sort of medal do you reckon they'll give me for that, sir?"

Mallory took the boots, looked at Stevens a long moment in silence, then turned as the tarpaulin was pushed aside. Brown stumbled in, lowered the transmitter and telescopic aerial to the floor of the cave and pulled out a tin of cigarettes. They slipped from his frozen fingers, fell into the icy mud at his feet, became brown and sodden on the instant. He swore, briefly, and without enthusiasm, beat his numbed hands across his chest, gave it up and sat down heavily on a convenient boulder. He looked tired and cold and thoroughly miserable.

Mallory lit a cigarette and passed it across to him.

" How did it go, Casey? Manage to raise them at all? "

" They managed to raise me—more or less. Reception was lousy." Brown drew the grateful tobacco smoke deep down into his lungs. " And I couldn't get through at all. Must be that damned great hill to the south there."

" Probably," Mallory nodded. " And what news from our friends in Cairo. Exhorting us to greater efforts? Telling us to get on with the job? "

" No news at all. Too damn' worried about the silence at this end. Said that from now on they were going to come through every four hours, acknowledgment or no. Repeated that about ten times, then signed off."

" That'll be a great help," Miller said acidly. " Nice to know they're on our side. Nothin' like moral support." He jerked his thumb towards the mouth of the cave. " Reckon them bloodhounds would be scared to death if they knew. . . . Did you take a gander at them before you came in? "

" I didn't have to," Brown said morosely. " I could hear them—sounded like the officer in charge shouting directions." Mechanically, almost, he picked up his automatic rifle, eased the clip in the magazine. " Must be less than a mile away now."

The search party, more closely bunched by this time, was less than a mile, was barely half a mile distant from the cave when the Oberleutnant in charge saw that the right wing of his line, on the steeper slopes to the south, was lagging behind once more. Impatiently he lifted his whistle to his mouth for the three sharp, peremptory blasts that would bring his weary men stumbling into line again. Twice the whistle shrilled out its imperative urgency, the piercing notes echoing flatly along the snowbound slopes and dying away in the valley below: but the third *wheep* died at birth, caught up again and tailed off in a wailing, eldritch diminuendo that merged with dreadful harmony into a long, bubbling scream of agony. For two or three seconds the Oberleutnant stood motionless in his tracks, his face shocked and contorted: then he jack-knifed violently forward and pitched down into the crusted snow. The burly sergeant beside him stared down at the fallen officer, looked up in sudden horrified understanding, opened his mouth to shout, sighed and toppled wearily over the body at his feet, the evil, whip-lash crack of the Mauser in his ears as he died.

High up on the western slopes of Mount Kostos, wedged in the V between two great boulders, Andrea gazed down the darkening mountainside over the depressed telescopic sights of his rifle and pumped another three rounds into the wavering, disorganised line of searchers. His face was quite still, as immobile as the eyelids that never flickered to the regular crashing of his Mauser, and drained of all feeling. Even his eyes reflected the face, eyes neither hard nor pitiless, but simply empty and almost frighteningly remote, a remoteness that mirrored his mind, a mind armoured for the moment against all thought and sensation, for Andrea knew that he must not think about this thing. To kill, to take the life of his fellows, that was the supreme evil, for life was a gift that it was not his to take away. Not even in fair fight. And this was murder.

Slowly Andrea lowered the Mauser, peered through the drifting gun-smoke that hung heavily in the frosty evening air. The enemy had vanished, completely, rolled behind scattered boulders or burrowed frantically into the blanketing anonymity of the snow. But they were still there, still potentially as dangerous as ever. Andrea knew that they would recover fast from the death of their officer—there were no finer, no more tenacious fighters in Europe than the ski-troops of the Jaeger mountain battalion—and would come after him, catch and kill him if humanly possible. That was why Andrea's first care had been to kill their officer—he might not have come after him, might have stopped to puzzle out the reason for this unprovoked flank attack.

Andrea ducked low in reflex instinct as a sudden burst of automatic fire whined in murderous ricochet off the boulders before him. He had expected this. It was the old classic infantry attack pattern—advance under covering fire, drop, cover your mate and come again. Swiftly Andrea rammed home another charge into the magazine of his Mauser, dropped flat on his face and inched his way along behind the low line of broken rock that extended fifteen or twenty yards to his right—he had chosen his ambush point with care—and then petered out. At the far end he pulled his snow hood down to the level of his brows and edged a wary eye round the corner of the rock.

Another heavy burst of automatic fire smashed into the boulders he had just left, and half a dozen men—three from either end of the line—broke cover, scurried along the slope in a stumbling, crouching run, then pitched forward into the snow again. *Along* the slope—the two parties had run in opposite directions. Andrea lowered his head and rubbed the back of a massive hand across the stubbled grizzle of his chin. Awkward, damned awkward. No frontal attack for the foxes of the W.G.B. They were extending their lines on either side, the points hooking round in a great, encircling half-moon. Bad enough for himself, but he could have coped with that—a carefully reconnoitred escape gully wound up the slope behind him. But he hadn't foreseen what was obviously going to happen: the curving crescent of line to the west was going to sweep across the rock-shelter where the others lay hidden.

Andrea twisted over on his back and looked up at the evening sky. It was darkening by the moment, darkening with the gloom of coming snow, and daylight was beginning to fail. He twisted again and looked across the great swelling shoulder of Mount Kostos, looked at the few scattered rocks and shallow depressions that barely dimpled the smooth convexity of the slope. He took a second quick look round the rock as the rifles of the W.G.B. opened up once more, saw the same encircling manœuvre being executed again, and waited no longer. Firing blindly downhill, he half-rose to his feet and flung himself out into the open, finger squeezing on the trigger, feet driving desperately into the frozen snow as he launched himself towards the nearest rock-cover, forty yards away if an inch. Thirty-five yards to go, thirty, twenty and still not a shot fired, a slip, a stumble on the sliding scree, a catlike recovery, ten yards, still miraculously immune, and then he had dived into shelter to land on chest and stomach with a sickening impact that struck cruelly into his ribs and emptied his lungs with an explosive gasp.

Fighting for breath, he struck the magazine cover, rammed home another charge, risked a quick peep over the top of the rock and catapulted himself to his feet again, all inside ten seconds. The Mauser held across his body opened up again, firing downhill at vicious random, for Andrea had eyes only for the smoothly-treacherous ground at his feet, for the scree-lined depression so impossibly far ahead. And then the Mauser was empty, useless in his hand, and every gun far below had opened up, the shells whistling above his head or blinding him with spurting gouts of snow as they ricocheted off the solid rock. But twilight was touching the hills, Andrea was only a blur, a swiftly-flitting blur against a ghostly background, and uphill accuracy was notoriously difficult at any time. Even so, the massed fire from below was steadying and converging, and

Andrea waited no longer. Unseen hands plucking wickedly at the flying tails of his snow-smock, he flung himself almost horizontally forward and slid the last ten feet face down into the waiting depression.

Stretched full length on his back in the hollow, Andrea fished out a steel mirror from his breast pocket and held it gingerly above his head. At first he could see nothing, for the darkness was deeper below and the mirror misted from the warmth of his body. And then the film vanished in the chill mountain air and he could see two, three and then half a dozen men breaking cover, heading at a clumsy run straight up the face of the hill—and two of them had come from the extreme right of the line. Andrea lowered the mirror and relaxed with a long sigh of relief, eyes crinkling in a smile. He looked up at the sky, blinked as the first feathery flakes of falling snow melted on his eyelids and smiled again. Almost lazily he brought out another charger for the Mauser, fed more shells into the magazine.

" Boss? " Miller's voice was plaintive.

" Yes? What is it? " Mallory brushed some snow off his face and the collar of his smock and peered into the white darkness ahead.

" Boss, when you were in school did you ever read any stories about folks gettin' lost in a snowstorm and wanderin' round and round in circles for days? "

" We had exactly the same book in Queenstown," Mallory conceded.

" Wanderin' round and round until they died? " Miller persisted.

" Oh, for heaven's sake! " Mallory said impatiently. His feet, even in Stevens's roomy boots, hurt abominably. " How can we be wandering in circles if we're going downhill all the time? What do you think we're on—a bloody spiral staircase? "

Miller walked on in hurt silence, Mallory beside him, both

men ankle-deep in the wet, clinging snow that had been falling so silently, so persistently, for the past three hours since Andrea had drawn off the Jaeger search party. Even in mid-winter in the White Mountains in Crete Mallory could recall no snowfall so heavy and continuous. So much for the Isles of Greece and the eternal sunshine that gilds them yet, he thought bitterly. He hadn't reckoned on this when he'd planned on going down to Margaritha for food and fuel, but even so it wouldn't have made any difference to his decision. Although in less pain now, Stevens was becoming steadily weaker, and the need was desperate.

With moon and stars blanketed by the heavy snow-clouds —visibility, indeed, was hardly more than ten feet in any direction—the loss of their compasses had assumed a crippling importance. He didn't doubt his ability to find the village— it was simply a matter of walking downhill till they came to the stream that ran through the valley, then following that north till they came to Margaritha—but if the snow didn't let up their chances of locating that tiny cave again in the vast sweep of the hillsides . . .

Mallory smothered an exclamation as Miller's hand closed round his upper arm, dragged him down to his knees in the snow. Even in that moment of unknown danger he could feel a slow stirring of anger against himself, for his attention had been wandering along with his thoughts. . . . He lifted his hand as vizor against the snow, peered out narrowly through the wet, velvety curtain of white that swirled and eddied out of the darkness before him. Suddenly he had it—a dark, squat shape only feet away. They had all but walked straight into it.

" It's the hut," he said softly in Miller's ear. He had seen it early in the afternoon, half-way between their cave and Margaritha, and almost in a line with both. He was conscious of relief, an increase in confidence: they would be in the village in less than half an hour. " Elementary navigation, my dear Corporal," he murmured. " Lost and wandering in circles, my foot! Just put your faith . . ."

He broke off as Miller's fingers dug viciously into his arm, as Miller's head came close to his own.

" I heard voices, boss." The words were a mere breath of sound.

" Are you sure? " Miller's silenced gun, Mallory noticed, was still in his pocket.

Miller hesitated.

" Dammit to hell, boss, I'm sure of nothin'," he whispered irritably. " I've been imaginin' every damn' thing possible in the past hour! " He pulled the snow hood off his head, the better to listen, bent forward for a few seconds then sank back again. " Anyway, I'm sure I *thought* I heard somethin'."

" Come on. Let's take a look-see." Mallory was on his feet again. " I think you're mistaken. Can't be the Jaeger boys—they were half-way back across Mount Kostos when we saw them last. And the shepherds only use these places in the summer months." He slipped the safety catch of his Colt .455, walked slowly, at a half-crouch, towards the nearest wall of the hut, Miller at his shoulder.

They reached the hut, put their ears against the frail, tar-paper walls. Ten seconds passed, twenty, half a minute, then Mallory relaxed.

" Nobody at home. Or if they are, they're keeping mighty quiet. But no chances, Dusty. You go that way, I'll go this. Meet at the door—that'll be on the opposite side, facing into the valley. . . . Walk wide at the corners—never fails to baffle the unwary."

A minute later both men were inside the hut, the door shut behind them. The hooded beam of Mallory's torch probed into every corner of the ramshackle cabin. It was quite empty —an earthen floor, a rough wooden bunk, a dilapidated stove with a rusty lantern standing on it, and that was all. No table, no chair, no chimney, not even a window.

Mallory walked over to the stove, picked up the lamp and sniffed it.

"Hasn't been used for weeks. Still full of kerosene, though. Very useful in that damn' dungeon up there—if we can ever find the place. . . ."

He froze into a sudden listening immobility, eyes unfocused and head cocked slightly to one side. Gently, ever so gently, he set the lamp down, walked leisurely across to Miller.

"Remind me to apologise at some future date," he murmured. "We have company. Give me your gun and keep talking."

"Castelrosso again," Miller complained loudly. He hadn't even raised an eyebrow. "This is downright monotonous. A Chinaman—I'll bet it's a Chinaman this time." But he was already talking to himself.

The silenced automatic balanced at his waist, Mallory walked noiselessly round the hut, four feet out from the walls. He had passed two corners, was just rounding the third when, out of the corner of his eye, he saw a vague figure behind him rising up swiftly from the ground and lunging out with upraised arm. Mallory stepped back quickly under the blow, spun round, swung his balled fist viciously and backwards into the stomach of his attacker. There was a sudden explosive gasp of agony as the man doubled up, moaned and crumpled silently to the ground. Barely in time Mallory arrested the downward, clubbing swipe of his reversed automatic.

Gun reversed again, the butt settled securely in his palm, Mallory stared down unblinkingly at the huddled figure, at the primitive wooden baton still clutched in the gloved right hand, at the unmilitary looking knapsack strapped to his back. He kept his gun lined up on the fallen body, waiting: this had been just too easy, too suspicious. Thirty seconds passed and still the figure on the ground hadn't stirred. Mallory took a short step forward and carefully, deliberately and none too gently kicked the man on the outside of the right knee. It was an old trick, and he'd never known it to fail—the pain was brief, but agonising. But there was no movement, no sound at all.

Quickly Mallory stooped, hooked his free hand round the knapsack shoulder straps, straightened and made for the door, half-carrying, half-dragging his captive. The man was no weight at all. With a proportionately much heavier garrison than even in Crete, there would be that much less food for the islanders, Mallory mused compassionately. There would be very little indeed. He wished he hadn't hit him so hard.

Miller met him at the open door, stooped wordlessly, caught the unconscious man by the ankles and helped Mallory dump him unceremoniously on the bunk in the far corner of the hut.

"Nice goin', boss," he complimented. "Never heard a thing. Who's the heavyweight champ?"

"No idea." Mallory shook his head in the darkness. "Just skin and bones, that's all, just skin and bones. Shut the door, Dusty, and let's have a look at what we've got."

CHAPTER EIGHT

TUESDAY

1900-0015

A MINUTE passed, two, then the little man stirred, moaned and pushed himself to a sitting position. Mallory held his arm to steady him, while he shook his bent head, eyes screwed tightly shut as he concentrated on clearing the muzziness away. Finally he looked up slowly, glanced from Mallory to Miller and back at Mallory again in the feeble light of the newly-lit, shuttered lantern. Even as the men watched, they could see the colour returning to the swarthy cheeks, the indignant bristling of the heavy, dark moustache, the darkening anger in the eyes. Suddenly the man reached up, tore Mallory's hand away from his arm.

" Who are you? " He spoke in English, clear, precise, with hardly a trace of accent.

" Sorry, but the less you know the better." Mallory smiled, deliberately to rob the words of offence. " I mean that for your own sake. How are you feeling now? "

Tenderly the little man massaged his midriff, flexed his leg with a grimace of pain.

" You hit me very hard."

" I had to." Mallory reached behind him and picked up the cudgel the man had been carrying. " You tried to hit me with this. What did you expect me to do—take my hat off so you could have a better swipe at me? "

"You are very amusing." Again he bent his leg, experimentally, looked up at Mallory in hostile suspicion. " My knee hurts me," he said accusingly.

" First things first. Why the club? "

" I meant to knock you down and have a look at you," he explained impatiently. " It was the only safe way. You might have been one of the W.G.B. . . . Why is my knee——? "

" You had an awkward fall," Mallory said shamelessly. " What are you doing here? "

" Who are you? " the little man countered.

Miller coughed, looked ostentatiously at his watch.

" This is all very entertainin', boss—— "

" True for you, Dusty. We haven't all night." Quickly Mallory reached behind him, picked up the man's rucksack, tossed it across to Miller. " See what's in there, will you? " Strangely, the little man made no move to protest.

" Food! " Miller said reverently. " Wonderful, wonderful food. Cooked meat, bread, cheese—and wine." Reluctantly Miller closed the bag and looked curiously at their prisoner. " Helluva funny time for a picnic."

" So! An American, a Yankee." The little man smiled to himself. " Better and better! "

" What do you mean? " Miller asked suspiciously.

" See for yourself," the man said pleasantly. He nodded casually to the far corner of the room. " Look there."

Mallory spun round, realised in a moment that he had been tricked, jerked back again. Carefully he leaned forward and touched Miller's arm.

" Don't look round too quickly, Dusty. And don't touch your gun. It seems our friend was not alone." Mallory tightened his lips, mentally cursed himself for his obtuseness. Voices—Dusty had said there had been voices. Must be even more tired than he had thought. . . .

A tall, lean man blocked the entrance to the doorway. His face was shadowed under an enveloping snow-hood, but there was no mistaking the gun in his hand. A short Lee Enfield rifle, Mallory noted dispassionately.

" Do not shoot! " The little man spoke rapidly in Greek. " I am almost sure that they are those whom we seek, Panayis."

Panayis! Mallory felt the wave of relief wash over him. That was one of the names Eugene Vlachos had given him, back in Alexandria.

" The tables turned, are they not? " The little man smiled at Mallory, the tired eyes crinkling, the heavy black moustache lifting engagingly at one corner. " I ask you again, who are you ? "

" S.O.E.," Mallory answered unhesitatingly.

The man nodded in satisfaction. " Captain Jensen sent you? "

Mallory sank back on the bunk and sighed in long relief. " We are among friends, Dusty." He looked at the little man before him. " You must be Louki—the first plane tree in the square in Margaritha? "

The little man beamed. He bowed, stretched out his hand. " Louki. At your service, sir."

" And this, of course, is Panayis? "

The tall man in the doorway, dark, saturnine, unsmiling, inclined his head briefly but said nothing.

" You have us right! " The little man was beaming with delight. " Louki and Panayis. They know about us in Alexandria and Cairo, then? " he asked proudly.

" Of course! " Mallory smothered a smile. " They spoke highly of you. You have been of great help to the Allies before."

" And we will again," Louki said briskly. " Come, we are wasting time. The Germans are on the hills. What help can we give you? "

" Food, Louki. We need food—we need it badly."

" We have it! " Proudly, Louki gestured at the rucksacks. " We were on our way up with it."

" You were on your way. . . ." Mallory was astonished. " How did you know where we were—or even that we were on the island? "

Louki waved a deprecating hand.

" It was easy. Since first light German troops have been moving south through Margaritha up into the hills. All morning they combed the east col of Kostos. We knew someone must have landed, and that the Germans were looking for them. We heard, too, that the Germans had blocked the cliff path on the south coast, at both ends. So you must have come over the west col. They would not expect that—you fooled them. So we came to find you."

" But you would never have found us——"

" We would have found you." There was complete certainty in the voice. " Panayis and I—we know every stone, every blade of grass in Navarone." Louki shivered suddenly, stared out bleakly through the swirling snow. " You couldn't have picked worse weather."

" We couldn't have picked better," Mallory said grimly.

" Last night, yes," Louki agreed. " No one would expect you in that wind and rain. No one would hear the aircraft or even dream that you would try to jump——"

" We came by sea," Miller interrupted. He waved a negligent hand. " We climbed the south cliff."

" What? The south cliff! " Louki was frankly disbelieving. " No one could climb the south cliff. It is impossible! "

" That's the way we felt when we were about half-way up," Mallory said candidly. " But Dusty, here, is right. That's how it was."

Louki had taken a step back: his face was expressionless. " I say it is impossible," he repeated flatly.

" He is telling the truth, Louki," Miller cut in quietly. " Do you never read newspapers? "

" Of course I read newspapers! " Louki bristled with indignation. " Do you think I am—how you say—illiterate? "

" Then think back to just before the war," Miller advised.
" Think of mountaineerin'—and the Himalayas. You must
have seen his picture in the papers—once, twice, a hundred
times." He looked at Mallory consideringly. " Only he was
a little prettier in those days. You must remember. This is
Mallory, Keith Mallory of New Zealand."

Mallory said nothing. He was watching Louki, the puzzlement, the comical screwing up of the eyes, head cocked to one
side: then, all at once, something clicked in the little man's
memory and his face lit up in a great, crinkling smile that
swamped every last trace of suspicion. He stepped forward,
hand outstretched in welcome.

" By heaven, you are right! Mallory! Of course I know
Mallory! " He grabbed Mallory's hand, pumped it up and
down with great enthusiasm. " It is indeed as the American
says. You need a shave. . . . And you look older."

" I feel older," Mallory said gloomily. He nodded at Miller.
" This is Corporal Miller, an American citizen."

"Another famous climber? " Louki asked eagerly. "Another
tiger of the hills, yes? "

" He climbed the south cliff as it has never been climbed
before," Mallory answered truthfully. He glanced at his watch,
then looked directly at Louki. " There are others up in the hills.
We need help, Louki. We need it badly and we need it at
once. You know the danger if you are caught helping us? "

" Danger? " Louki waved a contemptuous hand. " Danger
to Louki and Panayis, the foxes of Navarone? Impossible!
We are the ghosts of the night." He hitched his pack higher up
on his shoulders. " Come. Let us take this food to your
friends."

" Just a minute." Mallory's restraining hand was on his
arm. " There are two other things. We need heat—a stove
and fuel, and we need——"

" Heat! A stove! " Louki was incredulous. " Your friends
in the hills—what are they? A band of old women? "

" And we also need bandages and medicine," Mallory went on patiently. " One of our friends has been terribly injured. We are not sure, but we do not think that he will live."

" Panayis! " Louki barked. " Back to the village." Louki was speaking in Greek now. Rapidly he issued his orders, had Mallory describe where the rock-shelter was, made sure that Panayis understood, then stood a moment in indecision, pulling at an end of his moustache. At length he looked up at Mallory.

" Could you find this cave again by yourself? "

" Lord only knows," Mallory said frankly. " I honestly don't think so."

" Then I must come with you. I had hoped—you see, it will be a heavy load for Panayis—I have told him to bring bedding as well—and I don't think——"

" I'll go along with him," Miller volunteered. He thought of his back-breaking labours on the caique, the climb up the cliff, their forced march through the mountains. " The exercise will do me good."

Louki translated his offer to Panayis—taciturn, apparently, only because of his complete lack of English—and was met by what appeared to be a torrent of protest. Miller looked at him in astonishment.

" What's the matter with old sunshine here? " he asked Mallory. " Doesn't seem any too happy to me."

" Says he can manage O.K. and wants to go by himself," Mallory interpreted. " Thinks you'll slow him up on the hills." He shook his head in mock wonder. " As if any man could slow Dusty Miller up! "

" Exactly! " Louki was bristling with anger. Again he turned to Panayis, fingers stabbing the empty air to emphasise his words. Miller turned, looked apprehensively at Mallory.

" What's he tellin' him now, boss? "

" Only the truth," Mallory said solemnly. " Saying he ought to be honoured at being given the opportunity of marching with Monsieur Miller, the world-famous American

climber." Mallory grinned. " Panayis will be on his mettle
to-night—determined to prove that a Navaronian can climb
as well and as fast as any man."

" Oh, my Gawd! " Miller moaned.

" And on the way back, don't forget to give Panayis a hand
up the steeper bits."

Miller's reply was luckily lost in a sudden flurry of snow-
laden wind.

That wind was rising steadily now, a bitter wind that
whipped the heavy snow into their bent faces and stung the
tears from their blinking eyes. A heavy, wet snow that melted
as it touched, and trickled down through every gap and chink
in their clothing until they were wet and chilled and thoroughly
miserable. A clammy, sticky snow that built up layer after
energy-sapping layer under their leaden-footed boots, until they
stumbled along inches above the ground, leg muscles aching
from the sheer accumulated weight of snow. There was no
visibility worthy of the name, not even of a matter of feet, they
were blanketed, swallowed up by an impenetrable cocoon of
swirling grey and white, unchanging, featureless: Louki strode
on diagonally upwards across the slope with the untroubled
certainty of a man walking up his own garden path.

Louki seemed as agile as a mountain goat, and as tireless.
Nor was his tongue less nimble, less unwearied than his legs.
He talked incessantly, a man overjoyed to be in action again,
no matter what action so long as it was against the enemy. He
told Mallory of the last three attacks on the island and how
they had so bloodily failed—the Germans had been somehow
forewarned of the seaborne assault, had been waiting for the
Special Boat Service and the Commandos with everything they
had and had cut them to pieces, while the two airborne groups
had had the most evil luck, been delivered up to the enemy by
misjudgment, by a series of unforeseeable coincidences; or how
Panayis and himself had on both occasions narrowly escaped

with their lives—Panayis had actually been captured the last time, had killed both his guards and escaped unrecognised; of the disposition of the German troops and check-points throughout the island, the location of the road blocks on the only two roads; and, finally, of what little he himself knew of the layout of the fortress of Navarone itself. Panayis, the dark one, could tell him more of that, Louki said: twice Panayis had been inside the fortress, once for an entire night: the guns, the control rooms, the barracks, the officers' quarters, the magazine, the turbo rooms, the sentry points—he knew where each one lay, to the inch.

Mallory whistled softly to himself. This was more than he had ever dared hope for. They had still to escape the net of searchers, still to reach the fortress, still to get inside it. But once inside—and Panayis must know how to get inside. . . . Unconsciously Mallory lengthened his stride, bent his back to the slope.

" Your friend Panayis must be quite something," he said slowly. " Tell me more about him, Louki."

" What can I tell you? " Louki shook his head in a little flurry of snowflakes. " What do I know of Panayis? What does anyone know of Panayis? That he has the luck of the devil, the courage of a madman and that sooner the lion will lie down with the lamb, the starving wolf spare the flock, than Panayis breathe the same air as the Germans? We all know that, and we know nothing of Panayis. All I know is that I thank God I am no German, with Panayis on the island. He strikes by stealth, by night, by knife and in the back." Louki crossed himself. " His hands are full of blood."

Mallory shivered involuntarily. The dark, sombre figure of Panayis, the memory of the expressionless face, the hooded eyes, were beginning to fascinate him.

" There's more to him than that, surely," Mallory argued. " After all, you are both Navaronians——"

" Yes, yes, that is so."

" This is a small island, you've lived together all your
lives——"

" Ah, but that is where the Major is wrong! " Mallory's
promotion in rank was entirely Louki's own idea: despite
Mallory's protests and explanations he seemed determined to
stick to it. " I, Louki, was for many years in foreign lands,
helping Monsieur Vlachos. Monsieur Vlachos," Louki said
with pride, " is a very important Government official."

" I know," Mallory nodded. " A consul. I've met him.
He is a very fine man."

" You have met him! Monsieur Vlachos? " There was no
mistaking the gladness, the delight in Louki's voice. " That
is good! That is wonderful! Later you must tell me more.
He is a great man. Did I ever tell you——"

" We were speaking about Panayis," Mallory reminded him
gently.

" Ah, yes, Panayis. As I was saying, I was away for a long
time. When I came back, Panayis was gone. His father had
died, his mother had married again and Panayis had gone to
live with his stepfather and two little stepsisters in Crete. His
stepfather, half-fisherman, half-farmer, was killed in fighting
the Germans near Candia—this was in the beginning. Panayis
took over the boat of his father, helped many of the Allies to
escape until he was caught by the Germans, strung up by his
wrists in the village square—where his family lived—not far
from Casteli. He was flogged till the white of his ribs, of his
backbone, was there for all to see, and left for dead. Then they
burnt the village and Panayis's family—disappeared. You
understand, Major? "

" I understand," Mallory said grimly. " But Panayis——"

" He should have died. But he is tough, that one, tougher
than a knot in an old carob tree. Friends cut him down during
the night, took him away into the hills till he was well again.
And then he arrived back in Navarone, God knows how. I
think he came from island to island in a small rowing-boat.

He never says why he came back—I think it gives him greater pleasure to kill on his own native island. I do not know, Major. All I know is that food and sleep, the sunshine, women and wine—all these are nothing and less than nothing to the dark one." Again Louki crossed himself. " He obeys me, for I am the steward of the Vlachos family, but even I am afraid of him. To kill, to keep on killing, then kill again—that is the very breath of his being." Louki stopped momentarily, sniffed the air like a hound seeking some fugitive scent, then kicked the snow off his boots and struck off up the hill at a tangent. The little man's unhesitating sureness of direction was uncanny.

" How far to go now, Louki? "

" Two hundred yards, Major. No more." Louki blew some snow of his heavy, dark moustache and swore. " I shall not be sorry to arrive."

" Nor I." Mallory thought of the miserable, draughty shelter in the dripping rocks almost with affection. It was becoming steadily colder as they climbed out of the valley, and the wind was rising, climbing up the register with a steady, moaning whine: they had to lean into it now, push hard against it, to make any progress. Suddenly both men stopped, listened, looked at each other, heads bent against the driving snow. Around them there was only the white emptiness and the silence: there was no sign of what had caused the sudden sound.

" You heard something, too? " Mallory murmured.

" It is only I." Mallory spun round as the deep voice boomed out behind him and the bulky, white-smocked figure loomed out of the snow. " A milk wagon on a cobbled street is as nothing compared to yourself and your friend here. But the snow muffled your voices and I could not be sure."

Mallory looked at him curiously. " How come you're here, Andrea? "

" Wood," Andrea explained. " I was looking for firewood. I was high up on Kostos at sunset when the snow lifted for a moment. I could have sworn I saw an old hut in a gully not far from here—it was dark and square against the snow. So I left——"

" You are right," Louki interrupted. " The hut of old Leri, the mad one. Leri was a goatherd. We all warned him, but Leri would listen and speak to no man, only to his goats. He died in his hut, in a landslide."

" It is an ill wind . . ." Andrea murmured. " Old Leri will keep us warm to-night." He checked abruptly as the gully opened up at his feet, then dropped quickly to the bottom, sure-footed as a mountain sheep. He whistled twice, a double high-pitched note, listened intently into the snow for the answering whistle, walked swiftly up the gully. Casey Brown, gun lowered, met them at the entrance to the cave and held back the canvas screen to let them pass inside.

The smoking tallow candle, guttering heavily to one side in the icy draught, filled every corner of the cave with dark and flickering shadows from its erratic flame. The candle itself was almost gone, the dripping wick bending over tiredly till it touched the rock, and Louki, snow-suit cast aside, was lighting another stump of candle from the dying flame. For a moment, both candles flared up together, and Mallory saw Louki clearly for the first time—a small, compact figure in a dark-blue jacket black-braided at the seams and flamboyantly frogged at the breast, the jacket tightly bound to his body by the crimson *tsanta* or cummerbund, and, above, the swarthy, smiling face, the magnificent moustache that he flaunted like a banner. A Laughing Cavalier of a man, a miniature d'Artagnan splendidly behung with weapons. And then Mallory's gaze travelled up to the lined, liquid eyes, eyes dark and sad and permanently tired, and his shock, a slow, uncomprehending shock, had barely time to register before the stub of the candle had flared up and died and Louki had sunk back into the shadows.

Stevens was stretched in a sleeping-bag his breathing harsh

and shallow and quick. He had been awake when they had arrived but had refused all food and drink, and turned away and drifted off into an uneasy jerky sleep. He seemed to be suffering no pain at all now: a bad sign, Mallory thought bleakly, the worst possible. He wished Miller would return. . . .

Casey Brown washed down the last few crumbs of bread with a mouthful of wine, rose stiffly to his feet, pulled the screen aside and peered out mournfully at the falling snow. He shuddered, let the canvas fall, lifted up his transmitter and shrugged into the shoulder straps, gathered up a coil of rope, a torch and a groundsheet. Mallory looked at his watch: it was fifteen minutes to midnight. The routine call from Cairo was almost due.

" Going to have another go, Casey? I wouldn't send a dog out on a night like this."

" Neither would I," Brown said morosely. " But I think I'd better, sir. Reception is far better at night and I'm going to climb uphill a bit to get a clearance from that damned mountain there: I'd be spotted right away if I tried to do that in daylight."

" Right you are, Casey. You know best." Mallory looked at him curiously. " What's all the extra gear for? "

" Putting the set under the groundsheet then getting below it myself with the torch," Brown explained. " And I'm pegging the rope here, going to pay it out on my way up. I'd like to be able to get back some time."

" Good enough," Mallory approved. " Just watch it a bit higher up. This gully narrows and deepens into a regular ravine."

" Don't you worry about me, sir," Brown said firmly. " Nothing's going to happen to Casey Brown." A snow-laden gust of wind, the flap of the canvas and Brown was gone.

" Well, if Brown can do it . . ." Mallory was on his feet now, pulling his snow-smock over his head. " Fuel, gentlemen —old Leri's hut. Who's for a midnight stroll? "

Andrea and Louki were on their feet together, but Mallory shook his head.

"One's enough. I think someone should stay to look after Stevens."

"He's sound asleep," Andrea murmured. "He can come to no harm in the short time we are away."

"I wasn't thinking of that. It's just that we can't take the chance of him falling into German hands. They'd make him talk, one way or another. It would be no fault of his—but they'd make him talk. It's too much of a risk."

"Pouf!" Louki snapped his fingers. "You worry about nothing, Major. There isn't a German within miles of here. You have my word."

Mallory hesitated, then grinned. "You're right. I'm getting the jumps." He bent over Stevens, shook him gently. The boy stirred and moaned, opened his eyes slowly.

"We're going out for some firewood," Mallory said. "Back in a few minutes. You be O.K.?"

"Of course, sir. What can happen? Just leave a gun by my side—and blow out the candle." He smiled. "Be sure to call out before you come in!"

Mallory stooped, blew out the candle. For an instant the flame flared then died and every feature, every person in the cave was swallowed up in the thick darkness of a winter midnight. Abruptly Mallory turned on his heel and pushed out through the canvas into the drifting, wind-blown snow already filling up the floor of the gully, Andrea and Louki close behind.

It took them ten minutes to find the ruined hut of the old goatherd, another five for Andrea to wrench the door off its shattered hinges and smash it up to manageable lengths, along with the wood from the bunk and table, another ten to carry back with them to the rock-shelter as much wood as they could conveniently rope together and carry. The wind, blowing straight north off Kostos, was in their faces now—faces numbed with the chill, wet lash of the driving snow, and blowing almost at gale force: they were not sorry to reach the gully again, drop down gratefully between the sheltering walls.

Mallory called softly at the mouth of the cave. There was no reply, no movement from inside. He called again, listened intently as the silent seconds went by, turned his head and looked briefly at Andrea and Louki. Carefully, he laid his bundle of wood in the snow, pulled out his Colt and torch, eased aside the curtain, lamp switch and Colt safety-catch clicking as one.

The spotlight beam lit up the floor at the mouth of the cave, passed on, settled, wavered, probed into the farthest corner of the shelter, returned again to the middle of the cave and steadied there as if the torch were clamped in a vice. On the floor there was only a crumpled, empty sleeping-bag. Andy Stevens was gone.

CHAPTER NINE

TUESDAY NIGHT

0015-0200

" So I was wrong," Andrea murmured. " He wasn't asleep."

" He certainly wasn't," Mallory agreed grimly. " He fooled me too—*and* he heard what I said." His mouth twisted. " He knows now why we're so anxious to look after him. He knows now that he was right when he spoke about a mill-stone. I should hate to feel the way he must be feeling right now."

Andrea nodded. " It is not difficult to guess why he has gone."

Mallory looked quickly at his watch, pushed his way out of the cave.

" Twenty minutes—he can't have been gone more than twenty minutes. Probably a bit less to make sure we were well clear. He can only drag himself—fifty yards at the most. We'll find him in four minutes. Use your torches and take the hoods off—nobody will see us in this damn' blizzard. Fan out uphill—I'll take the gully in the middle."

" Uphill? " Louki's hand was on his arm, his voice puzzled. " But his leg——"

" Uphill, I said," Mallory broke in impatiently. " Stevens has brains—and a damn' sight more guts than he thinks we credit him with. He'll figure we'll think he's taken the easy way." Mallory paused a moment then went on sombrely: " Any dying man who drags himself out in this lot is going to do nothing the easy way. Come on! "

They found him in exactly three minutes. He must have suspected that Mallory wouldn't fall for the obvious, or he had heard them stumbling up the slope, for he had managed to burrow his way in behind the overhanging snowdrift that sealed off the space beneath a projecting ledge just above the rim of the gully. An almost perfect place of concealment, but his leg betrayed him: in the probing light of his torch Andrea's sharp eyes caught the tiny trickle of blood seeping darkly through the surface of the snow. He was already unconscious when they uncovered him, from cold or exhaustion or the agony of his shattered leg: probably from all three.

Back in the cave again, Mallory tried to pour some ouzo—the fiery, breath-catching local spirit—down Stevens's throat. He had a vague suspicion that this might be dangerous—or perhaps it was only dangerous in cases of shock, his memory was confused on that point—but it seemed better than nothing. Stevens gagged, spluttered and coughed most of it back up again, but some at least stayed down. With Andrea's help Mallory tightened the loosened splints on the leg, staunched the oozing blood, and spread below and above the boy every dry covering he could find in the cave. Then he sat back tiredly and fished out a cigarette from his waterproof case. There was nothing more he could do until Dusty Miller returned with Panayis from the village. He was pretty sure that there was nothing that Dusty could do for Stevens either. There was nothing anybody could do for him.

Already Louki had a fire burning near the mouth of the cave, the old, tinder-dry wood blazing up in a fierce, crackling blaze with hardly a wisp of smoke. Almost at once its warmth began to spread throughout the cave, and the three men edged gratefully nearer. From half a dozen points in the roof thin, steadily-increasing streams of water from the melting snows above began to splash down on the gravelly floor beneath: with these, and with the heat of the blaze, the ground was soon a quagmire. But, especially to Mallory and Andrea, these discomforts were a small price to pay for the privilege of being warm for the first time in over thirty hours. Mallory felt the glow seep through him like a benison, felt his entire body relax, his eyelids grow heavy and drowsy.

Back propped against the wall, he was just drifting off to sleep, still smoking that first cigarette, when there was a gust of wind, a sudden chilling flurry of snow and Brown was inside the cave, wearily slipping the transmitter straps from his shoulders. Lugubrious as ever, his tired eyes lit up momentarily at the sight of the fire. Blue-faced and shuddering with cold—no joke, Mallory thought grimly, squatting motionless for half an hour on that bleak and frozen hillside—he hunched down silently by the fire, dragged out the inevitable cigarette and gazed moodily into the flames, oblivious alike of the clouds of steam that almost immediately enveloped him, of the acrid smell of his singeing clothes. He looked utterly despondent. Mallory reached for a bottle, poured out some of the heated *retsimo*—mainland wine heavily reinforced with resin—and passed it across to Brown.

" Chuck it straight down the hatch," Mallory advised. " That way you won't taste it." He prodded the transmitter with his foot and looked up at Brown again. " No dice this time either? "

" Raised them no bother, sir." Brown grimaced at the sticky sweetness of the wine. " Reception was first class—both here and in Cairo."

" You got through! " Mallory sat up, leaned forward eagerly. " And were they pleased to hear from their wandering boys to-night? "

" They didn't say. The first thing they told me was to shut up and stay that way." Brown poked moodily at the fire with a steaming boot. " Don't ask me how, sir, but they've been tipped off that enough equipment for two or three small monitoring stations has been sent here in the past fort-night."

Mallory swore.

" Monitoring stations! That's damned handy, that is! " He thought briefly of the fugitive, nomad existence these same monitoring stations had compelled Andrea and himself to lead in the White Mountains of Crete. " Dammit, Casey, on an island like this, the size of a soup plate, they can pin-point us with their eyes shut! "

" Aye, they can that, sir," Brown nodded heavily.

" Have you heard anything of these stations, Louki? " Mallory asked.

" Nothing, Major; nothing." Louki shrugged. " I am afraid I do not even know what you are talking about."

" I don't suppose so. Not that it matters—it's too late now. Let's have the rest of the good news, Casey."

" That's about it, sir. No sending for me—by order. Restricted to code abbreviations—affirmative, negative, repetitive, wilco and such-like. Continuous sending only in emergency or when concealment's impossible anyway."

" Like from the condemned cell in these ducky little dungeons in Navarone," Mallory murmured. " ' I died with my boots on, ma'.' "

" With all respects, sir, that's not funny," Brown said morosely. " Their invasion fleet—mainly caiques and E-boats —sailed this morning from the Piraeus," he went on. " About four o'clock this morning. Cairo expects they'll be holing up in the Cyclades somewhere to-night."

" That's very clever of Cairo. Where the hell else could they hole up? " Mallory lit a fresh cigarette and looked bleakly into the fire. " Anyway, it's nice to know they're on the way. That the lot, Casey? "

Brown nodded silently.

" Good enough, then. Thanks a lot for going out. Better turn in, catch up with some sleep while you can. . . . Louki reckons we should be down in Margaritha before dawn, hole up there for the day—he's got some sort of abandoned well all lined up for us—and push on to the town of Navarone to-morrow night."

" My God! " Brown moaned. " To-night a leaking cave. To-morrow night an abandoned well—half-full of water, probably. Where are we staying in Navarone, sir. The crypt in the local cemetery? "

" A singularly apt lodging, the way things are going," Mallory said dryly. " We'll hope for the best. We're leaving before five." He watched Brown lie down beside Stevens and transferred his attention to Louki. The little man was seated on a box on the opposite side of the fire, occasionally turning a heavy stone to be wrapped in cloth and put to Stevens's numbed feet, and blissfully hugging the flames. By and by he became aware of Mallory's close scrutiny and looked up.

" You look worried, Major." Louki seemed vexed. " You look—what is the word?—concerned. You do not like my plan, no? I thought we had agreed——"

" I'm not worried about your plan," Mallory said frankly. " I'm not even worried about you. It's that box you're sitting on. Enough H.E. in it to blow up a battleship—and you're only three feet from that fire. It's not just too healthy, Louki."

Louki shifted uneasily on his seat, tugged at one end of his moustache.

" I have heard that you can throw this T.N.T. into a fire and that it just burns up nicely, like a pine full of sap."

" True enough," Mallory acquiesced. " You can also bend it, break it, file it, saw it, jump on it and hit it with a sledge-hammer, and all you'll get is the benefit of the exercise. But if it starts to sweat in a hot, humid atmosphere—and then the exudation crystallises. Oh, brother! And it's getting far too hot and sticky in this hole."

" Outside with it! " Louki was on his feet, backing farther into the cave. " Outside with it! " He hesitated. " Unless the snow, the moisture——"

"You can also leave it immersed in salt water for ten years without doing it any harm," Mallory interrupted didactically. "But there are some primers there that might come to grief—not to mention that box of detonators beside Andrea. We'll just stick the lot outside, under a cape."

"Pouf! Louki has a far better idea!" The little man was already slipping into his cloak. "Old Leri's hut! The very place. Exactly! We can pick it up there whenever we want—and if you have to leave here in a hurry you do not have to worry about it." Before Mallory could protest, Louki had bent over the box, lifted it with an effort, half-walked, half-staggered round the fire, making for the screen. He had hardly taken three steps when Andrea was by his side, had relieved him firmly of the box and tucked it under one arm.

"If you will permit me——"

"No, no!" Louki was affronted. "I can manage easily. It is nothing."

"I know, I know," Andrea said pacifically. "But these explosives—they must be carried a certain way. I have been trained," he explained.

"So? I did not realise. Of course it must be as you say! I, then, will bring the detonators." Honour satisfied, Louki thankfully gave up the argument, lifted the little box and scuttled out of the cave close on Andrea's heels.

Mallory looked at his watch. One o'clock exactly. Miller and Panayis should be back soon, he thought. The wind had passed its peak and the snow was almost gone: the going would be all that easier, but there would be tracks in the snow. Awkward, these tracks, but not fatal—they themselves would be gone before light, cutting straight downhill for the foot of the valley. The snow wouldn't lie there—and even if there were patches they could take to the stream that wound through the valley, leaving no trace behind.

The fire was sinking and the cold creeping in on them again.

Mallory shivered in his still wet clothes, threw some more wood on the fire, watched it blaze up, and flood the cave with light. Brown, huddled on a groundsheet, was already asleep. Stevens, his back to him, was lying motionless, his breathing short and quick. God only knew how long the boy would stay alive: he was dying, Miller said, but " dying " was a very indefinite term: when a man, a terribly injured, dying man, made up his mind not to die he became the toughest, most enduring creature on earth. Mallory had seen it happen before. But maybe Stevens didn't want to live. To live, to overcome these desperate injuries—that would be to prove himself to himself, and to others, and he was young enough, and sensitive enough and had been hurt and had suffered so much in the past that that could easily be the most important thing in the world to him: on the other hand, he knew what an appalling handicap he had become—he had heard Mallory say so; he knew, too, that Mallory's primary concern was not for his welfare but the fear that he would be captured, crack under pressure and tell everything—he had heard Mallory say so; and he knew that he had failed his friends. It was all very difficult, impossible to say how the balance of contending forces would work out eventually. Mallory shook his head, sighed, lit a fresh cigarette and moved closer to the fire.

Andrea and Louki returned less than five minutes later, and Miller and Panayis were almost at their heels. They could hear Miller coming some distance away, slipping, falling and swearing almost continuously as he struggled up the gully under a large and awkward load. He practically fell across the threshhold of the cave and collapsed wearily by the fire. He gave the impression of a man who had been through a very great deal indeed. Mallory grinned sympathetically at him.

"Well, Dusty, how did it go? Hope Panayis here didn't slow you up too much."

Miller didn't seem to hear him. He was gazing incredulously at the fire, lantern jaw dropping open as its significance slowly dawned on him.

"Hell's teeth! Would you look at that!" He swore bitterly. "Here I spend half the gawddamned night climbing up a gawddamned mountain with a stove and enough kerosene to bath a bloody elephant. And what do I find?" He took a deep breath to tell them what he found, then subsided into a strangled, seething silence.

"A man your age should watch his blood pressure," Mallory advised. "How did the rest of it go?"

"Okay, I guess." Miller had a mug of ouzo in his hand and was beginning to brighten up again. "We got the beddin', the medicine kit——"

"If you'll give me the bedding I will get our young friend into it now," Andrea interrupted.

"And food?" Mallory asked.

"Yeah. We got the grub, boss. Stacks of it. This guy Panayis is a wonder. Bread, wine, goat-cheese, garlic sausages, rice—everything."

"Rice?" It was Mallory's turn to be incredulous. "But you can't get the stuff in the islands nowadays, Dusty."

"Panayis can." Miller was enjoying himself hugely now. "He got it from the German commandant's kitchen. Guy by the name of Skoda."

"The German commandant's—you're joking!"

"So help me, boss, that's Gospel truth." Miller drained half the ouzo at a gulp and expelled his breath in a long, gusty sigh of satisfaction. "Little ol' Miller hangs around the back door, knees knockin' like Carmen Miranda's castanets, ready for a smart take off in any direction while Junior here goes in and cracks the joint. Back home in the States he'd make a fortune as a cat-burglar. Comes back in about ten minutes, luggin' that damned suitcase there." Miller indicated it with a casual wave of his hand. "Not only cleans out the commandant's pantry, but also borrows his satchel to carry the

stuff in. I tell you, boss, associatin' with this character gives
me heart attacks."

" But—but how about guards, about sentries? "

" Taken the night off, I guess, boss. Old Panayis is like a
clam—never says a word, and even then I can't understand
him. My guess is that everybody's out lookin' for us."

" There and back and you didn't meet a soul." Mallory
filled him a mug of wine. " Nice going, Dusty."

" Panayis's doin', not mine. I just tagged along. Besides,
we did run into a couple of Panayis's pals—he hunted them up,
rather. Musta given him the tip-off about somethin'. He was
hoppin' with excitement just afterwards, tried to tell me all
about it." Miller shrugged his shoulders sadly. " We weren't
operatin' on the same wave-length, boss."

Mallory nodded across the cave. Louki and Panayis were
close together, Louki doing all the listening, while Panayis
talked rapidly in a low voice, gesticulating with both hands.

" He's still pretty worked up about something," Mallory
said thoughtfully. He raised his voice. " What's the matter,
Louki? "

" Matter enough, Major." Louki tugged ferociously at the
end of his moustache. " We will have to be leaving soon—
Panayis wants to go right away. He has heard that the German
garrison is going to make a house-to-house check in our village
during the night—about four o'clock, Panayis was told."

" Not a routine check, I take it? " Mallory asked.

" This has not happened for many months. They must
think that you have slipped their patrols and are hiding in the
village." Louki chuckled. " If you ask me, I don't think they
know *what* to think. It is nothing to you, of course. You will
not be there—and even if you were they would not find you:
and it will make it all the safer for you to come to Margaritha
afterwards. But Panayis and I—we must not be found out of
our beds. Things would go hard with us."

" Of course, of course. We must take no risks. But there is

plenty of time. You will go down in an hour. But first, the
fortress." He dug into his breast pocket, brought out the map
Eugene Vlachos had drawn for him, turned to Panayis and
slipped easily into the island Greek. " Come, Panayis. I hear
you know the fortress as Louki here knows his own vegetable
patch. I already know much, but I want you to tell me
everything about it—the layout, guns, magazines, power rooms,
barracks, sentries, guard routine, exits, alarm systems, even
where the shadows are deep and the others less deep—just
everything. No matter how tiny and insignificant the details
may seem to you, nevertheless you must tell me. If a door opens
outwards instead of inwards, you must tell me: that could save
a thousand lives."

" And how does the Major mean to get inside? " Louki
asked.

" I don't know yet. I cannot decide until I have seen the
fortress." Mallory was aware of Andrea looking sharply at
him, then looking away. They had made their plans on the
M.T.B. for entering the fortress. But it was the keystone upon
which everything depended, and Mallory felt that this knowledge should be confined to the fewest number possible.

For almost half an hour Mallory and the three Greeks
huddled over the chart in the light of the flames, Mallory
checking on what he had been told, meticulously pencilling in
all the fresh information that Panayis had to give him—and
Panayis had a very great deal to tell. It seemed almost impossible that a man could have assimilated so much in two brief
visits to the fortress—and clandestine visits in the darkness, at
that. He had an incredible eye and capacity for detail; and it
was a burning hatred of the Germans, Mallory felt certain, that
had imprinted these details on an all but photographic memory.
Mallory could feel his hopes rising with every second that
passed.

Casey Brown was awake again. Tired though he was, the
babble of voices had cut through an uneasy sleep. He crossed

over to where Andy Stevens, half-awake now, lay propped against the wall, talking rationally at times, incoherently at others. There was nothing for him to do there, Brown saw: Miller, cleaning, dusting and rebandaging the wounds had had all the help he needed—and very efficient help at that—from Andrea. He moved over to the mouth of the cave, listened blankly to the four men talking in Greek, moved out past the screen for a breath of the cold, clean night air. With seven people inside the cave and the fire burning continuously, the lack of almost all ventilation had made it uncomfortably warm.

He was back in the cave in thirty seconds, drawing the screen tightly shut behind him.

" Quiet, everybody! " he whispered softly. He gestured behind him. " There's something moving out there, down the slope a bit. I heard it twice, sir."

Panayis swore softly, twisted to his feet like a wild cat. A foot-long, two-edged throwing knife gleamed evilly in his hand and he had vanished through the canvas screen before anyone could speak. Andrea made to follow him, but Mallory stretched out his hand.

" Stay where you are, Andrea. Our friend Panayis is just that little bit too precipitate," he said softly. " There may be nothing—or it might be some diversionary move. . . . Oh, damn! " Stevens had just started babbling to himself in a loud voice. " He would start talking now. Can't you do something . . ."

But Andrea was already bent over the sick boy, holding his hand in his own, smoothing the hot forehead and hair with his free hand and talking to him soothingly, softly, continuously. At first he paid no attention, kept on talking in a rambling, inconsequential fashion about nothing in particular; gradually, however, the hypnotic effect of the stroking hand, the gentle caressing murmur took effect, and the babbling died away to a barely audible muttering ceased altogether. Suddenly his eyes opened and he was awake and quite rational.

" What is it, Andrea? Why are you——? "

" Shh! " Mallory held up his hand. " I can hear some-one——"

" It's Panayis, sir." Brown had his eye at a crack in the curtain. " Just moving up the gully."

Seconds later, Panayis was inside the cave, squatting down by the fire. He looked thoroughly disgusted.

" There is no one there," he reported. " Some goats I saw, down the hill, but that was all." Mallory translated to the others.

" Didn't sound like goats to me," Brown said doggedly. " Different kind of sound altogether."

" I will take a look," Andrea volunteered. " Just to make sure. But I do not think the dark one would make a mistake." Before Mallory could say anything he was gone, as quickly and silently as Panayis. He was back in three minutes, shaking his head. " Panayis is right. There is no one. I did not even see the goats."

" And that's what it must have been, Casey," Mallory said. " Still, I don't like it. Snow almost stopped, wind dropping and the valley probably swarming with German patrols—I think it's time you two were away. For God's sake, be careful. If anyone tries to stop you, shoot to kill. They'll blame it on us anyway."

" Shoot to kill! " Louki laughed dryly. " Unnecessary advice, Major, when the dark one is with us. He never shoots any other way."

" Right, away you go. Damned sorry you've got your-selves mixed up in all this—but now that you are, a thousand thanks for all you've done. See you at half-past six."

" Half-past six," Louki echoed. " The olive grove on the bank of the stream, south of the village. We will be waiting there."

Two minutes later they were lost to sight and sound and all was still inside the cave again, except for the faint crackling of the embers of the dying fire. Brown had moved out on guard, and Stevens had already fallen into a restless, pain-filled sleep. Miller bent over him for a moment or two, then moved softly across the cave to Mallory. His right hand held a crumpled heap of bloodstained bandages. He held them out towards Mallory.

"Take a sniff at that, boss," he asked quietly. "Easy does it."

Mallory bent forward, drew away sharply, his nose wrinkled in immediate disgust.

"Good lord, Dusty! That's vile!" He paused, paused in sure, sick certainty. He knew the answer before he spoke. "What on earth is it?"

"Gangrene." Miller sat down heavily by his side, threw the bandages into the fire. All at once he sounded tired, defeated. "Gas gangrene. Spreadin' like a forest fire—and he would have died anyway. I'm just wastin' my time."

CHAPTER TEN

TUESDAY NIGHT

0400-0600

THE GERMANS took them just after four o'clock in the morning, while they were still asleep. Bone-tired and deep-drugged with this sleep as they were, they had no chance, not the slightest hope of offering any resistance. The conception, timing and execution of the coup were immaculate. Surprise was complete.

Andrea was the first awake. Some alien whisper of sound had reached deep down to that part of him that never slept, and he twisted round and elbowed himself off the ground with the same noiseless speed as his hand reached out for his ready-cocked and loaded Mauser. But the white beam of the powerful torch lancing through the blackness of the cave had blinded him, frozen his stretching hand even before the clipped bite of command from the man who held the torch.

" Still! All of you! " Faultless English, with barely a trace of accent, and the voice glacial in its menace. " You move, and you die! " Another torch switched on, a third, and the cave was flooded with light. Wide awake, now, and motionless, Mallory squinted painfully into the dazzling beams: in the back-wash of reflected light, he could just discern the vague, formless shapes crouched in the mouth of the cave, bent over the dulled barrels of automatic rifles.

" Hands clasped above the heads and backs to the wall! "

184

A certainty, an assured competence in the voice that made for instant obedience. " Take a good look at them, Sergeant." Almost conversational now, the tone, but neither torch nor gun barrel had wavered a fraction. " No shadow of expression in their faces, not even a flicker of the eyes. Dangerous men, Sergeant. The English choose their killers well! "

Mallory felt the grey bitterness of defeat wash through him in an almost tangible wave, he could taste the sourness of it in the back of his mouth. For a brief, heart-sickening second he allowed himself to think of what must now inevitably happen and as soon as the thought had come he thrust it savagely away. Everything, every action, every thought, every breath must be on the present. Hope was gone, but not irrecoverably gone : not so long as Andrea lived. He wondered if Casey Brown had seen or heard them coming, and what had happened to him : he made to ask, checked himself just in time. Maybe he was still at large.

" How did you manage to find us ? " Mallory asked quietly.

" Only fools burn juniper wood," the officer said contemptuously. " We have been on Kostos all day and most of the night. A dead man could have smelt it."

" On Kostos ? " Miller shook his head. " How could——?"

" Enough ! " The officer turned to someone behind him. " Tear down that screen," he ordered in German, " and keep us covered on either side." He looked back into the cave, gestured almost imperceptibly with his torch. " All right, you three. Outside—and you had better be careful. Please believe me that my men are praying for an excuse to shoot you down, you murdering swine! " The venomous hatred in his voice carried utter conviction.

Slowly, hands still clasped above their heads, the three men stumbled to their feet. Mallory had taken only one step when the whip-lash of the German's voice brought him up short.

" Stop! " He stabbed the beam of his torch down at the

unconscious Stevens, gestured abruptly at Andrea. " One side, you! Who is this? "

" You need not fear from him," Mallory said quietly. " He is one of us but he is terribly injured. He is dying."

" We will see," the officer said tightly. " Move to the back of the cave! " He waited until the three men had stepped over Stevens, changed his automatic rifle for a pistol, dropped to his knees and advanced slowly, torch in one hand, gun in the other, well below the line of fire of the two soldiers who advanced unbidden at his heels. There was an inevitability, a cold professionalism about it all that made Mallory's heart sink.

Abruptly the officer reached out his gun-hand, tore the covers off the boy. A shuddering tremor shook the whole body, his head rolled from side to side as he moaned in unconscious agony. The officer bent quickly over him, the hard, clean lines of the face, the fair hair beneath the hood high-lit in the beam of his own torch. A quick look at Stevens's pain-twisted, emaciated features, a glance at the shattered leg, a brief, distasteful wrinkling of the nose as he caught the foul stench of the gangrene, and he had hunched back on his heels, gently replacing the covers over the sick boy.

" You speak the truth," he said softly. " We are not barbarians. I have no quarrel with a dying man. Leave him there." He rose to his feet, walked slowly backwards. " The rest of you outside."

The snow had stopped altogether, Mallory saw, and stars were beginning to twinkle in the clearing sky. The wind, too, had fallen away and was perceptibly warmer. Most of the snow would be gone by midday, Mallory guessed.

Carelessly, incuriously, he looked around him. There was no sign of Casey Brown. Inevitably Mallory's hopes began to rise. Petty Officer Brown's recommendation for this operation had come from the very top. Two rows of ribbons to which he was entitled but never wore bespoke his gallantry, he had a

formidable reputation as a guerrilla fighter—and he had had
an automatic rifle in his hand. If he were somewhere out there.
. . . Almost as if he had divined his hopes, the German smashed
them at a word.

"You wonder where your sentry is, perhaps?" he asked
mockingly. "Never fear, Englishman, he is not far from here,
asleep at his post. Very sound asleep, I'm afraid."

"You've killed him?" Mallory's hands clenched until his
palms ached.

The other shrugged his shoulder in vast indifference.

"I really couldn't say. It was all too easy. One of my men
lay in the gully and moaned. A masterly performance—really
pitiable—he almost had me convinced. Like a fool your man
came to investigate. I had another man waiting above, the
barrel of his rifle in his hand. A very effective club, I assure
you. . . ."

Slowly Mallory unclenched his fists and stared bleakly down
the gully. Of course Casey would fall for that, he was bound to
after what had happened earlier in the night. He wasn't going
to make a fool of himself again, cry "wolf" twice in succession:
inevitably, he had gone to check first. Suddenly the thought
occurred to Mallory that maybe Casey Brown *had* heard something earlier on, but the thought vanished as soon as it had
come. Panayis did not look like the man to make a mistake:
and Andrea never made a mistake; Mallory turned back to
the officer again.

"Well, where do we go from here?"

"Margaritha, and very shortly. But one thing first." The
German, his own height to an inch, stood squarely in front of
him, levelled revolver at waist height, switched-off torch
dangling loosely from his right hand. "Just a little thing,
Englishman. Where are the explosives?" He almost spat the
words out.

"Explosives?" Mallory furrowed his brow in perplexity.
"What explosives?" he asked blankly, then staggered and fell

to the ground as the heavy torch swept round in a vicious half-circle, caught him flush on the side of the face. Dizzily he shook his head and climbed slowly to his feet again.

" The explosives." The torch was balanced in the hand again, the voice silky and gentle. " I asked you where they were."

" I don't know what you are talking about." Mallory spat out a broken tooth, wiped some blood off his smashed lips. " Is this the way the Germans treat their prisoners? " he asked contemptuously.

" Shut up! "

Again the torch lashed out. Mallory was waiting for it, rode the blow as best he could: even so the torch caught him heavily high up on the cheek-bone, just below the temple, stunning him with his jarring impact. Seconds passed, then he pushed himself slowly off the snow, the whole side of his face afire with agony, his vision blurred and unfocused.

" We fight a clean war! " The officer was breathing heavily, in barely controlled fury. " We fight by the Geneva Conventions. But these are for soldiers, not for murdering spies——"

" We are no spies! " Mallory interrupted. He felt as if his head was coming apart.

" Then where are your uniforms? " the officer demanded. " Spies, I say—murdering spies who stab in the back and cut men's throats! " The voice was trembling with anger. Mallory was at a loss—nothing spurious about this indignation.

" Cut men's throats? " He shook his head in bewilderment. " What the hell are you talking about? "

" My own batman. A harmless messenger, a boy only—and he wasn't even armed. We found him only an hour ago. Ach, I waste my time! " He broke off as he turned to watch two men coming up the gully. Mallory stood motionless for a moment, cursing the ill luck that had led the dead man across the path of Panayis—it could have been no one else—then turned to see what had caught the officer's attention. He focused his aching eyes with difficulty, looked at the bent figure struggling up the slope, urged on by the ungentle prodding of a bayoneted rifle. Mallory let go a long, silent breath of relief. The left side of Brown's face was caked with blood from a gash above the temple, but he was otherwise unharmed.

" Right! Sit down in the snow, all of you! " He gestured to several of his men. " Bind their hands! "

" You are going to shoot us now, perhaps? " Mallory asked quietly. It was suddenly, desperately urgent that he should know: there was nothing they could do but die, but at least they could die on their feet, fighting; but if they weren't to die just yet, almost any later opportunity for resistance would be less suicidal than this.

" Not yet, unfortunately. My section commander in Margaritha, Hauptmann Skoda, wishes to see you first—maybe it would be better for you if I *did* shoot you now. Then the Herr Kommandant in Navarone—Officer Commanding of the whole island." The German smiled thinly. " But only a postponement, Englishman. You will be kicking your heels before the sun sets. We have a short way with spies in Navarone."

" But, sir! Captain! " Hands raised in appeal, Andrea took a step forward, brought up short as two rifle muzzles ground into his chest.

" Not Captain—Lieutenant," the officer corrected him. " Oberleutnant Turzig, at your service. What is it you want, fat one? " he asked contemptuously.

" Spies! You said spies! I am no spy! " The words rushed and tumbled over one another, as if he could not get them out fast enough. " Before God, I am no spy! I am not one of them." The eyes were wide and staring, the mouth working soundlessly between the gasped-out sentences. " I am only a Greek, a poor Greek. They forced me to come along as an interpreter. I swear it, Lieutenant Turzig, I swear it! "

" You yellow bastard! " Miller ground out viciously, then

grunted in agony as a rifle butt drove into the small of his back, just above the kidney. He stumbled, fell forward on his hands and knees, realised even as he fell that Andrea was only playing a part, that Mallory had only to speak half a dozen words in Greek to expose Andrea's lie. Miller twisted on his side in the snow, shook his fist weakly and hoped that the contorted pain on his face might be mistaken for fury. " You two-faced, double-crossing dago! You gawddamned swine, I'll get you . . ." There was a hollow, sickening thud and Miller collapsed in the snow: the heavy ski-boot had caught him just behind the ear.

Mallory said nothing. He did not even glance at Miller. Fists balled helplessly at his sides and mouth compressed, he glared steadily at Andrea through narrowed slits of eyes. He knew the lieutenant was watching him, felt he must back Andrea up all the way. What Andrea intended he could not even begin to guess—but he would back him to the end of the world.

" So! " Turzig murmured thoughtfully. " Thieves fall out, eh? " Mallory thought he detected the faintest overtones of doubt, of hesitancy, in his voice. But the lieutenant was taking no chances. " No matter, fat one. You have cast your lot with these assassins. What is it the English say? ' You have made your bed, you must lie on it.' " He looked at Andrea's vast bulk dispassionately. " We may need to strengthen a special gallows for you."

" No, no, no! " Andrea's voice rose sharply, fearfully, on the last word. " It is true what I tell you! I am not one of them, Lieutenant Turzig, before God I am not one of them! " He wrung his hands in distress, his great moon-face contorted in anguish. " Why must I die for no fault of my own? I didn't want to come. I am no fighting man, Lieutenant Turzig! "

" I can see that," Turzig said dryly. " A monstrous deal of skin to cover a quivering jelly-bag your size—and every inch of it precious to you." He looked at Mallory, and at Miller, still lying face down in the snow. "I cannot congratulate your friends on their choice of companion."

"I can tell you everything, Lieutenant, I can tell you everything!" Andrea pressed forward excitedly, eager to consolidate his advantage, to reinforce the beginnings of doubt. "I am no friend of the Allies—I will prove it to you—and then perhaps——"

"You damned Judas!" Mallory made to fling himself forward, but two burly soldiers caught him and pinioned his arms from behind. He struggled briefly, then relaxed, looked balefully at Andrea. "If you dare to open your mouth, I promise you you'll never live to——"

"Be quiet!" Turzig's voice was very cold. "I have had enough of recriminations, of cheap melodrama. Another word and you join your friend in the snow there." He looked at him a moment in silence, then swung back to Andrea. "I promise nothing. I will hear what you have to say." He made no attempt to disguise the repugnance in his voice.

"You must judge for yourself." A nice mixture of relief, earnestness and the dawn of hope, of returning confidence. Andrea paused a minute and gestured dramatically at Mallory, Miller and Brown. "These are no ordinary soldiers—they are Jellicoe's men, of the Special Boat Service!"

"Tell me something I couldn't have guessed myself," Turzig growled. "The English Earl has been a thorn in our flesh these many months past. If that is all you have to tell me, fat one——"

"Wait!" Andrea held up his hand. "They are still no ordinary men but a specially picked force—an assault unit, they call themselves—flown last Sunday night from Alexandria to Castelrosso. They left that same night from Castelrosso in a motor-boat."

"A torpedo boat," Turzig nodded. "So much we know already. Go on."

" You know already! But how——? "

" Never mind how. Hurry up! "

" Of course, Lieutenant, of course." Not a twitch in his face betrayed Andrea's relief. This had been the only dangerous point in his story. Nicolai, of course, had warned the Germans, but never thought it worth while mentioning the presence of a giant Greek in the party. No reason, of course, why he should have selected him for special mention—but if he had done, it would have been the end.

" The torpedo boat landed them somewhere in the islands, north of Rhodes. I do not know where. There they stole a caique, sailed it up through Turkish waters, met a big German patrol boat—and sunk it." Andrea paused for effect. " I was less than half a mile away at the time in my fishing boat."

Turzig leaned forward. " How did they manage to sink so big a boat? " Strangely, he didn't doubt that it had been sunk.

" They pretended to be harmless fishermen like myself. I had just been stopped, investigated and cleared," Andrea said virtuously. " Anyway, your patrol boat came alongside this old caique. Close alongside. Suddenly there were guns firing on both sides, two boxes went flying through the air—into the engine-room of your boat, I think. Pouf! " Andrea threw up his hands dramatically. " That was the end of that! "

" We wondered . . ." Turzig said softly. " Well, go on."

" You wondered what, Lieutenant? " Turzig's eyes narrowed and Andrea hurried on.

" Their interpreter had been killed in the fight. They tricked me into speaking English—I spent many years in Cyprus—kidnapped me, let my sons sail the boat——"

" Why should they want an interpreter? " Turzig demanded suspiciously. " There are many British officers who speak Greek."

" I am coming to that," Andrea said impatiently. " How

in God's name do you expect me to finish my story if you keep interrupting all the time? Where was I? Ah, yes. They forced me to come along, and their engine broke down. I don't know what happened—I was kept below. I think we were in a creek somewhere, repairing the engine, and then there was a wild bout of drinking—you will not believe this, Lieutenant Turzig, that men on so desperate a mission should get drunk—and then we sailed again."

"On the contrary, I do believe you." Turzig was nodding his head slowly, as if in secret understanding. "I believe you indeed."

"You do?" Andrea contrived to look disappointed. "Well, we ran into a fearful storm, wrecked the boat on the south cliff of this island and climbed——"

"Stop!" Turzig had drawn back sharply, suspicion flaring in his eyes. "Almost I believed you! I believed you because we know more than you think, and so far you have told the truth. But not now. You are clever, fat one, but not so clever as you think. One thing you have forgotten—or maybe you do not know. We are of the *Wurttembergische Gebirgsbataillon*—we *know* mountains, my friend, better than any troops in the world. I myself am a Prussian, but I have climbed everything worth climbing in the Alps and Transylvania— and I tell you that the south cliff cannot be climbed. It is impossible!"

"Impossible perhaps for you." Andrea shook his head sadly. "These cursed Allies will beat you yet. They are clever, Lieutenant Turzig, damnably clever!"

"Explain yourself," Turzig ordered curtly.

"Just this. They knew men thought the south cliff could not be climbed. So they determined to climb it. You would never dream that this could be done, that an expedition could land on Navarone that way. But the Allies took a gamble, found a man to lead the expedition. He could not speak Greek, but that did not matter, for what they wanted was a man who could climb—and so they picked the greatest rock-climber in the world to-day." Andrea paused for effect, flung out his arm dramatically. "And this is the man they picked, Lieutenant Turzig! You are a mountaineer yourself and you are bound to know him. His name is Mallory—Keith Mallory of New Zealand!"

There was a sharp exclamation, the click of a switch, and Turzig had taken a couple of steps forward, thrust the torch almost into Mallory's eyes. For almost ten seconds he stared into the New Zealander's averted, screwed-up face, then slowly lowered his arm, the harsh spotlight limning a dazzling white circle in the snow at his feet. Once, twice, half a dozen times Turzig nodded his head in slow understanding.

"Of course!" he murmured. "Mallory—Keith Mallory! Of course I know him. There's not a man in my *Abteilung* but has heard of Keith Mallory." He shook his head. "I should have known him, I should have known him at once." He stood for some time with his head bent, aimlessly screwing the toe of his right boot into the soft snow then looked up abruptly. "Before the war, even during it, I would have been proud to have known you, glad to have met you. But not here, not now. Not any more. I wish to God they had sent someone else." He hesitated, made to carry on, then changed his mind, turned wearily to Andrea. "My apologies, fat one. Indeed you speak the truth. Go on."

"Certainly!" Andrea's round moon face was one vast smirk of satisfaction. "We climbed the cliff, as I said—although the boy in the cave there was badly hurt—and silenced the guard. Mallory killed him," Andrea added unblushingly. "It was fair fight. We spent most of the night crossing the divide and found this cave before dawn. We were almost dead with hunger and cold. We have been here since."

"And nothing has happened since?"

"On the contrary." Andrea seemed to be enjoying himself

hugely, revelling in being the focus of attention. " Two people came up to see us. Who they were I do not know—they kept their faces hidden all the time—nor do I know where they came from."

" It is as well that you admitted that," Turzig said grimly. " I knew someone had been here. I recognised the stove—it belongs to Hauptmann Skoda! "

" Indeed? " Andrea raised his eyebrows in polite surprise. " I did not know. Well, they talked for some time and——"

" Did you manage to overhear anything they were talking about? " Turzig interrupted. The question came so naturally, so spontaneously, that Mallory held his breath. It was beautifully done. Andrea would walk into it—he couldn't help it. But Andrea was a man inspired that night.

" Overhear them! " Andrea clamped his lips shut in sorely-tried forbearance, gazed heavenwards in exasperated appeal. " Lieutenant Turzig, how often must I tell you that I am the interpreter? They *could* only talk through me. Of course I know what they were talking about. They are going to blow up the big guns in the harbour."

" I didn't think they had come here for their health! " Turzig said acidly.

" Ah, but you don't know that they have the plans of the fortress. You don't know that Kheros is to be invaded on Saturday morning. You don't know that they are in radio contact with Cairo all the time. You don't know that destroyers of the British Navy are coming through the Maidos Straits on Friday night as soon as the big guns have been silenced. You don't know——"

" Enough! " Turzig clapped his hands together, his face alight with excitement. " The Royal Navy, eh? Wonderful, wonderful! *That* is what we want to hear. But enough! Keep it for Hauptmann Skoda and the Kommandant in the fortress. We must be off. But first—one more thing. The explosives—where are they? "

Andrea's shoulders slumped in dejection. He spread out his arms, palms upward.

" Alas, Lieutenant Turzig, I do not know. They took them out and hid them—some talk about the cave being too hot." He waved a hand towards the western col, in the diametrically opposite direction to Leri's hut. " That way, I think. But I cannot be sure, for they would not tell me." He looked bitterly at Mallory. " These Britishers are all the same. They trust nobody."

" Heaven only knows that I don't blame them for that! " Turzig said feelingly. He looked at Andrea in disgust. " More than ever I would like to see you dangling from the highest scaffold in Navarone. But Herr Kommandant in the town is a kindly man and rewards informers. You may yet live to betray some more comrades."

" Thank you, thank you, thank you! I knew you were fair and just. I promise you, Lieutenant Turzig——"

" Shut up! " Turzig said contemptuously. He switched into German. " Sergeant, have these men bound. And don't forget the fat one! Later we can untie him, and he can carry the sick man back to the post. Leave a man on guard. The rest of you come with me—we must find those explosives."

" Could we not make one of them tell us, sir? " the sergeant ventured.

" The only man who would tell us, can't. He's already told us all he knows. As for the rest—well, I was mistaken about them, Sergeant." He turned to Mallory, inclined his head briefly, spoke in English. " An error of judgment, Herr Mallory. We are all very tired. I am almost sorry I struck you." He wheeled abruptly, climbed swiftly up the bank. Two minutes later only a solitary soldier was left on guard.

For the tenth time Mallory shifted his position uncomfortably, strained at the cord that bound his hands together behind his back, for the tenth time recognised the futility of both these actions. No matter how he twisted and turned, the wet snow soaked icily through his clothes until he was chilled to the bone and shaking continually with the cold; and the man who had tied these knots had known his job all too well. Mallory wondered irritably if Turzig and his men meant to spend all night searching for the explosives: they had been gone for more than half an hour already.

He relaxed, lay back on his side in the cushioning snow of the gully bank, and looked thoughtfully at Andrea who was sitting upright just in front of him. He had watched Andrea, with bowed head and hunched and lifting shoulders, making one single, titanic effort to free himself seconds after the guard had gestured to them to sit down, had seen the cords bite and gouge until they had almost disappeared in his flesh, the fractional slump of his shoulders as he gave up. Since then the giant Greek had sat quite still and contented himself with scowling at the sentry in the injured fashion of one who has been grievously wronged. That solitary test of the strength of his bonds had been enough. Oberleutnant Turzig had keen eyes, and swollen, chafed and bleeding wrists would have accorded ill with the character Andrea had created for himself.

A masterly creation, Mallory mused, all the more remarkable for its spontaneity, its improvisation. Andrea had told so much of the truth, so much that was verifiable or could be verified, that belief in the rest of his story followed almost automatically. And at the same time he had told Turzig nothing of importance, nothing the Germans could not have found out for themselves—except the proposed evacuation of Kheros by the Navy. Wryly Mallory remembered his dismay, his shocked unbelief when he heard Andrea telling of it—but Andrea had been far ahead of him. There was a fair chance that the Germans might have guessed anyway—they would reason, perhaps, that an assault by the British on the guns of Navarone at the same time as the German assault on Kheros would be just that little bit too coincidental: again, escape for them all quite clearly depended upon how thoroughly Andrea managed to convince his captors that he was all he claimed, and the relative freedom of action that he could thereby gain —and there was no doubt at all that it was the news of the proposed evacuation that had tipped the scales with Turzig: and the fact that Andrea had given Saturday as the invasion date would only carry all the more weight, as that had been Jensen's original date—obviously false information fed to his agents by German counter-Intelligence, who had known it impossible to conceal the invasion preparations themselves; and finally, if Andrea hadn't told Turzig of the destroyers, he might have failed to carry conviction, they might all yet finish on the waiting gallows in the fortress, the guns would remain intact and destroy the naval ships anyway.

It was all very complicated, too complicated for the state his head was in. Mallory sighed and looked away from Andrea towards the other two. Brown and a now conscious Miller were both sitting upright, hands bound behind their backs, staring down into the snow, occasionally shaking muzzy heads from side to side. Mallory could appreciate all too easily how they felt—the whole right-hand side of his face ached cruelly, continuously. Nothing but aching, broken heads everywhere, Mallory thought bitterly. He wondered how Andy Stevens was feeling, glanced idly past the sentry towards the dark mouth of the cave, stiffened in sudden, almost uncomprehending shock.

Slowly, with an infinitely careful carelessness, he let his eyes wander away from the cave, let them light indifferently on the sentry who sat on Brown's transmitter, hunched watchfully over the Schmeisser cradled on his knees, finger crooked on the trigger. Pray God he doesn't turn round, Mallory said to himself over and over again, pray God he doesn't turn round. Let him sit like that just for a little while longer, only a little while longer. . . . In spite of himself, Mallory felt his gaze shifting, being dragged back again towards that cave-mouth. Andy Stevens was coming out of the cave. Even in the dim starlight every movement was terribly plain as he inched forward agonisingly on chest and belly, dragging his shattered leg behind him. He was placing his hands beneath his shoulders, levering himself upward and forward while his head dropped below his shoulders with pain and the exhaustion of the effort, lowering himself slowly on the soft and sodden snow, then repeating the same heart-sapping process over and over again. Exhausted and pain-filled as the boy might be, Mallory thought, his mind was still working: he had a white sheet over his shoulders and back as camouflage against the snow, and he carried a climbing spike in his right hand. He must have heard at least some of Turzig's conversation: there were two or three guns in the cave, he could easily have shot the guard without coming out at all—but he must have known that the sound of a shot would have brought the Germans running, had them back at the cave long before he could have crawled across the gully, far less cut loose any of his friends.

Five yards Stevens had to go, Mallory estimated, five yards at the most. Deep down in the gully where they were, the south wind passed them by, was no more than a muted whisper in the night; that apart, there was no sound at all, nothing but their own breathing, the occasional stirring as someone stretched a cramped or frozen leg. He's bound to hear him if he comes any closer, Mallory thought desperately, even in that soft snow he's bound to hear him.

Mallory bent his head, began to cough loudly, almost continuously. The sentry looked at him, in surprise first, then in irritation as the coughing continued.

" Be quiet! " the sentry ordered in German. " Stop that coughing at once! "

" *Hüsten? Hüsten?* Coughing, is it? I can't help it," Mallory protested in English. He coughed again, louder, more persistently than before. " It is your Oberleutnant's fault," he gasped. " He has knocked out some of my teeth." Mallory broke into a fresh paroxysm of coughing, recovered himself with an effort. " Is it my fault that I'm choking on my own blood? " he demanded.

Stevens was less than ten feet away now, but his tiny reserves of strength were almost gone. He could no longer raise himself to the full stretch of his arms, was advancing only a few pitiful inches at a time. At length he stopped altogether, lay still for half a minute. Mallory thought he had lost consciousness, but by and by he raised himself up again, to the full stretch this time, had just begun to pivot himself forward when he collapsed, fell heavily in the snow. Mallory began to cough again, but he was too late. The sentry leapt off his box and whirled round all in one movement, the evil mouth of the Schmeisser lined up on the body almost at his feet. Then he relaxed as he realised who it was, lowered the barrel of his gun.

" So! " he said softly. " The fledgling has left its nest. Poor little fledgling! " Mallory winced as he saw the back-swing of the gun ready to smash down on Stevens's defenceless head, but the sentry was a kindly enough man, his reaction had been purely automatic. He arrested the swinging butt inches above the tortured face, bent down and almost gently removed the spike from the feebly threatening hand, sent it spinning over the edge of the gully. Then he lifted Stevens carefully by the shoulders, slid in the bunched-up sheet as pillow for the unconscious head against the bitter cold of the snow, shook his head wonderingly, sadly, went back to his seat on the ammunition box.

Hauptmann Skoda was a small, thin man in his late thirties, neat, dapper, debonair and wholly evil. There was something innately evil about the long, corded neck that stretched up scrawnily above his padded shoulders, something repellent about the incongruously small bullet head perched above. When the thin, bloodless lips parted in a smile, which was often, they revealed a perfect set of teeth: far from lighting his face, the smile only emphasised the sallow skin stretched abnormally taut across the sharp nose and high cheek-bones, puckered up the sabre scar that bisected the left cheek from eyebrow to chin: and whether he smiled or not, the pupils of the deep-set eyes remained always the same, still and black and empty. Even at that early hour—it was not yet six o'clock—he was immaculately dressed, freshly shaven, the wetly-gleaming hair—thin, dark, heavily indented above the temples—brushed straight back across his head. Seated behind a flat-topped table, the sole article of furniture in the bench-lined guardroom, only the upper half of his body was visible: even so, one instinctively knew that the crease of the trousers, the polish of the jackboots, would be beyond reproach.

He smiled often, and he was smiling now as Oberleutnant Turzig finished his report. Leaning far back in his chair, elbows on the arm-rests, Skoda steepled his lean fingers under his chin, smiled benignly round the guardroom. The lazy, empty eyes missed nothing—the guard at the door, the two guards behind the bound prisoners, Andrea sitting on the bench where he had just laid Stevens—one lazy sweep of those eyes encompassed them all.

"Excellently done, Oberleutnant Turzig!" he purred. "Most efficient, really most efficient!" He looked speculatively at the three men standing before him, at their bruised and blood-caked faces, switched his glance to Stevens, lying barely conscious on the bench, smiled again and permitted himself a fractional lift of his eyebrows. "A little trouble, perhaps, Turzig? The prisoners were not too—ah—co-operative?"

"They offered no resistance, sir, no resistance at all," Turzig said stiffly. The tone, the manner, were punctilious, correct, but the distaste, the latent hostility were mirrored in his eyes. "My men were maybe a little enthusiastic. We wanted to make no mistake."

"Quite right, Lieutenant, quite right," Skoda murmured

approvingly. " These are dangerous men and one cannot take
chances with dangerous men." He pushed back his chair, rose
easily to his feet, strolled round the table and stopped in front
of Andrea. " Except maybe this one, Lieutenant? "

" He is dangerous only to his friends," Turzig said shortly.
" It is as I told you, sir. He would betray his mother to save
his own skin."

" And claiming friendship with us, eh?" Skoda asked
musingly. " One of our gallant allies, Lieutenant." Skoda
reached out a gentle hand, brought it viciously down and across
Andrea's cheek, the heavy signet ring on his middle finger
tearing skin and flesh. Andrea cried out in pain, clapped one
hand to his bleeding face and cowered away, his right arm
raised above his head in blind defence.

" A notable addition to the armed forces of the Third
Reich," Skoda murmured. " You were not mistaken, Lieutenant. A poltroon—the instinctive reaction of a hurt man is
an infallible guide. It is curious," he mused, " how often very
big men are thus. Part of nature's compensatory process, I
suppose. . . . What is your name, my brave friend? "

" Papagos," Andrea muttered sullenly. " Peter Papagos."
He took his hand away from his cheek, looked at it with eyes
slowly widening with horror, began to rub it across his trouser
leg with jerky, hurried movements, the repugnance on his face
plain for every man to see. Skoda watched him with amuse-
ment.

" You do not like to see blood, Papagos, eh? " he suggested.
" Especially your own blood? "

A few seconds passed in silence, then Andrea lifted his head
suddenly, his fat face screwed up in misery. He looked as if he
were going to cry.

" I am only a poor fisherman, your Honour! " he burst out.
" You laugh at me and say I do not like blood, and it is true.
Nor do I like suffering and war. I want no part of any of these
things! " His great fists were clenched in futile appeal, his

face puckered in woe, his voice risen an octave. It was a masterly exhibition of despair, and even Mallory found himself almost believing in it. "Why wasn't I left alone?" he went on pathetically. "God only knows I am no fighting man——"

"A highly inaccurate statement," Skoda interrupted dryly. "That fact must be patently obvious to every person in the room by this time." He tapped his teeth with a jade cigarette-holder, his eyes speculative. "A fisherman you call yourself——"

"He's a damned traitor!" Mallory interrupted. The commandant was becoming just that little bit too interested in Andrea. At once Skoda wheeled round, stood in front of Mallory with his hands clasped behind his back, teetering on heels and toes, and looked him up and down in mocking inspection.

"So!" he said thoughtfully. "The great Keith Mallory! A rather different proposition from our fat and fearful friend on the bench there, eh, Lieutenant?" He did not wait for an answer. "What rank are you, Mallory?"

"Captain," Mallory answered briefly.

"Captain Mallory, eh? Captain Keith Mallory, the greatest mountaineer of our time, the idol of pre-war Europe, the conqueror of the world's most impossible climbs." Skoda shook his head sadly. "And to think that it should all end like this. . . . I doubt whether posterity will rank your last climb as among your greatest: there are only ten steps leading to the gallows in the fortress of Navarone." Skoda smiled. "Hardly a cheerful thought, is it, Captain Mallory?"

"I wasn't even thinking about it," the New Zealander answered pleasantly. "What worries me is your face." He frowned. "Somewhere or other I'm sure I've seen it or something like it before." His voice trailed off into silence.

"Indeed?" Skoda was interested. "In the Bernese Alps, perhaps? Often before the war——"

" I have it now! " Mallory's face cleared. He knew the risk he was taking, but anything that concentrated attention on himself to the exclusion of Andrea was justified. He beamed at Skoda. " Three months ago, it was, in the zoo in Cairo. A plains buzzard that had been captured in the Sudan. A rather old and mangy buzzard, I'm afraid," Mallory went on apologetically, " but exactly the same scrawny neck, the same beaky face and bald head——"

Mallory broke off abruptly, swayed back out of reach as Skoda, his face livid and gleaming teeth bared in rage, swung at him with his fist. The blow carried with it all Skoda's wiry strength, but anger blurred his timing and the fist swung harmlessly by: he stumbled, recovered, then fell to the floor with a shout of pain as Mallory's heavy boot caught him flush on the thigh, just above the knee. He had barely touched the floor when he was up like a cat, took a pace forward and collapsed heavily again as his injured leg gave under him.

There was a moment's shocked stillness throughout the room, then Skoda rose painfully, supporting himself on the edge of the heavy table. He was breathing quickly, the thin mouth a hard, white line, the great sabre scar flaming redly in the sallow face drained now of all colour. He looked neither at Mallory nor anyone else, but slowly, deliberately, in an almost frightening silence, began to work his way round to the back of the table, the scuffing of his sliding palms on the leather top rasping edgily across over-tautened nerves.

Mallory stood quite still, watching him with expressionless face, cursing himself for his folly. He had overplayed his hand. There was no doubt in his mind—there could be no doubt in the mind of anyone in that room—that Skoda meant to kill him; and he, Mallory, would not die. Only Skoda and Andrea would die: Skoda from Andrea's throwing knife—Andrea was rubbing blood from his face with the inside of his sleeve, finger-tips only inches from the sheath—and Andrea from the guns of the guards, for the knife was all he had. You fool, you fool, you bloody stupid fool, Mallory repeated to himself over and over again. He turned his head slightly and glanced out of the corner of his eye at the sentry nearest him. Nearest him—but still six or seven feet away. The sentry would get him, Mallory knew, the blast of the slugs from that Schmeisser would tear him in half before he could cover the distance. But he would try. He must try. It was the least he owed to Andrea.

Skoda reached the back of the table, opened a drawer and lifted out a gun. An automatic, Mallory noted with detachment—a little, blue-metal, snub-nosed toy—but a murderous toy, the kind of gun he would have expected Skoda to have. Unhurriedly Skoda pressed the release button, checked the magazine, snapped it home with the palm of his hand, flicked off the safety catch and looked up at Mallory. The eyes hadn't altered in the slightest—they were cold, dark and empty as ever. Mallory flicked a glance at Andrea and tensed himself for one convulsive fling backwards. Here it comes, he thought savagely, this is how bloody fools like Keith Mallory die—and then all of a sudden, and unknowingly, he relaxed, for his eyes were still on Andrea and he had seen Andrea doing the same, the huge hand slipping down unconcernedly from the neck, empty of any sign of knife.

There was a scuffle at the table and Mallory was just in time to see Turzig pin Skoda's gun-hand to the table-top.

"Not that, sir!" Turzig begged. "For God's sake, not that way!"

"Take your hands away," Skoda whispered. The staring, empty eyes never left Mallory's face. "Take your hands away, I say—unless you want to go the same way as Captain Mallory."

"You can't kill him, sir!" Turzig persisted doggedly. "You just can't. Herr Kommandant's orders were very clear, Hauptmann Skoda. The leader must be brought to him alive."

"He was shot while trying to escape," Skoda said thickly.

"It's no good." Turzig shook his head. "We can't kill

them all—and the other prisoners would talk." He released his grip on Skoda's hands. "Alive, Herr Kommandant said, but he didn't say how much alive." He lowered his voice confidentially. "Perhaps we may have some difficulty in making Captain Mallory talk," he suggested.

"What? What did you say?" Abruptly the death's head smile flashed once more, and Skoda was completely on balance again. "You are over-zealous, Lieutenant. Remind me to speak to you about it some time. You underestimate me: that was exactly what I was trying to do—frighten Mallory into talking. And now you've spoilt it all." The smile was still on his face, the voice light, almost bantering, but Mallory was under no illusions. He owed his life to the young W.G.B. lieutenant—how easily one could respect, form a friendship with a man like Turzig if it weren't for this damned, crazy war. . . . Skoda was standing in front of him again: he had left his gun on the table.

"But enough of this fooling, eh, Captain Mallory?" The German's teeth fairly gleamed in the bright light from the naked lamps overhead. "We haven't all night, have we?"

Mallory looked at him, then turned away in silence. It was warm enough, stuffy almost, in that little guardroom, but he was conscious of a sudden, nameless chill; he knew all at once, without knowing why, but with complete certainty, that this little man before him was utterly evil.

"Well, well, well, we are not quite so talkative now, are we, my friend?" He hummed a little to himself, looked up abruptly, the smile broader than ever. "Where are the explosives, Captain Mallory?"

"Explosives?" Mallory lifted an interrogatory eyebrow. "I don't know what you are talking about."

"You don't remember, eh?"

"I don't know what you are talking about."

"So." Skoda hummed to himself again and walked over in front of Miller. "And what about you, my friend?"

" Sure I remember," Miller said easily. " The captain's got it all wrong."

" A sensible man! " Skoda purred—but Mallory could have sworn to an undertone of disappointment in the voice. " Proceed, my friend."

" Captain Mallory has no eye for detail," Miller drawled. " I was with him that day. He is malignin' a noble bird. It was a vulture, not a buzzard."

Just for a second Skoda's smile slipped, then it was back again, as rigidly fixed and lifeless as if it had been painted on.

" Very, very witty men, don't you think, Turzig? What the British would call music-hall comedians. Let them laugh while they may, until the hangman's noose begins to tighten. . . ." He looked at Casey Brown. " Perhaps you——"

" Why don't you go and take a running jump to yourself? " Brown growled.

" A running jump? The idiom escapes me, but I fear it is hardly complimentary." Skoda selected a cigarette from a thin case, tapped it thoughtfully on a thumb nail. " Hmm. Not just what one might call too co-operative, Lieutenant Turzig."

" You won't get these men to talk, sir." There was a quiet finality in Turzig's voice.

" Possibly not, possibly not." Skoda was quite unruffled. " Nevertheless, I shall have the information I want, and within five minutes." He walked unhurriedly across to his desk, pressed a button, screwed his cigarette into its jade holder, and leaned against the table, an arrogance, a careless contempt in every action, even to the leisurely crossing of the gleaming jack-boots.

Suddenly a side door was flung open and two men stumbled into the room, prodded by a rifle barrel. Mallory caught his breath, felt his nails dig savagely into the palms of his hands. Louki and Panayis! Louki and Panayis, bound and bleeding, Louki from a cut above the eye, Panayis from a scalp wound.

So they'd got them too, and in spite of his warnings. Both men were shirt-sleeved; Louki, minus his magnificently frogged jacket, scarlet *tsanta* and the small arsenal of weapons that he carried stuck beneath it, looked strangely pathetic and woe-begone—strangely, for he was red-faced with anger, the moustache bristling more ferociously than ever. Mallory looked at him with eyes empty of all recognition, his face expression-less.

" Come now, Captain Mallory," Skoda said reproachfully. " Have you no word of greeting for two old friends? No? Or perhaps you are just overwhelmed? " he suggested smoothly. " You had not expected to see them so soon again, eh, Captain Mallory."

" What cheap trick is this? " Mallory asked contemptuously. " I've never seen these men before in my life." His eyes caught those of Panayis, held there involuntarily: the black hate that stared out of those eyes, the feral malevolence—there was something appalling about it.

" Of course not," Skoda sighed wearily. " Oh, of course not. Human memory is so short, is it not, Captain Mallory." The sigh was pure theatre—Skoda was enjoying himself im-mensely, the cat playing with the mouse. " However, we will try again." He swung round, crossed over to the bench where Stevens lay, pulled off the blanket and, before anyone could guess his intentions, chopped the outside of his right hand against Stevens's smashed leg, just below the knee. . . . Stevens's entire body leapt in a convulsive spasm, but without even the whisper of a moan: he was still fully conscious, smiling at Skoda, blood trickling down his chin from where his teeth had gashed his lower lip.

" You shouldn't have done that, Hauptmann Skoda," Mallory said. His voice was barely a whisper, but unnaturally loud in the frozen silence of the room. " You are going to die for that, Hauptmann Skoda."

" So? I am going to die, am I? " Again he chopped his

hand against the fractured leg, again without reaction. " Then I may as well die twice over—eh, Captain Mallory? This young man is very, very tough—but the British have soft hearts, have they not, my dear Captain? " Gently his hand slid down Stevens's leg, closed round the stockinged ankle. " You have exactly five seconds to tell me the truth, Captain Mallory, and then I fear I will be compelled to rearrange these splints— *Gott in Himmel!* What's the matter with that great oaf? "

Andrea had taken a couple of steps forward, was standing only a yard away, swaying on his feet.

" Outside! Let me outside! " His breath came in short, fast gasps. He bowed his head, one hand to his throat, one over his stomach. " I cannot stand it! Air! Air! I must have air! "

" Ah, no, my dear Papagos, you shall remain here and enjoy—Corporal! Quickly! " He had seen Andrea's eyes roll upwards until only the whites showed. " The fool is going to faint! Take him away before he falls on top of us! "

Mallory had one fleeting glimpse of the two guards hurrying forwards, of the incredulous contempt on Louki's face, then he flicked a glance at Miller and Brown, caught the lazy droop of the American's eyelid in return, the millimetric inclination of Brown's head. Even as the two guards came up behind Andrea and lifted the flaccid arms across their shoulders, Mallory glanced half-left, saw the nearest sentry less than four feet away now, absorbed in the spectacle of the toppling giant. Easy, dead easy—the gun dangling by his side: he could hit him between wind and water before he knew what was happening. . . .

Fascinated, Mallory watched Andrea's forearms slipping nervelessly down the shoulders of the supporting guards till his wrists rested loosely beside their necks, palms facing inwards. And then there was the sudden leap of the great shoulder muscles and Mallory had hurled himself convulsively sidewards and back, his shoulder socketing with vicious force into the guard's stomach, inches below the breast-bone: an explosive *ouf*! of agony, the crash against the wooden walls of the room and Mallory knew the guard would be out of action for some time to come.

Even as he dived, Mallory had heard the sickening thud of heads being swept together. Now, as he twisted round on his side, he had a fleeting glimpse of another guard thrashing feebly on the floor under the combined weights of Miller and Brown, and then of Andrea tearing an automatic rifle from the guard who had been standing at his right shoulder: the Schmeisser was cradled in his great hands, lined up on Skoda's chest even before the unconscious man had hit the floor.

For one second, maybe two, all movement in the room ceased, every sound sheared off by a knife edge: the silence was abrupt, absolute—and infinitely more clamorous than the clamour that had gone before. No one moved, no one spoke, no one even breathed: the shock, the utter unexpectedness of what had happened held them all in thrall.

And then the silence erupted in a staccato crashing of sound, deafening in that confined space. Once, twice, three times, wordlessly, and with great care, Andrea shot Hauptmann Skoda through the heart. The blast of the shells lifted the little man off his feet, smashed him against the wall of the hut, pinned him there for one incredible second, arms outflung as though nailed against the rough planks in spreadeagle crucifixion; and then he collapsed, fell limply to the ground, a grotesque and broken doll that struck its heedless head against the edge of the bench before coming to rest on its back on the floor. The eyes were still wide open, as cold, as dark, as empty in death as they had been in life.

His Schmeisser waving in a gentle arc that covered Turzig and the sergeant, Andrea picked up Skoda's sheath knife, sliced through the ropes that bound Mallory's wrists.

" Can you hold this gun, my Captain? "

Mallory flexed his stiffened hands once or twice, nodded, took the gun in silence. In three steps Andrea was behind the blind side of the door leading to the ante-room, pressed to the wall, waiting, gesturing to Mallory to move as far back as possible out of the line of sight.

Suddenly the door was flung open. Andrea could just see the tip of the rifle barrel projecting beyond it.

" Oberleutnant Turzig! *Was ist los? Wer schoss . . .*" The voice broke off in a coughing grunt of agony as Andrea smashed the sole of his foot against the door. He was round the outside of the door in a moment, caught the man as he fell, pulled him clear of the doorway and peered into the adjacent hut. A brief inspection, then he closed the door, bolted it from the inside.

" Nobody else there, my Captain," Andrea reported. " Just the one gaoler, it seems."

" Fine! Cut the others loose, will you, Andrea? " He wheeled round towards Louki, smiled at the comical expression on the little man's face, the tentative, spreading, finally ear-to-ear grin that cut through the baffled incredulity.

" Where do the men sleep, Louki—the soldiers, I mean? "

" In a hut in the middle of the compound, Major. This is the officers' quarters."

" Compound? You mean——? "

" Barbed wire," Louki said succinctly. " Ten feet high— and all the way round."

" Exits? "

" One and one only. Two guards."

" Good! Andrea—everybody into the side room. No, not you, Lieutenant. You sit down here." He gestured to the chair behind the big desk. " Somebody's bound to come. Tell him you killed one of us—trying to escape. Then send for the guards at the gate."

For a moment Turzig didn't answer. He watched un-seeingly as Andrea walked past him, dragging two unconscious soldiers by their collars. Then he smiled. It was a wry sort of smile.

" I am sorry to disappoint you, Captain Mallory. Too much

has been lost already through my blind stupidity. I won't do it."

" Andrea! " Mallory called softly.

" Yes? " Andrea stood in the ante-room doorway.

" I think I hear someone coming. Is there a way out of that side room? "

Andrea nodded silently.

" Outside! The front door. Take your knife. If the Lieutenant . . ." But he was talking to himself. Andrea was already gone, slipping out through the back door, soundless as a ghost.

" You will do exactly as I say," Mallory said softly. He took position himself in the doorway to the side room, where he could see the front entrance between door and jamb: his automatic rifle was trained on Turzig. " If you don't, Andrea will kill the man at the door. Then we will kill you and the guards inside. Then we will knife the sentries at the gate. Nine dead men—and all for nothing, for we will escape anyway. . . . Here he is now." Mallory's voice was barely a whisper, eyes pitiless in a pitiless face. " Nine dead men, Lieutenant—and just because your pride is hurt." Deliberately, the last sentence was in German, fluent, colloquial, and Mallory's mouth twisted as he saw the almost imperceptible sag of Turzig's shoulders. He knew he had won, that Turzig had been going to take a last gamble on his ignorance of German, that this last hope was gone.

The door burst open and a soldier stood on the threshhold, breathing heavily. He was armed, but clad only in a singlet and trousers, oblivious of the cold.

" Lieutenant! Lieutenant! " He spoke in German. " We heard the shots——"

" It is nothing, Sergeant." Turzig bent his head over an open drawer, pretended to be searching for something to account for his solitary presence in the room. " One of our prisoners tried to escape. . . . We stopped him."

" Perhaps the medical orderly——"

" I'm afraid we stopped him rather permanently." Turzig smiled tiredly. " You can organise a burial detail in the morning. Meantime, you might tell the guards at the gate to come here for a minute. Then get to bed yourself—you'll catch your death of cold! "

" Shall I detail a relief guard——"

" Of course not! " Turzig said impatiently. " It's just for a minute. Besides, the only people to guard against are already in here." His lips tightened for a second as he realised what he had said, the unconscious irony of the words. " Hurry up, man! We haven't got all night! " He waited till the sound of the running footsteps died away, then looked steadily at Mallory. " Satisfied? "

" Perfectly. And my very sincere apologies," Mallory said quietly. " I hate to do a thing like this to a man like you." He looked round the door as Andrea came into the room. "Andrea, ask Louki and Panayis if there's a telephone switch-board in this block of huts. Tell them to smash it up and any receivers they can find." He grinned. " Then hurry back for our visitors from the gate. I'd be lost without you on the reception committee."

Turzig's gaze followed the broad retreating back.

" Captain Skoda was right. I still have much to learn." There was neither bitterness nor rancour in his voice. " He fooled me completely, that big one."

" You're not the first," Mallory reassured him. " He's fooled more people than I'll ever know. . . . You're not the first," he repeated. " But I think you must be just about the luckiest."

" Because I'm still alive? "

" Because you're still alive," Mallory echoed.

Less than ten minutes later the two guards at the gates had joined their comrades in the back room, captured, disarmed, bound and gagged with a speed and noiseless efficiency that excited Turzig's professional admiration, chagrined though he was. Securely tied hand and foot, he lay in a corner of the room, not yet gagged.

" I think I understand now why your High Command chose you for this task, Captain Mallory. If anyone could succeed, you would—but you must fail. The impossible must always remain so. Nevertheless, you have a great team."

" We get by," Mallory said modestly. He took a last look round the room, then grinned down at Stevens.

" Ready to take off on your travels again, young man, or do you find this becoming rather monotonous? "

" Ready when you are, sir." Lying on a stretcher which Louki had miraculously procured, he sighed in bliss. " First-class travel, this time, as befits an officer. Sheer luxury. I don't mind how far we go! "

" Speak for yourself," Miller growled morosely. He had been allocated first stint at the front or heavy end of the stretcher. But the quirk of his eyebrows robbed the words of all offence.

" Right then, we're off. One last thing. Where is the camp radio, Lieutenant Turzig? "

" So you can smash it, I suppose? "

" Precisely."

" I have no idea."

" What if I threaten to blow your head off? "

" You won't." Turzig smiled, though the smile was a trifle lopsided. " Given certain circumstances, you would kill me as you would a fly. But you wouldn't kill a man for refusing such information."

" You haven't as much to learn as your late and un-lamented captain thought," Mallory admitted. " It's not all that important. . . . I regret we have to do all this. I trust we do not meet again—not, at least, until the war is over. Who knows, some day we might even go climbing together." He signed to Louki to fix Turzig's gag and walked quickly out of the room. Two minutes later they had cleared the barracks and were safely lost in the darkness and the olive groves that stretched to the south of Margaritha.

When they cleared the groves, a long time later, it was almost dawn. Already the black silhouette of Kostos was softening in the first feathery greyness of the coming day. The wind was from the south, and warm, and the snow was beginning to melt on the hills.

CHAPTER ELEVEN

WEDNESDAY

1400-1600

ALL DAY long they lay hidden in the carob grove, a thick clump of stunted, gnarled trees that clung grimly to the treacherous, scree-strewn slope abutting what Louki called the "Devil's Playground." A poor shelter and an uncomfortable one, but in every other way all they could wish for: it offered concealment, a first-class defensive position immediately behind, a gentle breeze drawn up from the sea by the sun-baked rocks to the south, shade from the sun that rode from dawn to dusk in a cloudless sky—and an incomparable view of a sun-drenched, shimmering Ægean.

Away to their left, fading through diminishing shades of blue and indigo and violet into faraway nothingness, stretched the islands of the Lerades, the nearest of them, Maidos, so close that they could see isolated fisher cottages sparkling whitely in the sun: through that narrow, intervening gap of water would pass the ships of the Royal Navy in just over a day's time. To the right, and even farther away, remote, featureless, back-dropped by the towering Anatolian mountains, the coast of Turkey hooked north and west in a great curving scimitar: to the north itself, the thrusting spear of Cape Demirci, rock-rimmed but dimpled with sandy coves of white, reached far out into the placid blue of the Ægean: and north again beyond the Cape, haze-blurred in the purple distance, the island of Kheros lay dreaming on the surface of the sea.

It was a breath-taking panorama, a heart-catching beauty sweeping majestically through a great semi-circle over the sunlit sea. But Mallory had no eyes for it, had spared it only a passing glance when he had come on guard less than half an hour previously, just after two o'clock. He had dismissed it with one quick glance, settled by the bole of a tree, gazed for endless minutes, gazed until his eyes ached with strain at what he had so long waited to see. Had waited to see and come to destroy—the guns of the fortress of Navarone.

The town of Navarone—a town of from four to five thousand people, Mallory judged—lay sprawled round the deep, volcanic crescent of the harbour, a crescent so deep, so embracing, that it was almost a complete circle with only a narrow bottleneck of an entrance to the north-west, a gateway dominated by searchlights and mortar and machine-gun batteries on either side. Less than three miles distant to the north-east from the carob grove, every detail, every street, every building, every caique and launch in the harbour were clearly visible to Mallory and he studied them over and over again until he knew them by heart: the way the land to the west of the harbour sloped up gently to the olive groves, the dusty streets running down to the water's edge: the way the ground rose more sharply to the south, the streets now running parallel to the water down to the old town: the way the cliffs to the east—cliffs pock-marked by the bombs of Torrance's Liberator Squadron—stretched a hundred and fifty sheer feet above the water, then curved dizzily out over and above the harbour, and the great mound of volcanic rock towering above that again, a mound barricaded off from the town below by the high wall that ended flush with the cliff itself: and, finally, the way the twin rows of A.A. guns, the great radar scanners and the barracks of the fortress, squat, narrow-embrasured, built of big blocks of masonry, dominated everything in sight—including that great, black gash in the rock, below the fantastic overhang of the cliff.

Unconsciously, almost, Mallory nodded to himself in slow

218

THE GUNS OF NAVARONE

understanding. This was the fortress that had defied the Allies for eighteen long months, that had dominated the entire naval strategy in the Sporades since the Germans had reached out from the mainland into the isles, that had blocked all naval activity in that 2,000 square mile triangle between the Lerades and the Turkish coast. And now, when he saw it, it all made sense. Impregnable to land attack—the commanding fortress saw to that: impregnable to air attack—Mallory realised just how suicidal it had been to send out Torrance's squadron against the great guns protected by that jutting cliff, against those bristling rows of anti-aircraft guns: and impregnable to sea attack—the waiting squadrons of the Luftwaffe on Samos saw to that. Jensen had been right—only a guerrilla sabotage mission stood any chance at all: a remote chance, an all but suicidal chance, but still a chance, and Mallory knew he couldn't ask for more.

Thoughtfully he lowered the binoculars and rubbed the back of his hand across aching eyes. At last he felt he knew exactly what he was up against, was grateful for the knowledge, for the opportunity he'd been given of this long-range reconnaissance, this familiarising of himself with the terrain, the geography of the town. This was probably the one vantage point in the whole island that offered such an opportunity together with concealment and near immunity. No credit to himself, the leader of the mission, he reflected wryly, that they had found such a place: it had been Louki's idea entirely.

And he owed a great deal more than that to the sad-eyed little Greek. It had been Louki's idea that they first move up-valley from Margaritha, to give Andrea time to recover the explosives from old Leri's hut, and to make certain there was no immediate hue and cry and pursuit—they could have fought a rear-guard action up through the olive groves, until they had lost themselves in the foothills of Kostos: it was he who had guided them back past Margaritha when they had doubled on their tracks, had halted them opposite the village

1. MAIN GATE
2. POWER HOUSE
3. WATER STORAGE TANK
4. FIRE CONTROL TOWER
5. ENTRANCE TO MAGAZINE
6. HOUSE IN CHAPTERS 15 & 16
7. TAVERN IN CHAPTER 15
8. HOUSE IN CHAPTER 13

TO VYGOS

FORTRESS WALL

A.A. GUNS

OFFICERS' QUARTERS
ORDNANCE DEPOT
BARRACKS

BATTERIES & SEARCHLIGHTS

CLIFF OVERHANG

THE GUNS
IMMEDIATELY BELOW OVERHANG

JETTIES

TO MARGARITHA

TO DEVIL'S PLAYGROUND

CHARLES GREEN.

BATTERY & SEARCHLIGHT
CLIFF OVERHANG
CAVE WITH GUNS
FORTRESS BUILDINGS BEHIND CLIFF TOP
FORTRESS WALL
W. SIDE OF SQUARE
JETTIES

VIEW FROM WEST OF EAST SIDE OF HARBOUR

while he and Panayis had slipped wraith-like through the lifting twilight, picked up outdoor clothes for themselves, and, on the return journey, slipped into the *Abteilung* garage, torn away the coil ignitions of the German command car and truck—the only transport in Margaritha—and smashed their distributors for good measure; it was Louki who had led them by a sunken ditch right up to the road-block guard post at the mouth of the valley—it had been almost ludicrously simple to disarm the sentries, only one of whom had been awake—and, finally, it was Louki who had insisted that they walk down the muddy centre of the valley track till they came to the metalled road, less than two miles from the town itself. A hundred yards down this they had branched off to the left across a long, sloping field of lava that left no trace behind, arrived in the carob copse just on sunrise.

And it had worked. All these carefully engineered pointers, pointers that not even the most sceptical could have ignored and denied, had worked magnificently. Miller and Andrea, who had shared the forenoon watch, had seen the Navarone garrison spending long hours making the most intensive house-to-house search of the town. That should make it doubly, trebly safe for them the following day, Mallory reckoned: it was unlikely that the search would be repeated, still more unlikely that, if it were, it would be carried out with a fraction of the same enthusiasm. Louki had done his work well.

Mallory turned his head to look at him. The little man was still asleep—wedged on the slope behind a couple of tree-trunks, he hadn't stirred for five hours. Still dead tired himself, his legs aching and eyes smarting with sleeplessness, Mallory could not find it in him to grudge Louki a moment of his rest. He'd earned it all—and he'd been awake all though the previous night. So had Panayis, but Panayis was already awakening, Mallory saw, pushing the long, black hair out of his eyes: awake, rather, for his transition from sleep to full awareness was immediate, as fleeting and as complete as a cat's. A dangerous man, Mallory knew, a desperate man, almost, and a bitter enemy, but he knew nothing of Panayis, nothing at all. He doubted if he ever would.

Farther up on the slope, almost in the centre of the grove, Andrea had built a high platform of broken branches and twigs against a couple of carob poles maybe five feet apart, gradually filling up the space between slope and trees until he had a platform four feet in width, as nearly level as he could make it. Andy Stevens lay on this, still on his stretcher, still conscious. As far as Mallory could tell, Stevens hadn't closed his eyes since they had been marched away by Turzig from their cave in the mountains. He seemed to have passed beyond the need for sleep, or had crushed all desire for it. The stench from the gangrenous leg was nauseating, appalling, poisoned all the air around. Mallory and Miller had had a look at the leg shortly after their arrival in the copse, uncovered it, examined it, smiled at one another, tied it up again and assured Stevens that the wound was closing. Below the knee, the leg had turned almost completely black.

Mallory lifted his binoculars to have another look at the town, but lowered them almost at once as someone came sliding down the slope, touched him on the arm. It was Panayis, upset, anxious, almost angry looking. He gesticulated towards the westering sun.

" The time, Captain Mallory? " He spoke in Greek, his voice low, sibilant, urgent—an inevitable voice, Mallory thought, for the lean, dark mysteriousness of the man. " What is the time? " he repeated.

" Half-past two, or thereabouts." Mallory lifted an interrogatory eyebrow. " You are concerned, Panayis. Why? "

" You should have wakened me. You should have wakened me hours ago! " He *was* angry, Mallory decided. " It is my turn to keep watch."

" But you had no sleep last night," Mallory pointed out reasonably. " It just didn't seem fair——"

" It is my turn to keep watch, I tell you! " Panayis insisted stubbornly.

" Very well, then. If you insist." Mallory knew the high, fierce pride of the islanders too well to attempt to argue. " Heaven only knows what we would have done without Louki and yourself. . . . I'll stay and keep you company for a while."

" Ah, so that is why you let me sleep on! " There was no disguising the hurt in the eyes, the voice. " You do not trust Panayis——"

" Oh, for heaven's sake! " Mallory began in exasperation, checked himself and smiled. " Of course we trust you. Maybe I should go and get some more sleep anyway; you are kind to give me the chance. You will shake me in two hour's time? "

" Certainly, certainly! " Panayis was almost beaming. " I shall not fail."

Mallory scrambled up to the centre of the grove and stretched out lazily along the ledge he had levelled out for himself. For a few idle moments he watched Panayis pacing restlessly to and fro just inside the perimeter of the grove, lost interest when he saw him climbing swiftly up among the branches of a tree, seeking a high lookout vantage point and decided he might as well follow his own advice and get some sleep while he could.

" Captain Mallory! Captain Mallory! " An urgent, heavy hand was shaking his shoulder. " Wake up! Wake up! "

Mallory stirred, rolled over on his back, sat up quickly, opening his eyes as he did so. Panayis was stooped over him, the dark, saturnine face alive with anxiety. Mallory shook his head to clear away the mists of sleep and was on his feet in one swift, easy movement.

" What's the matter, Panayis? "

" Planes! " he said quickly. " There is a squadron of planes coming our way! "

" Planes? What planes? Whose planes? "

" I do not know, Captain. They are yet far away. But——"

" What direction? " Mallory snapped.

" They come from the north."

Together they ran down to the edge of the grove. Panayis gestured to the north, and Mallory caught sight of them at once, the afternoon sun glinting off the sharp dihedral of the wings. Stukas, all right, he thought grimly. Seven—no, eight of them—less than three miles away, flying in two echelons of four, two thousand, certainly not more than twenty-five hundred feet. . . . He became aware that Panayis was tugging urgently at his arm.

" Come, Captain Mallory! " he said excitedly. " We have no time to lose! " He pulled Mallory round, pointed with out-stretched arm at the gaunt, shattered cliffs that rose steeply behind them, cliffs crazily riven by rock-jumbled ravines that wound their aimless way back into the interior—or stopped as abruptly as they had begun. " The Devil's Playground! We must get in there at once! At once, Captain Mallory! "

" Why on earth should we? " Mallory looked at him in astonishment. " There's no reason to suppose that they're after us. How can they be? No one knows we're here."

" I do not care! " Panayis was stubborn in his conviction. " I know. Do not ask me how I know, for I do not know that myself. Louki will tell you—Panayis knows these things. I know, Captain Mallory, I *know*! "

Just for a second Mallory stared at him, uncomprehending. There was no questioning the earnestness, the utter sincerity—but it was the machine-gun staccato of the words that tipped the balance of instinct against reason. Almost without realising it, certainly without realising why, Mallory found himself running uphill, slipping and stumbling in the scree. He found the others already on their feet, tense, expectant, shrugging on their packs, the guns already in their hands.

" Get to the edge of the trees up there! " Mallory shouted. " Quickly! Stay there and stay under cover—we're going to have to break for that gap in the rocks." He gestured through the trees at a jagged fissure in the cliff-side, barely forty yards from where he stood, blessed Louki for his foresight in choosing a hideout with so convenient a bolt-hole. " Wait till I give the word. Andrea! " He turned round, then broke off, the words unneeded. Andrea had already scooped up the dying boy in his arms, just as he lay in stretcher and blankets and was weaving his way uphill in and out among the trees.

" What's up, boss? " Miller was by Mallory's side as he plunged up the slope. " I don't see nothin'."

" You can hear something if you'd just stop talking for a moment," Mallory said grimly. " Or just take a look up there."

Miller, flat on his stomach now and less than a dozen feet from the edge of the grove, twisted round and craned his neck upwards. He picked up the planes immediately.

" Stukas! " he said incredulously. " A squadron of gawd-damned Stukas! It can't be, boss! "

" It can and it is," Mallory said grimly. " Jensen told me that Jerry has stripped the Italian front of them—over two hundred pulled out in the last few weeks." Mallory squinted up at the squadron, less than half a mile away now. " And he's brought the whole damn' issue down to the Ægean."

" But they're not lookin' for us," Miller protested.

" I'm afraid they are," Mallory said grimly. The two bomber echelons had just dove-tailed into line ahead formation. " I'm afraid Panayis was right."

" But—but they're passin' us by——"

" They aren't," Mallory said flatly. " They're here to stay. Just keep your eyes on that leading plane."

Even as he spoke, the flight-commander tilted his gull-winged Junkers 87 sharply over to port, half-turned, fell straight out of the sky in a screaming power-dive, plummeting straight for the carob grove.

" Leave him alone! " Mallory shouted. " Don't fire! " The

Stuka, airbrakes at maximum depression, had steadied on the centre of the grove. Nothing could stop him now—but a chance shot might bring him down directly on top of them: the chances were poor enough as it was. . . . "Keep your hands over your heads—and your heads down!"

He ignored his own advice, his gaze following the bomber every foot of the way down. Five hundred, four hundred, three, the rising crescendo of the heavy engine was beginning to hurt his ears, and the Stuka was pulling sharply out of its plunging fall, its bomb gone.

Bomb! Mallory sat up sharply, screwing up his eyes against the blue of the sky. Not one bomb but dozens of them, clustered so thickly that they appeared to be jostling each other as they arrowed into the centre of the grove, striking the gnarled and stunted trees, breaking off branches and burying themselves to their fins in the soft and shingled slope. Incendiaries! Mallory had barely time to realise that they had been spared the horror of a 500-kilo H.E. bomb when the incendiaries erupted into hissing, guttering life, into an incandescent magnesium whiteness that reached out and completely destroyed the shadowed gloom of the carob grove. Within a matter of seconds the dazzling coruscation had given way to thick, evil-smelling clouds of acrid black smoke, smoke laced with flickering tongues of red, small at first then licking and twisting resinously upwards until entire trees were enveloped in a cocoon of flame. The Stuka was still pulling upwards out of its dive, had not yet levelled off when the heart of the grove, old and dry and tindery, was fiercely ablaze.

Miller twisted up and round, nudging Mallory to catch his attention through the crackling roar of the flames.

"Incendiaries, boss," he announced.

"What did you think they were using?" Mallory asked shortly. "Matches? They're trying to smoke us out, to burn us out, get us in the open. High explosive's not so good among trees. Ninety-nine times out of a hundred this would have worked." He coughed as the acrid smoke bit into his lungs, peered up with watering eyes through the tree-tops. " But not this time. Not if we're lucky. Not if they hold off another half-minute or so. Just look at that smoke! "

Miller looked. Thick, convoluted, shot through with fiery sparks, the rolling cloud was already a third of the way across the gap between grove and cliff, borne uphill by the wandering catspaws from the sea. It was the complete, the perfect smoke-screen. Miller nodded.

" Gonna make a break for it, huh, boss? "

" There's no choice—we either go, or we stay and get fried—or blown into very little bits. Probably both." He raised his voice. " Anybody see what's happening up top? "

" Queuing up for another go at us, sir," Brown said lugubriously. " The first bloke's still circling around."

" Waiting to see how we break cover. They won't wait long. This is where we take off." He peered uphill through the rolling smoke, but it was too thick, laced his watering eyes until everything was blurred through a misted sheen of tears. There was no saying how far uphill the smoke-bank had reached, and they couldn't afford to wait until they were sure. Stuka pilots had never been renowned for their patience.

" Right, everybody! " he shouted. " Fifteen yards along the tree-line to that wash, then straight up into the gorge. Don't stop till you're at least a hundred yards inside. Andrea, you lead the way. Off you go! " He peered through the blinding smoke. " Where's Panayis? "

There was no reply.

" Panayis! " Mallory called. " Panayis! "

" Perhaps he went back for somethin'." Miller had stopped, half-turned. " Shall I go——"

" Get on your way! " Mallory said savagely. " And if anything happens to young Stevens I'll hold you . . ." But Miller, wisely, was already gone, Andrea stumbling and coughing by his side.

For a couple of seconds Mallory stood irresolute, then plunged back downhill towards the centre of the grove. Maybe Panayis had gone back for something—and he couldn't understand English. Mallory had hardly gone five yards when he was forced to halt and fling his arm up before his face: the heat was searing. Panayis couldn't be down there; no one could have been down there, could have lived for seconds in that furnace. Gasping for air, hair singeing and clothes smouldering with fire, Mallory clawed his way back up the slope, colliding with trees, slipping, falling, then stumbling desperately to his feet again.

He ran along to the east end of the wood. No one there. Back to the other end again, towards the wash, almost completely blind now, the super-heated air searing viciously through throat and lungs till he was suffocating, till his breath was coming in great, whooping, agonised breaths. No sense in waiting longer, nothing he could do, nothing anyone could do except save himself. There was a noise in his ears, the roaring of the flames, the roaring of his own blood—and the screaming, heart-stopping roar of a Stuka in a power-dive. Desperately he flung himself forward over the sliding scree, stumbled and pitched headlong down to the floor of the wash.

Hurt or not, he did not know and he did not care. Sobbing aloud for breath, he rose to his feet, forced his aching legs to drive him somehow up the hill. The air was full of the thunder of engines, he knew the entire squadron was coming in to the attack, and then he had flung himself uncaringly to the ground as the first of the high explosive bombs erupted in its concussive blast of smoke and flame—erupted not forty yards away, to his left and ahead of him. *Ahead* of him! Even as he struggled upright again, lurched forward and upward once more, Mallory cursed himself again and again and again. You madman, he thought bitterly, confusedly, you damned crazy madman. Sending the others out to be killed. He should have thought of it—oh, God, he should have thought of it, a five-year-old could have thought of it. Of course Jerry wasn't going to bomb the grove: they had seen the obvious, the inevitable, as quickly as he had, were dive-bombing the pall of smoke between the grove and the cliff! A five-year-old—the earth exploded beneath his feet, a giant hand plucked him up and smashed him to the ground and the darkness closed over him.

CHAPTER TWELVE

WEDNESDAY

1600-1800

ONCE, twice, half a dozen times, Mallory struggled up from the depths of a black, trance-like stupor and momentarily touched the surface of consciousness only to slide back into the darkness again. Desperately, each time, he tried to hang on to these fleeting moments of awareness, but his mind was like the void, dark and sinewless, and even as he knew that his mind was slipping backwards again, loosing its grip on reality, the knowledge was gone, and there was only the void once more. Nightmare, he thought vaguely during one of the longer glimmerings of comprehension, I'm having a nightmare, like when you know you are having a nightmare and that if you could open your eyes it would be gone, but you can't open your eyes. He tried it now, tried to open his eyes, but it was no good, it was still as dark as ever and he was still sunk in this evil dream, for the sun had been shining brightly in the sky. He shook his head in slow despair.

"Aha! Observe! Signs of life at last!" There was no mistaking the slow, nasal drawl. "Ol' Medicine Man Miller triumphs again!" There was a moment's silence, a moment in which Mallory was increasingly aware of the diminishing thunder of aero engines, the acrid, resinous smoke that stung his nostrils and eyes, and then an arm had passed under his shoulders and Miller's persuasive voice was in his ear. "Just

229

try a little of this, boss. Ye olde vintage brandy. Nothin' like it anywhere."

Mallory felt the cold neck of the bottle, tilted his head back, took a long pull. Almost immediately he had jerked himself upright and forward to a sitting position, gagging, spluttering and fighting for breath as the raw, fiery ouzo bit into the mucous membrane of cheeks and throat. He tried to speak but could do no more than croak, gasp for fresh air and stare indignantly at the shadowy figure that knelt by his side. Miller, for his part, looked at him with unconcealed admiration.

"See, boss? Just like I said—nothin' like it." He shook his head admiringly. "Wide awake in an instant, as the literary boys would say. Never saw a shock and concussion victim recover so fast! "

"What the hell are you trying to do? " Mallory demanded. The fire had died down in his throat, and he could breathe again. "Poison me? " Angrily he shook his head, fighting off the pounding ache, the fog that still swirled round the fringes of his mind. "Bloody fine physician you are! Shock, you say, yet the first thing you do is administer a dose of spirits——"

"Take your pick," Miller interrupted grimly. "Either that or a damned sight bigger shock in about fifteen minutes or so when brother Jerry gets here."

"But they've gone away. I can't hear the Stukas any more."

"This lot's comin' up from the town," Miller said morosely. "Louki's just reported them. Half a dozen armoured cars and a couple of trucks with field guns the length of a telegraph pole."

"I see." Mallory twisted round, saw a gleam of light at a bend in the wall. A cave—a tunnel, almost. Little Cyprus, Louki had said some of the older people had called it—the Devil's Playground was riddled with a honeycomb of caves. He grinned wryly at the memory of his momentary panic when he thought his eyes had gone and turned again to Miller.

"Trouble again, Dusty, nothing but trouble. Thanks for bringing me round."

"Had to," Miller said briefly. "I guess we couldn't have carried you very far, boss."

Mallory nodded. "Not just the flattest of country hereabouts."

"There's that, too," Miller agreed. "What I really meant is that there's hardly anyone left to carry you. Casey Brown and Panayis have both been hurt, boss."

"What! Both of them?" Mallory screwed his eyes shut, shook his head in slow anger. "My God, Dusty, I'd forgotten all about the bomb—the bombs." He reached out his hand, caught Miller by the arm. "How—how bad are they?" There was so little time left, so much to do.

"How bad?" Miller shook out a pack of cigarettes and offered one to Mallory. "Not bad at all—if we could get them into hospital. But hellish painful and cripplin' if they gotta start hikin' up and down those gawddamned ravines hereabouts. First time I've seen canyon floors more nearly vertical than the walls themselves."

"You still haven't told me——"

"Sorry, boss, sorry. Shrapnel wounds, both of them, in exactly the same place—left thigh, just above the knee. No bones gone, no tendons cut. I've just finished tying up Casey's leg—it's a pretty wicked-lookin' gash. He's gonna know all about it when he starts walkin'."

"And Panayis?"

"Fixed his own leg," Miller said briefly. "A queer character. Wouldn't even let me look at it, far less bandage it. I reckon he'd have knifed me if I'd tried."

"Better to leave him alone anyway," Mallory advised. "Some of these islanders have strange taboos and superstitions. Just as long as he's alive. Though I still don't see how the hell he managed to get here."

"He was the first to leave," Miller explained. "Along with

Casey. You must have missed him in the smoke. They were climbin' together when they got hit."

"And how did I get here?"

"No prizes for the first correct answer." Miller jerked a thumb over his shoulder at the huge form that blocked half the width of the cave. "Junior here did his St. Bernard act once again. I wanted to go with him, but he wasn't keen. Said he reckoned it would be difficult to carry both of us up the hill. My feelin's were hurt considerable." Miller sighed. "I guess I just wasn't born to be a hero, that's all."

Mallory smiled. "Thanks again, Andrea."

"Thanks!" Miller was indignant. "A guy saves your life and all you can say is 'thanks'!"

"After the first dozen times or so you run out of suitable speeches," Mallory said dryly. "How's Stevens?"

"Breathin'."

Mallory nodded forward towards the source of light, wrinkled his nose. "Just round the corner, isn't he?"

"Yeah, it's pretty grim," Miller admitted. "The gangrene's spread up beyond the knee."

Mallory rose groggily to his feet, picked up his gun. "How is he really, Dusty?"

"He's dead, but he just won't die. He'll be gone by sundown. Gawd only knows what's kept him goin' so far."

"It may sound presumptuous," Mallory murmured; "but I think I know too."

"The first-class medical attention?" Miller said hopefully.

"Looks that way, doesn't it?" Mallory smiled down at the still kneeling Miller. "But that wasn't what I meant at all. Come, gentlemen, we have some business to attend to."

"Me, all I'm good for is blowin' up bridges and droppin' a handful of sand in engine bearin's," Miller announced. "Strategy and tactics are far beyond my simple mind. But I

still think those characters down there are pickin' a very stupid
way of committin' suicide. It would be a damned sight easier
for all concerned if they just shot themselves."

"I'm inclined to agree with you." Mallory settled himself
more firmly behind the jumbled rocks in the mouth of the
ravine that opened on the charred and smoking remains of the
carob grove directly below and took another look at the
Alpenkorps troops advancing in extended order up the steep,
shelterless slope. "They're no children at this game. I bet
they don't like it one little bit, either."

"Then why the hell are they doin' it, boss?"

"No option, probably. First off, this place can only be
attacked frontally." Mallory smiled down at the little Greek
lying between himself and Andrea. "Louki here chose the
place well. It would require a long detour to attack from the
rear—and it would take them a week to advance through that
devil's scrap-heap behind us. Secondly, it'll be sunset in a
couple of hours, and they know they haven't a hope of getting
us after it's dark. And finally—and I think this is more important than the other two reasons put together—it's a hundred
to one that the commandant in the town is being pretty
severely prodded by his High Command. There's too much at
stake, even in the one in a thousand chance of us getting at the
guns. They can't afford to have Kheros evacuated under their
noses, to lose——"

"Why not?" Miller interrupted. He gestured largely with
his hands. "Just a lot of useless rocks——"

"They can't afford to lose face with the Turks," Mallory
went on patiently. "The strategic importance of these islands
in the Sporades is negligible, but their political importance is
tremendous. Adolph badly needs another ally in these parts.
So he flies in Alpenkorps troops by the thousand and Stukas by
the hundred, the best he has—and he needs them desperately
on the Italian front. But you've got to convince your potential
ally that you're a pretty safe bet before you can persuade him

to give up his nice, safe seat on the fence and jump down on your side."

"Very interestin'," Miller observed. "So?"

"So the Germans are going to have no compunction about thirty or forty of their best troops being cut into little pieces. It's no trouble at all when you're sitting behind a desk a thousand miles away.... Let 'em come another hundred yards or so closer. Louki and I will start from the middle and work out: you and Andrea start from the outside."

"I don't like it, boss," Miller complained.

"Don't think that I do either," Mallory said quietly. "Slaughtering men forced to do a suicidal job like this is not my idea of fun—or even of war. But if we don't get them, they get us." He broke off and pointed across the burnished sea to where Kheros lay peacefully on the hazed horizon, striking golden glints off the westering sun. "What do you think they would have us do, Dusty?"

"I know, I know, boss." Miller stirred uncomfortably. "Don't rub it in." He pulled his woollen cap low over his forehead and stared bleakly down the slope. "How soon do the mass executions begin?"

"Another hundred yards, I said." Mallory looked down the slope again towards the coast road and grinned suddenly, glad to change the topic. "Never saw telegraph poles shrink so suddenly before, Dusty."

Miller studied the guns drawn up on the roads behind the two trucks and cleared his throat.

"I was only sayin' what Louki told me," he said defensively.

"What Louki told you!" The little Greek was indignant. "Before God, Major, the Americano is full of lies!"

"Ah, well, mebbe I was mistaken," Miller said magnanimously. He squinted again at the guns, forehead lined in puzzlement. "That first one's a mortar, I reckon. But what in the universe that other weird-looking contraption can be——"

"Also a mortar," Mallory explained. "A five-barrelled

job, and very nasty. The *Nebelwerfer* or Moanin' Minnie. Howls like all the lost souls in hell. Guaranteed to turn the knees to jelly, especially after nightfall—but it's still the other one you have to watch. A six-inch mortar, almost certainly using fragmentation bombs—you use a brush and shovel for clearing up afterwards."

"That's right," Miller growled. "Cheer us all up." But he was grateful to the New Zealander for trying to take their minds off what they had to do. "Why don't they use them?"

"They will," Mallory assured him. "Just as soon as we fire and they find out where we are."

"Gawd help us," Miller muttered. "Fragmentation bombs, you said!" He lapsed into gloomy silence.

"Any second now," Mallory said softly. "I only hope that our friend Turzig isn't among this lot." He reached out for his field-glasses but stopped in surprise as Andrea leaned across Louki and caught him by the wrist before he could lift the binoculars. "What's the matter, Andrea?"

"I would not be using these, my Captain. They have betrayed us once already. I have been thinking, and it can be nothing else. The sunlight reflecting from the lenses . . ."

Mallory stared at him, slowly released his grip on the glasses, nodded several times in succession.

"Of course, of course! I had been wondering. . . . Someone has been careless. There was no other way, there *could* have been no other way. It would only require a single flash to tip them off." He paused, remembering, then grinned wryly. "It could have been myself. All this started just after I had been on watch—and Panayis didn't have the glasses." He shook his head in mortification. "It *must* have been me, Andrea."

"I do not believe it," Andrea said flatly. "You couldn't make a mistake like that, my Captain."

"Not only could, but did, I'm afraid. But we'll worry about that afterwards." The middle of the ragged line of advancing soldiers, slipping and stumbling on the treacherous scree, had almost reached the lower limits of the blackened, stunted remains of the copse. " They've come far enough. I'll take the white helmet in the middle, Louki." Even as he spoke he could hear the soft scrape as the three others slid their automatic barrels across and between the protective rocks in front of them, could feel the wave of revulsion that washed through his mind. But his voice was steady enough as he spoke, relaxed and almost casual. " Right. Let them have it now! "

His last words were caught up and drowned in the tearing, rapid-fire crash of the automatic carbines. With four machine-guns in their hands—two Brens and two 9 mm. Schmeissers—it was no war, as he had said, but sheer, pitiful massacre, with the defenceless figures on the slope below, figures still stunned and uncomprehending, jerking, spinning round and collapsing like marionettes in the hands of a mad puppeteer, some to lie where they fell, others to roll down the steep slope, legs and arms flailing in the grotesque disjointedness of death. Only a couple stood still where they had been hit, vacant surprise mirrored in their lifeless faces, then slipped down tiredly to the stony ground at their feet. Almost three seconds had passed before the handful of those who still lived—about a quarter of the way in from either end of the line where the converging streams of fire had not yet met—realised what was happening and flung themselves desperately to the ground in search of the cover that didn't exist.

The phrenetic stammering of the machine-guns stopped abruptly and in unison, the sound sheared off as by a guillotine. The sudden silence was curiously oppressive, louder, more obtrusive than the clamour that had gone before. The gravelly earth beneath his elbows grated harshly as Mallory shifted his weight slightly, looked at the two men to his right, Andrea with his impassive face empty of all expression, Louki with the sheen of tears in his eyes. Then he became aware of the low murmuring to his left, shifted round again. Bitter-mouthed, savage, the American was swearing softly and continuously, oblivious to the pain as he pounded his fist time and again into the sharp-edged gravel before him.

"Just one more, Gawd." The quiet voice was almost a prayer. "That's all I ask. Just one more."

Mallory touched his arm. "What is it, Dusty?"

Miller looked round at him, eyes cold and still and empty of all recognition, then he blinked several times and grinned, a cut and bruised hand automatically reaching for his cigarettes.

"Jus' daydreamin', boss," he said easily. "Jus' day-dreamin'." He shook out his pack of cigarettes. "Have one?"

"That inhuman bastard that sent these poor devils up that hill," Mallory said quietly. "Make a wonderful picture seen over the sights of your rifle, wouldn't he?"

Abruptly Miller's smile vanished and he nodded.

"It would be all of that." He risked a quick peep round one of the boulders, eased himself back again. "Eight, mebbe ten of them still down there, boss," he reported. "The poor bastards are like ostriches—trying to take cover behind stones the size of an orange. . . . We leave them be?"

"We leave them be!" Mallory echoed emphatically. The thought of any more slaughter made him feel almost physically sick. "They won't try again." He broke off suddenly, flattened himself in reflex instinct as a burst of machine-gun bullets struck the steep-walled rock above their heads and whined up the gorge in vicious ricochet.

"Won't try again, huh?" Miller was already sliding his gun around the rock in front of him when Mallory caught his arm and pulled him back.

"Not them? Listen!" Another burst of fire, then another, and now they could hear the savage chatter of the machine-gun, a chatter rhythmically interrupted by a weird, half-human sighing as its belt passed through the breech. Mallory could feel the prickling of the hairs on the nape of his neck.

"A Spandau. Once you've heard a Spandau you can never forget it. Leave it alone—it's probably fixed on the back of one of the trucks and can't do us any harm. . . . I'm more worried about these damned mortars down there."

" I'm not," Miller said promptly. " They're not firing at us."

"That's why I'm worried. . . . What do you think, Andrea?"

" The same as you, my Captain. They are waiting. This Devil's Playground, as Louki calls it, is a madman's maze, and they can only fire as blind men——"

" They won't be waiting much longer," Mallory interrupted grimly. He pointed to the north. " Here come their eyes."

At first only specks above the promontory of Cape Demirci, the planes were soon recognisable for what they were, droning in slowly over the Ægean at about fifteen hundred feet. Mallory looked at them in astonishment, then turned to Andrea.

" Am I seeing things, Andrea? " He gestured at the first of the two planes, a high-winged little monoplane fighter. " That can't be a PZL? "

" It can be and it is," Andrea murmured. " An old Polish plane we had before the war," he explained to Miller. " And the other is an old Belgian plane—Breguets, we called them." Andrea shaded his eyes to look again at the two planes, now almost directly overhead. " I thought they had all been lost during the invasion."

" Me too," Mallory said. " Must have patched up some bits and pieces. Ah, they've seen us—beginning to circle. But why on earth they use these obsolete death traps——"

" I don't know and I don't care," Miller said rapidly. He had just taken a quick look round the boulder in front of him. " These damned guns down there are just linin' up on us, and muzzle-on they look a considerable sight bigger than telegraph poles. Fragmentation bombs, you said! Come on, boss, let's get the hell outa here! "

Thus the pattern was set for the remainder of that brief November afternoon, for the grim game of tip-and-run, hide-

and-seek among the ravines and shattered rocks of the Devil's
Playground. The planes held the key to the game, cruised high
overhead observing every move of the hunted group below,
relaying the information to the guns on the coast road and the
company of Alpenkorps that had moved up through the ravine
above the carob grove soon after the planes reported that the
positions there had been abandoned. The two ancient planes
were soon replaced by a couple of modern Henschels—Andrea
said that the PZL couldn't remain airborne for more than an
hour anyway.

Mallory was between the devil and the deep sea. Inaccurate
though the mortars were, some of the deadly fragmentation
bombs found their way into the deep ravines where they took
temporary shelter, the blast of metal lethal in the confined
space between the sheering walls. Occasionally they came so
close that Mallory was forced to take refuge in some of the deep
caves that honeycombed the walls of the canyons. In these they
were safe enough, but the safety was an illusion that could lead
only to ultimate defeat and capture; in the lulls, the Alpenkorps, whom they had fought off in a series of brief, skirmishing
rear-guard actions during the afternoon, could approach closely
enough to trap them inside. Time and time again Mallory and
his men were forced to move on to widen the gap between
themselves and their pursuers, following the indomitable Louki
wherever he chose to lead them, and taking their chance, often
a very slender and desperate chance, with the mortar bombs.
One bomb arced into a ravine that led into the interior, burying
itself in the gravelly ground not twenty yards ahead of them,
by far the nearest anything had come during the afternoon.
By one chance in a thousand, it didn't explode. They gave it as
wide a berth as possible, almost holding their breaths until they
were safely beyond.

About half an hour before sunset they struggled up the last
few boulder-strewn yards of a steeply-shelving ravine floor,
halted just beyond the shelter of the projecting wall where the

ravine dipped again and turned sharply to the right and the north. There had been no more mortar bombs since the one that had failed to explode. The six-inch and the weirdly-howling *Nebelwerfer* had only a limited range, Mallory knew, and though the planes still cruised overhead, they cruised uselessly: the sun was dipping towards the horizon and the floors of the ravines were already deep-sunk in shadowed gloom, invisible from above. But the Alpenkorps, tough, dogged, skilful soldiers, soldiers living only for the revenge of their massacred comrades, were very close behind. And they were highly-trained mountain troops, fresh, resilient, the reservoir of their energies barely tapped: whereas his own tiny band, worn out from continuous days and sleepless nights of labour and action. . . .

Mallory sank to the ground near the angled turn of the ravine where he could keep lookout, glanced at the others with a deceptive casualness that marked his cheerless assessment of what he saw. As a fighting unit they were in a pretty bad way. Both Panayis and Brown were badly crippled, the latter's face grey with pain. For the first time since leaving Alexandria, Casey Brown was apathetic, listless and quite indifferent to everything: this Mallory took as a very bad sign. Nor was Brown helped by the heavy transmitter still strapped to his back—with point-blank truculence he had ignored Mallory's categorical order to abandon it. Louki was tired, and looked it: his physique, Mallory realised now, was no match for his spirit, for the infectious smile that never left his face, for the panache of that magnificently upswept moustache that contrasted so oddly with the sad, tired eyes above. Miller, like himself, was tired, but, like himself, could keep on being tired for a long time yet. And Stevens was still conscious, but even in the twilit gloom of the canyon floor his face looked curiously transparent, while the nails, lips and eyelids were drained of blood. And Andrea, who had carried him up and down all these killing canyon tracks—where there had been tracks—

for almost two interminable hours, looked as he always did: immutable, indestructible.

Mallory shook his head, fished out a cigarette, made to strike a light, remembered the planes still cruising overhead and threw the match away. Idly his gaze travelled north along the canyon and he slowly stiffened, the unlit cigarette crumpling and shredding between his fingers. This ravine bore no resemblance to any of the others through which they had so far passed—it was broader, dead straight, at least three times as long—and, as far as he could see in the twilight, the far end was blocked off by an almost vertical wall.

"Louki!" Mallory was on his feet now, all weariness forgotten. "Do you know where you are. Do you know this place?"

"But certainly, Major!" Louki was hurt. "Have I not told you that Panayis and I, in the days of our youth——"

"But this is a cul-de-sac, a dead-end!" Mallory protested. "We're boxed in, man, we're trapped!"

Louki grinned impudently and twirled a corner of his moustache. The little man was enjoying himself.

"So? The Major does not trust Louki, is that it?" He grinned again, relented, patted the wall by his side. "Panayis and I, we have been working this way all afternoon. Along this wall there are many caves. One of them leads through to another valley that leads down to the coast road."

"I see, I see." Relief washing through his mind, Mallory sank down on the ground again. "And where does this other valley come out?"

"Just across the strait from Maidos."

"How far from the town?"

"About five miles, Major, maybe six. Not more."

"Fine, fine! And you're sure you can find this cave?"

"A hundred years from now and my head in a goat-skin bag!" Louki boasted.

"Fair enough!" Even as he spoke, Mallory catapulted

himself violently to one side, twisted in mid-air to avoid falling across Stevens and crashed heavily into the wall between Andrea and Miller. In a moment of unthinking carelessness he had exposed himself to view from the ravine they had just climbed: the burst of machine-gun fire from its lower end— a hundred and fifty yards away at the most—had almost blown his head off. Even as it was, the left shoulder of his jacket had been torn away, the shell just grazing his shoulder. Miller was already kneeling by his side, fingering the gash, running a gently exploratory hand across his back.

" Careless, damn careless," Mallory murmured. " But I didn't think they were so close." He didn't feel as calm as he sounded. If the mouth of that Schmeisser had been another sixteenth of an inch to the right, he'd have had no head left now.

" Are you all right, boss? " Miller was puzzled. " Did they——"

"Terrible shots," Mallory assured him cheerfully. "Couldn't hit a barn." He twisted round to look at his shoulder. " I hate to sound heroic, but this really is just a scratch. . . ." He rose easily to his feet, and picked up his gun. " Sorry and all that, gentlemen, but it's time we were on our way again. How far along is this cave, Louki? "

Louki rubbed his bristly chin, the smile suddenly gone. He looked quickly at Mallory, then away again.

" Louki! "

" Yes, yes, Major. The cave." Louki rubbed his chin again. " Well, it is a good way along. In fact, it is at the end," he finished uncomfortably.

" The *very* end? " asked Mallory quietly.

Louki nodded miserably, stared down at the ground at his feet. Even the ends of his moustache seemed to droop.

" That's handy," Mallory said heavily. " Oh, that's very handy! " He sank down to the ground again. " Helps us no end, that does."

He bowed his head in thought and didn't even lift it as Andrea poked a Bren round the angle of the rock, and fired a short downhill burst more in token of discouragement than in any hope of hitting anything. Another ten seconds passed, then Louki spoke again, his voice barely audible.

"I am very, very sorry. This is a terrible thing. Before God, Major, I would not have done it but that I thought they were still far behind."

"It's not your fault, Louki." Mallory was touched by the little man's obvious distress. He touched his ripped shoulder jacket. "I thought the same thing."

"Please!" Stevens put his hand on Mallory's arm. "What's wrong? I don't understand."

"Everybody else does, I'm afraid, Andy. It's very, very simple. We have half a mile to go along this valley here—and not a shred of cover. The Alpenkorps have less than two hundred yards to come up that ravine we've just left." He paused while Andrea fired another retaliatory short burst, then continued. "They'll do what they're doing now—keep probing to see if we're still here. The minute they judge we're gone, they'll be up here in a flash. They'll nail us before we're half-way, quarter way to the cave—you know we can't travel fast. And they're carrying a couple of Spandaus—they'll cut us to ribbons."

"I see," Stevens murmured. "You put it all so nicely, sir."

"Sorry, Andy, but that's how it is."

"But could you not leave two men as a rear-guard, while the rest——"

"And what happens to the rear-guard?" Mallory interrupted dryly.

"I see what you mean," he said in a low voice. "I hadn't thought of that."

"No, but the rear-guard would. Quite a problem, isn't it?"

"There is no problem at all," Louki announced. "The Major is kind, but this is all my fault. I will——"

"You'll do damn all of the kind!" Miller said savagely. He tore Louki's Bren from his hand and laid it on the ground. "You heard what the boss said—it wasn't your fault." For a moment Louki stared at him in anger, then turned dejectedly away. He looked as if he were going to cry. Mallory, too, stared at the American, astonished at the sudden vehemence, so completely out of character. Now that he came to think of it, Dusty had been strangely taciturn and thoughtful during the past hour or so—Mallory couldn't recall his saying a word during all that time. But time enough to worry about that later on. . . .

Casey Brown eased his injured leg, looking hopefully at Mallory. "Couldn't we stay here till it's dark—real dark—then make our way——"

"No good. The moon's almost full to-night—and not a cloud in the sky. They'd get us. Even more important, we have to get into the town between sunset and curfew to-night. Our last chance. Sorry, Casey, but it's no go."

Fifteen seconds, half a minute passed, and passed in silence, then they all started abruptly as Andy Stevens spoke.

"Louki *was* right, you know," he said pleasantly. The voice was weak, but filled with a calm certainty that jerked every eye towards him. He was propped up on one elbow, Louki's Bren cradled in his hands. It was a measure of their concentration on the problem on hand that no one had heard or seen him reach out for the machine-gun. "It's all very simple," Stevens went on quietly. "Just let's use our heads, that's all. . . . The gangrene's right up past the knee, isn't it, sir?"

Mallory said nothing: he didn't know what to say, the complete unexpectedness had knocked him off balance. He was vaguely aware that Miller was looking at him, his eyes begging him to say "No."

" Is it or isn't it? " There was patience, a curious understanding in the voice, and all of a sudden Mallory knew what
to say.

" Yes," he nodded. " It is." Miller was looking at him in
horror.

" Thank you, sir." Stevens was smiling in satisfaction.
" Thank you very much indeed. There's no need to point out
all the advantages of my staying here." There was an assurance
in his voice no one had ever heard before, the unthinking
authority of a man completely in charge of a situation. " Time
I did something for my living anyway. No fond farewells,
please. Just leave me a couple of boxes of ammo, two or three
thirty-six grenades and away you go."

" I'll be damned if we will! " Miller was on his feet,
making for the boy, then brought up abruptly as the Bren
centred on his chest.

" One step nearer and I'll shoot you," Stevens said calmly.
Miller looked at him in long silence, sank slowly back to the
ground.

" I would, you know," Stevens assured him. " Well,
good-bye, gentlemen. Thank you for all you've done for
me."

Twenty seconds, thirty, a whole minute passed in a queer,
trance-like silence, then Miller heaved himself to his feet again,
a tall, rangy figure with tattered clothes and a face curiously
haggard in the gathering gloom.

" So long, kid. I guess—waal, mebbe I'm not so smart after
all." He took Stevens's hand, looked down at the wasted face
for a long moment, made to say something else, then changed
his mind. " Be seein' you," he said abruptly, turned and walked
off heavily down the valley. One by one the others followed
him, wordlessly, except for Andrea who stopped and whispered
in the boy's ear, a whisper that brought a smile and a nod of
complete understanding, and then there was only Mallory left.
Stevens grinned up at him.

" Thank you, sir. Thanks for not letting me down. You and Andrea—you understand. You always did understand."

" You'll—you'll be all right, Andy?" God, Mallory thought, what a stupid, what an inane thing, to say.

" Honest, sir, I'm O.K." Stevens smiled contentedly. " No pain left—I can't feel a thing. It's wonderful!"

" Andy, I don't——"

" It's time you were gone, sir. The others will be waiting. Now if you'll just light me a gasper and fire a few random shots down that ravine . . ."

Within five minutes Mallory had overtaken the others, and inside fifteen they had all reached the cave that led to the coast. For a moment they stood in the entrance, listening to the intermittent firing from the other end of the valley, then turned wordlessly and plunged into the cave. Back where they had left him, Andy Stevens was lying on his stomach, peering down into the now almost dark ravine. There was no pain left in his body, none at all. He drew deeply on a cupped cigarette, smiled as he pushed another clip home into the magazine of the Bren. For the first time in his life Andy Stevens was happy and content beyond his understanding, a man at last at peace with himself. He was no longer afraid.

CHAPTER THIRTEEN

WEDNESDAY EVENING

1800-1915

EXACTLY FORTY MINUTES later they were safely in the heart of the town of Navarone, within fifty yards of the great gates of the fortress itself.

Mallory, gazing out at the gates and the still more massive arch of stone that encased them, shook his head for the tenth time and tried to fight off the feeling of disbelief and wonder that they should have reached their goal at last—or as nearly as made no difference. They had been due a break some time, he thought, the law of averages had been overwhelmingly against the continuation of the evil fortune that had dogged them so incessantly since they had arrived on the island. It was only right, he kept telling himself, it was only just that this should be so: but even so, the transition from that dark valley where they had left Andy Stevens to die to this tumbledown old house on the east side of the town square of Navarone had been so quick, so easy, that it still lay beyond immediate understanding or unthinking acceptance.

Not that it had been too easy in the first fifteen minutes or so, he remembered. Panayis's wounded leg had given out on him immediately after they had entered the cave, and he had collapsed; he must have been in agony, Mallory had thought, with his torn, roughly-bandaged leg, but the failing light and the dark, bitter, impassive face had masked the pain. He had begged Mallory to be allowed to remain where he was, to hold off the Alpenkorps when they had overcome Stevens and reached the end of the valley, but Mallory had roughly refused him permission. Brutally he had told Panayis that he was far too valuable to be left there—and that the chances of the Alpenkorps picking that cave out of a score of others were pretty remote. Mallory had hated having to talk to him like that, but there had been no time for gentle blandishments, and Panayis must have seen his point for he had made neither protest nor struggle when Miller and Andrea picked him up and helped him to limp through the cave. The limp, Mallory had noticed, had been much less noticeable then, perhaps because of the assistance, perhaps because now that he had been baulked of the chance of killing a few more Germans it had been pointless to exaggerate his hurt.

They had barely cleared the mouth of the cave on the other side and were making their way down the tree-tufted, sloping valley side towards the sea, the dark sheen of the Ægean clearly visible in the gloom, when Louki, hearing something, had gestured them all to silence. Almost immediately Mallory, too, heard it, a soft guttural voice occasionally lost in the crunch of approaching feet on gravel, had seen that they were providentially screened by some stunted trees, given the order to stop and sworn in quick anger as he had heard the soft thud and barely muffled cry behind them. He had gone back to investigate and found Panayis stretched on the ground unconscious. Miller, who had been helping him along, had explained that Mallory had halted them so suddenly that he'd bumped into Panayis, that the Greek's bad leg had given beneath him, throwing him heavily, his head striking a stone as he had fallen. Mallory had stooped down in instantly renewed suspicion—Panayis was a throw-back, a natural-born killer, and he was quite capable of faking an accident if he thought he could turn it to his advantage, line a few more of the enemy up on the sights of his rifle . . . but there had been no fake about that: the bruised and bloodied gash above the temple was all too real.

The German patrol, having had no inkling of their presence, moved noisily up the valley till they had finally gone out of earshot. Louki had thought that the commandant in Navarone was becoming desperate, trying to seal off every available exit from the Devil's Playground. Mallory had thought it unlikely, but had not stayed to argue the point. Five minutes later they had cleared the mouth of the valley, and in another five had not only reached the coast road but silenced and bound two sentries—the drivers, probably—who had been guarding a truck and command car parked by the roadside, stripped them of denims and helmets and bundled them out of sight behind some bushes.

The trip into Navarone had been ridiculously simple, but the entire lack of opposition was easily understandable, because of the complete unexpectedness of it all. Seated beside Mallory on the front seat, clad, like Mallory, in captured clothes, Louki had driven the big car, and driven it magnificently, an accomplishment so unusual to find in a remote Ægean island that Mallory had been completely mystified until Louki had reminded him that he had been Eugene Vlachos's Consulate chauffeur for many years. The drive into town had taken less than twelve minutes—not only did the little man handle the car superbly, but he knew the road so well that he got the utmost possible out of the big machine, most of the time without benefit of any lights at all.

Not only a simple journey, but quite uneventful. They had passed several parked trucks at intervals along the road, and less than two miles from the town itself had met a group of about twenty soldiers marching in the opposite direction in column of twos. Louki had slowed down—it would have been highly suspicious had he accelerated, endangering the lives of the marching men—but had switched on the powerful headlights, blinding them, and blown raucously on the horn, while

Mallory had leaned out of the right-hand window, sworn at them in perfect German and told them to get out of his damned way. This they had done, while the junior officer in charge had come smartly to attention, throwing up his hand in punctilious salute.

Immediately afterwards they had run through an area of high-walled, terraced market gardens, passed between a decaying Byzantine church and a whitewashed orthodox monastery that faced each other incongruously across the same dusty road, then almost at once were running through the lower part of the old town. Mallory had had a vague impression of narrow, winding, dim-lit streets only inches wider than the car itself, hugely cobbled and with almost knee-high pavements, then Louki was making his way up an arched lane, the car climbing steeply all the time. He had stopped abruptly, and Mallory had followed his quick survey of the darkened lane: completely deserted though over an hour yet to curfew. Beside them had been a flight of white stone steps innocent of any hand-rail, running up parallel to the wall of a house, with a highly ornamented lattice-work grill protecting the outside landing at the top. A still groggy Panayis had led them up these stairs, through a house—he had known exactly where he was—across a shallow roof, down some more steps, through a dark courtyard and into this ancient house where they were now. Louki had driven the car away even before they had reached the top of the stairs; it was only now that Mallory remembered that Louki hadn't thought it worth while to say what he intended to do with the car.

Still gazing out the windowless hole in the wall at the fortress gate, Mallory found himself hoping intensely that nothing would happen to the sad-eyed little Greek, and not only because in his infinite resource and local knowledge he had been invaluable to them and was likely to prove so again; all these considerations apart, Mallory had formed the deepest affection for him, for his unvarying cheerfulness, his enthusiasm, his eagerness to help and to please, above all for his complete disregard of self. A thoroughly lovable little man, and Mallory's heart warmed to him. More than he could say for Panayis, he thought sourly, and then immediately regretted the thought: it was no fault of Panayis's that he was what he was, and in his own dark and bitter way he had done as much for them as Louki. But the fact remained that he was sadly lacking in Louki's warm humanity.

He lacked also Louki's quick intelligence, the calculated opportunism that amounted almost to genius. It had been a brilliant idea on Louki's part, Mallory mused, that they should take over this abandoned house: not that there had been any difficulty in finding an empty house—since the Germans had taken over the old castle the inhabitants of the town had left in their scores for Margaritha and other outlying villages, none more quickly than those who had lived in the town square itself; the nearness of the fortress wall that formed the north side of the square had been more than many of them could stomach, with the constant coming and going of their conquerors through the fortress gates, the sentries marching to and fro, the never-ceasing reminders that their freedom was a vanished thing. So many had gone that more than half the houses on the west side of the square—those nearest the fortress —were now occupied by German officers. But this same enforced close observation of the fortress's activities had been exactly what Mallory had wanted. When the time came to strike they had only yards to go. And although any competent garrison commander would always be prepared against the unexpected, Mallory considered it unlikely indeed that any reasonable man could conceive of a sabotage group so suicidally minded as to spend an entire day within a literal stone's throw of the fortress wall.

Not that the house as such had much to recommend it. As a home, a dwelling place, it was just about as uncomfortable as possible, as dilapidated as it could be without actually falling

down. The west side of the square—the side perched precariously on the cliff-top—and the south side were made up
of fairly modern buildings of whitewashed stone and Parian
granite, huddled together in the invariable fashion of houses
in these island towns, flat-roofed to catch as much as possible
of the winter rains. But the east side of the square, where they
were, was made up of antiquated timber and turf houses, of the
kind much more often found in remote mountain villages.

The beaten earth floor beneath his feet was hummocky,
uneven, and the previous occupants had used one corner of it
—obviously—for a variety of purposes, not least as a refuse
dump. The ceiling was of rough-hewn, blackened beams, more
or less covered with planks, these in turn being covered with a
thick layer of trodden earth: from previous experience of such
houses in the White Mountains, Mallory knew that the roof
would leak like a sieve whenever the rain came on. Across one
end of the room was a solid ledge some thirty inches high, a
ledge that served, after the fashion of similar structures in
Eskimo igloos, as bed, table or settee as the occasion demanded.
The room was completely bare of furniture.

Mallory started as someone touched him on the shoulder
and turned round. Miller was behind him, munching away
steadily, the remains of a bottle of wine in his hand.

" Better get some chow, boss," he advised. " I'll take a
gander through this hole from time to time."

" Right you are, Dusty. Thanks." Mallory moved gingerly
towards the back of the room—it was almost pitch dark inside
and they dared not risk a light—and felt his way till he brought
up against the ledge. The tireless Andrea had gone through
their provisions and prepared a meal of sorts—dried figs, honey,
cheese, garlic sausages and pounded roast chestnuts. A horrible
mixture, Mallory thought, but the best Andrea could do:
besides he was too hungry, ravenously so, to worry about such
niceties as the pleasing of his palate. And by the time he had
washed it down with some of the local wine that Louki and

Panayis had provided the previous day, the sweetly-resinous rawness of the drink had obliterated every other taste.

Carefully, shielding the match with his hand, Mallory lit a cigarette and began to explain for the first time his plan for entering the fortress. He did not have to bother lowering his voice—a couple of looms in the next house, one of the few occupied ones left on that side of the square, clacked incessantly throughout the evening. Mallory had a shrewd suspicion that this was more of Louki's doing, although it was difficult to see how he could have got word through to any of his friends. But Mallory was content to accept the situation as it was, to concentrate on making sure that the others understood his instructions.

Apparently they did, for there were no questions. For a few minutes the talk became general, the usually taciturn Casey Brown having the most to say, complaining bitterly about the food, the drink, his injured leg and the hardness of the bench where he wouldn't be able to sleep a wink all night long. Mallory grinned to himself but said nothing; Casey Brown was definitely on the mend.

" I reckon we've talked enough, gentlemen." Mallory slid off the bench and stretched himself. God, he was tired! " Our first and last chance to get a decent night's sleep. Two hour watches—I'll take the first."

" By yourself? " It was Miller calling softly from the other end of the room. " Don't you think we should share watches, boss? One for the front, one for the back. Besides, you know we're all pretty well done up. One man by himself might fall asleep." He sounded so anxious that Mallory laughed.

" Not a chance, Dusty. Each man will keep watch by the window there and if he falls asleep he'll damn' soon wake up when he hits the floor. And it's because we're so darned bushed that we can't afford to have anyone lose sleep unnecessarily. Myself first, then you, then Panayis, then Casey, then Andrea."

"Yeah, I suppose that'll be O.K.," Miller conceded grudgingly.

He put something hard and cold into his hand. Mallory recognised it at once—it was Miller's most cherished possession, his silenced automatic.

"Just so's you can fill any nosy customers full of little holes without wakin' the whole town." He ambled off to the back of the room, lit a cigarette, smoked it quietly for a few moments, then swung his legs up on the bench. Within five minutes everyone except the silently watchful man at the window was sound asleep.

Two or three minutes later Mallory jerked to unmoving attention as he heard a stealthy sound outside—from the back of the house, he thought. The clacking of the looms next door had stopped, and the house was very still. Again there came the noise, unmistakable this time, a gentle tapping at the door at the end of the passage that led from the back of the room.

"Remain there, my Captain." It was Andrea's soft murmur, and Mallory marvelled for the hundredth time at Andrea's ability to rouse himself from the deepest of sleeps at the slightest alien sound: the violence of a thunderstorm would have left him undisturbed. "I will see to it. It must be Louki."

It was Louki. The little man was panting, near exhaustion, but extraordinarily pleased with himself. Gratefully he drank the cup of wine that Andrea poured for him.

"Damned glad to see you back again!" Mallory said sincerely. "How did it go? Someone after you?"

Mallory could almost see him drawing himself up to his full height in the darkness.

"As if any of these clumsy fools could see Louki, even on a moonlit night, far less catch him," he said indignantly. He paused to draw some deep breaths. "No, no, Major, I knew you would be worried about me so I ran back all the way. Well, nearly all the way," he amended. "I am not so young as I was, Major Mallory."

" All the way from where," Mallory asked. He was glad of the darkness that hid his smile.

" From Vygos. It is an old castle that the Franks built there many generations ago, about two miles from here along the coast road to the east." He paused to drink another mouthful of wine. " More than two miles, I would say—and I only walked twice, a minute at a time, on the way back." Mallory had the impression that Louki already regretted his momentary weakness in admitting that he was no longer a young man.

" And what did you do there? " Mallory asked.

" I was thinking, after I left you," Louki answered indirectly. " Me, I am always thinking," he explained. " It is a habit of mine. I was thinking that when the soldiers who are looking for us out in the Devil's Playground find out that the car is gone, they will know that we are no longer in that accursed place."

" Yes," Mallory agreed carefully. " Yes, they will know that."

" Then they will say to themselves, ' Ha, those *verdammt Englanders* have little time left. They will know that we will know that they have little hope of catching us in the island— Panayis and I, we know every rock and tree and path and cave. So all they can do is to make sure that we do not get into the town—they will block every road leading in, and to-night is our last chance to get in. You follow me? " he asked anxiously.

" I'm trying very hard."

" But first—" [Louki spread his hands dramatically] " but first they will make sure we are not in the town. They would be fools to block the roads if we were already in the town. They *must* make sure we are not in the town. And so—the search. The very great search. With—how do you say?— the teeth-comb! "

Mallory nodded his head in slow understanding.

" I'm afraid he's right, Andrea."

" I, too, fear so," Andrea said unhappily. " We should have

thought of this. But perhaps we could hide—the roof-tops or——"

"With a teeth-comb, I said!" Louki interrupted impatiently. "But all is well. I, Louki have thought it all out. I can smell rain. There will be clouds over the moon before long, and it will be safe to move. . . . You do not want to know what I have done with the car, Major Mallory?" Louki was enjoying himself immensely.

"Forgotten all about it," Mallory confessed. "What *did* you do with the car?"

"I left it in the courtyard of Vygos castle. Then I emptied all the petrol from the tank and poured it over the car. Then I struck a match."

"You did *what*?" Mallory was incredulous.

"I struck a match. I think I was standing too near the car, for I do not seem to have any eyebrows left." Louki sighed. "A pity—it was such a splendid machine." Then he brightened. "But before God, Major, it burned magnificently."

Mallory stared at him.

"Why on earth——?"

"It is simple," Louki explained patiently. "By this time the men out in the Devil's Playground must know that their car has been stolen. They see the fire. They hurry back to—how do you say?"

"Investigate?"

"So. Investigate. They wait till the fire dies down. They investigate again. No bodies, no bones in the car, so they search the castle. And what do they find?"

There was silence in the room.

"Nothing!" Louki said impatiently. "They find nothing. And then they search the countryside for half a mile around. And what do they find? Again nothing. So then they know that they have been fooled, and that we are in the town, and will come to search the town."

"With the teeth-comb," Mallory murmured.

"With the teeth-comb. And what do they find?" Louki paused, then hurried on before anyone could steal his thunder. "Once again, they will find nothing," he said triumphantly. "And why? For by then the rain will have come, the moon will have vanished, the explosives will be hidden—and we will be gone!"

"Gone where?" Mallory felt dazed.

"Where but to Vygos castle, Major Mallory. Never while night follows day will they think to look for us there!"

Mallory looked at him in silence for long seconds without speaking, then turned to Andrea.

"Captain Jensen's only made one mistake so far," he murmured. "He picked the wrong man to lead this expedition. Not that it matters anyway. With Louki here on our side, how can we lose?"

Mallory lowered his rucksack gently to the earthen roof, straightened and peered up into the darkness, both hands shielding his eyes from the first drizzle of rain. Even from where they stood—on the crumbling roof of the house nearest the fortress on the east side of the square—the wall stretched fifteen, perhaps twenty feet above their heads; the wickedly out- and down-curving spikes that topped the wall were all but lost in the darkness.

"There she is, Dusty," Mallory murmured. "Nothing to it."

"Nothin' to it!" Miller was horrified. "I've—I've gotta get over *that*?"

"You'd have a ruddy hard time going through it," Mallory answered briefly. He grinned, clapped Miller on the back and prodded the rucksack at his feet. "We chuck this rope up, the hook catches, you shin smartly up——"

"And bleed to death on those six strands of barbed wire," Miller interrupted. "Louki says they're the biggest barbs he's ever seen."

"We'll use the tent for padding," Mallory said soothingly.

"I have a very delicate skin, boss," Miller complained. "Nothin' short of a spring mattress——"

"Well, you've only an hour to find one," Mallory said indifferently. Louki had estimated that it would be at least an hour before the search party would clear the northern part of the town, give himself and Andrea a chance to begin a diversion. "Come on, let's cache this stuff and get out of here. We'll shove the rucksacks in this corner and cover 'em with earth. Take the rope out first, though; we'll have no time to start undoing packs when we get back here."

Miller dropped to his knees, hands fumbling with straps, then exclaimed in sudden annoyance.

"This can't be the pack," he muttered in disgust. Abruptly his voice changed. "Here, wait a minute, though."

"What's up, Dusty?"

Miller didn't answer immediately. For a few seconds his hands explored the contents of the pack, then he straightened.

"The slow-burnin' fuse, boss." His voice was blurred with anger, with a vicious anger that astonished Mallory. "It's gone!"

"What!" Mallory stooped, began to search through the pack. "It can't be, Dusty, it just *can't*! Dammit to hell, man, you packed the stuff yourself!"

"Sure I did, boss," Miller grated. "And then some crawlin' bastard comes along behind my back and unpacks it again."

"Impossible!" Mallory protested. "It's just downright impossible, Dusty. *You* closed that rucksack—I saw you do it in the grove this morning—and Louki has had it all the time since then. And I'd trust Louki with my life."

"So would I, boss."

"Maybe we're both wrong," Mallory went on quietly. "Maybe you did miss it out. We're both helluva tired, Dusty."

Miller looked at him queerly, said nothing for a moment, then began to swear again. " It's my own fault, boss, my own gawddamned fault."

" What do you mean, your own fault? Heavens above, man, I was there when . . ." Mallory broke off, rose quickly to his feet and stared through the darkness at the south side of the square. A single shot had rung out there, the whiplash crack of a carbine followed the thin, high whine of a ricochet, and then silence.

Mallory stood quite still, hands clenched by his sides. Over ten minutes had passed since he and Miller had left Panayis to guide Andrea and Brown to the Castle Vygos—they should have been well away from the square by this time. And almost certainly Louki wouldn't be down there. Mallory's instructions to him had been explicit—to hide the remainder of the T.N.T. blocks in the roof and then wait there to lead himself and Miller to the keep. But something could have gone wrong, something could always go wrong. Or a trap, maybe, a ruse. But what kind of trap?

The sudden, off-beat stammering of a heavy machine-gun stilled his thoughts, and for a moment or two he was all eyes and straining ears. And then another, and lighter machine-gun cut in, just for a few seconds: as abruptly as they had started, both guns died away, together. Mallory waited no longer.

" Get the stuff together again," he whispered urgently. " We're taking it with us. Something's gone wrong." Within thirty seconds they had ropes and explosives back in their knapsacks, had strapped them on their backs and were on their way.

Bent almost double, careful to make no noise whatsoever, they ran across the roof-tops towards the old house where they had hidden earlier in the evening, where they were now to rendezvous with Louki. Still running, they were only feet away from the house when they saw his shadowy figure rise up, only it wasn't Louki, Mallory realised at once, it was far too tall for

Louki and without breaking step he catapulted the horizontal
driving weight of his 180 pounds at the unknown figure in a
homicidal tackle, his shoulder catching the man just below
the breast-bone, emptying every last particle of air from the
man's lungs with an explosive, agonised *whoosh*. A second later
both of Miller's sinewy hands were clamped round the man's
neck, slowly choking him to death.

And he would have choked to death, neither of the two men
were in any mind for half-measures, had not Mallory, prompted
by some fugitive intuition, stooped low over the contorted face,
the staring, protruding eyes, choked back a cry of sudden
horror.

" Dusty! " he whispered hoarsely. " For God's sake, stop!
Let him go! It's Panayis! "

Miller didn't hear him. In the gloom his face was like stone,
his head sunk farther and farther between hunching shoulders
as he tightened his grip, strangling the Greek in a weird and
savage silence.

" It's Panayis, you bloody fool, Panayis! " Mallory's mouth
was at the American's ear, his hands clamped round the other's
wrists as he tried to drag him off Panayis's throat. He could
hear the muffled drumming of Panayis's heels on the turf of
the roof, tore at Miller's wrists with all his strength: twice
before he had heard that sound as a man had died under
Andrea's great hands, and he knew with sudden certainty that
Panayis would go the same way, and soon, if he didn't make
Miller understand. But all at once Miller understood, relaxed
heavily, straightened up, still kneeling, hands hanging limply
by his sides. Breathing deeply he stared down in silence at the
man at his feet.

" What the hell's the matter with you? " Mallory demanded
softly. " Deaf or blind or both? "

" Just one of these things, I guess." Miller rubbed the back
of a hand across his forehead, his face empty of expression.
" Sorry, boss, sorry."

" Why the hell apologise to me? " Mallory looked away from him, looked down at Panayis: the Greek was sitting up now, hands massaging his bruised throat, sucking in long draughts of air in great, whooping gasps. " But maybe Panayis here might appreciate——"

" Apologies can wait," Miller interrupted brusquely. " Ask him what's happened to Louki."

Mallory looked at him for a moment, made to reply, changed his mind, translated the question. He listened to Panayis's halting answer—it obviously hurt him even to try to speak—and his mouth tightened in a hard, bitter line. Miller watched the fractional slump of the New Zealander's shoulders, felt he could wait no longer.

" Well, what is it, boss? Somethin's happened to Louki, is that it? "

" Yes," Mallory said tonelessly. " They'd only got as far as the lane at the back when they found a small German patrol blocking their way. Louki tried to draw them off and the machine-gunner got him through the chest. Andrea got the machine-gunner and took Louki away. Panayis says he'll die for sure."

CHAPTER FOURTEEN

WEDNESDAY NIGHT

1915-2000

THE THREE MEN cleared the town without any difficulty, striking out directly across country for the castle Vygos and avoiding the main road. It was beginning to rain now, heavily, persistently, and the ground was mired and sodden, the few ploughed fields they crossed almost impassable. They had just struggled their way through one of these and could just see the dim outline of the keep—less than a cross-country mile from the town instead of Louki's exaggerated estimate—when they passed by an abandoned earthen house and Miller spoke for the first time since they had left the town square of Navarone.

" I'm bushed, boss." His head was sunk on his chest, and his breathing was laboured. " Ol' man Miller's on the downward path, I reckon, and the legs are gone. Couldn't we squat inside here for a couple of minutes, boss, and have a smoke? "

Mallory looked at him in surprise, thought how desperately weary his own legs felt and nodded in reluctant agreement. Miller wasn't the man to complain unless he was near exhaustion.

" Okay, Dusty, I don't suppose a minute or two will harm." He translated quickly into Greek and led the way inside, Miller at his heels complaining at length about his advancing age. Once inside, Mallory felt his way across to the inevitable wooden bunk, sat down gratefully, lit a cigarette then looked up in puzzlement. Miller was still on his feet, walking slowly round the hut, tapping the walls as he went.

"Why don't you sit down?" Mallory asked irritably. "That was why you came in here in the first place, wasn't it?"

"No, boss, not really." The drawl was very pronounced. "Just a low-down trick to get us inside. Two-three very special things I want to show you."

"Very special. What the devil are you trying to tell me?"

"Bear with me, Captain Mallory," Miller requested formally. "Bear with me just a few minutes. I'm not wastin' your time. You have my word, Captain Mallory."

"Very well." Mallory was mystified, but his confidence in Miller remained unshaken. "As you wish. Only don't be too long about it."

"Thanks, boss." The strain of formality was too much for Miller. "It won't take long. There'll be a lamp or candles in here—you said the islanders never leave an abandoned house without 'em?"

"And a very useful superstition it's been to us, too." Mallory reached under the bunk with his torch, straightened his back. "Two or three candles here."

"I want a light, boss. No windows—I checked. O.K.?"

"Light one and I'll go outside to see if there's anything showing." Mallory was completely in the dark about the American's intentions. He felt Miller didn't want him to say anything, and there was a calm surety about him that precluded questioning. Mallory was back in less than a minute. "Not a chink to be seen from the outside," he reported.

"Fair enough. Thanks, boss." Miller lit a second candle, then slipped the rucksack straps from his shoulders, laid the pack on the bunk and stood in silence for a moment.

Mallory looked at his watch, looked back at Miller.

"You were going to show me something," he prompted.

"Yeah, that's right. Three things, I said." He dug into the

pack, brought out a little black box hardly bigger than a match-box. " Exhibit A, boss."

Mallory looked at it curiously. " What's that? "

" Clockwork fuse." Miller began to unscrew the back panel. " Hate the damned things. Always make me feel like one of those Bolshevik characters with a dark cloak, a moustache like Louki's and carryin' one of those black cannon-ball things with a sputterin' fuse stickin' outa it. But it works." He had the back off the box now, examining the mechanism in the light of his torch. " But this one doesn't, not any more," he added softly. " Clock's O.K., but the contact arm's been bent right back. This thing could tick till Kingdom Come and it couldn't even set off a firework."

" But how on earth——? "

" Exhibit B." Miller didn't seem to hear him. He opened the detonator box, gingerly lifted a fuse from its felt and cotton-wool bed and examined it closely under his torch. Then he looked at Mallory again. " Fulminate of mercury, boss. Only seventy-seven grains, but enough to blow your fingers off. Unstable as hell, too—the littlest tap will set it off." He let it fall to the ground, and Mallory winced and drew back involuntarily as the American smashed a heavy heel down on top of it. But there was no explosion, nothing at all.

" Ain't workin' so good either, is it, boss? A hundred to one the rest are all empty, too." He fished out a pack of cigarettes, lit one, and watched the smoke eddy and swirl above the heat of the candles. He slid the cigarettes into his pocket.

" There was a third thing you were going to show me," Mallory said quietly.

" Yeah, I was goin' to show you somethin' else." The voice was very gentle, and Mallory felt suddenly cold. " I was goin' to show you a spy, a traitor, the most vicious, twistin', murderin', double-crossin' bastard I've ever known." The American had his hand out of his pocket now, the silenced automatic sitting snugly against his palm, the muzzle trained over Panayis's heart. He went on, more gently than ever. "Judas Iscariot had nothin' on the boy-friend, here, boss. . . . Take your coat off, Panayis."

"What the devil are you doing! Are you crazy?" Mallory started forward, half-angry, half-amazed, but brought up sharply against Miller's extended arm, rigid as a bar of iron. "What bloody nonsense is this? He doesn't understand English!"

"Don't he, though? Then why was he out of the cave like a flash when Casey reported hearin' sounds outside . . . and why was he the first to leave the carob grove this afternoon if he didn't understand your order? Take your coat off, Judas, or I'll shoot you through the arm. I'll give you two seconds."

Mallory made to throw his arms round Miller and bring him to the ground, but halted in mid-step as he caught the look on Panayis's face—teeth bared, murder glaring out from the coal-black eyes. Never before had Mallory seen such malignity in a human face, a malignity that yielded abruptly to shocked pain and disbelief as the .32 bullet smashed into his upper arm, just below the shoulder.

"Two seconds and then the other arm," Miller said woodenly. But Panayis was already tearing off his jacket, the dark, bestial eyes never leaving Miller's face. Mallory looked at him, shivered involuntarily, looked at Miller. Indifference, he thought, that was the only word to describe the look on the American's face. Indifference. Unaccountably, Mallory felt colder than ever.

"Turn round!" The automatic never wavered.

Slowly Panayis turned round. Miller stepped forward, caught the black shirt by the collar, ripped it off his back with one convulsive jerk.

"Waal, waal, now, whoever woulda thought it?" Miller drawled. "Surprise, surprise, surprise! Remember, boss, this was the character that was publicly flogged by the Germans in

Crete, flogged until the white of his ribs showed through. His back's in a helluva state, isn't it? "

Mallory looked but said nothing. Completely off balance, his mind was in a kaleidoscopic whirl, his thoughts struggling to adjust themselves to a new set of circumstances, a complete reversal of all his previous thinking. Not a scar, not a single blemish, marked the dark smoothness of that skin.

"Just a natural quick healer," Miller murmured. "Only a nasty, twisted mind like mine would think that he had been a German agent in Crete, became known to the Allies as a fifth columnist, lost his usefulness to the Germans and was shipped back to Navarone by fast motor-launch under cover of night. Floggin'! Island-hoppin' his way back here in a row-boat! Just a lot of bloody eyewash! " Miller paused, and his mouth twisted. " I wonder how many pieces of silver he made in Crete before they got wise to him? "

" But heavens above, man, you're not going to condemn someone just for shooting a line! " Mallory protested. Strangely, he didn't feel nearly as vehement as he sounded. " How many survivors would there be among the Allies if——"

" Not convinced yet, huh? " Miller waved his automatic negligently at Panayis. " Roll up the left trouser leg, Iscariot. Two seconds again."

Panayis did as he was told. The black, venomous eyes never looked away from Miller's. He rolled the dark cloth up to the knee.

" Farther yet? That's my little boy," Miller encouraged him. " And now take that bandage off—right off." A few seconds passed, then Miller shook his head sadly. " A ghastly wound, boss, a ghastly wound! "

" I'm beginning to see your point," Mallory said thoughtfully. The dark sinewy leg wasn't even scratched. " But why on earth——"

" Simple. Four reasons at least. Junior here is a treacherous, slimy bastard—no self-respectin' rattlesnake would come within

a mile of him—but he's a clever bastard. He faked his leg so
he could stay in the cave in the Devil's Playground when the
four of us went back to stop the Alpenkorps from comin' up the
slope below the carob grove."

" Why? Frightened he'd stop something? "

Miller shook his head impatiently.

" Junior here's scared o' nothin'. He stayed behind to write
a note. Later on he used his leg to drop behind us some place,
and leave the note where it could be seen. Early on, this must
have been. Note probably said that we would come out at such
and such a place, and would they kindly send a welcomin'
committee to meet us there. They sent it, remember: it was
their car we swiped to get to town. . . . That was the
first time I got real suspicious of the boy-friend: after he'd
dropped behind he made up on us again real quick—too
damn' quick for a man with a game leg. But it wasn't till I
opened that rucksack in the square this evenin' that I really
knew."

" You only mentioned two reasons," Mallory prompted.

" Comin' to the others. Number three—he could fall
behind when the welcomin' committee opened up in front—
Iscariot here wasn't goin' to get himself knocked off before he
collected his salary. And number four—remember that real
touchin' scene when he begged you to let him stay at the far
end of the cave that led into the valley we came out? Goin' to
do his Horatio-on-the-bridge act? "

" Going to show them the right cave to pick, you mean."

" Check. After that he was gettin' pretty desperate. I still
wasn't sure, but I was awful suspicious, boss. Didn't know
what he might try next. So I clouted him good and hard when
that last patrol came up the valley."

" I see," Mallory said quietly. " I see indeed." He looked
sharply at Miller. " You should have told me. You had no
right——"

" I was goin' to, boss. But I hadn't a chance—Junior here

was around all the time. I was just startin' to tell you half an hour back, when the guns started up."

Mallory nodded in understanding. " How did you happen on all this in the first place, Dusty? "

" Juniper," Miller said succinctly. " Remember that's how Turzig said he came to find us? He smelt the juniper."

" That's right. We *were* burning juniper."

" Sure we were. But he said he smelt it on Kostos—and the wind was blowin' off Kostos all day long."

" My God! " Mallory whispered. " Of course, of course! And I missed it completely."

" But Jerry knew we were there. How? Waal, he ain't got second sight no more than I have. So he was tipped off— he was tipped off by the boy-friend here. Remember I said he'd talked to some of his pals in Margaritha when we went down there for the supplies? " Miller spat in disgust. " Fooled me all along the line. Pals? I didn't know how right I was. Sure they were his pals—his German pals! And that food he said he got from the commandant's kitchen—he got it from the kitchen all right. Almost certainly he goes in and asks for it—and old Skoda hands him his own suitcase to stow it in."

" But the German he killed on the way back to the village? Surely to God——"

" Panayis killed him." There was a tired certainty in Miller's voice. " What's another corpse to Sunshine here. Probably stumbled on the poor bastard in the dark and had to kill him. Local colour. Louki was there, remember, and he couldn't have Louki gettin' suspicious. He would have blamed it on Louki anyway. The guy ain't human. . . . And remember when he was flung into Skoda's room in Margaritha along with Louki, blood pourin' from a wound in his head? "

Mallory nodded.

" High-grade ketchup. Probably also from the com-

mandant's kitchen," Miller said bitterly. " If Skoda had failed
by every other means, there would still have been the boy-
friend here as a stool-pigeon. Why he never asked Louki where
the explosives were I don't know."

" Obviously he didn't know Louki knew."

" Mebbe. But one thing the bastard did know—how to use
a mirror. Musta heliographed the garrison from the carob
grove and given our position. No other way, boss. Then sometime this morning he must have got hold of my rucksack,
whipped out all the slow fuse and fixed the clock fuse and
detonators. He should have had his hands blown off tamperin'
with them fulminates. Lord only knows where he learnt to
handle the damn' things."

" Crete," Mallory said positively. " The Germans would
see to that. A spy who can't also double as a saboteur is no
good to them."

" And he was very good to them," Miller said softly. "Very,
very good. They're gonna miss their little pal. Iscariot here
was a very smart baby indeed."

" He was. Except to-night. He should have been smart
enough to know that at least one of us would be suspicious——"

" He probably was," Miller interrupted. " But he was mis-
informed. I think Louki's unhurt. I think Junior here talked
Louki into letting him stay in his place—Louki was always a
bit scared of him—then he strolled across to his pals at the
gate, told 'em to send a strong-arm squad out to Vygos to pick
up the others, asked them to fire a few shots—he was very
strong on local colour, was our loyal little pal—then strolls
back across the square, hoists himself up on the roof and waits
to tip off his pals as soon as we came in the back door. But
Louki forgot to tell him just one thing—that we were goin' to
rendezvous on the roof of the house, not inside. So the boy-
friend here lurks away for all he's worth up top, waiting to
signal his friends. Ten to one that he's got a torch in his
pocket."

Mallory picked up Panayis's coat and examined it briefly. "He has."

"That's it, then." Miller lit another cigarette, watched the match burn down slowly to his fingers, then looked up at Panayis. "How does it feel to know that you're goin' to die, Panayis, to feel like all them poor bastards who've felt just as you're feeling now, just before they died—all the men in Crete, all the guys in the sea-borne and air landings on Navarone who died because they thought you were on their side? How does it feel, Panayis?"

Panayis said nothing. His left hand clutching his torn right arm, trying to stem the blood, he stood there motionless, the dark, evil face masked in hate, the lips still drawn back in that less than human snarl. There was no fear in him, none at all, and Mallory tensed himself for the last, despairing attempt for life that Panayis must surely make, and then he had looked at Miller and knew there would be no attempt, because there was a strange sureness and inevitability about the American, an utter immobility of hand and eye that somehow precluded even the thought, far less the possibility of escape.

"The prisoner has nothin' to say." Miller sounded very tired. "I suppose I should say somethin'. I suppose I should give out with a long spiel about me bein' the judge, the jury and the executioner, but I don't think I'll bother myself. Dead men make poor witnesses. . . . Mebbe it's not your fault, Panayis, mebbe there's an awful good reason why you came to be what you are. Gawd only knows. I don't, and I don't much care. There are too many dead men. I'm goin' to kill you, Panayis, and I'm goin' to kill you now." Miller dropped his cigarette, ground it into the floor of the hut. "Nothin' at all to say?"

And he had nothing at all to say, the hate, the malignity of the black eyes said it all for him and Miller nodded, just once, as if in secret understanding. Carefully, accurately, he shot Panayis through the heart, twice, blew out the candles, turned his back and was half-way towards the door before the dead man had crashed to the ground.

"I am afraid I cannot do it, Andrea." Louki sat back wearily, shook his head in despair. "I am very sorry, Andrea. The knots are too tight."

"No matter." Andrea rolled over from his side to a sitting position, tried to ease his tightly-bound legs and wrists. "They are cunning, these Germans, and wet cords can only be cut." Characteristically, he made no mention of the fact that only a couple of minutes previously he had twisted round to reach the cords on Louki's wrist and undone them with half a dozen tugs of his steel-trap fingers. "We will think of something else."

He looked away from Louki, glanced across the room in the faint light of the smoking oil-lamp that stood by the grille door, a light so yellow, so dim that Casey Brown, trussed like a barnyard fowl and loosely secured, like himself, by a length of rope to the iron hooks suspended from the roof, was no more than a shapeless blur in the opposite corner of the stone-flagged room. Andrea smiled to himself, without mirth. Taken prisoner again, and for the second time that day—and with the same ease and surprise that gave no chance at all of resistance: completely unsuspecting, they had been captured in an upper room, seconds after Casey had finished talking to Cairo. The patrol had known exactly where to find them—and with their leader's assurance that it was all over, with his gloating explanation of the part Panayis had played, the unexpectedness, the success of the coup was all too easy to understand. And it was difficult not to believe his assurance that neither Mallory nor Miller had a chance. But the thought of ultimate defeat never occurred to Andrea.

His gaze left Casey Brown, wandered round the room, took in what he could see of the stone walls and floor, the hooks, the ventilation ducts, the heavy grille door. A dungeon, a torture dungeon, one would have thought, but Andrea had seen such places before. A castle, they called this place, but it was really only an old keep, no more than a manor house built round the crenellated towers. And the long-dead Frankish nobles who had built these keeps had lived well. No dungeon this, Andrea knew, but simply the larder where they had hung their meat and game, and done without windows and light for the sake of . . .

The light! Andrea twisted round, looked at the smoking oil lamp, his eyes narrowing.

" Louki! " he called softly. The little Greek turned round to look at him.

" Can you reach the lamp? "

" I think so. . . . Yes, I can."

" Take the glass off," Andrea whispered. " Use a cloth—it will be hot. Then wrap it in the cloth, hit it on the floor—gently. The glass is thick—you can cut me loose in a minute or two."

Louki stared at him for an uncomprehending moment, then nodded in understanding. He shuffled across the floor—his legs were still bound—reached out, then halted his hand abruptly, only inches from the glass. The peremptory, metallic clang had been only feet away, and he raised his head slowly to see what had caused it.

He could have stretched out his hand, touched the barrel of the Mauser that protruded threateningly through the bars of the grille door. Again the guard rattled the rifle angrily between the bars, shouted something he didn't understand.

" Leave it alone, Louki," Andrea said quietly. His voice was tranquil, unshadowed by disappointment. " Come back here. Our friend outside is not too pleased." Obediently Louki moved back, heard the guttural voice again, rapid and alarmed this time, the rattle as the guard withdrew his rifle quickly from the bars of the door, the urgent pounding of his feet on the flagstones outside as he raced up the passage.

" What's the matter with our little friend? " Casey Brown was as lugubrious, as weary as ever. " He seems upset."

" He is upset." Andrea smiled. " He's just realised that Louki's hands are untied."

" Well, why doesn't he tie them up again? "

" Slow in the head he may be, but he is no fool," Andrea explained. " This could be a trap and he's gone for his friends."

Almost at once they heard a thud, like the closing of a distant door, the sound of more than one pair of feet running down the passage, the tinny rattling of keys on a ring, the rasp of a key against the lock, a sharp click, the squeal of rusty hinges and then two soldiers were in the room, dark and menacing with their jackboots and ready guns. Two or three seconds elapsed while they looked around them, accustoming their eyes to the gloom, then the man nearest the door spoke.

" A terrible thing, boss, nothin' short of deplorable! Leave 'em alone for a couple of minutes and see what happens? The whole damn' bunch tied up like Houdini on an off night! "

There was a brief, incredulous silence, then all three were sitting upright, staring at them. Brown recovered first.

" High time, too," he complained. " Thought you were never going to get here."

" What he means is that he thought we were never going to see you again," Andrea said quietly. " Neither did I. But here you are, safe and sound."

" Yes," Mallory nodded. " Thanks to Dusty and his nasty suspicious mind that cottoned on to Panayis while all the rest of us were asleep."

" Where is he? " Louki asked.

" Panayis? " Miller waved a negligent hand. " We left him behind—he met with a sorta accident." He was across at the other side of the room now, carefully cutting the cords that pinioned Brown's injured leg, whistling tunelessly as he sawed away with his sheath knife. Mallory, too, was busy, slicing through Andrea's bonds, explaining rapidly what had happened, listening to the big Greek's equally concise account of what had befallen the others in the keep. And then Andrea was on his feet, massaging his numbed hands, looking across at Miller.

" That whistling, my Captain. It sounds terrible and, what is worse, it is very loud. The guards——"

" No worry there," Mallory said grimly. " They never expected to see Dusty and myself again. . . . They kept a poor watch." He turned round to look at Brown, now hobbling across the floor.

" How's the leg, Casey? "

" Fine, sir." Brown brushed it aside as of no importance. " I got through to Cairo, to-night, sir. The report——"

" It'll have to wait, Casey. We must get out as fast as we can. You all right, Louki? "

" I am heart-broken, Major Mallory. That a countryman of mine, a trusted friend——"

" That, too, will have to wait. Come on! "

" You are in a great hurry," Andrea protested mildly. They were already out in the passage, stepping over the cell guard lying in a crumpled heap on the floor. " Surely if they're all like our friend here——"

" No danger from this quarter," Mallory interrupted impatiently. " The soldiers in the town—they're bound to know by now that we've either missed Panayis or disposed of him. In either case they'll know that we're certain to come hot-footing out here. Work it out for yourself. They're probably half-way here already, and if they do come . . ." He broke off, stared at the smashed generator and the ruins of Casey Brown's transmitter set lying in one corner of the entrance hall. " Done a pretty good job on these, haven't they? " he said bitterly.

" Thank the Lord," Miller said piously. " All the less to tote around, is what I say. If you could only see the state of my back with that damned generator——"

" Sir! " Brown had caught Mallory's arm, an action so foreign to the usually punctilious petty officer that Mallory halted in surprise. " Sir, it's terribly important—the report, I mean. You *must* listen, sir! "

The action, the deadly earnestness, caught and held Mallory's full attention. He turned to face Brown with a smile.

" O.K., Casey, let's have it," he said quietly. " Things can't possibly be any worse than they are now."

" They can, sir." There was something tired, defeated about Casey Brown, and the great, stone hall seemed strangely chill. " I'm afraid they can, sir. I got through to-night. First-class reception. Captain Jensen himself, and he was hopping mad. Been waiting all day for us to come on the air. Asked how things were, and I told him that you were outside the fortress just then, and hoped to be inside the magazine in an hour or so."

" Go on."

" He said that was the best news he'd ever had. He said his information had been wrong, he'd been fooled, that the invasion fleet didn't hole up overnight in the Cyclades, that they had come straight through under the heaviest air and E-boat escort ever seen in the Med., and are due to hit the beaches on Kheros some time before dawn to-morrow. He said our destroyers had been waiting to the south all day, moved up at dusk and were waiting word from him to see whether they would attempt the passage of the Maidos Straits. I told him maybe something could go wrong, but he said not with Captain Mallory and Miller inside and besides he wasn't —he couldn't risk the lives of twelve hundred men on Kheros just on the off chance that he might be wrong." Brown broke off suddenly and looked down miserably at his feet. No one else in the hall moved or made any sound at all.

" Go on. " Mallory repeated in a whisper. His face was very pale.

" That's all, sir. That's all there is. The destroyers are

coming through the Straits at midnight." Brown looked down at his luminous watch. " Midnight. Four hours to go."

" Oh, God! Midnight! " Mallory was stricken, his eyes for the moment unseeing, ivory-knuckled hands clenched in futility and despair. " They're coming through at midnight! God help them! God help them all now! "

CHAPTER FIFTEEN

WEDNESDAY NIGHT

2000-2115

EIGHT-THIRTY, his watch said. Eight-thirty. Exactly half an hour to curfew. Mallory flattened himself on the roof, pressed himself as closely as possible against the low retaining wall that almost touched the great, sheering sides of the fortress, swore softly to himself. It only required one man with a torch in his hand to look over the top of the fortress wall—a cat-walk ran the whole length of the inside of the wall, four feet from the top —and it would be the end of them all. The wandering beam of a torch and they were bound to be seen, it was impossible not to be seen: he and Dusty Miller—the American was stretched out behind him and clutching the big truck battery in his arms —were wide open to the view of anyone who happened to glance down that way. Perhaps they should have stayed with the others a couple of roofs away, with Casey and Louki, the one busy tying spaced knots in a rope, the other busy splicing a bent wire hook on to a long bamboo they had torn from a bamboo hedge just outside the town, where they had hurriedly taken shelter as a convoy of three trucks had roared past them heading for the castle Vygos.

Eight thirty-two. What the devil was Andrea doing down there, Mallory wondered irritably and at once regretted his irritation. Andrea wouldn't waste an unnecessary second. Speed was vital, haste fatal. It seemed unlikely that there would be any officers inside—from what they had seen, practi-

277

cally half the garrison were combing either the town or the
countryside out in the direction of Vygos—but if there were and
even one gave a cry it would be the end.

Mallory stared down at the burn on the back of his hand,
thought of the truck they had set on fire and grinned wryly to
himself. Setting the truck on fire had been his only contribution
to the night's performance so far. All the other credit went to
either Andrea or Miller. It was Andrea who had seen in this
house on the west side of the square—one of several adjoining
houses used as officers' billets—the only possible answer to their
problem. It was Miller, now lacking all time-fuses, clockwork,
generator and every other source of electric power who had
suddenly stated that he must have a battery, and again it was
Andrea, hearing the distant approach of a truck, who had
blocked the entrance to the long driveway to the keep with
heavy stones from the flanking pillars, forcing the soldiers to
abandon their truck at the gates and run up the drive towards
their house. To overcome the driver and his mate and bundle
them senseless into a ditch had taken seconds only, scarcely
more time than it had taken Miller to unscrew the terminals
of the heavy battery, find the inevitable jerri-can below the
tail-board and pour the contents over engine, cab and body.
The truck had gone up in a roar and *whoosh* of flames: as
Louki had said earlier in the night, setting petrol-soaked
vehicles on fire was not without its dangers—the charred patch
on his hand stung painfully—but, again as Louki had said, it
had burned magnificently. A pity, in a way—it had attracted
attention to their escape sooner than was necessary—but it had
been vital to destroy the evidence, the fact that a battery was
missing. Mallory had too much experience of and respect for
the Germans ever to underrate them: they could put two and
two together better than most.

He felt Miller tug at his ankle, started, twisted round
quickly. The American was pointing beyond him, and he
turned again and saw Andrea signalling to him from the raised

trap in the far corner: he had been so engrossed in his thinking, the giant Greek so catlike in his silence, that he had completely failed to notice his arrival. Mallory shook his head, momentarily angered at his own abstraction, took the battery from Miller, whispered to him to get the others, then edged slowly across the roof, as noiselessly as possible. The sheer deadweight of the battery was astonishing, it felt as if it weighed a ton, but Andrea plucked it from his hands, lifted it over the trap coaming, tucked it under one arm and nimbly descended the stairs to the tiny hall-way as if it weighed nothing at all.

Andrea moved out through the open doorway to the covered balcony that overlooked the darkened harbour, almost a hundred vertical feet beneath. Mallory, following close behind, touched him on the shoulder as he lowered the battery gently to the ground.

" Any trouble? " he asked softly.

" None at all, my Keith." Andrea straightened. " The house is empty. I was so surprised that I went over it all, twice, just to make sure."

" Fine! Wonderful! I suppose the whole bunch of them are out scouring the country for us—interesting to know what they would say if they were told we were sitting in their front parlour? "

" They would never believe it," Andrea said without hesitation. " This is the last place they would ever think to look for us."

" I've never hoped so much that you're right! " Mallory murmured fervently. He moved across to the latticed railing that enclosed the balcony, gazed down into the blackness beneath his feet and shivered. A long, long drop and it was very cold; that sluicing, vertical rain chilled one to the bone. . . . He stepped back, shook the railing.

" This thing strong enough, do you think? " he whispered.

" I don't know, my Keith, I don't know at all." Andrea shrugged. " I hope so."

" I hope so," Mallory echoed. " It doesn't really matter.
This is how it has to be." Again he leaned far out over the
railing, twisted his head to the right and upwards. In the rain-
filled gloom of the night he could just faintly make out the still
darker gloom of the mouth of the cave housing the two great
guns, perhaps forty feet away from where he stood, at least
thirty feet higher—and all vertical cliff-face between. As far as
accessibility went, the cave mouth could have been on the
moon.

He drew back, turned round as he heard Brown limping on
to the balcony.

" Go to the front of the house and stay there, Casey, will
you? Stay by the window. Leave the front door unlocked. If
we have any visitors, let them in."

" Club 'em, knife 'em, no guns," Brown murmured. " Is
that it, sir? "

" That's it, Casey."

" Just leave this little thing to me," Brown said grimly. He
hobbled away through the doorway.

Mallory turned to Andrea. " I make it twenty-three
minutes."

" I, too. Twenty-three minutes to nine."

" Good luck," Mallory murmured. He grinned at Miller.
" Come on, Dusty. Opening time."

Five minutes later, Mallory and Miller were seated in a
taverna just off the south side of the town square. Despite the
garish blue paint with which the *tavernaris* had covered everything in sight—walls, tables, chairs, shelves all in the same
execrably vivid colour (blue and red for the wine shops, green
for the sweetmeats shops was the almost invariable rule throughout the islands)—it was a gloomy, ill-lit place, as gloomy almost
as the stern, righteous, magnificently-moustached heroes of the
Wars of Independence whose dark, burning eyes glared down
at them from a dozen faded prints scattered at eye-level along

the walls. Between each pair of portraits was a brightly-coloured wall advertisement for Fix's beer: the effect of the décor, taken as a whole, was indescribable, and Mallory shuddered to think what it would have been like had the *tavernaris* had at his disposal any illumination more powerful than the two smoking oil lamps placed on the counter before him.

As it was, the gloom suited him well. Their dark clothes, braided jackets, *tsantas* and jackboots looked genuine enough, Mallory knew, and the black-fringed turbans Louki had mysteriously obtained for them looked as they ought to look in a tavern where every islander there—about eight of them—wore nothing else on their heads. Their clothes had been good enough to pass muster with the *tavernaris*—but then even the keeper of a wine shop could hardly be expected to know every man in a town of five thousand, and a patriotic Greek, as Louki had declared this man to be, wasn't going to lift even a faintly suspicious eyebrow as long as there were German soldiers present. And there were Germans present—four of them, sitting round a table near the counter. Which was why Mallory had been glad of the semi-darkness. Not, he was certain, that he and Dusty Miller had any reason to be physically afraid of these men. Louki had dismissed them contemptuously as a bunch of old women—headquarters clerks, Mallory guessed—who came to this tavern every night of the week. But there was no point in sticking out their necks unnecessarily.

Miller lit one of the pungent, evil-smelling local cigarettes, wrinkling his nose in distaste.

" Damn' funny smell in this joint, boss."

" Put your cigarette out," Mallory suggested.

" You wouldn't believe it, but the smell I'm smelling is a damn' sight worse than that."

" Hashish," Mallory said briefly. " The curse of these island ports." He nodded over towards a dark corner. " The lads of the village over there will be at it every night in life. It's all they live for."

"Do they have to make that gawddamned awful racket when they're at it?" Miller asked peevishly. "Toscanini should see this lot!"

Mallory looked at the small group in the corner, clustered round the young man playing a *bouzouko*—a long-necked mandolin—and singing the haunting, nostalgic *rembetika* songs of the hashish smokers of the Piraeus. He supposed the music did have a certain melancholy, lotus-land attraction, but right then it jarred on him. One had to be in a certain twilit, untroubled mood to appreciate that sort of thing; and he had never felt less untroubled in his life.

"I suppose it *is* a bit grim," he admitted. "But at least it lets us talk together, which we couldn't do if they all packed up and went home."

"I wish to hell they would," Miller said morosely. "I'd gladly keep my mouth shut." He picked distastefully at the *meze*—a mixture of chopped olives, liver, cheese and apples—on the plate before him; as a good American and a bourbon drinker of long standing he disapproved strongly of the invariable Greek custom of eating when drinking. Suddenly he looked up and crushed his cigarette against the table top. "For Gawd's sake, boss, how much longer?"

Mallory looked at him, then looked away. He knew exactly how Dusty Miller felt, for he felt that way himself—tense, keyed-up, every nerve strung to the tautest pitch of efficiency. So much depended on the next few minutes; whether all their labour and their suffering had been necessary, whether the men on Kheros would live or die, whether Andy Stevens had lived and died in vain. Mallory looked at Miller again, saw the nervous hands, the deepened wrinkles round the eyes, the tightly compressed mouth, white at the outer corners, saw all these signs of strain, noted them and discounted them. Excepting Andrea alone, of all the men he had ever known he would have picked the lean, morose American to be his companion that night. Or maybe even including Andrea. " The finest saboteur in southern Europe " Captain Jensen had called him back in Alexandria. Miller had come a long way from Alexandria, and he had come for this alone. To-night was Miller's night.

Mallory looked at his watch.

" Curfew in fifteen minutes," he said quietly. " The balloon goes up in twelve minutes. For us, another four minutes to go."

Miller nodded, but said nothing. He filled his glass again from the beaker in the middle of the table, lit a cigarette. Mallory could see a nerve twitching high up in his temple and wondered dryly how many twitching nerves Miller could see in his own face. He wondered, too, how the crippled Casey Brown was getting on in the house they had just left. In many ways he had the most responsible job of all—and at the critical moment he would have to leave the door unguarded, move back to the balcony. One slip up there. . . . He saw Miller look strangely at him and grinned crookedly. This had to come off, it just had to: he thought of what must surely happen if he failed, then shied away from the thought. It wasn't good to think of these things, not now, not at this time.

He wondered if the other two were at their posts, unmolested; they should be, the search party had long passed through the upper part of the town; but you never knew what could go wrong, there was so much that could go wrong, and so easily. Mallory looked at his watch again: he had never seen a second hand move so slowly. He lit a last cigarette, poured a final glass of wine, listened without really hearing to the weird, keening threnody of the *rembetika* song in the corner. And then the song of the hashish singers died plaintively away, the glasses were empty and Mallory was on his feet.

" Time bringeth all things," he murmured. " Here we go again."

He sauntered easily towards the door, calling good night to the *tavernaris*. Just at the doorway he paused, began to search impatiently through his pockets as if he had lost something: it was a windless night, and it was raining, he saw, raining heavily, the lances of rain bouncing inches off the cobbled street—and the street itself was deserted as far as he could see in either direction. Satisfied, Mallory swung round with a curse, forehead furrowed in exasperation, started to walk back towards the table he had just left, right hand now delving into the capacious inner pocket of his jacket. He saw without seeming to that Dusty Miller was pushing his chair back, rising to his feet. And then Mallory had halted, his face clearing and his hands no longer searching. He was exactly three feet from the table where the four Germans were sitting.

"Keep quite still!" He spoke in German, his voice low but as steady, as menacing, as the Navy Colt .455 balanced in his right hand. "We are desperate men. If you move we will kill you."

For a full three seconds the soldiers sat immobile, expressionless except for the shocked widening of their eyes. And then there was a quick flicker of the eyelids from the man sitting nearest the counter, a twitching of the shoulder and then a grunt of agony as the .32 bullet smashed into his upper arm. The soft thud of Miller's silenced automatic couldn't have been heard beyond the doorway.

"Sorry, boss," Miller apologised. "Mebbe he's only sufferin, from St. Vitus' Dance." He looked with interest at the pain-twisted face, the blood welling darkly between the fingers clasped tightly over the wound. "But he looks kinda cured to me."

"He is cured," Mallory said grimly. He turned to the innkeeper, a tall, melancholy man with a thin face and mandarin moustache that drooped forlornly over either corner of his mouth, spoke to him in the quick, colloquial speech of the islands. "Do these men speak Greek?"

The *tavernaris* shook his head. Completely unruffled and unimpressed, he seemed to regard armed hold-ups in his tavern as the rule rather than the exception.

" Not them! " he said contemptuously. " English a little, I think—I am sure. But not our language. That I do know."

" Good. I am a British Intelligence officer. Have you a place where I can hide these men? "

" You shouldn't have done this," the *tavernaris* protested mildly. " I will surely die for this."

" Oh, no, you won't." Mallory had slid across the counter, his pistol boring into the man's midriff. No one could doubt that the man was being threatened—and violently threatened —no one, that is, who couldn't see the broad wink that Mallory had given the inn-keeper. " I'm going to tie you up with them. All right? "

" All right. There is a trap-door at the end of the counter here. Steps lead down to the cellar."

" Good enough. I'll find it by accident." Mallory gave him a vicious and all too convincing shove that sent the man staggering, vaulted back across the counter walked over to the *rembetiks* singers at the far corner of the room."

" Go home," he said quickly. " It is almost curfew time anyway. Go out the back way, and remember—you have seen nothing, no one. You understand? "

" We understand." It was the young *bouzouko* player who spoke. He jerked his thumb at his companions and grinned. " Bad men—but good Greeks. Can we help you? "

" No! " Mallory was emphatic. " Think of your families —these soldiers have recognised you. They must know you well—you and they are here most nights, is that not so? "

The young man nodded.

" Off you go, then. Thank you all the same."

A minute later, in the dim, candle-lit cellar, Miller prodded the soldier nearest him—the one most like himself in height and build. " Take your clothes off! " he ordered.

" English pig! " the German snarled.

" Not *English*," Miller protested. " I'll give you thirty seconds to get your coat and pants off."

The man swore at him, viciously, but made no move to obey. Miller sighed. The German had guts, but time was running out. He took a careful bead on the soldier's hand and pulled the trigger. Again the soft *plop* and the man was staring down stupidly at the hole torn in the heel of his left hand.

" Mustn't spoil the nice uniforms, must we? " Miller asked conversationally. He lifted the automatic until the soldier was staring down the barrel of the gun. " The next goes between the eyes." The casual drawl carried complete conviction. " It won't take me long to undress you, I guess." But the man had already started to tear his uniform off, sobbing with anger and the pain of his wounded hand.

Less than another five minutes had passed when Mallory, clad like Miller in German uniform, unlocked the front door of the tavern and peered cautiously out. The rain, if anything, was heavier than ever—and there wasn't a soul in sight. Mallory beckoned Miller to follow and locked the door behind him. Together the two men walked up the middle of the street, making no attempt to seek either shelter or shadows. Fifty yards took them into the town square, where they turned right along the south side of the square, then left along the east side, not breaking step as they passed the old house where they had hidden earlier in the evening, not even as Louki's hand appeared mysteriously behind the partly opened door, a hand weighted down with two German Army rucksacks—rucksacks packed with rope, fuses, wire and high explosive. A few yards farther on they stopped suddenly, crouched down behind a couple of huge wine barrels outside a barber's shop, gazed at the two armed guards in the arched gateway, less than a hundred feet away, as they shrugged into their packs and waited for their cue.

They had only moments to wait—the timing had been

split-second throughout. Mallory was just tightening the waist-belt of his rucksack when a series of explosions shook the centre of the town, not three hundred yards away, explosions followed by the vicious rattle of a machine-gun, then by further explosions. Andrea was doing his stuff magnificently with his grenades and home-made bombs.

Both men suddenly shrank back as a broad, white beam of light stabbed out from a platform high above the gateway, a beam that paralleled the top of the wall to the east, showed up every hooked spike and strand of barbed wire as clearly as sunlight. Mallory and Miller looked at each other for a fleeting moment, their faces grim. Panayis hadn't missed a thing: they would have been pinned on these strands like flies on fly-paper and cut to ribbons by machine-guns.

Mallory waited another half-minute, touched Miller's arm, rose to his feet and started running madly across the square, the long hooked bamboo pressed close to his side, the American pounding behind him. In a few seconds they had reached the gates of the fortress, the startled guards running the last few feet to meet them.

" Every man to the Street of Steps! " Mallory shouted. " Those damned English saboteurs are trapped in a house down there! We've got to have some mortars. Hurry, man, hurry, in the name of God! "

" But the gate! " one of the two guards protested. " We cannot leave the gate! " The man had no suspicions, none at all: in the circumstances—the near darkness, the pouring rain, the German-clad soldier speaking perfect German, the obvious truth that there was a gun-battle being fought near-hand—it would have been remarkable had he shown any signs of doubt.

" Idiot! " Mallory screamed at him. " *Dummkopf*! What is there to guard against here? The English swine are in the Street of Steps. They must be destroyed! For God's sake, hurry! " he shouted desperately. " If they escape again it'll be the Russian Front for all of us! "

Mallory had his hand on the man's shoulder now, ready to push him on his way, but his hand fell to his side unneeded. The two men were already gone, running pell-mell across the square, had vanished into the rain and the darkness already. Seconds later Mallory and Miller were deep inside the fortress of Navarone.

Everywhere there was complete confusion—a bustling, purposeful confusion as one would expect with the seasoned troops of the Alpenkorps, but confusion nevertheless, with much shouting of orders, blowing of whistles, starting of truck engines, sergeants running to and fro chivvying their men into marching order or into the waiting transports. Mallory and Miller ran too, once or twice through groups of men milling round the tailboard of a truck. Not that they were in any desperate hurry for themselves, but nothing could have been more conspicuous—and suspicious—than the sight of a couple of men walking calmly along in the middle of all that urgent activity. And so they ran, heads down or averted whenever they passed through a pool of light, Miller cursing feelingly and often at the unaccustomed exercise.

They skirted two barrack blocks on their right, then the power-house on their left, then an ordnance depot on their right and then the *Abteilung* garage on their left. They were climbing, now, almost in darkness, but Mallory knew where he was to the inch: he had so thoroughly memorised the closely tallying descriptions given him by Vlachos and Panayis that he would have been confident of finding his way with complete accuracy even if the darkness had been absolute.

" What's that, boss? " Miller had caught Mallory by the arm, was pointing to a large, uncompromisingly rectangular building that loomed gauntly against the horizon. " The local hoosegow? "

" Water storage tank," Mallory said briefly. " Panayis estimates there's half a million gallons in there—magazine

flooding in an emergency. The magazines are directly below."
He pointed to a squat, box-like, concrete structure a little
farther on. " The only entrance to the magazine. Locked and
guarded."

They were approaching the senior officers' quarters now—
the commandant had his own flat on the second story, directly
overlooking the massive, reinforced ferro-concrete control tower
that controlled the two great guns below. Mallory suddenly
stopped, picked up a handful of dirt, rubbed it on his face and
told Miller to do the same.

" Disguise," he explained. " The experts would consider it
a bit on the elementary side, but it'll have to do. The lighting's
apt to be a bit brighter inside this place."

He went up the steps to the officers' quarters at a dead run,
crashed through the swing doors with a force that almost took
them off their hinges. The sentry at the keyboard looked at
him in astonishment, the barrel of his sub-machine-gun lining
up on the New Zealander's chest.

" Put that thing down, you damned idiot! " Mallory
snapped furiously. " Where's the commandant? Quickly, you
oaf! It's life or death! "

"Herr—Herr Kommandant? " the sentry stuttered. " He's
left—they are all gone, just a minute ago."

" What? All gone? " Mallory was staring at him with
narrowed, dangerous eyes. " Did you say ' all gone '? " he
asked softly.

" Yes. I—I'm sure they're . . ." He broke off abruptly as
Mallory's eyes shifted to a point behind his shoulder.

" Then who the hell is that? " Mallory demanded savagely.

The sentry would have been less than human not to fall for
it. Even as he was swinging round to look, the vicious judo
cut took him just below the left ear. Mallory had smashed open
the glass of the keyboard before the unfortunate guard had hit
the floor, swept all the keys—about a dozen in all—off their
rings and into his pocket. It took them another twenty seconds

to tape the man's mouth and hands and lock him in a convenient cupboard; then they were on their way again, still running.

One more obstacle to overcome, Mallory thought as they pounded along in the darkness, the last of the triple defences. He did not know how many men would be guarding the locked door to the magazine, and in that moment of fierce exaltation he didn't particularly care. Neither, he felt sure, did Miller. There were no worries now, no taut-nerved tensions or nameless anxieties. Mallory would have been the last man in the world to admit it, or even believe it, but this was what men like Miller and himself had been born for.

They had their hand-torches out now, the powerful beams swinging in wild arcs as they plunged along, skirting the massed batteries of A.A. guns. To anyone observing their approach from the front, there could have been nothing more calculated to disarm suspicion than the sight and sound of the two men running towards them without any attempt at concealment, one of them shouting to the other in German, both with lit torches whose beams lifted and fell, lifted and fell as the men's arms windmilled by their sides. But these same torches were deeply hooded, and only a very alert observer indeed would have noticed that the downward arc of the lights never passed backwards beyond the runners' feet.

Suddenly Mallory saw two shadows detaching themselves from the darker shadow of the magazine entrance, steadied his torch for a brief second to check. He slackened speed.

"Right!" he said softly. "Here they come—only two of them. One each—get as close as possible first. Quick and quiet—a shout, a shot, and we're finished. And for God's sake don't start clubbing 'em with your torch. There'll be no lights on in that magazine and I'm not going to start crawling around there with a box of bloody matches in my hand!" He transferred his torch to his left hand, pulled out his Navy Colt, reversed it, caught it by the barrel, brought up sharply only inches away from the guards now running to meet them.

" Are you all right? " Mallory gasped. " Anyone been here? Quickly, man, *quickly!* "

" Yes, yes, we're all right." The man was off guard, apprehensive. " What in the name of God is all that noise——"

" Those damned English saboteurs! " Mallory swore viciously. " They've killed the guards and they're inside! Are you sure no one's been here? Come, let me see."

He pushed his way past the guard, probed his torch at the massive padlock, then straightened his back.

" Thank heaven for that anyway! " He turned round, let the dazzling beam of his torch catch the man square in the eyes, muttered an apology and switched off the light, the sound of the sharp click lost in the hollow, soggy thud of the heel of his Colt catching the man behind the ear, just below the helmet. The sentry was still on his feet, just beginning to crumple, when Mallory staggered as the second guard reeled into him, staggered, recovered, clouted him with the Colt for good measure, then stiffened in sudden dismay as he heard the vicious, hissing *plop* of Miller's automatic, twice in rapid succession.

" What the hell——"

" Wily birds, boss," Miller murmured. " Very wily indeed. There was a third character in the shadows at the side. Only way to stop him." Automatic cocked in his ready hand, he stooped over the man for a moment, then straightened. " Afraid he's been stopped kinda permanent, boss." There was no expression in his voice.

" Tie up the others." Mallory had only half-heard him; he was already busy at the magazine door, trying a succession of keys in the lock. The third key fitted, the lock opened and the heavy steel door gave easily to his touch. He took a last swift look round, but there was no one in sight, no sound but the revving engine of the last of the trucks clearing the fortress gates, the distant rattle of machine-gun fire. Andrea was doing a magnificent job—if only he didn't overdo it, leave his withdrawal till it was too late. . . . Mallory turned quickly, switched on his torch, stepped inside the door. Miller would follow when he was ready.

A vertical steel ladder fixed to the rock led down to the floor of the cave. On either side of the ladder were hollow liftshafts, unprotected even by a cage, oiled wire ropes glistening in the middle, a polished metal runner at each side of the square to guide and steady the spring-loaded side-wheels of the lift itself. Spartan in their simplicity but wholly adequate, there was no mistaking these for anything but what they were—the shell hoist shafts going down to the magazine.

Mallory reached the solid floor of the cave and swept his torch round through a 180-degree arc. This was the very end of that great cave that opened out beneath the towering overhang of rock that dominated the entire harbour. Not the natural end, he saw after a moment's inspection, but a man-made addition: the volcanic rock around him had been drilled and blasted out. There was nothing here but the two shafts descending into the pitchy darkness and another steel ladder, also leading to the magazine. But the magazine could wait: to check that there were no more guards down here and to ensure an emergency escape route—these were the two vital needs of the moment.

Quickly Mallory ran along the tunnel, flipping his torch on and off. The Germans were past-masters of booby traps—explosive booby traps—for the protection of important installations, but the chances were that they had none in that tunnel—not with several hundred tons of high explosive stored only feet away.

The tunnel itself, dripping-damp and duck-board floored, was about seven feet high and even wider, but the central passage was very narrow—most of the space was taken up by the roller conveyors, one on either side, for the great cartridges and shells.

Suddenly the conveyors curved away sharply to left and right, the sharply-sheering tunnel roof climbed steeply up into the near-darkness of the vaulted dome above, and, almost at his feet, their burnished steel caught in the beam from his torch, twin sets of parallel rails, imbedded in the solid stone and twenty feet apart, stretched forward into the lightened gloom ahead, the great, gaping mouth of the cave. And just before he switched off the torch—searchers returning from the Devil's Playground might easily catch the pin-point of light in the darkness—Mallory had a brief glimpse of the turn-tables that crowned the far end of these shining rails and, crouched massively above, like some nightmare monsters from an ancient and other world, the evil, the sinister silhouettes of the two great guns of Navarone.

Torch and revolver dangling loosely in his hands, only dimly aware of the curious tingling in the tips of his fingers, Mallory walked slowly forward. Slowly, but not with the stealthy slowness, the razor-drawn expectancy of a man momentarily anticipating trouble—there was no guard in the cave, Mallory was quite sure of that now—but with that strange, dream-like slowness, the half-belief of a man who has accomplished something he had known all along he could never accomplish, with the slowness of a man at last face to face with a feared but long-sought enemy. I'm here at last, Mallory said to himself over and over again, I'm here at last, I've made it, and these are the guns of Navarone: these are the guns I came to destroy, the guns of Navarone, and I have come at last. But somehow he couldn't quite believe it. . . .

Slowly still Mallory approached the guns, walked half-way round the perimeter of the turn-table of the gun on the left, examined it as well as he could in the gloom. He was staggered by the sheer size of it, the tremendous girth and reach of the barrel that stretched far out into the night. He told himself that the experts thought it was only a nine-inch crunch gun, that the crowding confines of the cave were bound to exaggerate its size. He told himself these things, discounted them: twelve-inch bore if an inch, that gun was the biggest thing he had ever seen. Big? Heavens above, it was gigantic! The fools, the blind, crazy fools who had sent the *Sybaris* out against these . . .

The train of thought was lost, abruptly. Mallory stood quite still, one hand resting against the massive gun carriage and tried to recall the sound that had jerked him back to the present. Immobile, he listened for it again, eyes closed the better to hear, but the sound did not come again, and suddenly he knew that it was no sound at all but the absence of sound that had cut through his thoughts, triggered off some un-conscious warning bell. The night was suddenly very silent, very still: down in the heart of the town the guns had stopped firing.

Mallory swore softly to himself. He had already spent far too much time day-dreaming, and time was running short. It *must* be running short—Andrea had withdrawn, it was only a matter of time until the Germans discovered that they had been duped. And then they would come running—and there was no doubt where they would come. Swiftly Mallory shrugged out of his rucksack, pulled out the hundred-foot wire-cored rope coiled inside. Their emergency escape route— whatever else he did he must make sure of that.

The rope looped round his arm, he moved forward cautiously, seeking a belay but had only taken three steps when his right knee-cap struck something hard and unyielding. He checked the exclamation of pain, investigated the obstacle with his free hand, realised immediately what it was—an iron railing stretched waist-high across the mouth of the cave. Of course! There had been bound to be something like this, some barrier to prevent people from falling over the edge, especially in the darkness of the night. He hadn't been able to pick it up with the binoculars from the carob grove that afternoon— close though it was to the entrance, it had been concealed in the gloom of the cave. But he should have thought of it.

Quickly Mallory felt his way along to the left, to the very end of the railing, crossed it, tied the rope securely to the base of the vertical stanchion next to the wall, paid out the rope as he moved gingerly to the lip of the cave mouth. And then, almost at once, he was there and there was nothing below his probing foot but a hundred and twenty feet of sheer drop to the land-locked harbour of Navarone.

Away to his right was a dark, formless blur lying on the water, a blur that might have been Cape Demirci: straight ahead, across the darkly velvet sheen of the Maidos Straits, he could see the twinkle of far-away lights—it was a measure of the enemy's confidence that they permitted these lights at all, or, more likely, these fisher cottages were useful as a bearing marker for the guns at night: and to the left, surprisingly near, barely thirty feet away in a horizontal plane, but far below the level where he was standing, he could see the jutting end of the outside wall of the fortress where it abutted on the cliff, the roofs of the houses on the west side of the square beyond that, and, beyond that again, the town itself curving sharply downwards and outwards, to the south first, then to the west, close-girdling and matching the curve of the crescent harbour. Above—but there was nothing to be seen above, that fantastic overhang above blotted out more than half the sky; and below, the darkness was equally impenetrable, the surface of the harbour inky and black as night. There were vessels down there, he knew, Grecian caiques and German launches, but they might have been a thousand miles away for any sign he could see of them.

The brief, all encompassing glance had taken barely ten seconds, but Mallory waited no longer. Swiftly he bent down, tied a double bowline in the end of the rope and left it lying on the edge. In an emergency they could kick it out into the darkness. It would be thirty feet short of the water, he estimated

—enough to clear any launch or masted caique that might be moving about the harbour. They could drop the rest of the way, maybe a bone-breaking fall on to the deck of a ship, but they would have to risk it. Mallory took one last look down into the Stygian blackness and shivered: he hoped to God that he and Miller wouldn't have to take that way out.

Dusty Miller was kneeling on the duck-boards by the top of the ladder leading down to the magazine as Mallory came running back up the tunnel, his hands busy with wires, fuses, detonators and explosives. He straightened up as Mallory approached.

" I reckon this stuff should keep 'em happy, boss." He set the hands of the clockwork fuse, listened appreciatively to the barely audible hum, then eased himself down the ladder. " In here among the top two rows of cartridges, I thought."

" Wherever you say," Mallory acquiesced. " Only don't make it too obvious—or too difficult to find. Sure there's no chance of them suspecting that we knew the clock and fuses were dud? "

" None in the world," Miller said confidently. " When they find this here contraption they'll knock holes in each others' backs congratulatin' themselves—and they'll never look any further."

" Fair enough." Mallory was satisfied. " Lock the door up top? "

" Certainly I locked the door! " Miller looked at him reproachfully. " Boss, sometimes I think . . ."

But Mallory never heard what he thought. A metallic, reverberating clangour echoed cavernously through the cave and magazine, blotting out Miller's words, then died away over the harbour. Again the sound came, while the two men stared bleakly at one another, then again and again, then escaped for a moment of time.

" Company," Mallory murmured. " Complete with sledgehammers. Dear God, I only hope that door holds." He was already running along the passage towards the guns, Miller close behind him.

"Company!" Miller was shaking his head as he ran. "How in the hell did they get here so soon?"

"Our late lamented little pal," Mallory said savagely. He vaulted over the railing, edged back to the mouth of the cave. "And we were suckers enough to believe he told the whole truth. But he never told us that opening that door up top triggered off an alarm bell in the guard-room."

CHAPTER SIXTEEN

WEDNESDAY NIGHT

2115-2345

SMOOTHLY, skilfully, Miller paid out the wire-cored rope—double-turned round the top rail—as Mallory sank out of sight into the darkness. Fifty feet had gone, he estimated, fifty-five, sixty, then there came the awaited sharp double tug on the signal cord looped round his wrist and he at once checked the rope, stooped and tied it securely to the foot of the stanchion.

And then he had straightened again, belayed himself to the rail with the rope's end, leaned far out over the edge, caught hold of the rope with both hands as far down as he could reach and began, slowly, almost imperceptibly at first, then with gradually increasing momentum, to swing man and rope from side to side, pendulum-wise. As the swings of the pendulum grew wider, the rope started to twist and jump in his hands, and Miller knew that Mallory must be striking outcrops of rock, spinning uncontrollably as he bounced off them. But Miller knew that he couldn't stop now, the clanging of the sledges behind him was almost continuous: he only stooped the lower over the rope, flung all the strength of his sinewy arms and shoulders into the effort of bringing Mallory nearer and still nearer to the rope that Brown would by now have thrown down from the balcony of the house where they had left him.

Far below, half-way between the cave mouth and the invisible waters of the harbour, Mallory swung in a great arc through the rain-filled darkness of the sky, forty rushing, bone-bruising feet between the extremities of the swings. Earlier he had struck his head heavily on an outcrop of rock, all but losing consciousness and his grip on the rope. But he knew where to expect that projection now and pushed himself clear each time as he approached it, even although this made him spin in a complete circle every time. It was as well, he thought, that it was dark, that he was independent of sight anyway: the blow had reopened an old wound Turzig had given him, his whole upper face was masked with blood, both eyes completely gummed.

But he wasn't worried about the wound, about the blood in his eyes. The rope—that was all that mattered. Was the rope there? Had anything happened to Casey Brown? Had he been jumped before he could get the rope over the side? If he had, then all hope was gone and there was nothing they could do, no other way they could span the forty sheer feet between house and cave. It just *had* to be there. But if it were there, why couldn't he find it? Three times now, at the right extremity of a swing, he had reached out with his bamboo pole, heard the hook scrape emptily, frustratingly, against the bare rock.

And then, the fourth time, stretched out to the straining limit of both arms, he felt the hook catch on! Immediately he jerked the pole in, caught the rope before he dropped back on the downward swing, jerked the signal cord urgently, checked himself gradually as he fell back. Two minutes later, near exhaustion from the sixty-foot climb up the wet, slippery rope, he crawled blindly over the lip of the cave and flung himself to the ground, sobbing for breath.

Swiftly, without speaking, Miller bent down, slipped the twin loops of the double bowline from Mallory's legs, undid the knot, tied it to Brown's rope, gave the latter a tug and watched the joined ropes disappear into the darkness. Within two minutes the heavy battery was across, underslung from the two ropes, lowered so far by Casey Brown then hauled up by Mallory and Miller. Within another two minutes, but with infinitely more caution, this time, the canvas bag with the nitro, primers and detonators, had been pulled across, lay on the stone floor beside the battery.

All noise had ceased, the hammering of the sledges against the steel door had stopped completely. There was something threatening, foreboding about the stillness, the silence was more menacing than all the clamour that had gone before. Was the door down, the lock smashed, the Germans waiting for them in the gloom of the tunnel, waiting with cradled machine-carbines that would tear the life out of them? But there was no time to wonder, no time to wait, no time now to stop to weigh the chances. The time for caution was past, and whether they lived or died was of no account any more.

The heavy Colt .455 balanced at his waist, Mallory climbed over the safety barrier, padded silently past the great guns and through the passage, his torch clicking on half-way down its length. The place was deserted, the door above still intact. He climbed swiftly up the ladder, listened at the top. A subdued murmur of voices, he thought he heard, and a faint hissing sound on the other side of the heavy steel door, but he couldn't be sure. He leaned forward to hear better, the palm of his hand against the door, drew back with a muffled exclamation of pain. Just above the lock, the door was almost red-hot. Mallory dropped down to the floor of the tunnel just as Miller came staggering up with the battery.

" That door's hot as blazes. They must be burning——"
" Did you hear anything? " Miller interrupted.
" There was a kind of hissing——"
" Oxy-acetylene torch," Miller said briefly. " They'll be burnin' out the lock. It'll take time—that door's made of armoured steel."

" Why don't they blow it in—gelignite or whatever you use for that job? "

" Perish the thought," Miller said hastily. " Don't even *talk* about it, boss. Sympathetic detonation's a funny thing— there's an even chance that the whole damned lot would go up. Give me a hand with this thing, boss, will you? "

Within seconds Dusty Miller was again a man absorbed in his own element, the danger outside, the return trip he had yet to make across the face of the cliff, completely forgotten for the moment. The task took him four minutes from begin- ning to end. While Mallory was sliding the battery below the floored well of the lift, Miller squeezed in between the shining steel runners of the lift shaft itself, stooped to examine the rear one with his torch and establish, by the abrupt transition from polished to dull metal, exactly where the spring-loaded wheel of the shell-hoist came to rest. Satisfied, he pulled out a roll of sticky black tape, wound it a dozen times round the shaft, stepped back to look at it: it was quite invisible.

Quickly he taped the ends of two rubber-covered wires on the insulated strip, one at either side, taped these down also until nothing was visible but the bared steel cores at the tips, joined these to two four-inch strips of bared wire, taped these also, top and bottom, to the insulated shaft, vertically and less than half an inch apart. From the canvas bag he removed the T.N.T., the primer and the detonator—a bridge mercury detonator lugged and screwed to his own specification—fitted them together and connected one of the wires from the steel shaft to a lug on the detonator, screwing it firmly home. The other wire from the shaft he led to the positive terminal on the battery, and a third wire from the negative terminal to the detonator. It only required the ammunition hoist to sink down into the magazine—as it would do as soon as they began firing— and the spring-loaded wheel would short out the bare wires, completing the circuit and triggering off the detonator. A last check on the position of the bared vertical wires and he sat back satisfied. Mallory had just descended the ladder from the tunnel. Miller tapped him on the leg to draw his attention, negligently waving the steel blade of his knife within an inch of the exposed wires.

"Are you aware, boss," he said conversationally, "that if I touched this here blade across those terminals, the whole gawddamned place would go up in smithereens." He shook his head musingly. "Just one little slip of the hand, just one teeny little touch and Mallory and Miller are among the angels."

"For God's sake put that thing away!" Mallory snapped nervously. "And let's get the hell out of here. They've got a complete half-circle cut through that door already!"

Five minutes later Miller was safe—it had been a simple matter of sliding down a 45-degree tautened rope to where Brown waited. Mallory took a last look back into the cave, and his mouth twisted. He wondered how many soldiers manned the guns and magazine during action stations. One thing, he thought, they'll never know anything about it, the poor bastards. And then he thought, for the hundredth time, of all the men on Kheros and the destroyers, and his lips tightened and he looked away. Without another backward glance he slipped over the edge, dropped down into the night. He was half-way there, at the very lowest point of the curve and about to start climbing again, when he heard the vicious, staccato rattle of machine-gun fire directly overhead.

It was Miller who helped him over the balcony rail, an apprehensive-looking Miller who glanced often over his shoulder in the direction of the gun-fire—and the heaviest concentration of fire, Mallory realised with sudden dismay, was coming from their own, the west side of the square, only three or four houses away. Their escape route was cut off.

"Come on, boss!" Miller said urgently. "Let's get away from this joint. Gettin' downright unhealthy round these parts."

Mallory jerked his head in the direction of the fire. " Who's down there? " he asked quickly.

" A German patrol."

" Then how in the hell can we get away? " Mallory demanded. " And where's Andrea? "

" Across the other side of the square, boss. That's who those birds along there are firing at."

" The other side of the square! " He glanced at his watch. " Heavens above, man, what's he doing there? " He was moving through the house now, speaking over his shoulder. " Why did you let him go? "

" I didn't let him go, boss," Miller said carefully. " He was gone when I came. Seems that Brown here saw a big patrol start a house to house search of the square. Started on the other side and were doin' two or three houses at a time. Andrea— he'd come back by this time—thought it a sure bet that they'd work right round the square and get here in two or three minutes, so he took off like a bat across the roofs."

" Going to draw them off? " Mallory was at Louki's side staring out of the window. " The crazy fool! He'll get himself killed this time—get himself killed for sure! There are soldiers everywhere. Besides, they won't fall for it again. He tricked them once up in the hills, and the Germans——"

" I'm not so sure, sir," Brown interrupted excitedly. " Andrea's just shot out the searchlight on his side. They'll think for certain that we're going to break out over the wall and —look, sir, look! There they go! " Brown was almost dancing with excitement, the pain of his injured leg forgotten. " He's done it, sir, he's done it! "

Sure enough, Mallory saw, the patrol had broken away from their shelter in the house to their right and were running across the square in extended formation, their heavy boots clattering on the cobbles, stumbling, falling, recovering again as they lost footing on the slippery wetness of the uneven stones. At the same time Mallory could see torches flickering on the roofs of the houses opposite, the vague forms of men crouching low to escape observation and making swiftly for the spot where Andrea had been when he had shot out the great Cyclops eye of the searchlight.

"They'll be on him from every side." Mallory spoke quietly enough, but his fists clenched until the nails cut into the palms of his hands. He stood stock-still for some seconds, stooped quickly and gathered a Schmeisser up from the floor. "He hasn't a chance. I'm going after him." He turned abruptly, brought up with equal suddenness: Miller was blocking his way to the door.

"Andrea left word that we were to leave him be, that he'd find his own way out." Miller was very calm, very respectful. "Said that no one was to help him, not on any account."

"Don't try to stop me, Dusty." Mallory spoke evenly, mechanically almost. He was hardly aware that Dusty Miller was there. He only knew that he must get out at once, get to Andrea's side, give him what help he could. They had been together too long, he owed too much to the smiling giant to let him go so easily. He couldn't remember how often Andrea had come after *him*, more than once when he had thought hope was gone. . . . He put his hand against Miller's chest.

"You'll only be in his way, boss," Miller said urgently. "That's what you said . . ."

Mallory pushed him aside, strode for the door, brought up his fist to strike as hands closed round his upper arm. He stopped just in time, looked down into Louki's worried face.

"The American is right," Louki said insistently. "You must not go. Andrea said you were to take us down to the harbour."

"Go down yourselves," Mallory said brusquely. "You know the way, you know the plans."

"You would let us all go, let us all——"

" I'd let the whole damn' world go if I could help him."
There was an utter sincerity in the New Zealander's voice.
" Andrea would never let me down."

" But you would let him down," Louki said quietly. " Is
that it, Major Mallory? "

" What the devil do you mean? "

" By not doing as he wishes. He may be hurt, killed even,
and if you go after him and are killed too, that makes it all
useless. He would die for nothing. Is it thus you would repay
your friend? "

" All right, all right, you win," Mallory said irritably.

" That is how Andrea would want it," Louki murmured.
" Any other way you would be——"

" Stop preaching at me! Right, gentlemen, let's be on our
way." He was back on balance again, easy, relaxed, the
primeval urge to go out and kill well under control. " We'll
take the high road—over the roofs. Dig into that kitchen stove
there, rub the ashes all over your hands and faces. See that
there's nothing white on you anywhere. And no talking! "

The five-minute journey down to the harbour wall—a
journey made in soft-footed silence with Mallory hushing even
the beginnings of a whisper—was quite uneventful. Not only
did they see no soldiers, they saw no one at all. The inhabitants
of Navarone were wisely observing the curfew, and the streets
were completely deserted. Andrea had drawn off pursuit with
a vengeance. Mallory began to fear that the Germans had
taken him, but just as they reached the water's edge he heard
the gunfire again, a good deal farther away this time, in the
very north-east corner of the town, round the back of the
fortress.

Mallory stood on the low wall above the harbour, looked
at his companions, gazed out over the dark oiliness of the
water. Through the heavy rain he could just distinguish, to his
right and left, the vague blurs of caiques moored stern on to
the wall. Beyond that he could see nothing.

"Well, I don't suppose we can get much wetter than we are right now," he observed. He turned to Louki, checked something the little man was trying to say about Andrea. "You sure you can find it all right in the darkness?" "It" was the commandant's personal launch, a thirty-six-foot ten-tonner always kept moored to a buoy a hundred feet offshore. The engineer, who doubled as guard, slept aboard, Louki had said.

"I am already there," Louki boasted. "Blindfold me as you will and I——"

"All right, all right," Mallory said hastily. "I'll take your word for it. Lend me your hat, will you, Casey?" He jammed the automatic into the crown of the hat, pulled it firmly on to his head, slid gently into the water and struck out by Louki's side.

"The engineer," Louki said softly. "I think he will be awake, Major."

"I think so, too," Mallory said grimly. Again there came the chatter of machine-carbines, the deeper whiplash of a Mauser. "So will everyone else in Navarone, unless they're deaf or dead. Drop behind as soon as we see the boat. Come when I call."

Ten seconds, fifteen passed, then Louki touched Mallory on the arm.

"I see it," Mallory whispered. The blurred silhouette was less than fifteen yards away. He approached silently, neither legs nor arms breaking water, until he saw the vague shape of a man standing on the poop, just aft of the engine-room hatchway. He was immobile, staring out in the direction of the fortress and the upper town: Mallory slowly circled round the stern of the boat and came up behind him, on the other side. Carefully he removed his hat, took out the gun, caught the low gunwale with his left hand. At the range of seven feet he knew he couldn't possibly miss, but he couldn't shoot the man, not then. The guard-rails were token affairs only, eighteen inches high at the most, and the splash of the man falling into the water would almost certainly alert the guards at the harbour mouth emplacements.

" If you move I will kill you! " Mallory said softly in German. The man stiffened. He had a carbine in his hand, Mallory saw.

" Put the gun down. Don't turn round." Again the man obeyed, and Mallory was out of the water and on to the deck, in seconds, neither eye nor automatic straying from the man's back. He stepped softly forward, reversed the automatic, struck, caught the man before he could fall overboard and lowered him quietly to the deck. Three minutes later all the others were safely aboard.

Mallory followed the limping Brown down to the engine-room, watched him as he switched on his hooded torch, looked around with a professional eye, looked at the big, gleaming, six-cylinder in line Diesel engine.

" This," said Brown reverently, " is an engine. What a beauty! Operates on any number of cylinders you like. I know the type, sir."

" I never doubted but you would. Can you start her up, Casey? "

" Just a minute till I have a look round, sir." Brown had all the unhurried patience of the born engineer. Slowly, methodically, he played the spotlight round the immaculate interior of the engine-room, switched on the fuel and turned to Mallory. " A dual control job, sir. We can take her from up top."

He carried out the same painstaking inspection in the wheelhouse, while Mallory waited impatiently. The rain was easing off now, not much, but sufficiently to let him see the vague outlines of the harbour entrance. He wondered for the tenth time if the guards there had been alerted against the possibility of an attempted escape by boat. It seemed unlikely —from the racket Andrea was making, the Germans would think that escape was the last thing in their minds. . . . He leaned forward, touched Brown on the shoulder.

"Twenty past eleven, Casey," he murmured. "If these destroyers come through early we're apt to have a thousand tons of rock falling on our heads."

"Ready now, sir," Brown announced. He gestured at the crowded dash-board beneath the screen. "Nothing to it really."

"I'm glad you think so," Mallory murmured fervently. "Start her moving, will you? Just keep it slow and easy."

Brown coughed apologetically. "We're still moored to the buoy. And it might be a good thing, sir, if we checked on the fixed guns, searchlights, signalling lamps, life-jackets and buoys. It's useful to know where these things are," he finished depreciatingly.

Mallory laughed softly, clapped him on the shoulder.

"You'd make a great diplomat, Chief. We'll do that." A landsman first and last, Mallory was none the less aware of the gulf that stretched between him and a man like Brown, made no bones about acknowledging it to himself. "Will you take her out, Casey?"

"Right, sir. Would you ask Louki to come here—I think it's steep to both sides, but there may be snags or reefs. You never know."

Three minutes later the launch was half-way to the harbour mouth, purring along softly on two cylinders, Mallory and Miller, still clad in German uniform, standing on the deck for'ard of the wheelhouse, Louki crouched low inside the wheelhouse itself. Suddenly, about sixty yards away, a signal lamp began to flash at them, its urgent clacking quite audible in the stillness of the night.

"Dan'l Boone Miller will now show how it's done," Miller muttered. He edged closer to the machine-gun on the starboard bow. "With my little gun I shall . . ."

He broke off sharply, his voice lost in the sudden clacking

from the wheelhouse behind him, the staccato off-beat chattering of a signal shutter triggered by professional fingers. Brown had handed the wheel over to Louki, was morsing back to the harbour entrance, the cold rain lancing palely through the flickering beams of the lamp. The enemy lamp had stopped but now began flashing again.

" My, they got a lot to say to each other," Miller said admiringly. " How long do the exchange of courtesies last, boss ? "

" I should say they are just about finished." Mallory moved back quickly to the wheelhouse. They were less than a hundred feet from the harbour entrance. Brown had confused the enemy, gained precious seconds, more time than Mallory had ever thought they could gain. But it couldn't last. He touched Brown on the arm.

" Give her everything you've got when the balloon goes up." Two seconds later he was back in position in the bows, Schmeisser ready in his hands. " Your big chance, Dan'l Boone. Don't give the searchlights a chance to line up—they'll blind you."

Even as he spoke, the light from the signal lamp at the harbour mouth cut off abruptly and two dazzling white beams, one from either side of the harbour entrance, stabbed blindingly through the darkness, bathing the whole harbour in their savage glare—a glare that lasted for only a fleeting second of time, yielded to a contrastingly Stygian darkness as two brief bursts of machine-gun fire smashed them into uselessness. From such short range it had been almost impossible to miss.

" Get down, everyone! " Mallory shouted. " Flat on the deck! "

The echoes of the gunfire were dying away, the reverberations fading along the great sea wall of the fortress when Casey Brown cut in all six cylinders of the engine and opened the throttle wide, the surging roar of the big Diesel blotting out all other sounds in the night. Five seconds, ten seconds, they were passing through the entrance, fifteen, twenty, still not a shot fired, half a minute and they were well clear, bows lifting high out of the water, the deep-dipped stern trailing its long, seething ribbon of phosphorescent white as the engine crescendoed to its clamorous maximum power and Brown pulled the heeling craft sharply round to starboard, seeking the protection of the steep-walled cliffs.

" A desperate battle, boss, but the better men won." Miller was on his feet now, clinging to a mounted gun for support as the deck canted away beneath his feet. " My grandchildren shall hear of this."

" Guards probably all up searching the town. Or maybe there *were* some poor blokes behind these searchlights. Or maybe we just took 'em all by surprise." Mallory shook his head. " Anyway you take it, we're just plain damn' lucky."

He moved aft, into the wheelhouse. Brown was at the wheel, Louki almost crowing with delight.

" That was magnificent, Casey," Mallory said sincerely. " A first-class job of work. Cut the engine when we come to the end of the cliffs. Our job's done. I'm going ashore."

" You don't have to, Major."

Mallory turned. " What's that? "

" You don't have to. I tried to tell you on the way down, but you kept telling me to be quiet." Louki sounded injured, turned to Casey. " Slow down, please. The last thing Andrea told me, Major, was that we were to come this way. Why do you think he let himself be trapped against the cliffs to the north instead of going out into the country, where he could have hidden easily."

" Is this true, Casey? " Mallory asked.

" Don't ask me, sir. Those two—they always talk in Greek."

" Of course, of course." Mallory looked at the low cliffs close of the starboard beam, barely moving now with the engine shut right down, looked back at Louki. " Are you quite sure . . ."

He stopped in mid-sentence, jumped out through the wheel-house door. The splash—there had been no mistaking the noise—had come from almost directly ahead. Mallory, Miller by his side, peered into the darkness, saw a dark head surfacing above the water less than twenty feet away, leaned far over with outstretched arm as the launch slid slowly by. Five seconds later Andrea stood on the deck, dripping mightily and beaming all over his great moon face. Mallory led him straight into the wheelhouse, switched on the soft light of the shaded chart-lamp.

" By all that's wonderful, Andrea, I never thought to see you again. How did it go? "

" I will soon tell you," Andrea laughed. " Just after——"

" You've been wounded! " Miller interrupted. " Your shoulder's kinda perforated." He pointed to the red stain spreading down the sea-soaked jacket.

" Well, now, I believe I have." Andrea affected vast surprise. " Just a scratch, my friend."

" Oh, sure, sure, just a scratch! It would be the same if your arm had been blown off. Come on down to the cabin—this is just a kindergarten exercise for a man of my medical skill."

" But the captain——"

" Will have to wait. And your story. Ol' Medicine Man Miller permits no interference with his patients. Come on! "

" Very well, very well," Andrea said docilely. He shook his head in mock resignation, followed Miller out of the cabin.

Brown opened up to full throttle again, took the launch north almost to Cape Demirci to avoid any hundred to one chance the harbour batteries might make, turned due east for a few miles then headed south into the Maidos Straits. Mallory stood by his side in the wheelhouse, gazing out over the dark, still waters. Suddenly he caught a gleam of white in the distance, touched Brown's arm and pointed for'ard.

" Breakers ahead, Casey, I think. Reefs, perhaps? "

Casey looked in long silence, finally shook his head.

" Bow-wave," he said unemotionally. " It's the destroyers coming through."

CHAPTER SEVENTEEN

WEDNESDAY NIGHT

Midnight

COMMANDER VINCENT RYAN, R.N., Captain (Destroyers) and Commanding Officer of His Majesty's latest S-class destroyer *Sirdar*, looked round the cramped chart-room and tugged thoughtfully at his magnificent Captain Kettle beard. A scruffier, a more villainous, a more cut and battered-looking bunch of hard cases he had never seen, he reflected, with the possible exception of a Bias Bay pirate crew he had helped round up when a very junior officer on the China Station. He looked at them more closely, tugged his beard again, thought there was more to it than mere scruffiness. He wouldn't care to be given the task of rounding this lot up. Dangerous, highly dangerous, he mused, but impossible to say why, there was only this quietness, this relaxed watchfulness that made him feel vaguely uncomfortable. His " hatchet-men," Jensen had called them: Captain Jensen picked his killers well.

" Any of you gentlemen care to go below," he suggested. " Plenty of hot water, dry clothes—and warm bunks. We won't be using them to-night."

" Thank you very much, sir." Mallory hesitated. " But we'd like to see this through."

" Right, then, the bridge it is," Ryan said cheerfully. The *Sirdar* was beginning to pick up speed again, the deck throbbing beneath their feet. " It is at your own risk, of course."

" We lead charmed lives," Miller drawled. " Nothin' ever happens to us."

The rain had stopped and they could see the cold twinkling of stars through broadening rifts in the clouds. Mallory looked around him, could see Maidos broad off the port bow and the great bulk of Navarone slipping by to starboard. Aft, about a cable length away, he could just distinguish two other ships, high-curving bow-waves piled whitely against tenebrious silhouettes. Mallory turned to the captain.

" No transports, sir? "

" No transports." Ryan felt a vague mixture of pleasure and embarrassment that this man should called him " sir." " Destroyers only. This is going to be a smash-and-grab job. No time for dawdlers to-night—and we're behind schedule already."

" How long to clear the beaches? "

" Half an hour."

" What! Twelve hundred men? " Mallory was incredulous.

" More." Ryan sighed. " Half the ruddy inhabitants want to come with us, too. We could still do it in half an hour, but we'll probably take a bit longer. We'll embark all the mobile equipment we can."

Mallory nodded, let his eye travel along the slender outlines of the *Sirdar*. " Where are you going to put 'em all, sir? "

" A fair question," Ryan admitted. " Five p.m. on the London Underground will be nothing compared to this little lot. But we'll pack them in somehow."

Mallory nodded again and looked across the dark waters at Navarone. Two minutes, now, three at the most, and the fortress would open behind that headland. He felt a hand touch his arm, half-turned and smiled down at the sad-eyed little Greek by his side.

" Not long now, Louki," he said quietly.

" The people, Major," he murmured. " The people in the town. Will they be all right? "

" They'll be all right. Dusty says the roof of the cave will go straight up. Most of the stuff will fall into the harbour."

" Yes, but the boats——? "

" Will you stop worrying! There's nobody aboard them— you know they have to leave at curfew time." He looked round as someone touched his arm.

" Captain Mallory, this is Lieutenant Beeston, my gunnery officer." There was a slight coolness in Ryan's voice that made Mallory think that he wasn't overfond of his gunnery officer. " Lieutenant Beeston is worried."

" I *am* worried! " The tone was cold, aloof, with an indefinable hint of condescension. " I understand that you have advised the captain not to offer any resistance? "

" You sound like a B.B.C. communiqué," Mallory said shortly. " But you're right. I did say that. You couldn't locate the guns except by searchlight and that would be fatal. Similarly with gunfire."

" I'm afraid I don't understand." One could almost see the lift of the eyebrows in the darkness.

" You'd give away your position," Mallory said patiently. " They'd nail you first time. Give 'em two minutes and they'd nail you anyway. I have good reason to believe that the accuracy of their gunners is quite fantastic."

" So has the Navy," Ryan interjected quietly. " Their third shell got the *Sybaris's* B magazine."

" Have you got any idea why this should be, Captain Mallory? " Beeston was quite unconvinced.

" Radar-controlled guns," Mallory said briefly. " They have two huge scanners atop the fortress."

" The *Sirdar* had radar installed last month," Beeston said stiffly. " I imagine we could register some hits ourselves if——"

" You could hardly miss." Miller drawled out the words, the tone dry and provocative. " It's a helluva big island, Mac."

" Who—who are you? " Beeston was rattled. " What the devil do you mean? "

" Corporal Miller." The American was unperturbed. " Must be a very selective instrument, Lootenant, that can pick out a cave in a hundred square miles of rock."

There was a moment's silence, then Beeston muttered something and turned away.

" You've hurt Guns's feelings, Corporal," Ryan murmured. " He's very keen to have a go—but we'll hold our fire. . . . How long till we clear that point, Captain? "

" I'm not sure." He turned. " What do you say, Casey? "

" A minute, sir. No more."

Ryan nodded, said nothing. There was a silence on the bridge, a silence only intensified by the sibilant rushing of the waters, the weird, lonesome pinging of the Asdic. Above, the sky was steadily clearing, and the moon, palely luminous, was struggling to appear through a patch of thinning cloud. Nobody spoke, nobody moved. Mallory was conscious of the great bulk of Andrea beside him, of Miller, Brown and Louki behind. Born in the heart of the country, brought up on the foothills of the Southern Alps, Mallory knew himself as a landsman first and last, an alien to the sea and ships: but he had never felt so much at home in his life, never really known till now what it was to belong. He was more than happy, Mallory thought vaguely to himself, he was content. Andrea and his new friends and the impossible well done—how could a man be but content? They weren't all going home, Andy Stevens wasn't coming with them, but strangely he could feel no sorrow, only a gentle melancholy. . . . Almost as if he had divined what Mallory was thinking, Andrea leaned towards him, towering over him in the darkness.

" He should be here," he murmured. " Andy Stevens should be here. That is what you are thinking, is it not? "

Mallory nodded and smiled, and said nothing.

" It doesn't really matter, does it, my Keith? " No anxiety, no questioning, just a statement of fact. " It doesn't really matter."

" It doesn't matter at all."

Even as he spoke, he looked up quickly. A light, a bright orange flame had lanced out from the sheering wall of the fortress; they had rounded the headland and he hadn't even noticed it. There was a whistling roar—Mallory thought incongruously of an express train emerging from a tunnel—directly overhead, and the great shell had crashed into the sea just beyond them. Mallory compressed his lips, unconsciously tightened his clenched fists. It was easy now to see how the *Sybaris* had died.

He could hear the gunnery officer saying something to the captain, but the words failed to register. They were looking at him and he at them and he did not see them. His mind was strangely detached. Another shell, would that be next? Or would the roar of the gunfire of that first shell come echoing across the sea? Or perhaps . . . Once again, he was back in that dark magazine entombed in the rocks, only now he could see men down there, doomed, unknowing men, could see the overhead pulleys swinging the great shells and cartridges towards the well of the lift, could see the shell hoist descending slowly, the bared, waiting wires less than half an inch apart, the shining, spring-loaded wheel running smoothly down the gleaming rail, the gentle bump as the hoist . . .

A white pillar of flame streaked up hundreds of feet into the night sky as the tremendous detonation tore the heart out of the great fortress of Navarone. No after-fire of any kind, no dark, billowing clouds of smoke, only that one blinding white column that lit up the entire town for a single instant of time, reached up incredibly till it touched the clouds, vanished as if it had never been. And then, by and by, came the shock waves, the solitary thunderclap of the explosion, staggering even at that distance, and finally the deep-throated rumbling as thousands of tons of rock toppled majestically into the harbour—thousands of tons of rock and the two great guns of Navarone.

The rumbling was still in their ears, the echoes fading away far out across the Ægean, when the clouds parted and the moon broke through, a full moon silvering the darkly-rippling waters to starboard, shining iridescently through the spun phosphorescence of the *Sirdar's* boiling wake. And dead ahead, bathed in the white moonlight, mysterious, remote, the island of Kheros lay sleeping on the surface of the sea.

THE END